MYSTERY IN MAY

A British Murder Mystery

MICHAEL CAMPLING

Shadowstone
Books

Published by Shadowstone Books
ISBN: 978-1-915507-04-4

BECOME A VIP READER

MEMBERS GET FREE BOOKS,
EXCLUSIVE CONTENT AND MORE

Visit: michaelcampling.com / freebooks

For Alien (who is from another planet), Chris and Reggie.
Old friends and true.

It is one of the blessings of old friends that you can afford to be stupid with them.

— *RALPH WALDO EMERSON*

FRIDAY

PROLOGUE

A HISS ON the line.

"Did you get it?" The woman's voice is uncertain. Tense. But the man who replies is unhurried, matter of fact: "I'm downloading it now."

"Okay. Tell me when it's done."

"Yeah." He hesitates. "Hang on. There's someone… I'll be right back."

"What's up? What's the matter?"

A pause, and then: "Sorry. I thought… I thought someone was coming up the stairs, but there's no one there."

"It was probably just your mum or your dad or—"

"No," he interrupts. "They've all gone out. Getting ready for tomorrow."

"Right. Are you going? To the May thing, I mean."

"No way."

"Maybe you should. You never go anywhere. You're starting to get…"

"What?"

"I don't know. Paranoid or something."

"Don't worry about me. I'm fine. Fine."

"Okay. But you can't freak out on me. Not now." She pauses. "You sound tired."

"I'm knackered."

"Get some sleep. Are we done?"

"Yeah. The internet here is crap, but I've got the whole file. I'll get started."

"Leave it for now. You can look at it tomorrow."

"I want to make sure it's okay. Hang on."

"Seriously, I think you ought to—"

"Bloody hell!"

"What? What's wrong?"

"Nothing. It's all good. Better. It's bloody amazing. We've got everything. It's going to take me ages to get through. I'd better hang up."

"You're starting now?"

"Hell yeah. When it's this good, you don't sit on it. I've got to work fast."

"It's up to you, I suppose, but you know what? You don't sound tired anymore."

"I'm wide awake. Buzzing." He laughs. "It's going to be a good night."

"You're crazy."

"I know. But listen, I've got to go. Talk soon, yeah?"

"Definitely. Tomorrow? Come to the May Fair. We could grab a beer, sit in the sunshine."

He doesn't answer, so she adds, "I'll call you tomorrow anyway. You might be ready for a drink by then."

"Okay. But don't call too early. I'm going to be up half the night."

"How about one o'clock?"

"Make it two."

"Sure." She takes a breath, whispers, "Love you."

"What's that?"

"Nothing. Bye."

A hiss on the line.

SATURDAY

CHAPTER 1

T HE ROPE SPRUNG tight. Trapped in its coils, the length of wood whirled on its axis, and a razor-sharp blade bit deep, sending the delicately curled shavings to tumble onto the grass.

Standing in the show field, so called because it was where Embervale's village show was held every August, Dan watched the display of woodworking, fascinated.

The simple lathe was powered only by the man whose foot pressed against its treadle, and he bent close to his task, his hands steady, his gaze unwavering. The man's weather-beaten brow was furrowed in concentration, and he worked to the insistent rhythm of the treadle, advancing the chisel a hair's breadth to cut on each downstroke, then releasing the blade to let the wood spin free as the piece reversed.

The whole set-up has a kind of rustic efficiency, Dan thought. *It does the job and nothing more.*

The lathe's operator cast a fleeting glance at Dan, then he returned his attention to his work. "All right?" he asked.

"Yes, I was just admiring your handiwork," Dan replied. "Very impressive."

The man stopped the treadle and studied the slender piece

of smooth wood he'd been working on. "Well, it'll do, I suppose. 'Tis nothing like as good as I want it, but we've got to work with what we've got, and that's that."

"It looks good to me. Is it a chair leg?"

"Hopefully." The man pulled a white handkerchief from his trouser pocket, then he removed his straw hat and mopped his brow. "It's powerful warm work on a day like this, that's for sure." Pocketing his handkerchief, he said, "I'm Reg, by the way. Reg Stoddard."

"I'm Dan Corrigan."

"Right. That name rings a bell, but you're not local, are you?"

"I am now. I moved to the village last summer. I'm in the Old Shop."

"Ah yes. I've seen your card on the pub noticeboard. You fix people's computers."

"That's right," Dan said. It had been Alan's idea, and it was simple: Dan was good with computers, so why not offer IT support? At first, Dan hadn't taken the suggestion seriously, but he needed the money. He'd been living on the income from his small portfolio of investments, but it was never quite enough. He'd had savings when he arrived in Embervale, but the renovations on the Old Shop had pared them to the bone.

So, Dan had ordered some business cards, taken out an advert in the *Mid-Devon Advertiser*, and after a slow start, the calls had come in. And much to Dan's surprise, it suited him. He set his own schedule, he enjoyed the work, and although his fledgling business was small, it was *his*.

Reg thought for a moment and nodded as if coming to a decision. "I've been meaning to get one of them laptops. I've got a brother up in Sheffield, and I call him every week. He's always telling me to get Skype or some such thing. But I don't know. It sounds complicated."

"It needn't be. I'd be happy to source a laptop for you, and

I'd bring it to your house and set it up. You'll need a decent internet connection, but I can help with that too. And the laptop could be a fairly basic model. You could probably get by with a tablet instead, or a lot of people make video calls on their phones."

Reg sniffed. "I've got a phone with a little screen, but I don't reckon much to it. And I don't like the look of them tablets. I'd rather have a proper keyboard. I know where I am with that."

"Okay." Dan took out his phone. "If you tell me your number, I'll give you a call and we'll take it from there."

"How much is all this going to cost?"

"I'll work out an estimate, and there'll be no obligation. I'll set it all down in writing, and if you're not happy, it won't cost you a penny. Fair enough?"

Reg nodded slowly. "All right." He reeled off his phone number, and Dan stored it in his contacts.

"Corrigan," Reg said. "That an Irish name?"

"I believe so, but I'm from London."

"Ah." Reg smiled as though this explained everything. "Well, since you're so quick to get me roped into your business, how about you have a go at mine?" He held his chisel out to Dan. "Go on. Try your hand."

"Oh, I'd spoil your work."

"That doesn't matter," Reg said. "It's only a practice piece, and anyway, that's what I'm here for: to get folk interested, keep the craft alive."

Dan hesitated. He could saw a piece of timber in half and make the cut reasonably straight, but that was the limit of his skill with wood. The lathe was a simple machine, but using it properly was sure to be much harder than it looked, and Dan was in no rush to make a fool of himself.

"Go on," Reg insisted. "Give it a whirl. Do an old man a favour." He smiled, a twinkle in his eyes, and Dan couldn't refuse.

"All right." Taking the chisel, Dan turned the unfamiliar tool around in his hand, testing its weight. The wooden handle was worn smooth from use and its steel blade was tinted with the patina of age, but its cutting edge gleamed bright, catching the sunlight. "Do I need gloves or anything?" Dan asked. "Safety goggles?"

Reg's eyebrows shot up his forehead. "You're going to be doing a bit of woodturning, not chopping down a tree. I've been doing this for more years than I care to remember, and I've still got all my fingers." He held up his hands, adding, "Most of them, at any rate."

Dan stared at Reg's right forefinger, which was little more than a stump. He could scarcely believe he hadn't noticed it before, but Reg had been so deft with the chisel that he'd clearly learned to make up for his missing finger. "Sorry," Dan said, averting his gaze. "I didn't mean…"

"Think nothing of it. Anyway, it wasn't a chisel that took my finger. It was a dog. A mangy old sheepdog that belonged to my uncle Bob. It bit me when I was a boy." He sniffed. "After it went for me, Bob took the dog behind the barn and didn't bring it back. I can still remember the sound of his shotgun echoing across the yard."

"That's terrible."

"Is it?" Reg shrugged. "It had to be done. The old dog had gone demented. They get like that sometimes. It was a farm dog, see, not a pet. Bob had a little place out on the moor. He farmed a few sheep, but he had no one except his dog to keep him company. I reckon the pair of them went a bit wild, man and dog alike. It was a hard life. A different time."

"It certainly sounds like it," Dan said. "What became of him? Bob, I mean."

"After he killed that dog, he was never the same. He wouldn't get another sheepdog, so he lived out his days on the moor all alone. One day, in the middle of winter, they found him lying on the ground, all but frozen solid. They reckon he must've gone out in the night to check on his sheep, got lost in the mist and never found his way back. Died of exposure not two hundred yards from his door." Reg sighed. "I've often wondered… if he'd still had that dog, would it have taken him home? Would old Bob have had a few more years of life? We'll never know."

Dan wasn't sure what to say. He'd lived in Embervale for almost a full year, and it was his home now. But there were times when it felt like he'd never understand the place or its people; they were so far removed from his old life in London that it beggared belief.

Reg chuckled. "Listen to me, blathering on when we should be getting you started." He patted the lathe. "Hold the chisel on the edge, then put your foot on the treadle and press it up and down a few times. Get the feel of it. When you've got it running nice and smooth, we'll have a go at doing a bit of work."

Dan did as he was told, but the treadle bucked beneath his foot, and the rope whipped up and down, the whole lathe juddering.

"Easy now," Reg said. "Nice and gentle."

"I'm not sure…"

"Keep at it. There's no hurry. You'll get it in a minute."

Dan frowned, but he persisted, pressing more gently on the treadle, and he soon found the rhythm. The rope moved smoothly, and the half-formed chair leg spun backward and forward.

Reg clapped his hands together. "Now, pick the spot where you want to cut and press the blade in on the downstroke. Not too far, mind. Just enough to cut. Then pull it back sharpish. Keep your hands in time with your foot."

"Like this?" Dan followed Reg's instructions. The chisel bit into the wood, and as he watched the wood shavings curl away, Dan grinned.

"Blimey," Reg said. "We'll make a bodger of you yet."

"Oh. Am I doing so badly?"

Reg laughed. "Bodging is what you're doing! It's the proper name for woodturning when you do it on a pole lathe like this. Time was, a man would live in the woods and build his lathe on the spot, working every day to fill his quota. Then he'd move on, set up somewhere else. It was a craft carried down through the generations. To be called a bodger is a wonderful thing. It means you've got real skill."

"I must try to remember that." Dan stopped working the treadle, then he stood back while Reg leaned in to inspect his work.

"Mm."

"How did I do?" Dan asked.

"It's passable. For a beginner." Reg tipped him a wink. "I dare say you'd get the hang of it with a bit more practice. It shouldn't take more than five or six years." He paused. "I could get you started if you like. Since you're local."

"That's very kind, but I don't think I'm cut out for it."

"Nobody starts off by tackling a whole chair. Start small, that's the secret. Look." Reg stepped across to a table where a selection of chopping boards, platters and other small items were on display. From a rack at the end of the table, he lifted a walking stick with a carved handle and showed it to Dan. "See? This kind of thing would make a good place to start. No turning involved. Just a bit of carving. I could show you how to get going."

"Thanks, but I won't have the time."

"Ah, well. I expect you're always rushing about, same as most people. But if you change your mind, you can generally find me in the pub on a Friday night. I go in nice and early for the meat raffle, then I toddle off home."

"That's the one time I steer clear of the Wild Boar," Dan replied. "I don't eat meat."

Reg's smile faded. "If you're going to the barbecue stall later, stick to the sausages is my advice. They're mainly breadcrumbs and pink food colouring, so you should be all right."

"I'll bear that in mind. Well, thanks for showing me the bodging. I think I'll go and see if I can find a cold drink."

"The beer tent's over by the barn."

"There's a beer tent?"

"Course there is," Reg said. "Have you never been to a village fair before?"

"This is my first. I was expecting scones and jam and a cup of tea."

"We can do a good deal better than that. Get yourself over to the beer tent and wet your whistle. A pint of ale is the only thing that'll do on a warm day like this."

"I might do that," Dan said.

But Reg wasn't listening. He looked past Dan, and his good humour vanished. "Hello," he muttered. "Here comes trouble."

Dan tried to follow his gaze, but all he could see was a crowd of people milling aimlessly around, mainly in family groups. Then, with a sickening jolt, Dan realised that Reg was staring with undisguised animosity at a young black man: the only person of colour in view.

Dan fought down the surge of anger stirring in his gut, then he turned on Reg. "How can you say that?"

"Oh, I know what you think. But I'm not some ignorant bigot. I don't care what the bloke looks like. It's what he's been up to that folks don't appreciate."

"And what's that, precisely?" Dan demanded. "All I can see is a young man enjoying a day out with his girlfriend."

"Trespassing. They've been camping in Brandle Wood, and they've no business being there."

"I've no idea where you mean, but where's the harm? A couple of young people camping in the woods, getting out into the countryside; I'd have thought you'd be all in favour."

"If they were local kids, maybe. But all these bloody

townies, they don't know how to behave. They've got no respect. They chuck their rubbish all over the place and then go home. Plastic bags, empty cans, broken bottles and God knows what else."

"Have you actually seen their campsite?"

"No need. I know what it'll be."

"No, you don't," Dan insisted. "You're judging those young people before you've given them a chance. Whether you care to admit or not, you're being prejudiced."

Reg grunted under his breath. "You know, it's just come back to me. Dan Corrigan. I've heard all about you. And it's true what they say, you really are an awkward bugger." Before Dan could reply, Reg raised a warning finger. "It's all very well coming out with fancy words, but trespassing is trespassing, and you can't have folks tramping all over the place, damaging crops and leaving their rubbish everywhere."

"You've no reason to think—"

"*Think!*" Reg interrupted. "I *know* what they'll do. And they're asking for trouble. If Sid Sturridge catches them, he'll give them what for."

"Not if they've already asked for permission to camp."

"Sid wouldn't allow it."

"Why not?"

"Because he's the gamekeeper, that's why. All the land around Brandle Wood belongs to Mr Benning, and he runs a shoot every week in the season. Pheasants. Sid's out there every day, tending to those birds, and he always has his gun and his dogs. If he finds those townies, he'll skin them alive."

Dan took another look at the young couple. The woman wore a summer dress, her bare arms tanned and her long dark hair hanging loose. She strolled hand in hand with her partner, smiling and chatting, relaxed. The young man at her side was square shouldered, and he moved with a certain self-confidence: not swaggering but proud, his back as straight as a rod.

"Maybe someone should warn them," Dan said. "About the gamekeeper."

"You could try," Reg muttered. "Won't do any good though."

"We'll see." Dan offered the chisel back to Reg. "Thanks, but I'll leave you to it."

"My pleasure." The warmth had gone from Reg's expression, and he eyed the chisel warily without taking it. "Other way around. When you pass a tool to someone, you give them the handle, never the blade. That's how accidents happen."

"Sorry." Dan flipped the chisel around and Reg took it carefully.

"That's better," Reg said. "Always handle your tools properly, that's the golden rule. It was drummed into me a long time ago. Better safe than sorry."

"Right. Well, thanks again. It was… instructional."

Reg nodded then went back to his work, and Dan strode away.

The young couple had joined a queue at a food stall, and if he was quick, Dan could stand next to them and strike up a conversation. But he was beaten to it by a middle-aged man in the uniform attire of the landowning classes: olive corduroys and a checked shirt with the Barbour logo discreetly displayed on the breast pocket. The man was below average height, but perhaps in an attempt to compensate, he walked stiff legged with his head held high and his nose in the air. The effect might've been comical if it hadn't been for the coldness of his glare and the mean set of his jaw.

The man marched up to the young couple and accosted them as though he owned the place. *He probably does*, Dan decided, and the thought rankled him. Just because the man owned a bit of land, it didn't give him the right to treat people as if they were his serfs. If there was one thing Dan couldn't stand, it was a bully.

"Look here!" the man called out. "I know what you've been doing, and I won't have it. You can't just make yourself at home on my land. It's against the law."

The young man regarded his accuser, then he folded his arms very slowly. But he didn't say a word.

His companion was less reserved. Her eyes ablaze, she squared up to the man, gesticulating as she spoke, and Dan caught a hint of her eastern European accent. "We're not doing any harm. What's it to you if we sleep out for a few nights?"

"How dare you speak to me like that?" the man spluttered. He pulled himself up to his full height, ready to launch into a verbal attack. But before he could begin, Dan arrived, and he placed himself between the aggrieved parties.

"Hello," Dan said with a broad smile. "You must be Mr Benning. Lovely to meet you. I'm Dan Corrigan." He extended his hand for a shake, but the man merely glanced at it.

"What do you want?"

"To help." Dan kept his hand in the air. "Come on now, Mr Benning. You'll shake the hand of a neighbour, won't you?"

"You're a local?"

Dan nodded. "I live in the village. The Old Shop. I've been there for almost a year."

"Hm. I thought I recognised the name. Craig Ellington mentioned you. Said you helped him out of a tight spot."

"That's right. Craig's a friend."

"I see." Begrudgingly, the man shook Dan's hand. "Scott Benning." His lips straightened for a second, but that was as close as he got to a smile. "Now, if you'll excuse me, Mr Corrigan…"

"Please, call me Dan." Ignoring Scott's glare, Dan turned to the couple. "And you are?"

"Why do you want to know?" the woman asked.

"So that we can talk properly," Dan said. "If you don't mind, that is."

The young man spoke for the first time, holding his hand out to Dan. "I'm Adedayo. People call me Ade."

Ade pronounced his name with a final *ay* sound, and Dan made sure to say it correctly as he shook his hand and said, "Nice to meet you, Ade." He looked expectantly at the young woman, and after a sullen second, she offered her hand for a shake.

"I'm Maria."

"Excellent. Now, maybe we can discuss the problem and find a way forward."

Scott shook his head. "There's nothing to discuss. I appreciate that you're trying to help, Dan, but you're wasting your time. These two are trespassing on my land. Either they pack up and leave, or I call the police and have them arrested. That's all there is to it."

"That's just ridiculous," Maria shot back. "Trespass is not a criminal offence. We haven't damaged anything, so you can call the police if you want, but they won't do a thing."

Scott's cheeks suffused with colour. "We'll see about that, you bloody little—"

"Scott!" Dan interrupted. "Let's not turn this into a slanging match."

"No, go on." Maria lifted her chin in defiance. "What were you going to call us? Let's hear it. What've you got?"

Scott growled, but Dan held up his hands. "Listen. All three of you. This isn't getting us anywhere."

"*Us?*" Maria asked. "What's it got to do with you, anyway?"

Dan offered a reassuring smile. "Believe it or not, I'm on your side."

"We can take care of ourselves. I'm in the final year of a law degree, and Ade's studying medicine. He's practically a doctor already, and he's in the OTC."

Scott's eyebrows lowered. "You're in the Officer Training Corps? Where?"

"Exeter OTC," Ade said. "Coming up to five years in the corps, and after I finish my degree, I'll be applying to Sandhurst."

"Who's your commanding officer?" Scott said.

"Why? Thinking of joining up?" Ade didn't quite manage to hide his smirk.

"Don't be facetious. I have friends in the forces. Powerful friends."

If Ade takes him down a peg, I won't stand in his way, Dan thought. *I might even cheer.* But rallying his powers of persuasion, he said, "Let's get back to the issue."

"No," Scott snapped. "This is important. I won't have this chap trying to pull the wool over my eyes. I don't believe a word he says."

"Why is that?" Ade asked. "Because I'm black? Is that it?"

Scott sneered. "Don't play that card with me. I just don't believe your story, not for one second. A medical student, tramping about in the woods like some hippie. It doesn't add up."

"Colonel Brampton," Ade said. "That's the name of my CO. Do you want to see my ID?"

Scott's expression soured even further. "No. I know John Brampton. And I'll be sure to tell him how you've behaved. He'll say you've brought his regiment into disrepute."

"Be my guest," Ade replied. "But you'll be wasting your time. He's got more important things on his mind right now."

"Like what?" Scott demanded.

But Ade shook his head, tight lipped.

In the ensuing silence, Dan said, "Here's a thought. Let

them stay there tonight, Scott. And tomorrow, they can move on, leaving the wood as they found it. Okay?"

"What if we don't want to move on?" Maria said. "We were going to stay for a week."

"I really think you'd be wise to find somewhere else," Dan replied. "There are campsites—"

"We don't want those places," Maria interrupted. "I can't stand them."

Undeterred, Dan said, "If it's wild camping you want, I believe there are places on Dartmoor where you can pitch a tent."

Ade and Maria exchanged a look, unconvinced.

"I'll tell you what," Dan went on. "My neighbour will know a good place. He's around here somewhere. I'll go and ask him, and then I'll get back to you. Okay?"

"It can't hurt," Ade said. Maria looked as though she was about to argue, but Ade disarmed her with a smile. "Listen, we don't want to stay where we're not wanted."

"I should bloody well think not," Scott grumbled. "In fact, you should go today. Right now."

Ade fixed the man with a stare. "We'll figure out an alternative spot, then we'll go this afternoon. All right?"

"That's perfectly reasonable," Dan said. "What do you say, Scott? Fair enough?"

Scott grunted as if unimpressed.

"Excellent. Situation resolved." Dan rubbed his hands together. "I'll go and pick Alan's brains. Ade, Maria, I'll find you in ten minutes or so."

He made to move away but changed his mind. "There's just one thing. Scott, I've heard your gamekeeper can be a bit overzealous. Will you let him know what's going on?"

"Oh, I'll tell Sturridge what to do in no uncertain terms. But the problem with Sturridge..." Scott broke off to send them a humourless grin. "Let's just say he tends to be a law unto himself. He looks after my estate, and God help anyone who gets in his way. He has a temper. And those dogs of his… One word from him and they'll tear your throat out."

"That's not helpful," Dan said. "You've asked these people to move on and they've agreed. There's no need for threats and intimidation."

"I've had enough of this." Maria pulled a phone from her shoulder bag. "You know what? I'm the one calling the police. I've got good grounds. Harassment, hate speech, causing an affray. And that's just for starters. Plus, we've got Dan for a witness."

"Don't bother," Ade said. "It's not worth the trouble. *He's* not worth it."

Maria held his gaze, then she sighed. "You're right. Let's go and get something to eat. I'm hungry, and apparently we've got to move the tent this afternoon."

"Sounds like a plan." Ade nodded to Dan. "Later."

"Later," Dan replied, then he watched Ade and Maria walk away.

"Bloody people," Scott muttered. "The nerve. Making out like I was the one in the wrong. *Unbelievable.*"

Dan took a breath. "They may have been trespassing, and you were within your rights to ask them to leave, but that's it. Everything else you said was over the top. Maria was right, they could've made a complaint. And you know how people talk in the village. Imagine if the police had turned up at the fair. It wouldn't have looked good for you."

Scott waved his words aside. "I don't care about a bit of gossip. If you ask me, it wouldn't have done any harm. You've got to let people know you won't put up with that kind of nonsense, or before you know it, you'll have hordes of people swarming all over the place, knocking down fences and leaving the gates open. And don't get me started on the junk they leave behind. Not just litter but great piles of stuff. We've had furniture, broken glass, old tyres, even builders' rubble."

"That's hardly fair," Dan protested. "Ade and Maria came out for a little camping trip. They're not fly-tippers."

Scott made a dismissive noise in the back of his throat. "It's plain to see where your sympathies lie. But you'd better hope those people are off my land by the close of play, or I won't be answerable for what happens to them."

Dan's only reply was a hard stare; he'd heard more than enough from Scott Benning. But the man hadn't finished.

"And here's a word of advice, Mr Corrigan. If you plan on staying in Embervale, you'd do well to choose your friends more wisely."

"I'm more than happy with my choices," Dan said. "Goodbye, Scott. I'll see you around."

Dan turned on his heel and marched away across the show field. He took out his phone to call Alan, but a familiar message flashed onto the screen: *Emergency Calls Only.* Sighing, he thrust his phone back into his pocket. *I know phone masts are ugly*, he thought. *But a few more wouldn't hurt, would they?*

Never mind. It shouldn't be too hard to find Alan, and surely he'd know some potential campsites for Ade and Maria. But there might not be much time. He assumed Scott had laid it on a bit thick with his dire warnings about the unpredictable gamekeeper. But then again, Reg Stoddard had mentioned Sid Sturridge as well, so perhaps there was cause for concern.

Would this Sturridge character really threaten Ade and Maria? It was impossible to be sure. The safest bet was to find Alan as soon as possible, and then they could advise Ade and Maria accordingly. *Where would Alan be?* Dan wondered. At that moment, a group of young men wandered past, all with plastic pint glasses in hand. *Of course!* Dan took a quick look around and quickly spotted a large tent with a hand-painted sign above the entrance. He started walking, strutting confidently across the field without a shadow of doubt in his mind. Alan would be in the beer tent. Where else?

CHAPTER 2

ALAN CLAPPED ALONG with the rest of the audience as the maypole dance came to a close. The children, resplendent in their freshly laundered school uniforms, had skipped around each other, trailing the long, brightly coloured maypole ribbons, weaving them together then reversing the steps to unravel the patterns. In the end, the ribbons were straight once more, and the absence of tangles meant that the dance had been completed successfully. The children grinned from ear to ear, and as the music faded, they bowed to accept the applause.

A woman in a cream linen trouser suit stepped forward to address the crowd. She was, Alan guessed, a few years younger than him, and with her short blonde hair and glowing complexion, she radiated health and vigour. And it was clear that she was the children's teacher: she had that unmistakable air of authority.

"Thank you so much for all your support," she began. "I know the children really appreciate your encouragement. They've worked very hard to perfect each dance. We've had some fine tangles over the last few weeks, but they kept trying, and I hope you'll agree that their efforts have paid off. It's too nice a day for long speeches, and you all want to go and enjoy the rest of the fair, but before you go, please pop into our tent, which is next to the community orchard. We've got lots for you to see, including some games the children have made and organised themselves, and of course we're selling tickets for our prize draw. I hope to see you there. Thanks again, and perhaps we can have one last round of applause for our maypole dancers!"

The audience obediently clapped and then they began to disperse. But Alan lingered, watching as the maypole was taken down and the long, colourful ribbons folded away. There were times when he missed being a teacher, missed being part of something so special, and he wandered toward the community orchard and stood in front of the tent where proud parents were bravely trying their hands at the games on offer.

"Would you care to whack a rat?" someone asked, and Alan turned to find the teacher regarding him with a smile. "Or perhaps," she went on, "you'd prefer to have a go at the tombola."

"I'm not sure I could choose between them," Alan replied. "So I'll just have to try both."

The teacher smiled, the light dancing in her lively green eyes. "Forgive me, but aren't you Alan Hargreaves, our famous author?"

Alan stood a little taller. "Yes. I don't know about famous, but I'm certainly an author."

"I thought so. I'm Miss Nickleton." She laughed. "Sorry, force of habit. Let's start again. I'm Gemma. Pleased to meet you." She held out her hand for a shake and Alan took it.

"I'm Alan, although you already knew that of course." Alan took a breath. "The maypole dancing was wonderful."

"Thank you. I must admit to being rather nervous. I'm from Embervale originally, so I know how important the May Fair is to the children, but I've only been at the school since

September. After my training I moved away for a few years, and inner-city kids aren't so keen on dancing around the maypole. This was my first attempt at teaching the dances, and I was told in no uncertain terms that we have a reputation to maintain."

"You needn't worry on that score. The children were particularly good this year."

"Flatterer," Gemma replied, though she was clearly pleased.

"I mean it. The children were a credit to you. You must've put in a lot of work."

"It's all down to the children. They knew the dances already. It was all I could do to keep up with them."

"But you'll have given up a lot of your free time to help them," Alan said. "I used to be a teacher myself, so I know how much effort goes into these things."

"Ah, I remember reading that you were a teacher. It must've been in your bio. We have several of your books in the library. I must get you to sign them for us."

"Certainly, I'd be delighted. But I can do better than that. I've been thinking about doing some school visits. Would you like me to pop in and give a talk sometime? I could do a few readings, answer questions, maybe even run a little writing workshop."

Gemma's hand went to her chest. "Mr Hargreaves, when can we book you in? It sounds wonderful. Mind you, I'll have to check the literacy budget. Finances tend to get a bit stretched at this time of year."

"Oh, I wouldn't charge you. It's not as though I'd have to travel far, and to be honest, you'd be doing me a favour. I've been thinking of doing school visits for a while, so this would be an ideal opportunity for me to get my feet wet. Besides, I'd like to help out. It'll be my way of giving something back to the community."

"Well, that's even better. If you could give me your phone number, we can set a date."

"Sure." Alan rattled off his number and Gemma tapped it into her phone.

"I'll call you," she said. "Whenever I can find five minutes to sit down and go through my plans. You know what it's like."

"Yes. Never a dull moment. But listen, while we're both here, why don't we sit down and talk it over? I've been out of the classroom for a while and everything must've changed. Perhaps we could discuss it over a cup of tea."

"Oh." Gemma looked down, and Alan's heart sank.

"Sorry, I didn't mean to be presumptuous. I expect you have other things to do."

Gemma shook her head, and when she looked back up, her smile had returned. "It's not that. I'm expecting a visitor later today, and I was going to tidy the house. But apart from that, all I have waiting for me at home is a stack of books to mark and a weekly plan that looks like…" She lifted her arms then let them fall. "Put it this way, unless I can change the laws of space and time, the only way I'll be able to cover everything is if we cancel the summer holidays and work through until Christmas."

"I remember the feeling well. But you'll tackle your timetable all the better if you've had a break, so my offer still stands. A cup of tea or coffee will perk you up no end." Alan smiled and looked Gemma in the eye. "They have home-made scones. With clotted cream."

She held his gaze as if weighing him up, and then she laughed. "Go on then. I can't stay long, but ten minutes won't hurt."

"Excellent. And it was my idea, so you must let me pay."

Gemma's expression clouded. "There's no need. I'd rather pay my way."

"No problem," Alan said quickly. "They're serving refreshments in the barn. It's this way."

"I'll get my things." Gemma crossed the tent, exchanged a few words with a man standing behind the stall, then she gathered her possessions, stuffing them into a small leather satchel and slinging it over her shoulder.

Alan watched the way she moved. Gemma was slightly built and there was a lightness to her step, but she had a presence that seemed larger than her slim frame. When she chatted to the children behind the stall, they watched her with rapt attention, and when she bestowed her smile on them, they beamed in return.

I'll bet she's a great teacher, Alan thought. *She has the gift.* Alan had been confident in the classroom, but it had been hard work. He'd always admired those teachers who, seemingly without effort, could hold the attention of any number of children. Gemma, he guessed, could make a gaggle of excited children fall silent with nothing more than a raised eyebrow.

"I've just realised," Gemma began as she strode toward him. "You still haven't tried our games."

"Yes, I'd forgotten." Alan rummaged in his pocket for some change. Thankfully, he'd come prepared. "Which shall I try first?"

Gemma considered for a second. "Whack a rat. You look as though you have a keen eye."

"Right. Whack a rat it is."

Alan paid his money and stood by with the stubby wooden bat, while a boy picked up something that looked suspiciously like a stuffed woolly sock that had been adorned with plastic eyes and a bootlace tail. With due ceremony, the boy dangled the home-made rat above the vertical length of plastic drainpipe mounted on a wooden stand.

"When I let go, you have to hit the rat when it comes out

the end," he announced. "You get three goes, and if you hit it, you get a sweet from the tub."

"Got it," Alan replied. "Ready when you are."

But he wasn't. Without warning, the boy released the fluffy rat, and whatever it was stuffed with, it must've been heavy, because the dratted thing emerged from the pipe at lightning speed. Alan struck at it, but far too late.

"Try again," Gemma said. "Better luck next time."

Alan nodded, grinning. But when the rat whizzed past, and he mistimed his swipe for a second time, his smile faltered.

"You'll get it next time," Gemma said.

"Maybe I should close my eyes," Alan replied. "Like Luke Skywalker."

"Use the Force," the boy giggled as he retrieved the rat and made it ready.

Gemma leaned closer to Alan, and lowering her voice to a stage whisper, she said, "The trick is, you have to start your swing *before* you see it."

"Ah." Alan took a breath. "Release the rat."

This time, Alan's bat connected with the stuffed sock and sent it sailing against the tent wall.

"Well done!" Gemma said. "I'm impressed."

"Years of practice," Alan replied as he returned the bat to the young boy.

Gemma laughed. "Really? With rats?"

"Cricket. I was on the team at school. Until I discovered... other things."

Gemma cocked an eyebrow and looked as though she'd like to know more, but the young boy interrupted: "You get to choose a sweet."

"Thank you." Alan eyed the plastic tub of sweets in their lurid wrappers. "I don't go in much for sweets. I'll tell you what, young man, you have it. Call it a perk of running the stall."

The boy glanced at Gemma. "I'm not allowed. They're for the prizes."

"It would set a precedent," Gemma said. "We don't want to start arguments, so I'll settle the matter. I'll pick one." Her hand hovered over the tub. "A pear drop. My favourite." She plucked the sweet from the tub and unwrapped it, popping it into her mouth. "My guilty pleasure. Now, Mr Hargreaves, you said you'd try the tombola."

"Okay. Maybe I'll be on a winning streak."

Alan handed his money to the pair of girls running the stall, and once the small wooden drum had been turned, he dipped his hand inside and pulled out three folded raffle tickets.

"Numbers ending with a five or a zero win a prize," one of the girls told him.

The first ticket Alan unfolded bore the number 78, the second was 143, and he held his breath as he revealed the third number.

"Bad luck," Gemma said, peering at the ticket. "Fifty-nine. Just one away from a prize."

"A miss is as good as a mile." Alan sent Gemma a smile, but she didn't respond in kind. Instead, she looked pensive for a moment then said, "You know, I really should be heading for home. I've got so much to do before this afternoon."

"Oh. It's up to you, of course, but we could get our drinks to take out. I promise not to take up too much of your time, and you could take your scone home and eat it later. You could buy an extra one or two for your visitor."

"He's not really the scone type."

"Ah."

Gemma sighed. "Oh dear, you look crestfallen. And I did talk you into playing two of our games, so the least I can do is keep you company for a while. But I can't be long."

"Ten minutes. And it'll be my treat. I insist."

"All right," Gemma said. "Let's go."

They chatted about teaching as they strolled across the show field, and Gemma's face lit up when she talked about her class and her plans for the school. She was full of optimism and bursting with ideas, and Alan hung on her every word. By the time they reached the barn and the refreshments, Alan knew that he liked Gemma Nickleton. He liked her very much indeed.

CHAPTER 3

THE BEER TENT was large and old fashioned, its flapping sides held in place by hemp ropes, and as soon as Dan stepped inside, he was hit by the mingling aromas of ale and damp canvas. The bar had been rigged up at the far end of the tent, and behind it a row of barrels lay on their sides. Dan ran his tongue across his lips, but it wasn't even lunchtime yet, and besides, he still had to find Alan. He cast his eye over the customers sitting at the scattered tables, but only a few dedicated beer drinkers had decided to start early, and it was clear that Alan wasn't among them.

Behind the bar, Sam Ashford stood patiently, waiting for customers, her hands spread wide on the counter. Her eyes went straight to Dan, and an uncertain smile fluttered across her lips.

Dan lifted his hand in acknowledgement. *I can't stay and talk to her*, he told himself. *I have to go and find Alan.* But Sam tilted her head, flicking her eyes toward the bar, and without meaning to, Dan found himself walking toward her.

"All right?" Sam asked. "Enjoying the fair?"

"Yes, it's good, but have you seen Alan?"

"Not yet." Sam sighed. "I wish I was out there with you

instead of being stuck behind the bar." She grinned. "I don't mean *with* you, obviously. I just meant that I wish I was outside in the sunshine with everybody else."

"Maybe you'll get time later."

"I doubt it. Once it gets near lunchtime, they'll start rolling in and I'll be run off my feet." She paused. "I expect you and Alan will be popping in later."

"Probably. I thought he'd be here now. That's the only reason I came in."

"Oh. I see." Sam looked away as if put out.

"It's nice to see you, though," Dan said quickly. "As always."

Her gaze met his, and there was that smile again: hesitant, half formed. She seemed to be waiting for something, and Dan hunted for the right thing to say. But then she patted her hair.

"Ah, you've had your hair done," he said. "I knew there was something different about you. It's nice."

"*Nice?* I didn't drive to Exeter and pay an arm and a leg for *nice.*"

"It's great, really it is. Much shorter. And it's more sophisticated than your usual..." Dan's words died on his lips under the force of Sam's glare. "I'm sorry, Sam, I didn't mean to imply that you don't always look nice, but I've got something on my mind right now, and I need—"

"Excuse me," someone said, and Dan turned to see a man in his twenties standing beside him at the bar. He seemed agitated, gripping the bar's edge with both hands as though preparing to leap over it.

"Are you all right?" Sam asked him.

The man nodded. "Yeah, yeah. Listen. Sorry to interrupt and all that, but we were in here earlier, my girlfriend and me, and I lost something. A bag. You haven't seen a bag, have you?"

"No," Sam replied. "What kind of bag?"

"A messenger bag. Black." The man leaned forward, peering behind the bar. "I thought someone might've handed it in."

"Sorry. No one's handed anything in."

"Could you look anyway?" the man said. "It'll only take a second."

Sam folded her arms. "I've been here the whole time. No one has handed anything in."

"Okay, but please check."

"All right." Sam bent down to look beneath the counter. Dan heard the clink of empty glass bottles, the rustle of a plastic bag, then Sam straightened her back. "Nope. There's nothing here."

"Shit!" The man bit his lip. "Sorry. But I really need to find that bag. It's got my wallet inside."

"Oh dear," Sam said. "Are you sure you left it in here?"

"No. I thought my girlfriend had it and she thought…" The man let out an exasperated sigh. "You can guess the rest. Neither of us can remember when we last saw it. I'd better keep on looking. It could be anywhere."

"Good luck," Sam said. "But before you go, give me a number where I can reach you, and if it turns up, I'll give you a call."

"Thanks. That would be great. I'll give you a card." The man pulled a slim leather wallet from his pocket and began hunting through it.

Dan had been watching the proceedings carefully, and he said, "That's good."

The man's gaze darted to Dan. "What did you say?"

Dan gestured to the man's hand. "You said that your wallet was in your bag, but it looks like you haven't lost it after all."

"Are you kidding?" the man demanded. "I'm not making this stuff up. This thing is just for my cards. My proper wallet is in the bag. My driving licence, my cash. All kinds of stuff."

"Okay." Dan kept his tone neutral. "There's no need to overreact. I was only trying to help."

"Is that a fact?" The man sent Dan a mocking smile, then he turned back to Sam, holding out a business card. "I'm Paul. My numbers are all on there."

"Thanks." Taking the card, Sam glanced at it before stowing it under the bar. "I'll be sure to let you know if anything turns up."

"Thank you. I really appreciate it. You're a star. I'll go and look around." He gave Sam a broad smile, then he strode from the tent.

"Poor bloke," Sam said. "What a thing to happen."

"If he's to be believed," Dan muttered. "It all seemed a bit fishy to me."

"Why do you have to be so suspicious about everyone? He was a nice young man, and he's had a bit of bad luck. You ought to feel sorry for him."

"You might be right. He could've been telling the truth, but he seemed very overwrought. I think something was going on, something he was trying to hide."

"Weren't you listening?" Sam asked. "The guy just lost his wallet. If I was in his shoes, I'd be going spare. I lost my keys last week, and I practically tore the pub apart. Total meltdown."

"Mm. But what about that business with the two wallets? It didn't ring true."

"That's because you're turning into an old fart before your time."

"I beg your pardon?"

"It's true," Sam insisted. "Young men don't like to have great big wallets in their pockets, on account of the way it spoils the look of their clothes. Only middle-aged men walk around with their jeans bulging all over the place." She shuddered. "Just look at Jeremy Clarkson."

"For one thing, I am not middle aged. And for another…"

Dan broke off, staring at her, his eyes round with horror. "Did you just compare me to Clarkson?"

"If the cap fits."

"The cap is several sizes too large," Dan shot back. "And several decades too old. Clarkson could be my father, for God's sake."

"Really? I must tell the *Daily Mail*."

"Not literally," Dan groaned, then he buttoned his lip. Sam was winding him up, grinning from ear to ear, and Dan did the only thing he could: he raised his hands in surrender. "Can we start again? Can we go back to before we were so rudely interrupted?"

Sam made a show of considering his proposal. "All right. You were saying you had something on your mind."

"That's right." Dan smiled gratefully. "I need to find Alan. I want to ask him something. Unless you happen to know a place nearby where people can go wild camping."

"You're going camping? Who with?"

"No, it's for someone else. I said I'd help. I promised."

Sam thought for a second. "There are a couple of proper campsites along the valley, but apart from that, I wouldn't know. Most of the land around here is private. You can't just pitch a tent anywhere you like — not without someone blowing a fuse. Some of the folks around here would set their dogs on you, like as not."

"So I understand." Dan placed his hands on the bar as if to push himself away. "I must get going. I'll catch you later."

"All right. Run along, city boy. But don't wait too long or the place will be packed."

"Sure." Dan marched from the tent. *City boy*, he thought. *If only*. If he was in the city, his phone would have a proper signal, and there'd be free Wi-Fi and a place to get a good espresso and some decent sushi.

Food, Dan thought. If Alan wasn't sipping a pint, he'd

probably be chasing down a snack. Dan headed toward the food stalls.

The longest queue was for the barbecue and Dan grimaced when the acrid fumes of burnt fat caught in his nostrils. But at least he didn't have to linger; Alan was not in the line of people hungrily eying the sizzling sausages and burgers.

Dan stopped to scan the field. The fine weather had brought people out, and the crowd had grown larger over the last few minutes. Dan had never seen so many people at a village event, but he knew the reason for the good turnout; knew it all too well. Alan had warned him that the May Day bank holiday, coupled with the first warm days of spring, would herald the start of the annual influx of tourists into Devon. And so it had proved. Over the last week, Dan had noticed the increasing numbers of motorhomes and caravans on the roads, and on several occasions, he'd been held up in the lanes by drivers who were unused to the necessity of having to stop and reverse into a lay-by every time they met an oncoming vehicle.

I suppose this is what happens when you live in a beauty spot, he told himself. *I'll just have to get used to it.* After all, he didn't want to become one of those people who resented outsiders; he was still the newcomer himself.

Thinking of new arrivals, he looked for Ade and Maria. They were nowhere in sight, but a sign on one of the food stalls snagged his gaze, a single word standing out: *Vegan.*

Below the sign promising both hot and cold food, the menu was displayed on a chalkboard. Dan moved closer to read it properly, and his mouth watered. *Hot mushroom flatbreads, spiced falafel served with fresh salsa, homemade burgers.* The list went on. The stall was housed in a smart green tent with a proper counter at the front, and from the tent's shady interior came the reassuring sound of someone chopping vegetables with the speed of a professional chef.

I don't have time for this, Dan thought. But his stomach disagreed, and it growled to let him know. Dan glanced once more at the menu, then he strode up to the counter.

At the back of the tent, a young man looked up from his chopping board, and Dan was impressed to see that he was dressed in a chef's white jacket that could've been used to advertise washing powder. A pair of checked trousers and a black cap completed the outfit. The chef offered Dan a bright smile. "I'll be right with you, sir. I just need to get this chard into the dressing. If I leave it lying around on a day like this, it'll start to wilt, and it won't be the same."

He renewed his skilful attack on the vivid green leaves, the knife a blur, then he scooped up the chopped leaves between the knife's broad blade and the edge of his palm.

"That's an impressive-looking knife," Dan said.

"It's a Nakiri," the chef replied, depositing the chopped chard into a gleaming glass bowl then tilting the knife toward Dan. The knife's handle was made from polished wood with a distinctive dark grain, and its glittering blade had a curious marbled patina. Unusually, the knife had no pointed tip. Instead, the metal had been cut almost square. "It was made by Sakai Takayuki in Japan," the chef went on. "That pattern is where the steel has been folded and hammered. It cost a small fortune, but it was worth every penny. The balance is perfect." He laid the knife gently on the board then, returning his attention to the bowl, he used his fingers to toss the chopped chard, coating them with a glistening mixture.

Dan detected the earthy aroma of olive oil and the sharp tang of balsamic vinegar, and he was mesmerised. This was what he'd been missing. Dan didn't go in for fine dining — the ubiquitous presence of cream and butter saw to that — but back in London, he'd known where to find great food. It had taken him years, but he'd built a mental map of the best vegan cafes and restaurants across London. From almond cake to za'atar-spiced houmous, whatever he'd desired, he'd been able to find it. And all of it freshly prepared by people who cared.

And here, in the middle of a field, culinary paradise had been brought to his doorstep. Dan let out a sigh of contentment, and the chef eyed him warily.

"Are you all right, sir?"

"Yes," Dan replied. "Tell me, is this a local enterprise?"

"Very much so. I'm from the village. But this is all new." He gestured around the tent. "I've been working in restaurants across the South-West, but I've decided to set up on my own. That way, I can source everything myself and make sure it's all up to scratch." He smiled. "So, what can I get you? The falafel is particularly good, but if you want a treat, I recommend the mushroom flatbread wrap. I use shitake, hen of the woods and chanterelles. I cook it to order, and I add a few sprigs of fresh thyme. It only takes a minute." He raised his eyebrows in expectation.

"And the flatbreads?"

"I have a local supplier who makes them himself to an authentic Turkish recipe. These were made this morning. You won't find fresher or better."

"Okay," Dan said. "Sold."

"Excellent." The chef went into action, lighting a gas burner and sliding a skillet into place. He held a bottle of oil over the pan, but he paused for a second before pouring a glug onto the smoking metal. Then he plucked mushrooms from a row of plastic tubs, adding them carefully to the hot oil, watching them like a hawk. After a second or two, he shook the pan, flicking his wrist to toss the mushrooms from one end of the pan to the other.

"Where do you get the mushrooms?" Dan asked. "Can you find them in the wild?"

"We get plenty of porcini around here in the autumn, but you can't rely on foraging, and I need a regular supply. I go to a small farm near Exeter. They have everything you could want. If you're interested, I can send you their details."

"That would be great," Dan said. "Shall I give you my number?"

"It might be better if you take my email address and drop me a line. There are some flyers on the counter there."

Dan found the small stack of flyers tucked away beside a cluster of glass bottles containing salad dressings and spicy sauces. *George Hepworth*, Dan read. *Proprietor: Embervale Kitchen.* There was a website and an email address. Dan folded the flyer and tucked it into his pocket. "Thanks, George. I'll be in touch. My name's Dan, by the way. Dan Corrigan."

George looked up from his frying pan. "Hi, Dan." A cloud flitted across his expression, and he looked as though he was about to say something, but he went back to his furious activity, his attention focused on the mushrooms as he added herbs and seasoning. "Almost ready. I just want them to get a little more colour."

"They smell incredible," Dan said. "It reminds me of cooking around a campfire. What have you put in there?"

"That would be telling." George grinned, laying a flatbread in a cardboard tray then giving his pan a final shake. "Perfect." Plucking out the sprigs of thyme, he scooped up the glistening mushrooms, arranging them neatly and then folding the bread to form a neat parcel. "There we are." He presented the tray to Dan. "Can I get you anything else?"

"Not right now, thanks." Dan paid and then lifted his prize.

"I'm here all day, so if you'd like something sweet, I have a blackthorn sorbet. Very refreshing. Much better than ice cream on a day like this."

"Home made?"

George wrinkled his brow as if affronted. "Of course. I

only make it at this time of year. I gather the blossoms from the hedgerows, and it doesn't bloom for long."

"I think I've got some at the end of my garden. I was going to cut it back, but my neighbour told me I mustn't. He says it's good for the bees."

"He's probably right. The bugs certainly like it. I have to get up at the crack of dawn to beat them to it. But don't worry, I check it's all clean before it goes into the sorbet. Otherwise, it wouldn't be vegan, would it?"

Dan laughed. "I think you could be forgiven for accidentally freezing a bug or two. But anyway, I might pop by later and try it."

"Please do. Enjoy your mushrooms."

"I intend to." Dan headed away, sinking his teeth into the flatbread as he walked, savouring the taste. George was obviously a talented chef, but would he make a living? He used expensive ingredients, and he must've spent hours in preparation, but most of the fair-goers seemed to be opting for the familiar lure of barbecued meat.

Even so, Dan knew a promising entrepreneur when he saw one, and George was as keen as home-grown horseradish. He'd make it one day. After all, some of the biggest brands in the supermarkets had started from humble food stalls.

George would find a niche. *That young man has a bright future ahead of him*, Dan decided. *As soon as I find Alan, I'll drag him over to George's stall and persuade him to try some real food.* But he'd have to find the man first. Where *was* he?

CHAPTER 4

S ITTING AT A table in the barn, Alan dabbed at the crumbs of scone on his plate then licked his finger.

"Hungry?" Gemma arched an eyebrow. "You could always go and get another scone."

"One was plenty." Alan saw the way she was looking at him, and the blood rose to his cheeks. "But I'm sorry for my awful table manners. I've been living on my own for too long."

"There's no Mrs Hargreaves?"

"No. But there's no need to sound so surprised. Do I look married?"

"You look contented. Like a man who's settled down."

"I'm not quite ready to be put out to pasture. I have a nice life, and the career I'd dreamed of since I was a child. But I enjoy learning new skills and meeting new people. Like you, for instance."

Gemma smiled. "Earlier, when you said you gave up cricket for other things, what did you mean? Did you discover girls? Was that it?"

"I suppose so. And music. I swapped my trusty bat for a second-hand electric guitar, and my white trousers for ripped jeans. I was even in a band for a while. But that was later when I was at university."

"Were you any good?"

"Terrible. We must've been the only band in history to split up due to popular demand. There was a petition."

"That's quite an achievement."

"We were in student accommodation, and the other residents objected to our practice sessions. I can't say I blame them. I only knew three chords, and I used to get those mixed up."

Gemma laughed, and Alan asked the question that had been on the tip of his tongue for some time: "You said you had a visitor arriving today. Is it somebody special?"

"Erm, it's complicated."

"Ah. I didn't mean to be nosy."

"It's not…" Gemma sighed. "It's my brother. He's coming to stay with me for a bit."

"I see." Alan tried to hide his relief, but he didn't make a very good job of it. He grinned as he said, "That'll be nice."

"Yes. I haven't seen him for ages. He's been away."

"So, you'll have lots of catching up to do."

Gemma managed a weak smile. "Something like that. But I don't want to go into it." She rallied, leaning closer and patting the table as if to signal a change of subject. "Tell me more about your writing. It must be fascinating."

"It's not as glamorous as you might think. I spend a lot of time sitting on my own at the keyboard and tapping away. There's not much to tell."

"Oh. I see."

The spark vanished from Gemma's eyes. He was losing her attention, and without stopping to think, Alan blurted, "Mind you, I've had a few adventures over the last year. Just before Christmas I was involved in a murder investigation."

Gemma sat back, her posture stiffening. "Murder?"

"Yes, but there's nothing to worry about. It all worked out

in the end." Alan knew he should stop talking, but somehow he blundered on. "I was just helping, that's all. I wasn't a suspect. Not that time, anyway."

"What do you mean *not that time*? When *were* you a suspect?"

Alan's mouth was dry. He checked his cup but it was empty. He had no way of playing for time; he'd have to soldier on and explain. "Last summer. A man in the village was attacked. My neighbour and me, we tried to help, but we were too late. Sadly, the man died, and because we'd been there, I was questioned by the police. It was a dreadful mix-up, but of course, it was nothing to do with me and it was all cleared up."

Gemma shook her head in disbelief.

"I shouldn't have mentioned it," Alan said. "It's not a fit topic for a day like this."

"No." Gemma's voice was faint, and she cleared her throat. "Thank you for the tea and everything, but I really must be going."

"You're very welcome. It was lovely talking to you." Alan had no idea what to say next and into the strained silence a voice boomed: "There you are."

Alan turned to see Dan hurrying toward him, and a sinking feeling stirred in his stomach.

"I've been looking for you everywhere," Dan said. "I thought you'd be in the beer tent."

"No. It's a bit early in the day for me," Alan said pointedly. "Far too early." His gaze slid toward Gemma, and Dan seemed to take the hint.

"Ah, yes," Dan said. "I was forgetting the time." He smiled at Gemma. "Forgive me barging in. I'm Dan. Alan's neighbour."

Gemma eyed him warily before turning to Alan, an unspoken question in her eyes.

"Yes, he's the one I was telling you about," Alan

explained. "Gemma, meet the infamous Dan Corrigan. But whatever he tells you about me, ignore it. He has a strange sense of humour." In a stage whisper, he added, "He's from London."

"Why am I infamous?" Dan asked. "What have you been saying?"

"Nothing. Alan mentioned you, that's all." Gemma stood, hoisting her satchel onto her shoulder. "Anyway, it was nice to meet you both, but I have to go. Thanks again, Alan. Bye."

"Oh, but we never talked about the school visit," Alan said. "Shall I call you at the school?"

"Let me think about it," Gemma replied. "I'll need to check with the head teacher. And she may feel that, in the circumstances, a visit wouldn't be appropriate."

"But I did explain," Alan said. "I wasn't implicated in what happened. I was in the wrong place at the wrong time. And I did everything I could to help the police."

"That's true," Dan put in. "I'm not sure which case you're talking about, but you can blame me. I'm always the one who drags Alan into trouble."

Gemma stared at Dan. "How many *cases* have there been?"

"Four," Dan replied. "But only three were murders. The other one was an execution, although you could argue that—"

"Dan, you're not helping," Alan interrupted. He stood, facing Gemma. "Believe it or not, I can explain all this. It's nowhere near as bad as it sounds."

Gemma looked him in the eye, then slowly she nodded. "Alan, you seem like a decent man. I could be wrong — God knows I've been wrong about men before — but I'm pretty sure you're okay. I believe what you say, but even so, that doesn't mean the visit can go ahead. We have to be very careful about the school's reputation. It's a small village, and we can't afford the wrong kind of publicity. I hope you understand."

Alan nodded dumbly.

"Goodbye," Gemma said, then she hurried away, making for the barn door.

Alan watched her go, but before Gemma could step outside, a man loomed in the doorway, barring her way. Gemma halted, frozen in her tracks, her cheeks pale.

Dan turned to Alan. "Who's that?"

"I've no idea," Alan replied.

The buzz of conversation in the barn died away, and every head turned to stare at the silent confrontation taking place in front of their eyes.

The new arrival was tall, but his shoulders were stooped, and he stretched out one hand against the door frame. It was hard to tell whether he was trying to block the exit or simply seeking support. Either way, when he lurched into the barn, he was unsteady, swaying on his feet. Gemma took a faltering step back, and though the man's attention was fixed on her, he must've noticed the silence, because he lifted his gaze to send a jaded stare around the barn. Alan met the man's stare with one of his own, then without hesitation Alan started moving toward Gemma. He heard Dan following in his footsteps, and he was glad of it.

Leering at Alan, the man let out a humourless cackle. "What's this — an unwelcoming committee?"

"For God's sake, Billy!" Gemma hissed. "Why do you always have to make a scene?"

The man shrugged. "I dunno. It's more fun."

Reaching Gemma's side, Alan said, "Are you all right, Gemma? Do you need any help?"

"*Her?*" the man scoffed. "Never. She doesn't need anybody. Never has. That's right, isn't it, sis?"

"He's your brother?" Alan asked.

"Well, he's quick on the uptake, isn't he?" The man

grinned evilly at Gemma. "Who's your friend, sis? Aren't you going to introduce me?"

"No, I'm not playing your silly games," Gemma replied. "You were supposed to meet me at home. What are you doing here? How did you even know where I was?"

"The internet. Any idiot could've found you, so I wasn't going to have any trouble, was I?" Billy cackled under his breath, then adopting a snide tone, he said, "Miss Nickleton will be taking her class to dance at the May Fair. Miss Nickleton will be running the stalls. Miss Nickleton will be saving the day, as bloody usual."

"That's enough," Gemma snapped.

Billy goggled at her in mock horror. "Miss Nickleton! You're being rude. These kind gentlemen have come over here to help, and you haven't even let me say hello." He offered his hand to Dan, his arm wavering in the air. "Billy Nickleton. Troublemaker, layabout and general pain in the arse. Pleased to meet you."

Gemma's hand went to her brow, covering her eyes. "Please, Billy, don't do this."

Sudden anger boiled in Alan's chest, and he said, "I think you'd better go, Billy. You're upsetting your sister."

"Bollocks. We're just having fun. Maybe you're the one upsetting her." He took a staggering step toward Alan. "Who are you, anyway? And what's this got to do with you? I was having a private conversation with my sister. *Private*. None of your bloody business, pal."

Alan squared his shoulders, but before he could say a word, Dan stepped forward. Smiling, he gripped Billy's hand as if for a shake, his fingers closing tight. "Billy, I'm Dan."

Billy focused on Dan as though seeing him properly for the first time, and his ebullient expression crumpled. "Ow! My hand! Let go."

Dan's smile grew broader, and he said one word. "Outside."

"No," Billy growled. "You can't tell me what to do." But he winced, shaking his head. Through clenched teeth, he said, "Let go of my bloody hand!"

"Oh dear," Dan said. "Does it hurt?" He twisted his hand, forcing Billy's wrist back into an unnatural position.

Billy grimaced, and for a split second Alan thought the man might lash out. But Billy's head was down, the defiant glint in his eyes extinguished.

"Don't hurt him," Gemma said. "Let him go."

Dan nodded. "Certainly. As soon as he steps outside."

"No," Gemma insisted. "Let go of him now."

"If you're sure." Dan released Billy's hand, then he stood his ground, waiting.

Nursing his wrist, Billy glared at him. "Bastard."

Dan offered an amiable shrug as if accepting a compliment.

"My car's in the next field," Gemma said. "Start walking, Billy, and don't make any more fuss or I'll leave you here."

"All right. Stop going on." Billy scowled at Dan, then he turned and walked out.

Gemma turned on Dan. "That was unnecessary."

"I don't know if your brother's drunk or high, but he was one step away from starting trouble," Dan said. "I saved him from himself, and all I did was squeeze his hand a little. He'll get over it. But if I hadn't stopped him, we both know where he would've ended up — straight back where he's just come from." Dan paused. "Do you want me to spell it out, Gemma?"

Gemma locked eyes with Dan, then she shook her head, the gesture almost imperceptible. She glanced at Alan, and he thought he saw a hint of regret in her expression. But then she was gone, marching out without a word, her head held high.

Dan and Alan followed her outside, then they stood and watched as Gemma and Billy disappeared into the crowd.

"Thanks a bunch, Dan," Alan said. "You really managed

to stick your oar in. God knows what she must think of us. Of me."

"She'll calm down. And she'll realise that, as I said, I did her brother a favour."

"How do you work that out? And anyway, what was all that stuff about him going back where he came from? You don't know him from Adam, do you?"

"I know everything I need to know about Billy Nickleton," Dan replied. "Didn't you notice his pale complexion? His face was practically grey. And his skin had that weird, waxy look."

"So what? I know he was worse for wear. Perhaps he's ill."

"No," Dan said. "The last time I saw someone looking like that, I was on a train. The guy got talking to one of the other passengers, and I heard every word. Guess where he'd been."

"I'm in no mood for puzzles. Spit it out."

Dan lowered his voice. "He'd been in the only place where you end up looking like the life's been drained out of you. Prison."

"You can't be sure of that."

"They call it a *prison tan*," Dan replied, keeping his voice low. "I didn't think Gemma would want me to mention it with everyone watching. But when I hinted at it, she didn't deny it."

"Oh my God. That explains a lot." Alan's hand went to his jaw. "Do you think she'll be all right? We could probably still catch her if we run."

Alan made to leave, but Dan stopped him with a raised hand. "Gemma made her feelings plain. She doesn't want us to interfere, and although I've only just met her, I get the impression she can look after herself."

"But if he's violent…"

"I don't think he's the type. He's all bravado and no guts. I stopped him with a firm handshake."

"It was more than that. Where did you learn to do that, anyway?"

"Public school."

Alan stared at him in disbelief.

"Seriously," Dan went on. "It was a schoolboy trick. It wasn't self-defence or anything fancy. I just grabbed his fingers and squeezed them together as hard as I could. But he thought I was making a move, and his mind did the rest."

Alan let out a long breath. "After all that, I feel like going home. I was having a nice time until your shadow loomed large."

"Be fair. It was Billy who barged in."

Alan waved his objection aside. "It started going sour before then. I made the mistake of mentioning some of the cases we've helped with. When you meet someone for the first time, *murder* is not a word you want to hear."

"Ah. And then I came along and made matters worse." Dan offered a rueful grin. "Sorry about that."

"It can't be helped. I should've kept quiet."

"Probably," Dan said. "But I know something that might cheer you up. I found a food stall, and it's really good. I'm talking next level."

"I'm not hungry."

"Maybe later. In the meantime, there's always the beer tent. I want to ask your advice about something, so I'm buying."

"Seriously? You want my advice?"

"Yes. Anyway, after gatecrashing your date with Gemma, I owe you one."

"You owe me two. But it wasn't a date. We were having tea. And a chat."

"Whatever you say, Alan. Whatever you say."

Dan's grin was unbearably smug, but Alan chose to ignore it. There were times when it paid to argue with Dan, but this wasn't one of them. *Choose your battles,* he told himself. And he led the way to the beer tent.

CHAPTER 5

G EORGE HEPWORTH CLOSED the door of the portable toilet cubicle and checked his hands as he hurried back toward his stall. The hand-washing facilities had been rudimentary, but he'd been to plenty of fairs and festivals, and he'd come fully prepared. His stall was equipped with a small sink, and he'd brought liquid soap, paper towels and hand sanitiser. Since he handled neither meat nor fish, he'd decided not to adopt the blue disposable gloves popular among those who ran food stalls. Gloves made you careless, and he was a stickler for hygiene. *Work clean*, that was his motto. Nothing less would do.

He cast a glance at the barbecue stand as he passed, cringing as the 'cook' wiped the sweat from his brow on the back of his hand. Did the man have no idea what he was doing? *Probably not*, George decided. He knew that several of the refreshment stalls were being run by volunteers, the proceeds going to Embervale's village hall restoration fund, and he assumed that the people running the barbecue had been roped in to help. They meant well, and the barbecue's fierce heat would kill most pathogens, but there was always the risk of cross-contamination. A little training would go a long way. Maybe he could give them a few pointers, but it would have to be later. He'd left his stall unattended for too long already.

He picked up his pace and was almost bowled over by some lout barging through the crowd.

"Watch it, mate!" the man snarled.

"You ran into…" George's protest petered out. "Billy?"

Billy looked him up and down. "George. What have you come as? A dentist?"

"These are my whites. I'm a chef now. I have my own business."

"Bloody hell."

"Yeah."

They regarded each other for a while, and Billy's sister appeared at his side.

"Hi, Gemma," George said. "Nice to see you again. How did it go with the maypole?"

Gemma almost smiled. "Fine, thanks. It went really well."

"I was going to pop over and watch, but I got busy. You know how it is."

"That's okay, we had a good crowd," Gemma replied. "Anyway, it's good to see you, but we were just heading home." She laid her hand on Billy's arm. "Come on. We've got to go."

Billy brushed her hand aside, his gaze still on George. "Give me a minute. I want to catch up with an old mate."

"All right. I'll wait in the car. If you're not there in five minutes, you can walk home."

"Fine."

"Don't keep him too long, George," Gemma said, then she strode away.

George shook his head. "You shouldn't talk like that to your sister, Billy. She's all right. You're lucky to have her."

"Am I? I've only been here half an hour and I'm regretting it already. I was better off inside."

George flinched. "Was it bad?"

"What do you think?"

"Sorry. Stupid question."

"Yeah." Billy sniffed. "At least you asked. When you've been in prison, most people take one look at you then cross the street. Either that or they have a go at you, start a fight. I don't know which is worse."

"It'll get better."

"I'm not holding my breath. I'm all right on my own. I've got used to it. I haven't had much choice, have I?"

George hesitated. "I should've kept in touch. I was going to write, but I didn't know what to say."

"It doesn't matter. I'm glad you didn't bother. I was glad to see the back of you. You were always a pain, hanging around all the time."

"We were friends."

"No, we weren't," Billy said. "I put up with you because my mum thought you were okay. *Such a nice boy*, that's what she used to say. She reckoned you'd keep me out of trouble." He sent George a lascivious smile. "If only she knew."

George looked away. "I heard your mum passed away. I couldn't go to the funeral. I was working, over in Plymouth."

"Very convenient. What you mean is, you were worried I'd be there."

"No. I'd have been pleased to see you. I asked for time off, but the head chef said no."

"You didn't miss much. Still, she left the house to sis, so it wasn't all bad."

George stared at him in dismay. "What's happened to you, Billy? You never used to be like this."

"Like what?"

"I don't know. Bitter."

Billy shrugged. "I'm telling it like it is. Mum died. She went to sleep one night and didn't wake up. If I'd been there, maybe I could've done something. But that was never on the cards. She told me never to show my face in the village again, said she couldn't bear the shame. But Gemma getting the house, that was good for me. She was working here already, so she trotted back to the old house and said I could stay with her when I got out. Otherwise, I'd still be waiting for parole."

"Parole. Does that mean—"

"It means they can send me back inside whenever they feel like it. It means I've got to be a good boy."

George tried not to be too obvious when he glanced at Billy's ankle, but he didn't get away with it.

Billy grunted under his breath. "Yes, I've got an ankle tag. Curfew. Every bloody night."

"It could be worse. At least you're out." George mustered a smile. "Maybe you can turn things around. You've got a chance to make a fresh start."

"Don't make me laugh. Keeping me home at night won't do any good. Where do you think I was when I ran my little scheme? I was safe at home, mate. Just me and my laptop. That's the great thing about the internet: you can buy anything and sell it to anybody. Nobody cares where the stuff comes from, and you can do the whole thing on your own."

"But… you're not going to start trading in stolen goods again, are you?"

"Of course not. I'm not stupid. There's no way I'm going back inside."

"That's good. Really. I hope it all works out for you. But listen, I have to go. I've left my stall, and there's no one looking after it."

"No assistant to help?"

"Not yet. Are you applying for the post?"

Billy wrinkled his nose. "Me? Mopping the floor and peeling potatoes? Not bloody likely. I had enough of that inside."

"Just as well. I couldn't afford to pay you."

"Come off it. You must be raking it in. I mean, look at you." He plucked at George's sleeve. "You look like someone off the TV or something. Who do you think you are, Gordon Ramsay?"

George peered at his sleeve as though fearing dirty fingerprints.

"It's all right," Billy said. "I'm not contagious."

"I like to keep my whites clean, that's all. It's part of the image."

Billy nodded. "Image. Yeah, that's you, down to the ground."

"What do you mean?"

"False. Putting up a front. Making out you're something special when you're not."

George felt his cheeks colour. "And what about you? Swaggering about like a thug, but we both know what you're—"

Billy grabbed his arm. "Shut up!"

"Or what?" George held Billy's stare. "Are you going to hit me?"

"You're not worth the bother." Billy shoved him back, letting go of his arm. "Go back to your pots and pans."

"Gladly." George straightened his tunic. "You need to sort yourself out, Billy. A lot of people around here know your face, and they know what you did."

"I couldn't give a toss." Billy let out a derisive snort. "I'll see you around, Georgie boy." He started walking, his hands in his pockets.

"You'd better watch your step," George called after him. But Billy gave no sign of having heard.

George didn't watch him go. He headed back to his stall, his whole body tight with anger. *Bloody idiot!* he scolded himself. *You should've walked on by.* But he couldn't have done that. Not with Billy.

An image came to his mind's eye: Billy smiling, laughing,

his green eyes sparkling with mischief; Billy's hand in his. But he pushed the thought from his mind.

He's nothing but trouble, George thought. *I need to steer well clear of him.* And that would be easy enough. They'd been close once, but even before Billy had been caught and arrested, they'd drifted apart, lived in different worlds. Billy belonged to the past; a past that was best forgotten.

You had to make your own way, and Billy had chosen the wrong path. And the worst of it was, when they'd been kids, Billy had been the clever one. There wasn't much he couldn't turn his hand to. He could've done anything. But he'd been lazy, always looking for a shortcut, a way to cheat the system. And look where it had landed him.

Why did I say that I meant to write to him? George asked himself. Of course he'd written, at least a dozen times. And every letter had met the same fate: crumpled in the waste bin.

He'd broken away from Billy, like a snake shedding its skin, and that's the way it had to be. Billy could go to hell for all he cared. And if he never saw him again, it would be a day too soon.

CHAPTER 6

THERE WERE NO free tables in the beer tent, so Dan and Alan stood at the bar, sipping from their pints. Dan suppressed the urge to quiz Alan about campsites right away; the time wasn't right. He'd never known Alan to hold a grudge, but from the set of his jaw, he guessed Alan was still a little prickly. The man needed a little space to regain his equilibrium.

They drank in silence until Alan held his plastic glass up to the light and said, "That's a nice pint. Hoppy but not too heavy, and with an aftertaste of citrus."

"I'll take your word for it," Dan replied. "All I know is it hits the spot. But I thought you didn't approve of IPA."

"It has its place, and on a day like this, a drop of Dartmoor IPA is perfect." Alan took a long draught of beer then set his drink down with a sigh. "That's good. But I'd better pace myself. I haven't had lunch yet."

"After this, we could grab something."

"Maybe." Alan stared into space, and as if by some absent-minded reflex, lifted his drink to his lips.

"Sorry about earlier," Dan said, but Alan shook his head.

"Water under the bridge."

They stood for a while, nursing their drinks, and then Dan said, "I was talking to a young couple earlier, and they're looking for somewhere they can pitch a tent. Wild camping. I thought you'd know where they could go."

"On Dartmoor?"

"Yes."

Alan nodded. "There are plenty of places. It's not far to Trendlebere Down, and there's always Hound Tor. But you have to stick to the rules. No big tents, no groups and definitely no open fires. You have to be away from the road, and you can only stay two nights, then you have to move on."

"Ah. I didn't know that. They want to stay for a week."

"Not allowed. The wild camping areas are for hikers. The idea is that you walk, carrying everything you need. Then, after a break, you pack up and continue on your way."

"I see. That's a shame. I said I'd help, but it sounds like I've given them false hope."

"Maybe you've saved them from getting into trouble."

"It's a bit late for that," Dan said. "They've pitched camp in somewhere called Brandle Wood, and the landowner came over and started laying down the law."

"Scott Benning."

"Yes. Do you know him?"

"Only to say hello to. From what I gather, he's…" Alan chewed over his words. "Let's just say that we don't move in the same circles. He's done some good things for the village. He owns the field we're standing in, and he lets the village use it for the May Fair and the summer show every year. And he donated the land for the community orchard; we use that for the apple day."

"But?"

"Who says there's a *but*?"

"Your tone of voice," Dan said. "Also, having met the man, I'd say he's arrogant, overbearing and generally unpleasant."

"Well, don't say it too loud," Alan replied. "He's sitting over there."

Alan tilted his head toward the back of the tent, and Dan turned to see Scott ensconced in a corner, deep in conversation with a man Dan didn't recognise. Scott's attention was focused on his companion, and he was leaning in close to him, his chin thrust forward, and his lips moving rapidly. In contrast, the other man's eyes were on everyone but Scott; his gaze roamed the tent, darting from one person to the next. He caught Dan looking at him, and his eyes narrowed. He stared as if committing Dan's face to memory, and there was something unsettling in the intensity of the man's glare: something predatory.

Dan broke eye contact and shifted his position, turning his back on Scott and his friend. He took a gulp of beer, then lowering his voice, he said, "Who's that with Scott?"

"I don't know," Alan replied. "He's not a local. It's not a face you'd forget."

"He's a nasty-looking brute," Dan said, but Alan shushed him.

"They're coming over," Alan muttered. "You haven't antagonised Scott, have you?"

Dan shrugged. "Possibly."

"Oh hell. Whatever you do, don't make matters worse. Just smile and nod, that's the best way to deal with people like him."

"I'm not going to doff my cap, just because the guy owns a few fields."

"No, but you can be polite," Alan insisted. "Remember, you're still the new boy around here. *I'm* still considered a recent arrival, and I've lived here for more than five years."

Dan raised a palm to admit defeat. "All right. I'll be civil."

"Good." Alan took a swig of beer, then he turned to greet Scott and his friend with a smile. "Scott. Nice to see you."

Scott acknowledged Alan with a nod. "Alan, isn't it? The local author."

"That's right. And I think you've met my neighbour."

"Oh yes," Scott replied. "I know Dan."

"Hello again," Dan said. Scott and his companion watched him carefully, expecting more, but Dan decided to follow Alan's advice for once, and he buttoned his lip.

Breaking the silence, Alan turned to Scott's companion. "Are you enjoying the fair?"

The man frowned. "Mm. It's all very *quaint*."

"You'll have to forgive Harry," Scott said. "He's a city-dweller." Patting the man on the arm, he added, "Come on, Harry. Don't be antisocial. Say hello to my neighbours."

Harry lifted his chin a millimetre. "Hi."

"I'm afraid Harry doesn't take to the countryside," Scott explained. "It's the wide-open spaces; they make him angry."

"Surely not," Alan said. "You won't find better countryside anywhere."

Harry grunted. "But what's the point of it all? All that land, sitting there, empty, unused, unproductive. It's a waste."

"People need food," Dan said. "And as well as agriculture, there's tourism and leisure, forestry—"

"All of it shockingly underused," Harry interrupted. "It's like the dark ages. Practically medieval."

"We're going to change all that," Scott said. "But I mustn't talk shop." He gestured to Dan's half-empty glass. "Can I get you another?"

Dan shook his head. "No thanks. I'm fine."

"Come on," Scott insisted. "Peace offering. We got off on the wrong foot earlier. Let me buy you a pint. Both of you."

Alan nudged Dan with his elbow. "We've got time for another, haven't we? And we're not driving."

"Okay then," Dan said. "A pint of IPA would be nice. Thank you."

"That's the spirit." Scott stepped up to the bar. Sam was pouring a pint, but she looked up immediately, flashing a smile.

"Be right with you, Mr Benning," she called out. "One second."

"No rush," Scott said.

Sam reached up to grab a packet of nuts from a box on the shelf, and Dan saw the way Scott tilted his head, admiring the view. A familiar flicker of jealousy stirred in Dan's stomach, but he fought against it. He had no claim over Sam's affections. They weren't in a relationship, and for her part, Sam seemed quite comfortable with the attention she received from her male customers. *It's none of my business*, Dan told himself. *None whatsoever*.

Dan looked away from Scott and was surprised to find Harry staring him full in the face, watching him as if searching for a sign of weakness. An image of a hyena came to Dan's mind, but he didn't bat an eyelid. Smiling at Harry, he said, "I take it that you're here on business."

"What else is there?" Harry asked.

"Relaxation," Alan said. "Socialising with friends and neighbours."

Harry snorted in derision. "Right. For that, I'd need a helicopter out of here. I've told Scott he should buy one, but he won't have it."

"And where would you fly to?" Dan asked. "London?"

"Maybe. I've got friends all over."

Dan rephrased his question: "Where are you based?"

"I'm staying with Scott for a while," Harry replied. "But I have a place in Manchester, a flat in London and a cottage on the south-east coast."

"Very nice," Alan said. "But you're not from Manchester, are you? You haven't got an accent."

Harry shrugged. "I move around a lot."

Scott rejoined them, holding out a couple of plastic pint glasses to Dan and Alan. "IPA."

Alan and Dan barely had time to thank him and take their drinks before Scott marched back to the bar. He returned a moment later with two small plastic cups. "I can't believe we have to drink good whisky out of these things," he said, handing a cup to Harry, "but beggars can't be choosers."

"I've never seen myself as a beggar." Harry peered at his cup then took an experimental sip. "I thought you said this was good whisky."

"You're in a tent in a field," Scott shot back. "What do you expect?"

"Better," Harry said. "I expect better."

Scott rolled his eyes and lifted his cup. "Here's to another successful May Fair."

"I'll drink to that," Alan said, finishing off his first pint and picking up his second. "Cheers."

The others raised their drinks, but Dan didn't join in. "Scott, Alan was telling me that you own this field," he said. "It's very generous of you to let everyone use it."

Scott smiled. "I like to do my part for the community. I've done well for myself. It's good to give something back."

"And good PR," Dan said.

"That too," Scott admitted. "It certainly doesn't hurt."

Harry brightened. "Now we're talking. It makes good business sense to get the locals onside. It'll pay dividends down the line."

"What kind of business are you talking about?" Dan asked. "You didn't say before."

"I'm in *the* business," Harry replied. "Energy. It's the fundamental driving force of the economy, and it always will be."

Alan's face fell. "What kind of energy? Don't tell me you're talking about fracking."

Harry curled his lip. "Not here."

"What then?" Dan said.

"Renewables." Harry looked from Dan to Alan as though gauging their reaction. "I'd guess that you approve."

Dan nodded firmly. "Absolutely."

"Me too," Alan put in. "I quite like to see wind turbines. They add something to the landscape, so long as there aren't too many in one place."

Harry turned on Alan. "Define *too many*."

"It's not that there's a precise number," Alan replied. "But I'd hate to see crowds of them."

"And what's your alternative?" Harry kept his tone pleasant enough, but there was a cold glint in his eye. "Are you happy for coal to be mined and oil to be piped from the ground, so long as it's on someone else's doorstep? Or are you one of those people who complain about wind farms while you burn Russian gas to heat your home?"

Alan bristled. "Neither. I simply believe in a balanced economy. We have to set our needs against the needs of the planet."

"For *balanced*, read *stagnant*," Harry said. "Growth is all that matters. And for growth, we need more and more energy. So you shouldn't be worrying about having *too many* wind turbines, you should be complaining that we might not have *enough*."

Scott raised his voice: "Gentlemen. That's enough heated debate. Harry, you're being deliberately provocative. You know full well that we're not building a wind farm."

Harry smirked.

You led us by the nose into that argument, Dan thought. *Why?* Perhaps Harry liked to play games, and this one was called misdirection. Whatever they were planning, it was probably a large-scale development. But what kind of energy were they talking about? Dan clicked his fingers. There was only one type of renewable energy scheme for someone who owned a large area of land. "You're planning a solar power installation."

Harry mimed applause. "We certainly are. And no, you can't invest. We're oversubscribed as it is."

"There's one further along the valley," Alan said. "There was some fuss over it, wasn't there?"

"Nothing we couldn't handle," Scott replied.

"That's yours?" Alan asked. "But it's miles away."

"Yes." Scott raised his eyebrows. "What can I say? It's a big estate."

"Strictly speaking, the land is owned by our company," Harry said. "Scott is the chair of directors, but he likes to play the lord of the manor."

Scott grinned. "Somebody has to do it. Besides, I'm the majority shareholder. To all intents and purposes, I own the land beneath your feet, Harry. Remember that."

"Oh, I'm unlikely to forget it." Harry knocked back the last of his drink. "This stuff might be rough, but I need another. Anybody care to join me?"

"No thanks." Dan lifted his pint. "I've hardly touched this one."

"And I need to keep a clear head," Scott said. "But don't let me stop you."

Looking distinctly unimpressed, Harry moved to the bar, and Scott leaned closer to Dan, lowering his voice. "You'll understand that our plans are at an early stage, and these kinds of development can be sensitive. I've got some investors coming over on Sunday, and we're going to look at the site on Monday. It's next to Brandle Wood, and I can't have those students wandering about in the woods when my guests arrive. We'll be touring the estate, and I'll be telling everyone how safe and secure the place is. I can't afford any hiccups. These are high-powered investors, and they expect a certain level of discretion. Do you understand?"

"Yes," Dan said. "I understand perfectly."

"But have you got rid of those bloody people yet? Have they gone?"

"Not yet," Dan admitted.

Scott's expression darkened. "Why not? You said you'd deal with them."

"I haven't found anywhere for them to go," Dan said. "It turned out to be more complex than I thought."

"For God's sake," Scott hissed. "There's nothing complicated about it. If Harry finds out…" He broke off as Harry returned, drink in hand. Scott smiled. "Harry, Dan was just saying that he has to push off. Straight away."

Harry frowned. "What? But you haven't finished your drinks. Is the beer that bad?"

"It's fine, but I have something I need to do," Dan said. "Alan, are you coming? I could use your help."

Alan cast a regretful glance at his pint, then he nodded. "Of course. No problem."

They said their goodbyes, and Scott shook hands with Dan, leaning in and keeping hold of his hand for a second longer than was necessary. In a casual tone, he said, "Keep me updated, Dan. You can find my details online. Look for Ironbrand Farm. Leave me a message and it'll get to me."

Harry frowned. "What's this?"

"Nothing," Scott replied. "Village gossip. It's always good to keep up with local opinion and test the temperature, so to speak. Sometimes it pays to tread gently."

Harry's sneer eloquently expressed what he thought of treading gently, but he shook hands with Dan and Alan in a businesslike fashion.

The formalities over, Dan headed back into the field, Alan trailing in his wake. Outside, Dan squinted in the spring sunlight, feeling the effects of the beer.

"You know," Alan began, "this is my sixth May Fair since I've been in Embervale, and until now, the most shocking thing that's ever happened was when I won a hamper in the raffle."

"Have you bought a ticket?" Dan asked.

"Two strips. The draw is at three o'clock."

"Then you'd better hold on to them," Dan said. "Because I can't see any sign of that young couple. I need to tell them the bad news about the wild camping, but with the way things are going, we'll still be looking for them when the last prize is being handed out."

CHAPTER 7

A S ARRANGED, PAUL spotted Daisy near the entrance to
the show ring. She was easy to make out: everyone
around her had their backs to him while they watched
something going on inside the ring. But Daisy was looking for
him, almost standing on tiptoe as she searched the crowd.

Paul stalked toward her, and her eyes met his. He hoped
his expression told her what she needed to know: he'd had no
luck. The bag was gone. But Daisy smiled and started
walking to meet him, and as they drew closer, she unhooked
something from her shoulder. And there, dangling from her
hand, was the black messenger bag.

Paul rushed to her side and wrapped his arms around her,
planting a kiss on her forehead. "You beauty! You found it."

Daisy pushed him away. "Get off! Don't go slobbering all
over me, you great lummock."

"Why not? I'm only showing you a bit of affection. And
you deserve it. You're a star." Taking the bag from her, he
unfastened the catch and opened the flap. Inside, the laptop
looked fine, and the portable hard drive was still snug in its
padded case. His backup phone was there too, safely tucked

into its pocket. "It's all okay." He closed the bag and slung the strap over his shoulder. "Where did you find it?"

"You're not going to be so pleased with me when I tell you."

"Why? Where was it?"

Daisy blushed. "Promise you won't be cross with me."

"Just tell me, Daisy."

"All right. I'm sorry, but it turns out…" Daisy hesitated then spoke in a rush. "I didn't mean to, but I must've left it in the loo."

"What?"

"I put it down while I was, you know, on the toilet. But I knew you were waiting, and I'd been ages on account of the queue. So I must've dashed out and left it behind."

"Daisy! For God's sake!"

"You said you wouldn't be cross."

"No, I didn't." Paul pointed a finger at her face. "I've every right to be angry. How could you be so careless?"

She batted his hand away. "Don't be like that. People are staring."

Paul peered past Daisy and saw that she was right. More than one head had turned in their direction. He sent the onlookers a benign grin, keeping his expression fixed until the last nosy parker lost interest and looked away. Then he stared at Daisy, his lips pressed tight into a straight line and his eyes cold. "I don't know what I'm going to do with you. I really don't."

"There's no need to be such a pillock about it. Everything's fine. The bag was exactly where I left it, and I'm sure no one touched it."

"You can't know that. Anything could've happened."

Daisy held out her arms. "Paul! Nothing happened. You've got your precious bag back, all right? What more do you want?"

"Nothing. But from now on, this bag doesn't leave my sight. Not for one second."

"Suits me," Daisy said. "But maybe you shouldn't take it outside. Find somewhere at your house to hide it."

"What? And have my mum find it? Or my little brother? He's always poking around, messing with my stuff. You have no idea what you're talking about, no idea what it's like."

Daisy's brow furrowed. "That's not true. I've been to your place loads of times, and I know what you have to put up with. But that's why we're doing this, right?" She stepped closer to him, taking his hands in hers. "It'll be different when we've got a place of our own. We'll be able to do whatever we want."

He looked down into her dark eyes and felt his anger fading. Daisy could always do that for him. He got so frustrated sometimes, so wound up. He was forever snapping at everyone, like a mad dog straining at the end of its chain. But Daisy, she could lift the burden from his back and make everything all right. And he needed her; needed to see her every day. Like this. Just the two of them. Together against the world.

"There," she said. "You've come back to me."

Paul let out a long breath. "I don't mean to take it out on you. But I just get sick of it. I work all week, but the money goes nowhere. By the time I've paid for my car, there's hardly anything left. The bloody insurance is due next month, and I don't know how I'm going to be able to afford it. And if I can't drive, I'm out of a job. They'll give me the sack, and then I'll never be able to leave home." He looked Daisy in the eye, willing her to understand. "It's no use piddling about with a few hundred quid at a time. We need something bigger. Much bigger. And I can't wait much longer. We need the money now."

"Well, I might be able to do something about that." Daisy smiled.

"How?"

"I'll tell you. Just after we split up to look for your bag, I was going around the stalls, and I bumped into my uncle."

"So what? He hasn't got any money, has he? What did he do, give you a pound to buy sweeties?"

"Don't be daft. He was talking to someone, and when the bloke turned around, guess who it was."

"I don't know."

"Scott Benning," Daisy crowed. "The richest bloke for miles."

Paul tilted his head to one side. "Go on."

"Well, you know what my uncle's like. He started banging on, boasting about what a good worker I am. Then he told him about me cleaning houses, and how I set it all up on my own."

"With my help," Paul said.

Daisy wrinkled her nose. "It was my idea. Anyway, the point is, Mr Benning suddenly got all interested and said he could always use someone to help up at his place."

"Bloody hell," Paul breathed. "Seriously?"

"Definitely. I've got to go up to his house tomorrow at twelve. He says he'll show me the ropes, see what I think." Daisy giggled. "I reckon that's not all he wants to show me, the dirty sod."

Paul's body stiffened. "What did he say to you?"

"Nothing, but I know that look. He did ask me if I wanted to get a drink in the beer tent. He said he was meeting a friend, so it was all above board, but I said no."

"Bloody cheek! He fancied his chances. That's the end of that then. You can't go to his house. I won't let you."

Daisy tutted. "You're just being stupid. You can't stop me, and anyway, that would be ridiculous. He's loaded. This is our big chance."

"I don't know."

"Well, I do. It's not every day you get an opportunity like

this, and I say it's worth taking. You never know what might come of it."

"But he's not like the others," Paul protested. "If we try the same old routine, he'll be on to us. It won't work."

"Then we'll figure out something new. There's plenty of time." Daisy laid her hand on Paul's cheek. "Relax. All I'm going to do is talk to the man. And while I'm there, I'll see if I can get a good look around his house, check it out. If it looks too risky, I'll tell you, and we won't go near it."

Paul chewed at the inside of his cheek, but he didn't reply.

"What's got into you?" Daisy asked. "Normally, you'd be jumping at a chance like this."

"I don't know. Maybe it's because we lost the bag. It's got me rattled. I was picturing it all, you know? Imagining the cops taking me away, the questions, the trial. Prison."

"Poor thing. You worry too much." Daisy pulled him to her and hugged him, rubbing his back. "We found the bag and no harm done. That's a good sign, isn't it? And me running into Benning, that's got to be good luck. Seems like things are finally working out for us."

"Maybe."

"No maybe about it." Daisy ran her hand through his hair. "I'll tell you what we'll do. Tomorrow, you can give me a lift up to Benning's house, then you can wait in the car while I go in. I won't be long, and you'll be right outside."

"All right. But if he tries anything, if he so much as touches you, I'll kill him. I'll break his bloody neck."

Daisy hugged him harder. "He won't try anything. I know his type. He'll eye me up when he thinks no one's watching, but that's about his limit. He won't lay a hand on me. He wouldn't dare." She pushed herself back from Paul, grinning. "Anyway, who's to say I'd mind? I might fancy trading you in for an older man."

"Very funny."

"I'm not joking. A man like that, he could keep me in fine style. And he's not bad looking."

"Huh! Anyway, you needn't flatter yourself. You're nothing to a bloke like him. All he wants is someone to clean up after him and his posh friends. A servant to scrub the bath and polish the floor."

"I know that," Daisy said. "I'm not thick. I was trying to make you laugh." She stood back from him. "I think we should go home now. This was supposed to be fun, but I've had enough of your bad moods."

"That's not fair," Paul grumbled. "I'm knackered, that's all. I was up half the night. And you know why." He took a breath. "But you're right — let's get out of here. We could find somewhere quiet, park up for a bit."

"Hm. I know what you want. But I don't know if you deserve it."

"Come on, Daisy. I don't mind if we just sit and talk. But I need to get away from all these people, get my head straight." Paul's expression brightened. "We could go to Brandle Wood. It's just down the road, and there's a parking spot. We could go for a walk."

"And lie in the long grass, eh?"

Paul gave her a bashful smile. "Maybe. A bit of a cuddle might be nice. And no one will come by. Most of the locals are here at the fair. We'll have the whole wood to ourselves."

Daisy made a show of thinking it over. "It does sound nice. I wonder if it's too early for the bluebells. It's lovely up there when they're all out. Magical."

"You'll come then?"

"All right," Daisy said with a grin. "You talked me into it. Let's go."

"And that is the best news I've heard today." Paul took her arm, and together they headed across the field.

CHAPTER 8

D AN PAUSED IN the lane, turning to look back toward the show field. "Are you sure this is the right way?"

At his side, Alan halted. "Yes. We follow the road for a bit, and then Brandle Wood will be on our left. Don't you trust my navigation?"

"It's not that. But I've never seen this lane before, and I thought I knew most of the local roads; the ones leading out of the village, anyway."

"Don't you believe it. Devon lanes are a law unto themselves. I've lived here for years, and I find new ones all the time. It's almost as if they move around when no one's about, sneaking from one place to the next in the dead of night."

"That sounds like something from one of your books."

"It might be," Alan admitted with a smile. "I pinched the idea from J.K. Rowling, but as T.S. Eliot said, immature poets imitate; mature poets steal."

"I thought that was Picasso."

"Most people do," Alan said. "I blame Steve Jobs. He said it was Picasso, but he was wrong. I looked it up. Stravinsky said something similar, but Eliot beat him to it."

"You have too much free time on your hands."

"Not anymore," Alan said. "Not anymore."

They resumed their journey, and a short while later, they came to a lay-by where a couple of cars were parked in the shade of an unkempt hedgerow.

Alan pointed to a wooden gate. "That's where most people go in."

"Even though it's private land?"

"Yes. There's an old bridle path that runs right through," Alan said. "But I don't think you get all that many people up here. A few dog walkers, families with young children. Locals mainly. It's the sort of place you have to know about, or you'd never find it."

"The campers found it."

"Maybe they're good at reading maps. The bridle path is marked on the OS maps, and you said that the young man was an officer cadet."

"We can ask him when we find him," Dan said. "Assuming we do find him. How big is this wood?"

"It's a decent size. It's not all that wide, but it stretches for a few miles to the south." Alan opened the gate, and they made their way through. "It's a shame we didn't find that young couple back at the field. They must've left early."

"Yes." Dan loaded the word with dark significance, and Alan sent him a sharp look.

"You think there might've been more trouble?"

"It's a possibility," Dan said. "Is it this way?" He indicated a rough path that wove through the crowded trees and disappeared between clumps of holly and hawthorn. "I wouldn't like to ride a horse through there. You'd get knocked off by a branch or something."

"As far as I know, this is the only path," Alan replied, and he led the way. But they hadn't walked far when Alan said, "What makes you think there might've been another row at the fair?"

"It was the way Scott behaved. I can't help wondering if he'd have talked that way to someone who was white."

There was a pause before Alan replied. "This area isn't the most diverse, I'll admit. And I've heard some stupid remarks made by people who didn't know any better, but—"

"Ignorance is no excuse," Dan interrupted.

"No, I know. And I'm not defending Scott in any way, but you can't assume he's a racist. I get the impression he talks down to almost everyone. Unless you're rich and powerful, you don't count."

"You could be right."

Alan halted. "Did you hear that?"

"What?" Dan stopped to listen. There. Low voices. Someone pushing through the undergrowth. "Yes. And whoever it is, it sounds like they're coming this way. Fast."

"It could be the people we're looking for," Alan said. "Shall we…"

But before he could finish his sentence, two figures — a man and a woman — dashed into view, charging between the bushes. They ran clumsily, scarcely looking where they were going, and ignoring the thorns that snagged at their clothes.

I recognise him, Dan thought. And in that moment, the man saw Dan and Alan, and he halted, grabbing hold of his companion's arm, forcing her to stop. They stood, staring, breathing hard.

"Are you all right?" Dan asked.

"Fine," the woman said, but Dan ignored her. He was busy studying the young man, taking in the tight lines around his eyes, the film of sweat on his brow.

"It's Paul, isn't it?" Dan asked. "We met at the fair. In the beer tent."

Paul nodded reluctantly.

His partner took his hand, tugging it, and she whispered something.

"I know," Paul replied. Then to Dan: "We've got to go."

Still holding hands, and with their gaze on the ground, they trudged toward Dan and Alan.

Alan stood aside to give them room, but Dan stood his ground, forcing them to slow down. And as they passed, Dan said, "I see you've found it."

Paul stopped, turning sharply to face Dan. "What?"

Dan gestured to the messenger bag on Paul's shoulder. "Your bag. You were looking for it."

"Yeah." Paul seemed to weigh Dan up, then he added, "Listen, if I were you, I wouldn't go down there."

"Oh?" Dan said. "Why's that?"

"Paul," his partner warned. "Don't get involved."

"I'm not. But I've got to tell them."

"Tell us what?" Alan asked. "What's the problem?"

"It's Sid Sturridge," Paul said. "He's on the warpath. We heard shouting, and I went to look. He was…" He glanced at his partner, but she simply shrugged, making it clear he was on his own. "He found a couple of people camping in the wood, and he lost his rag," Paul went on. "He was effing and blinding, shouting the odds, making all kinds of threats."

"What happened?" Dan asked. "Was he armed?"

Paul's eyes clouded in confusion. "I don't think he had his gun. But he was squaring up to the bloke, spoiling for a fight. And the other guy, he was big, you know, like a rugby player or something. And he just stood there, taking it, calm as you like. But then…" Paul chewed at his bottom lip. "Maybe I should've done something, but Daisy held me back."

"Tell me what happened," Dan said. "Quickly."

"Sid shoved the bloke. Pushed him in the chest. And that was it. The next thing I know, Sid was on the ground."

"Did he get up again?" Alan said. "Was he all right?"

"I didn't hang around to find out," Paul replied. "When Sid got knocked down, Daisy screamed. They must've heard us, so we had to get out of there."

Daisy pouted. "It wasn't my fault. It was horrible."

Dan exchanged a look with Alan. There was no need to ask the question aloud, and Alan answered with a nod. They'd have to go and investigate.

Watching them carefully, Daisy said, "Are you two cops or something?"

"Certainly not," Dan replied. "But we'll go and find out what's happened. We might be able to help."

"That's not a good idea," Paul said. "I know what Sid's like. We used to come in here when we were kids, mucking about on our bikes, and he used to chase us off, put the fear of God into us."

"Never mind all that," Daisy put in. "Sid works for Mr Benning, and I've got my interview to think about. I don't want to ruin everything before I've even had a chance."

Dan sent her a questioning look, but she avoided his gaze. She focused on Paul, tugging at his sleeve. "Come on, Paul. Take me home. We should never have come here. I don't know what I was thinking."

"Okay," Paul replied. "Don't panic. We're going." Then to Dan, he said, "If you really want to risk it, they're down there. Follow the path for a few minutes, and you'll see them on your right. The tent's blue. You can't miss it."

"Thanks," Dan said, already turning away. He hurried along the path with Alan, looking from side to side as they went, searching the shady spaces between the trees. Beside Dan's feet, a bird launched itself from the undergrowth, flapping its wings and letting out a croaking cry. Startled, Dan missed his step, but Alan smiled and said, "Pheasant."

"I know," Dan replied. "Damned thing. It practically gave me a heart attack."

"Think of it as a cardiovascular workout. Better than a treadmill any day of the week."

"Remind me never to come to you for training advice," Dan said. "Any sign of a tent?"

"Not yet. But a minute ago, I thought I heard something."

"Probably more of the local wildlife, preparing to pounce."

"No," Alan insisted. "I thought I heard voices." He stopped to listen. "Over there." Alan abandoned the path and waded into the tangle of bracken and briars that sprawled across much of the forest floor.

"Paul said we'd see them from the path," Dan said, but Alan wasn't listening; he was forging ahead as though he knew where he was going.

Dan followed Alan's trail through the undergrowth. A bramble latched onto his trousers, and Dan stopped to tug his leg free. The bramble came away with an ominous ripping sound, and Dan cursed under his breath. His lightweight trekking trousers were Swedish, and for the price he'd paid, the fabric should've been able to withstand a couple of thorns. *I can't afford to buy another pair*, he thought. *Not from the same brand, at any rate.*

Dan straightened his back. "Alan?"

His friend was nowhere in sight, and Dan raised his voice, calling out again.

No reply.

He tilted his head to listen. And there it was. Alan's voice: "Over here!"

Dan pinpointed the source of the sound and set off toward it, striding through a patch of bracken and clambering up an uneven slope, grabbing onto tree trunks as he went. Cresting the ridge, he looked down into the hollow below. A blue tent lay partially dismantled on the ground, and Alan stood beside it, remonstrating with Maria while Ade circled the tent, pulling tent pegs from the ground. Ade was concentrating on his task, but as Dan scrambled down the slope toward him, Ade stood tall, his arms hanging loose at his sides. Eyeing Dan, he called out, "What do *you* want? If you've come to warn us off, you're too late. We're leaving."

"It's nothing like that," Dan replied, reaching the bottom

of the slope and catching his breath. "We wanted to check you're okay. We heard there was a problem."

Ade grunted. "You could call it that. Some bloke threatened us. But you probably know that. Friend of yours, is he?"

"We're nothing to do with the gamekeeper or the landowner," Alan replied. "That's what I've been trying to tell you."

"And we don't believe you," Maria snapped. "You turned up pretty fast. You're all in it together. Otherwise, how did you know what happened?"

Dan held up his hands. "It's a long story, so you'll just have to accept me at my word. If it was up to me, you could camp here for as long as you want, but the man who owns the wood doesn't see it that way."

"You've got that right," Ade said. "We got the message loud and clear, but he sent his hired hand to do his dirty work." He took a step closer to Dan, jabbing his finger in the air to emphasise each word as he spoke. "He threatened us, he was abusive and then he dared to try pushing me around. And that was a step too far."

"It was a hate crime," Maria put in. "Pure and simple. You should've heard what he said. It was extremely offensive. No one should have to listen to that. The man's a racist."

Dan's heart sank. "I'm so sorry to hear that. That's disgusting."

"There's no excuse for it," Alan added. "The man should pay for it. But if you hit him, then—"

"It was self-defence," Maria interrupted.

Ade nodded firmly. "I don't start fights. I'm training to be a doctor, for God's sake. I've done plenty of night shifts in A & E on a Friday night, so I know what happens when people start throwing punches. But that guy went too far. He laid his hands on me, so I shoved him back. It wasn't hard enough to knock him over, but he went down like a sack of potatoes. He must've tripped or something."

"He got off lightly," Maria added. "Ade could've made mincemeat of him, but he didn't. He was very restrained."

"There were some witnesses," Dan said carefully. "We ran into them, and they told us that you knocked Sid Sturridge down."

Ade and Maria shared a look. "I knew I heard something," Maria said. "What did they say?"

"Pretty much what I've told you," Dan replied. "But they definitely used the phrase *knocked down*. Not *shoved*."

"Then they can't have seen what actually happened," Ade said. "They must've been too far away."

Dan nodded. "That's possible but I can't be sure."

"Oh hell," Maria muttered. "This could change everything. It could be bad for us. Very bad."

"How?" Ade said. "Even if they couldn't see properly, they'll have heard the bloke shouting at us. That has to be in our favour. And it must've been obvious I was only defending myself."

"Don't count on it," Maria replied. "I don't like it, Ade. Eyewitnesses are notoriously unreliable, especially in a situation like this. It sounds like they've misinterpreted what they saw." She turned to Dan. "These witnesses, are they local people?"

"I believe so," Dan said. "At least, I know one of them is from the village, but I'm not sure that's important."

Maria tutted. "Are you kidding? They're biased. They'll be on that awful man's side."

"Not necessarily," Dan replied. "Paul told me that Sid Sturridge struck first."

"Paul," Ade said thoughtfully. "So, you know him, this witness. Where does he live?"

Maria laid her hand on Ade's arm. "Don't even think about it. You can't contact him. If it comes to court—"

"I can't let it get that far," Ade interrupted. "I could get kicked off my course. If I get charged with assault, they'll throw me out. It'll be five years of hard work down the drain. And what about Sandhurst? My whole future could go up in smoke."

Dan made a downward motion with his hands. "Let's not be too hasty. The first thing is to get you out of here in case Sturridge comes back."

"We're ahead of you," Maria said. "In half an hour, we'll be on our way back to Exeter."

"Good." Dan thought for a second. "I happen to know that the landowner has a big event coming up. He's hosting some important visitors over the next few days, and he won't want even a hint of trouble. Alan and I could talk to him, try and smooth things over. We can persuade him to handle it quietly."

"But what about the gamekeeper?" Maria asked. "He was furious. He's not going to let it go."

"If we set about this the right way, Sturridge will do exactly what his employer tells him to do," Dan said. "Trust me. I know how to pull the right levers. I can get this sorted out."

Maria and Ade stared at him.

"Why?" Maria asked. "Why would you do that for us?"

"Because I feel partly responsible," Dan replied. "I promised to find you a place to go, but I got sidetracked, and I left it too late. That's why we came up here; I wanted to try and put things right. But if I'd been quicker, this mess might've been avoided."

Maria glanced at Ade. Then, to Dan, she said, "Okay. If you think you can help, we'd be stupid to turn you down. But for what it's worth, you didn't cause this. You couldn't have known what that man would do. And the way he fell... it was pure chance. An accident. Nobody's fault."

"And that's what I'll tell Scott Benning," Dan said. "Now, do you need a hand packing up?"

"No, you're all right," Ade said. "We won't be long. But if you can sort that bloke out, and keep him from going to the police, that would be a huge help. Believe me."

"It won't be a problem," Dan said. "I'm only sorry it came to this."

"We'll leave you to it," Alan said. "And don't worry. Dan can be very persuasive."

Dan and Alan said goodbye and headed back the way they'd come.

"You know, at first I thought that trouble sort of followed you around," Alan began. "But now I realise that you go looking for it. You actively seek it out. And I know why."

"Is that so?" Dan replied. "Go on then. You're going to tell me anyway, so you may as well get on with it."

"Don't take this the wrong way, but you're an addict."

"Nonsense."

"It's true," Alan insisted. "You turn everything into a personal battle. You thrive on conflict. Just now, when you were taking charge, it was as if you came alive."

"I can keep my head in a crisis, I'll admit to that. But I'm not addicted to anything. With the possible exceptions of caffeine and IPA." He laughed, catching Alan's eye, inviting him to join in.

But Alan was not to be deflected. "I'm not criticising you," he went on. "Far from it. Plenty of people crave excitement one way or another. But maybe it would be better if you acknowledged your need for adrenaline; embraced it."

"What are you trying to say?"

Alan paused. "Don't get me wrong. It's been great to have you as a neighbour, and as a friend, but this quiet life in the village — is it really for you?"

"I'm perfectly happy," Dan said. "I'll go and talk to Benning because I've got to finish what I've started. But after that, I'm going to do some work in the garden. Pull up a couple of weeds. Cut the grass. That's hardly an adrenaline-filled afternoon."

"Fine. I was just making an observation."

"If you want to play amateur psychologist, take a look at yourself. You didn't have to come here. You hadn't even met Ade until a few minutes ago, but you still came along for the ride. So who's looking for excitement now?"

Alan held up his hands. "Guilty as charged. But our *adventures*, for want of a better word, are the exception for me: the pinch of salt that makes the meal worth eating. For you, they're the whole menu."

"I've never heard so much nonsensical psychobabble in my life," Dan said. But as they trudged out through the wood, he was already planning his conversation with Scott Benning, playing through scenarios in his mind, rehearsing new angles of attack. And though he'd never admit it to Alan, he was looking forward to it.

They reached the lane and headed back toward the village, and Dan said, "There's just one small problem."

"Let me guess," Alan replied. "You're not convinced that a phone message will get through to Benning in time, and you're thinking about going up to his house to beard him in his den. Am I right?"

"No. Whatever we think of him, Scott is a modern businessman, and he'll be plugged into his lines of communication night and day. I'll have no problem reaching him."

"What's bothering you then?"

"There's a glitch in my plans for this afternoon." Dan grinned. "My lawnmower's on the blink. Can I borrow yours?"

CHAPTER 9

SITTING IN THE passenger seat of his Vauxhall Corsa, Ade turned his head to read a sign as they passed. "What did that one say?"

Without taking her eyes from the road, Maria said, "No idea. But don't worry, I know where I'm going. I recognise that farm."

"I don't. None of this looks familiar."

"That's because you have no sense of direction. Some officer you'll make. You can't read a map to save your life." Maria sent him a grin to show she was kidding. "Fortunately, you have a lot of other qualities."

"Don't do me any favours."

"You're okay. You have your uses. When you're not wrapped up in your infectious diseases or whatever it is this week."

"Pharmacology," Ade said. "And it's kicking my arse. I should never have come on this trip. I can't afford the time."

"You were climbing the walls. You needed some time away. You have to clear your head now and then, or you'll run yourself into the ground. You have to give yourself a break."

"Yeah," Ade intoned. "And this has been so relaxing."

Maria sighed. "I'm sorry. It couldn't have worked out much worse, could it? But we'll figure something out. For a start, we could go out tonight. Pizza. A couple of drinks." She grinned. "And then home for a nice relaxing back rub."

Ade smiled. "That does sound good."

"The back rub is for me. My shoulders are very tense. And you do have such lovely strong hands."

"All right. I'll rub your back, but don't blame me if I get carried away."

"I'm counting on it."

They drove on in silence for a minute, but as they passed through a crossroads, Ade reached down into the footwell and grabbed his day bag. "We passed that sign ten minutes ago. I'm going to check on my phone."

"Seriously, Ade, relax. I *know* where we are."

"It won't hurt to check." Ade rifled through his bag. "Shit!"

"What? Don't tell me you've lost your phone."

"No, of course not. I never lose my phone. But—" He broke off, concentrating on his search. "Where is the damned thing?"

"What *are* you looking for?"

Ade stopped hunting through the bag. "My ID badge. I always keep it in the inside pocket, but it's not there."

"Maybe you didn't bring it with you."

"I always carry it. I never know when I might need it. Anyway, I definitely had it earlier. I saw it before we went to the fair." Ade scowled at the bag as though it were responsible for his loss. "It must've fallen out when we were packing up. We left in a rush and I stuffed everything into the nearest bag. All I could think about was that bloke coming back."

"I know. But don't worry. You can get another badge from the hospital, can't you?"

"Yeah, but it's not just the badge, it's my swipe card. They were both on my lanyard, and the whole thing is gone. That card is a big deal. It's a total hassle to replace." Ade glanced over his shoulder. "Maybe we should…"

"No. You don't want to go back for it, do you?"

Ade hesitated. "Not really, but it wouldn't take long. Easier than getting another badge."

"I'm sorry, but no. We can't go back there. Not after what happened. Anyway, we'll be on the main road soon. In another twenty minutes, we'll be home."

"Okay. I suppose you're right." Ade stuffed his bag back into the footwell. "What about tomorrow?"

"Seriously?"

"Yeah. We could go somewhere for lunch. A nice pub. And we could swing past on the way. If no one's around, I could run in, have a quick look, and then we'd be out of there. You could stay in the car if you like, keep the engine running."

"Hm."

They reached a T-junction and Maria brought the car to a halt while she checked in both directions.

"Ah, now we're going the right way," Ade said. "I knew this lane would be okay."

"Of course you did." Maria shook her head, then she pulled onto the main road and accelerated away.

CHAPTER 10

ALONE IN THE kitchen at the Old Shop, Dan switched on his laptop and searched for Ironbrand Farm. The website was impressively slick, and Scott had been right: his contact details were easy to find. Dan made the call, mentally preparing to do battle with an overprotective PA. But to his surprise, Scott answered the phone in person: "Benning here."

"Hello, it's Dan. You asked me to keep you up to date."

"Right. What's the state of play?"

"First, you'll be glad to know that when I left Ade and Maria, they were packing up their tent. They've probably left Brandle Wood already."

"That was quick work. Good man!"

"Unfortunately, the situation isn't quite as simple as we'd hoped," Dan said.

"In what way? Did they make a fuss?"

"They weren't the problem. Your gamekeeper arrived before I did, and he overstepped the mark."

"I warned them about Sturridge. He's a rough old diamond, and he doesn't care who knows it."

"It went further than that. He assaulted the young man, and that leaves him open to criminal charges."

"Their word against his."

Dan bit back a few choice words. Was that all the man could say? Didn't he want to know if anyone had been hurt? Dan cleared his throat and said, "Apparently not. There were witnesses."

"In my wood? Who?"

"That's not important," Dan said. "I've talked to Ade and Maria, and they're happy to forget the whole incident. However, Mr Sturridge might not be so keen to let the matter drop."

There was a pause before Scott replied. "What is that you're not telling me, Dan?"

"The young man was forced to defend himself. I don't think Sturridge was badly hurt, but he fell, and we're concerned he might harbour a grudge. As it stands, the matter is resolved, but if Sturridge goes to the police, it could inflame the situation."

"Oh well. I shan't lose any sleep over it."

"I suggest that you reconsider," Dan said. "We're talking about a couple of young people, one of whom is a law student—"

"So what?" Scott interrupted. "I'd bet on my legal team against a student on any day of the week."

"That's not the point, Scott. If you give them an axe to grind, you can't be surprised if they swing it in your direction. They'll know their way around social media, and to an outside observer, this will look like a clear case of racial harassment. Ask yourself one question: when your investors type Ironbrand Farm into Google, what do you want them to see?"

Dan stopped for a second, giving Scott time to join the dots, then he added, "This is all avoidable, Scott. You can control this before it gets started; before it becomes a news story."

"Hm. You make a fair point," Scott said. "I'll deal with it. I'll tear Sturridge off a strip and send him packing with his tail between his legs. It's one thing for him to throw his weight about, but I can't have him thumping passers-by, I suppose."

"It's up to you, but a gentler approach might be better. You don't want an employee with a grudge. If I were you, I'd calm Sturridge down, keep him onside."

"I know how to handle the man. I joke about him sometimes, but he needs putting in his place now and then. I'll give him a dressing-down, and he'll take it like a man. Then I'll give him a few quid and send him off to the pub to lick his wounds. And that will be that."

Dan rolled his eyes. What century was Scott living in? But all he said aloud was, "It's up to you."

"Yup. Thanks for calling Dan. Listen, you must come up to the farm sometime and have a drink. I have a decent cellar and very good whisky." He paused. "Hang on, Harry wants a word."

"I haven't got time," Dan said, but there was only a series of muffled noises as the phone changed hands.

Harry came on the line: "Dan. We're having a little drinks party up here. Tomorrow night. It's a business thing, very dull, but you'd be more than welcome."

"I'm not sure. I might be busy."

"Around here? What's to keep you busy?" Harry laughed. "Don't answer that. I don't want to know. But come tomorrow, anyway. You don't want to offend me by refusing my invitation. And besides, I think you might find it interesting. You could bring your friend, Alan. I enjoyed our little debate, and I think you'll find the evening stimulating. Both of you."

"Erm, can I get back to you?"

"No need," Harry said. "It's just drinks and snacks. If you come, we'll be pleased to see you. If you don't, no problem. But I've got to get going. Lots to do. Bye."

He ended the call before Dan could reply, and Dan slid his phone across the kitchen table. *What was all that about?* he wondered. When he'd met Harry, the man had been unpleasant from the start, as if he'd taken an active and immediate dislike to him. And yet, here he was, inviting him to a party.

Dan hit on the answer straight away. Harry wanted to drag him and Alan into his PR effort. He wanted to parade them in front of his investors. They'd be the acceptable face of the local community: a couple of educated guys who were keen on renewable energy and ready to show their support.

We'll see about that, Dan thought. *I've got a good mind to tell him where he can stick his party.* But if there was to be a large-scale solar farm on his doorstep, he'd like to know about it. And it was always better to be on the inside, getting information first hand.

Maybe he'd go along and judge for himself. If nothing else, it would be a change from the usual evening in the pub. He could mention it to Alan when he went around to borrow his lawnmower.

Thinking of which, he'd better get started. The afternoon was still warm, and the grass wasn't getting any shorter.

SUNDAY

CHAPTER 11

IT WAS MID-MORNING, and Dan had just pressed the button on his coffee machine when his phone rang. He glanced regretfully at the stream of steaming espresso already flowing into his cup, the crema forming perfectly. But coffee would have to wait while he answered his phone; it could be work.

Accepting the call, Dan smiled as he said, "Hello." It was supposed to make you sound friendly, or so he'd heard. But the caller was unlikely to be impressed; his greeting was brusque, and his voice commanding: "Hello. You must be the computer chappie."

Dan fought the urge to say, "Must I?" Judging by the man's aristocratic diction, he could prove to be a valuable customer. So Dan kept his tone pleasant and said, "That's right. I'm Dan Corrigan. How can I help you?"

"Jolly good. I'm Monty Albright. I don't think we've met, but I'm in the village, and a friend recommended you. Anyway, long story short, I've been having a few difficulties with my machine. I think it might have been hit with a virus. It's behaving in a most peculiar fashion."

"Oh dear. I'd be happy to take a look for you. But what kind of issues are you having? Do you get error messages?"

"Not exactly. It's when I'm logging into my various accounts that the problems crop up. I keep having to verify myself all the time. I get emails, phone calls, text messages. It's getting beyond a joke."

"That sounds like two-factor authentication."

"I know about all that," Monty said. "But it's happening more than it used to. And I have to keep resetting my passwords all the time. It's most irritating."

"It could be a malware problem," Dan said. "When would you like me to come around? I have time on Monday."

"Hm. Couldn't you come today? I need my machine for work, you see. I work with organisations all over the globe, and it's always a workday somewhere." He paused. "I know it's a Sunday, but I'll happily pay for your emergency call-out fee. It's rather urgent, you see."

"In that case, I'll be happy to come over. Whereabouts are you?"

"The Vicarage. Do you know it?"

"No. I'm sorry, you didn't say *Reverend*, but are you the vicar?"

"Good heavens, no. My place used to be the vicarage, back in the days when the church could afford to keep the clergy in style. I've lived here for a good many years, but it's always been called the Vicarage, and I suspect that's the way it's going to stay. Anyway, it's easy to find. It's slap-bang in the middle of the village. Not far from the hall."

"Right. I'll walk over. I can be there in half an hour."

"Excellent. I'll see you shortly. I'll put a pot of coffee on."

"Oh, that won't be necessary."

"Nonsense. It's the least I can do," Monty said, his tone brightening. "Cheerio."

"Goodbye."

Dan ended the call then he downed his espresso. There were some things he was willing to take a risk on, but the quality of other people's coffee wasn't one of them.

CHAPTER 12

L ISA STURRIDGE COULD tell a lot about her husband's mood from the way he came down the stairs. Today, he stomped down as though he was trying to put his feet through the floorboards. She fetched his mug from the rack and poured tea from the pot so that it would be waiting for him. Good. It was nice and strong; just the way he liked it.

But Sid didn't appear. Instead, she heard him rattling about in the hallway. She opened her mouth to call out, but she changed her mind when she noticed the way the dogs were behaving. Both spaniels, Skip and Charlie, had lifted their heads to listen, but they'd stayed on their bed, their eyes watchful but wary. *It's going to be one of those days*, the dogs seemed to say, and Lisa let out a small sigh.

Her husband had come home in a terrible temper the night before, but he'd calmed down after a few glasses of whisky. He'd had a good sleep and a lie-in, so he ought to be in better form; that was how it usually worked. But not today.

He has a bee in his bonnet, she told herself. *Keep out of the way and let him get on with it.* But what on earth was he doing in the hall? He was barging around, making a racket and muttering to himself. What was he up to?

A minute later, she found out. Sid appeared in the kitchen doorway, dressed for work: boots on, waxed cotton jacket over his arm, and hiking stick in hand.

"Morning," Lisa said. "There's a mug of tea for you there."

"Ta." Sid scarcely looked at her, but he marched across and grabbed the mug, taking a gulp before setting it down on the counter again. "That's all I've got time for."

"I was going to make you some bacon and eggs."

"Not today." He caught her eye for a moment and added, "Sorry. Too busy."

"On a Sunday?"

Sid simply nodded, then he stomped through to the utility room. She heard the jingle of keys in a lock, and Sid grumbling to himself. There was more clattering then he reappeared in the kitchen.

"You're taking your gun out?"

"Obviously." Sid patted the double-barrelled shotgun cradled in the crook of his arm.

"Where are you going?"

Sid lifted his chin. "Brandle Wood."

"Will you be long? I've got a nice piece of lamb for lunch. Your favourite."

"I'll be back in plenty of time for that," Sid said. "I'm taking the Land Rover. I'll be there and back in no time." He shifted his attention to the dogs. "Come on, you lazy sods. Time to earn your keep."

Both dogs leaped to their feet, bumbling into each other as they rushed to be the first to his side. Sid made for the door.

"Bye then," Lisa called after him. "Be careful."

"Bye," he replied. And then he was gone. She heard the growl of the Land Rover's engine, then the crunch of tyres on the gravel drive. And as the sound died away, the house was suddenly very quiet.

Lisa looked at her husband's half-drunk mug of tea, then

she picked it up and poured the remains into her own. It was a shame to waste good tea. She took a sip, but it was lukewarm and bitter. Disappointing.

She sat still for a minute or two, staring at the kitchen window. Then she picked herself up and poured the tea down the sink. There was plenty to be getting on with. And if she made a good lunch, maybe it would perk Sid up a bit. It was worth a try.

CHAPTER 13

A CCORDING TO DAN'S phone, he was standing right outside the Vicarage, but the house was hidden away behind a stone wall topped with a dense privet hedge. *I've walked along this road so many times*, he thought. *But I've never seen beyond the wall.* He hadn't even known that the vicarage existed. It was a wonder that Alan hadn't pointed it out. *Maybe he did*, Dan thought. *I probably tuned it out.* History had never been Dan's strong suit, and once you'd seen one thatched cottage, you'd seen them all.

Searching for a way in, Dan followed the wall, turning a corner into a narrow lane, and then again into an even narrower one. And there it was: a wrought-iron gate set into the wall. There was no name on the gate and no plaque on the wall, but this had to be the place.

Dan pushed the gate open and made his way down a path of crumbling red bricks that led through a venerable iron archway, its frame bedecked with climbing roses. Dan wandered through, and it was as if he'd stepped back in time.

Flawless lawns stretched out on either side, and around the garden's perimeter, flower beds were crammed with lush foliage and dotted with brightly coloured flowers. It was a garden from another age, profusely planted but not brash in any way, as if each plant had been carefully selected to harmonise with its neighbours. And presiding over the idyllic scene, the house exuded a quiet grandeur. It wasn't on the scale of a stately home, but it was certainly the largest cottage Dan had ever seen. Its walls were built from mellow stone, topped with a pristine thatched roof, and the small leaded windows reflected the morning sunlight.

Dan strolled toward the house, feeling as though he was intruding on the set of a Merchant–Ivory film. If he'd bumped into Helena Bonham-Carter and someone had yelled "Cut!" he would only have been mildly surprised.

But the only other person present was the immaculately turned-out gentleman who emerged from the front door. His grey hair was neatly combed in a side parting, and he wore a light-blue three-piece suit, a white shirt and a striped tie. He raised a hand in greeting. "Computer wizard?"

"I can't promise magic," Dan replied. "But I'll do my best."

"Jolly good. I'm Monty Albright, by the way. We spoke on the phone."

"Dan Corrigan."

They shook hands, and Dan added, "Your garden is very impressive."

"Do you think so? That's very kind." Monty cast a proprietorial glance over his domain. "It's hard to get it looking right at this time of year. Reg helps me out. He does all the back-breaking stuff. He's very good. Do you know Reg?"

"I met a man called Reg at the May Fair. He was making a chair leg on a lathe."

"That's the chap. Always making something or other." Monty looked at Dan, a twinkle in his eyes but his gaze sharp. "You're new to the village, aren't you?"

"I've been here for nearly a year."

"I thought as much. New." Monty smiled. "You must come another time and see the garden properly when everything's in bloom. There's a garden party here every August. It's run by the church to raise funds. Roof, windows, you know the kind of thing. Anyway, I let them have the run of the lawns and they do the rest. It's all good fun."

"That's very charitable of you."

"Well, we have to keep these traditions alive, and they're always very grateful." He paused. "I take it that you don't attend the church."

"No. Except for weddings and funerals."

Monty nodded. "Me neither. That's why we were both up and working on a Sunday morning, eh? No rest for the wicked!" He laughed, and Dan decided two things. The first was that he liked Monty Albright, and the second was that the man was as sharp as a tack. He might play the part of the elderly English eccentric, but his faculties were undiminished.

"Shall we take a look at your computer?" Dan asked.

"Quite right. Here I am, keeping you talking when you have a job to do." Monty extended his arm, beckoning Dan to enter. "Come in, come in. I'll introduce you to the patient."

He led Dan through a wood-panelled hallway and into a spacious lounge that looked out over the garden. Arranged around the fireplace, a pair of velvet-covered armchairs dominated the centre of the room, but in front of the window, an antique writing desk held a black PC tower along with a monitor, keyboard and mouse. A compact laser printer sat on a small metal filing cabinet beside the desk. Apart from the computer equipment, the desk was bare, with not a stray piece of paper in sight.

"My office," Monty said. "Please, have a look. I left the machine switched on."

Crossing the room, Dan wiggled the mouse to wake the computer, and a lock screen appeared on the monitor.

"Ah. I'll pop in the password." Monty joined him, taking the only seat: a modern office chair with a mesh back.

As Monty typed on the keyboard, Dan said, "You keep your workspace very tidy."

"Everything in its place and I don't print anything off unless I have to. If I need a hard copy of a document, I immediately file it away." Monty hit the return key with a flourish, and the monitor showed the familiar desktop, uncluttered by unnecessary icons or carelessly dropped files. Monty stood, gesturing to the chair. "Please, have a seat. Let the dog see the rabbit."

"Thanks. I'll start by running through a few checks." Dan took the chair and pulled the keyboard closer. "To begin with, do you have an up-to-date backup of all your important files?"

"I should be okay. I pay for a service called IDrive."

Dan raised his eyebrows. "Excellent. I'll check it's working properly." A few clicks were enough to tell Dan that Monty knew what he was doing. "I see that you have BitDefender installed and it's up to date. If a virus has slipped past that, I'd be surprised. When did you last run a scan?"

"This morning, before I called you. It gave me the green light, but I don't know whether to trust it. Since the problems started, I must've run it twenty times, but it always comes back with a clean bill of health."

"Hm." Dan opened the anti-virus program and started going through its logs. "According to this, you've had BitDefender installed for several months. When did the problems first appear?"

"A few days ago. It's when I log into my accounts that things go pear shaped. And then there are all the emails. Here, I'll show you." He reached across and used the mouse, opening Outlook and selecting an email from Barclays Bank. "There. They keep saying I've tried to reset my password, but I've done no such thing."

Dan groaned inwardly. "These emails, have you clicked on any of them?"

"I might have done, but I'm positive they were genuine."

"They might've looked genuine, but these scams can be very convincing. It's called phishing. The links take you to fake sites, and when you enter your passwords, the scammers capture them."

"I know about all that, and I'm almost certain I haven't been taken in. I almost got caught that way once, and BitDefender popped up and warned me."

"You're more vigilant than most," Dan admitted. "But even so, I'm concerned that you may have been the victim of identity theft. It sounds as though someone has stolen or somehow obtained your account details, and probably some passwords, and they're trying to use them. That's why you keep getting all these requests by email and on your phone."

"The blighters! What can I do about it?"

"The first thing I'd advise is that you go through all of your online accounts, starting with the critical ones, such as banks, and you change the password to a very secure alternative. You'll need at least twelve characters including numbers and punctuation, and each one must be unique."

"That's easily done. What next?"

"You should go through your bank accounts and credit cards, checking every transaction. Look out for anything unusual or unexpected. The amounts may not even be large. Sometimes the scammers take small amounts to avoid detection, but they do it several times."

"I see." Monty heaved a sigh. "The worst thing is I knew this could happen, but I didn't think it could happen to me. As you observed, I'm very careful." His face fell. "Oh God. This explains the phone."

"Did someone call you?"

"No. A phone arrived this morning — a mobile phone. Brand new. A courier brought it. The letter said it was an upgrade, but I wasn't expecting it. And as you say, anything unexpected could be suspicious."

Dan stood. "Could you show me the phone?"

"Yes, of course. I'll go and get it." Monty bustled from the room, returning a minute later with a small package: a cardboard box wrapped in a plastic bag. "Here it is." He held it out, and Dan took it from him, opening the box carefully.

"Wow!" Dan breathed. "This is the new Samsung. It's only been on sale for a few days. I was thinking about getting one, but it was too expensive."

"Oh no. And I suppose someone's used my credit card to pay for it."

"It's a possibility," Dan said.

"But it hasn't done them much good. I've got the phone, and I can send it back."

"Yes, but the scammers often try and intercept the package before it arrives." Dan paused. "Monty, you need to call your phone company and tell them you didn't order that phone, and then you need to call the police."

"All right. But why do you look so worried? I mean, we've won, haven't we? We've beaten them."

"Not yet. I'll try to explain, but we haven't got much time. Somebody will probably turn up very soon. A member of the gang."

"Here?"

"I'm afraid so," Dan said. "There's a chance that someone will turn up, posing as a courier. They'll say that the package was delivered by mistake, then they'll try and persuade you to hand it over. They'll say they're going to send it back, but whatever happens, you mustn't give it to them. I'll wait with you, at least until you've talked to the police. Okay?"

Monty nodded slowly. "That's very good of you. Thank you. I'll just go and get a glass of water. I think I need one of my pills. As soon as I've seen to that, I'll start making calls straight away. Get it done and dusted." He moved slowly to the door, halting by the threshold. "I suppose they chose me because they think I'm an old duffer."

"It's possible that they're targeting people of a certain age. And they may have figured out that you live alone. In their eyes, that makes you vulnerable."

"Little blighters! Just let them show their faces around here, and I'll show them vulnerable. I've got a good mind to fetch my shotgun!"

Monty's face and neck turned an alarming shade of puce, and Dan said, "Please, take a moment, Monty. You've had a nasty surprise, but we'll call the police and let them deal with it."

"I know, I know. You needn't worry. I'm not going to shoot anyone. I'm blowing off a bit of steam, that's all. But who can blame me?" Monty shook his head. "I used to be a magistrate, you know. Thought I'd seen it all. But *this*. It beggars belief. And in Embervale! Good God!" Monty trudged from the room, and Dan was left alone, listening to Monty's heavy footsteps on the stairs.

I hope he finds his pills in time, Dan thought. *I wonder what they're for*. For a moment, he imagined the dull thud of a body hitting the floor, and pictured the man sprawled on the carpet, an unopened brown bottle in his fist. But he pushed the thought away. Monty had the bearing of a man who'd kept himself fit and active. It would take more than this to lay him low. The man had been a little naïve, that was all. Living in a quiet village was no protection against cybercrime, and it was foolish to think otherwise.

But there was something wrong here, something Dan couldn't quite see. Monty was clearly security conscious, and every detail in the spotless room suggested that he was a meticulous man. Would he have been so careless as to click on a dodgy email?

It was unlikely, but everyone made mistakes, didn't they? Dan stared at Monty's computer. From what he'd seen, the machine was almost certainly free from malware. The damage had been done elsewhere: a series of fake websites had captured Monty's passwords and squirrelled them away, leading him on a dance as one link led to another.

It was the most impersonal of crimes: a life reduced to a string of data. Data that could be bought and sold in the uncharted back alleys of cyberspace.

But Monty would bounce back. The new phone could be returned, and if any money had been fraudulently withdrawn from his accounts, he could try to reclaim it. It would be an uphill struggle, but Monty seemed like the kind of person to relish a challenge.

In the meantime, a spurious courier could arrive at any moment. *It would be best if I answered the door*, Dan thought. *Otherwise, I could wind up with a murder on my hands. Again.*

Dan smiled to himself. Life had been quiet for the last few months, but this break from the routine was fine with him. It was absolutely fine.

CHAPTER 14

D AISY'S MUM HAD a conservatory at home, but it was
nothing like this. The conservatory at Ironbrand Farm
was so big, Daisy could only stand and stare, turning on the
spot to take in the size of the place.

Watching her, Scott smiled. "Don't worry, you won't have
to clean the glass. I have a man who comes in and takes care
of it."

"The roof as well?" Daisy asked, tipping back her head to
gaze up at the glass roof. "He must have a big ladder."

"He uses a cherry-picker," Scott said. "He's a specialist."

"Right." Daisy took a few faltering steps, then she laid her
hand on the back of a cane sofa. Turning to Scott, she smiled.
"It's all very grand."

"We like it. But that concludes the tour. I think it was all
self-explanatory, but is there anything you'd like to ask?"

"Erm. In the main house, there are a lot of wooden floors.
Do they need polishing? Because that would take ages."

"The floorboards are original. Four hundred years old. I
have them oiled and polished once or twice a year, but again,
I get a specialist to deal with all that. All you'd have to do is
run the Dyson over them every day. Keep them clean."

"Every day?"

"Well, weekdays. I'll need you for about four hours a day, in the mornings. Would that be a problem?"

"It might be. Most places, I go once a week. If you want me here every day, I'll have to do a bit of juggling to fit everything in. I don't know if I can manage it."

"This is a big house," Scott said. "And I like it kept just so. I entertain my business associates here, and it's important to create the right atmosphere. And there's the office across the yard. That's in the old barn. You'll have passed it on your way in. It all needs to be kept clean and tidy. I can't abide mess. So if you can't take the job on, you'd better tell me right away. But honestly, you'd be making a terrible mistake."

Daisy frowned. "Would I?"

"Yes. You see, I've got where I am by hiring the right people. I'm good at it, and I can always pick a winner. You, Daisy, are a winner."

"You make me sound like a racehorse."

Scott laughed and Daisy joined in.

"I wouldn't dream of making any such comparison," Scott said. "But I like you, Daisy. You arrived on time, you've come smartly dressed, and you've got something about you. A spark. Know what I mean?"

"I think so."

"Good. You've got potential, Daisy. I could see it right away. I'd like to have you on the team."

"Does that mean I've got the job?"

"If you want it," Scott said. "But I'll tell you what, we'll give you a trial run. Give it a week and we'll take it from there. You can start on Monday. Okay?"

He held out his hand and Daisy took it. "Okay."

Scott smiled as they shook hands. "Excellent. I'll work out an hourly rate and have someone send you the details. And I'll need a couple of references."

"Oh. I don't have anything written down. Usually, people

don't give me any paperwork or anything. But I could ask someone to write me a reference."

"That's okay. Tell me a couple of people you've been working for, and I'll give them a call."

"Right. Do you want the details now? I'm not sure who to pick."

"Don't fret, Daisy. It's just a formality. I'll take you over to the office and introduce you to Carol. She handles all my HR. You can give the names of your referees to her, and she'll do the rest. She's terribly efficient."

Scott led Daisy outside, taking her across the yard and into a large, converted barn. Inside, Daisy gazed around the modern open-plan workspace, her eyes wide.

"Are you all right?" Scott asked.

Daisy nodded. "I always wanted to work in an office. I learned to type at school, but I couldn't get a job. I was hopeless at maths, and I failed the exam. Twice."

"You never know," Scott said. "There are always opportunities for the right people." He led Daisy to the back of the room where a woman was watching them from behind an enormous white desk. She was the room's only occupant, and her desk was placed to give her a commanding view over the entire office. "This is Carol, my office manager," Scott said. "Carol, this is Daisy. I was just telling her that we're always on the lookout for raw talent."

"In principle, yes," Carol replied. "But I wouldn't like to give the young lady false expectations. I'm afraid we're fully staffed at the moment."

"We'll see about that," Scott said. "We're always expanding, so anything could happen. Anything at all." He winked at Daisy, then said, "Carol, I'd like you to set Daisy up for a trial week on our cleaning staff, starting tomorrow."

Carol looked Daisy up and down, apparently unimpressed. "That's very short notice, Mr Benning. Do we have a completed application form? A CV? References?"

"Don't pick holes," Scott replied. "You know perfectly well that Jasmine let us down, and we need a replacement. Daisy fits the bill."

"Even so," Carol began, "without references—"

"Daisy will give you some names, and you can give them a call," Scott interrupted. "Now, I have things to do, so I'll leave Daisy in your capable hands. Okay?"

"Of course." Carol tilted her head toward a vacant chair. "You'd better have a seat, Daisy."

Daisy sat down, her back straight. "Will this take very long? Only, my boyfriend's out in the lane, waiting in the car."

"You should've told me," Scott said. "He could've waited in here."

"He'll be all right. He's a bit…"

Scott sent Daisy a questioning look.

"He's sort of shy," Daisy said. "He's not very good at meeting new people."

"Oh dear," Scott said absently, taking out his phone and checking the screen. "Sorry, Carol, I must've missed your message earlier. What's it about?"

Carol sighed. "It's Sid Sturridge. His wife called a little while ago, and she's worried that he hasn't come home. She seems to think he came to work today, but he's not on the rota."

"You know what he's like," Scott said. "He probably came to check on the birds."

"Well, I wish he'd stick to the schedule," Carol replied. "We can't have people coming and going whenever they feel like it."

Scott shrugged. "I expect he's trying to get back into my good books. I had to have strong words with him last night."

"What's he done this time?" Carol asked.

"It's not worth going into. I'll let you two get acquainted. I've got a heap of things to check before tonight." Scott made to leave, then changed his mind. "Here's a thought, Daisy. How would you like to pick up a bit of extra cash?"

Daisy hesitated. "It depends..."

"It's nothing too arduous," Scott said. "I'm having a party tonight, and it's always good to have plenty of people to pass around the nibbles. It would only be for a few hours, but it'll be worth your while."

"That sounds all right," Daisy replied. "Would I need to wear anything special?"

Scott shook his head. "A white blouse and black trousers would be good."

"That would be fine," Daisy said. "What time?"

"Could you be here for six?"

Daisy nodded.

"Excellent. Carol will sort out your pay packet. I'll see you later."

Scott strode from the room, and Daisy puffed out her cheeks. "Crikey. Is he always like that?"

Carol's smile was tight. "No. This is one of Mr Benning's quieter days. Sometimes, he's through here like a whirlwind." She pulled her keyboard closer, her fingers poised over the keys. "Now, let's get the paperwork done, shall we?"

The paperwork completed, Daisy strolled across the yard with a spring in her step and a smile on her lips. She looked up at the wisps of cloud that streaked the sky and pictured herself mingling with the posh folks at the party. When she was thirteen, she'd had a craze for reading millionaire romance novels, and for a second she wondered what Scott would look like without his shirt. *He said I had potential*, she thought. *I could say the same about him.* Scott was nothing like the rugged men she'd dreamed about as an adolescent, but he'd mentioned that he'd had one of the outbuildings converted into a gym, so he probably worked out. He was married, of course, but there'd be other men at the party, and just maybe she'd catch someone's eye. Especially if she wore her new white blouse; the one that was just a little too tight.

Still smiling, she wandered out into the lane. The car was parked a short way from the gate, and Paul was leaning against it, his hands in his pockets. She waved, but he just said, "What took you?"

Her smile vanished. "I beg your pardon."

"Why were you so long? I've been waiting for ages."

"Aren't you going to ask how it went? Aren't you going to say something nice for a change?" She let out an exasperated sigh, then she stalked toward him. "I don't know what's wrong with you. I really don't."

"I was worried, that's all. You've been a long time, and I didn't know what to do."

"I said I'd call you if there was a problem, didn't I?"

Paul nodded dumbly.

"Well, I didn't call, so there wasn't a problem." She went to the passenger door and let herself in, throwing herself into the seat and wrestling with the safety belt.

Paul opened the door and sat beside her, watching her with baleful eyes. "I've missed the courier."

"And that's my fault is it?"

"I didn't say that, did I? But if you'd been a bit quicker…"

She turned on him. "It's no use moaning about it. Are you going to drive me home or what?"

"Yeah. But what happened with Benning?"

"Finally." Daisy drew a breath. "I got the job. A trial run, anyway. I start on Monday."

"That's good. I mean, it's great. Well done, babe."

Daisy giggled. "But that's not the best part."

"I know that laugh. What have you done?"

"Well, there's this woman, Carol, a right stuck-up cow. She runs the office. Anyway, she had to print off a contract for me to sign, but the printer had run out of paper, so she had to go and get some. She left me on my own, right next to her desk."

Paul's hand went to his mouth. "You didn't."

"I bloody well did. It only took me a second, and there it was, done."

"Jesus," Paul breathed. "That's risky."

"Why? She'll never spot it. Her computer was under the desk."

"But an office is different. People are more careful. They check stuff like that."

"Rubbish."

"And how would you know? I work in an office, and I know about this stuff. I'm telling you, you shouldn't have done it. Not there."

"I thought you'd be pleased."

Paul sat back. "Unbelievable. Absolutely bloody unbelievable."

Daisy bit her lower lip. "There's something else you're not going to like."

"What now?"

"I've got to come back here tonight. I've got another job, waitressing at his posh party."

Paul took hold of the steering wheel with both hands, his thumbnails digging into the plastic, picking at it. The insistent scratching sound set Daisy's teeth on edge, but it was best not to react. It was the kind of thing Paul did when he was calming himself down. He needed to get these tics over and done with; if she let him alone for a while, he'd be all right.

After a minute, he said, "You were going to come around to mine tonight."

"Yeah. Sorry, but I can't let Scott down. I've got to keep him sweet."

"Not too sweet though."

"Jealous?"

"No," Paul blurted. "But I don't want him taking advantage."

"Don't be daft. I can handle him."

"I'll handle the bugger," Paul said. "If he does anything to you, I'll smash his face in."

Daisy didn't bother to contradict him. Paul had some dark moods, but he wasn't a fighter; he was too soft for that. That was one of the things she liked about him. "Come on," she said. "I'll make it up to you. When we get to my house, you can come in for a bit. They've all gone out."

Paul's expression brightened. "Okay. That'll be nice."

"Yes," she said. "Yes, it will."

CHAPTER 15

D AN AND ALAN decided to walk up to Ironbrand Farm, and while they strolled along the lane, Dan told Alan about what had happened with Monty Albright.

"Did anyone turn up and try to claim the phone?" Alan asked.

"Not while I was there," Dan said. "I waited for a while, but once he'd got over the initial shock, Monty took it all in his stride. He insisted that I leave him to it."

"He's quite a character."

Dan smiled. "Definitely. I was there when he called his bank, and he wasn't going to stand for any nonsense."

"Good for him. But it's an awful thing to happen. You hear about these scams, but somehow you don't expect them in a little place like this."

"Cybercrime knows no boundaries," Dan said. "It can find you anywhere, at any time."

Alan considered this for a moment. "Was he targeted deliberately, do you think?"

"It's hard to be sure, but I suspect he fitted a profile. A single person of a certain age, living alone. His name might have been on a list that fell into the wrong hands, but it could be much simpler than that. He's a careful man, but he could easily have been caught in a phishing scam. All it takes is one click."

"Poor old Monty. It could happen to anyone."

"Almost anyone," Dan said.

"You're immune, are you? Or is it just that you're infallible?"

Dan summoned a wry smile. Alan had a habit of bringing him down to earth with a bump, but perhaps that was why they got on so well. In London, Dan had been part of a wide social circle: a gang of upwardly mobile go-getters. They'd shared a lot of good times, but they'd never criticised each other. At the time, Dan had thought this was because they shared a cast-iron belief in the value of positivity. But now, he realised, they simply hadn't cared about each other. When Dan had fallen from grace, in those dark days when he'd scarcely been able to look after himself, his so-called friends had all vanished without a trace.

Alan would never do that to him.

Dan checked his watch. "It's almost seven."

"It's not much further. We'll be on time."

Sure enough, a few minutes later, they arrived at a broad set of wrought-iron gates, both firmly closed. And worked into the pattern of metal bars were the words *Ironbrand Farm*.

Beside the main gates, the smaller entrance for pedestrians was less forbidding. Dan and Alan made their way through, following the path that led toward a broad yard and the house beyond. The yard was brightly lit, and Dan took in the expanse of spotless concrete, the array of converted outbuildings. It was like no farm he'd ever seen.

As if reading his mind, Alan said, "Not a chicken in sight."

"No sign of any animals at all. No farmyard smells, and nothing in the stone troughs except geraniums."

"Pelargoniums."

"What's the difference?"

"Never mind." Alan lowered his voice. "How much do you think this place is worth?"

"A lot," Dan said. "And if they build a big solar farm, it'll be worth even more."

They made their way to the front door, where a smartly dressed woman let them in, introducing herself as Carol, Mr Benning's office manager.

"Pleased to meet you," Dan said. "I'm Dan Corrigan and this is Alan Hargreaves."

"Yes, I've been expecting you. Welcome to Ironbrand."

"You didn't mistake us for a couple of high-powered businessmen, then?" Alan asked.

Carol returned his smile. "Everyone else arrived by car this afternoon. You're the only guests from Embervale. Can I take your coats?"

"Thanks." Dan slipped out of his coat, aware that Carol was watching him carefully. As he handed his coat to her, he said, "Is something wrong?"

She shook her head. "No. That is, unless…"

"Go on," Dan prompted.

Carol seemed to make her mind up. "Do you know Mr Sturridge?"

"I know of him," Dan said. "Why? What's happened?"

"It's nothing to worry about. But I thought that, since you walked here, you might've spotted him in the lane. He's probably lurking around out there somewhere."

"At this time in the evening?" Dan asked. "Is he after poachers?"

"I'm not sure what he gets up to, but never mind. Forget I asked. Give me a second to hang your coats, then I'll take you through."

She disappeared through a doorway, and Alan muttered, "What was all that about?"

"I don't know. But the more I hear about this Sturridge character, the less I like the sound of him."

"I don't really know him," Alan said. "I've seen him around the village, but he's not the type to stop and say hello."

Carol reappeared, and her calm and professional manner was back. "This way, gentlemen," she said, and Dan and Alan followed her through to a huge conservatory where a gaggle of men and women stood chatting, drinks in hand. The men were almost uniformly clad in suits of grey, though most had removed their ties. The women, however, had thought ahead and changed into cocktail dresses. It was the kind of gathering that Dan knew well and old instincts stirred. In the past, parties like this were all about networking, making connections, searching for opportunities. But not tonight. Tonight, he had nothing to gain and nothing to lose. He could relax, sample the wine and enjoy himself.

Carol showed them where they could get a drink, then she waltzed away, mingling with the guests and exchanging a word here and there.

Alan leaned closer to Dan. "I knew I should've worn my best suit."

"Alan, that *is* your best suit," Dan said.

"No, it isn't."

"Don't take this the wrong way, but that thing you call your best suit is… How can I put this tactfully? It's long past its best. It makes you look like a gangster."

Alan's face fell. "And that's your idea of tact, is it?"

"I was trying to help. You wouldn't want me to lie, would you?"

"Hm. You might go a little easy on the honesty once in a while," Alan said. "I think I'll grab a drink. I have a premonition that it's only a matter of time before we're asked to leave, and I want to have at least one glass of free fizz."

Alan strode over to a white-clothed table where a young

man was dispensing drinks. Dan waited a moment, and as he cast his eye over the gathering, a woman wearing an elegant black dress sashayed toward him.

"Hello," she said. "Have you only just arrived?"

"Yes. We're from the village. We were last-minute additions."

The woman arched an eyebrow, then she extended her hand. "I see. I'm Jocelyn, Scott's wife."

Dan shook her hand. "Delighted to meet you. It's a lovely place you have here."

"Yes." Jocelyn looked around the room as though seeing it anew. "I like to think we've added to the old buildings, modernising while keeping true to the traditional style." She pointed to a large octagonal table that held an arrangement of fresh flowers. "I had that table made from an oak that grew just outside. We had to have it felled to make way for a new barn. It was a shame to lose the tree, but there we are. Anyway, I did some research and found a design that was just perfect. A local craftsman turned the legs and made the frame, and we found a cabinetmaker in Exeter who made the top and put the whole thing together. It cost a fortune, but it was worth it to keep the memory of that old tree alive."

Or you could've just left the tree alone, Dan thought. But fortunately, Jocelyn had no intention of leaving a gap for him to speak, so he kept his thoughts to himself.

"I love to spend time in this room when I'm here," she went on. "But that isn't as often as I'd like. I have so many places to visit and so many people who I simply must see, so I'm always flitting from place to place."

"Do you travel for work?"

She grinned. "For pleasure. Pure pleasure. But I'm being a terrible hostess. You don't have a drink. Step this way."

She led him to the table where Alan was polishing off a glass of sparkling wine.

Dan introduced Jocelyn to Alan, and after a few

pleasantries, Jocelyn caught the eye of the young man behind the table. "Marco, three glasses of champagne. But run down to the cellar and get a bottle of the good stuff. I don't want this muck you're giving the others. I'll have the Krug 1988 and make sure you take it from the chiller."

A muscle in Marco's cheek twitched, and when he spoke, he stumbled over his words as though English wasn't his first language. "Erm, Mr Benning, he has left me the instructions, and he said—"

Jocelyn cut him off with a raised hand. "I don't care what he said. This is my house, and I'll drink my own damned champagne whenever I please. Understand?"

Marco nodded.

"You know where the cellar key is, don't you?"

"Yes, Mrs Benning."

"Well, go and get the Krug. And make sure it's the 1988. Check the label."

"Of course, Mrs Benning." Marco hurried away.

"Honestly," Jocelyn murmured. "I don't know where he finds these people, but they seem to get worse. I'm all in favour of immigration, I really am. But every time I come home, there's another domestic who doesn't know one end of a mop from the other. And some of them steal, I'm sure of it."

In the silence that followed, Alan caught Dan's eye then he looked away, self-consciously straightening his jacket.

Getting the message, Dan said, "This conservatory is amazing. It must be wonderful in summer. Does it face south?"

"More or less," Jocelyn replied absently. Her attention was on someone across the room. "There's a case in point. That girl with the tray. Where has she sprung from? I've never seen her before in my life."

"I have. She's a local girl." Dan smiled at the sight of the young woman struggling to balance a tray of canapés as she made her way through the throng. The last time he'd seen her had been in Brandle Wood. *Her name's Daisy*, he recalled. *A fish out of water if ever there was one.* Perhaps Daisy was overwhelmed, unused to being surrounded by the ostentatiously wealthy, because she was having difficulty putting one foot in front of the other. Still, Daisy looked the part, and with her hair tied back and her smart white blouse, she could pass as waiting staff in any high-end restaurant. Provided she could stand still.

Jocelyn narrowed her eyes. "Perhaps she came with the caterer. He's local. And for him, I'm prepared to make allowances. He's a genius. Have you tried the canapés yet?"

"Not yet," Dan said. "And it looks like I might be too late."

Her tray empty, Daisy was making a hasty retreat, and she disappeared through the doorway.

"Oh, she'll be back in a minute with some more. You must try everything. The blinis are divine."

"It depends on what's in them," Dan replied. "I'm pretty much a vegan."

Jocelyn's eyes widened and she laid her hand on his chest. "I'm incredibly careful what I eat, and honestly, you'll be fine with this chef. Vegan food is his speciality. He's marvellous."

"Is his name George, by any chance?" Dan asked.

"Yes. Do you know him?"

Dan nodded. "We've met. I must go and say hello."

"Later, perhaps," Jocelyn said. "He's in the kitchen, and he'll be rushed off his feet."

Behind them, Marco arrived, bearing a tray with three glasses. "Your champagne, Mrs Benning."

"Thank you." Jocelyn took her glass with barely a glance at Marco, then she turned to Dan and Alan. "I must go and schmooze, so I'll leave you to enjoy your drinks. But please, remember to try the food. It's to die for."

She strolled away, and Dan and Alan took pains to thank

Marco as they lifted their glasses. They sipped appreciatively, then Alan whispered, "Bloody hell!"

"Sir?" Marco leaned forward. "Is there a problem with the wine?"

"Not at all," Alan replied. "But if this is champagne, what have I been drinking all these years?"

Marco grinned nervously. "Mr Benning is particular about his wine. He keeps it very well."

"So I can see," Alan said. "Are you just here for this evening, Marco, or do you work here all the time?"

Marco's smile faltered. "I have been with Mr Benning for a while. I work mainly in the kitchen."

"Right. I can't quite place your accent," Dan said. "Where are you from?"

"Italy," Marco replied. "South Italy."

"In that case, *grazie mille*." Dan raised his glass, but Marco seemed put out by the gesture.

"Please. Thanks are not necessary. I hope you enjoy your champagne. Excuse me, but I must attend to the kitchen." Marco bowed his head then he bustled away.

Dan frowned.

"Poor chap," Alan said. "I bet the lady of the house gives him the runaround."

"Hm. He was certainly nervous. I wonder…"

"What?"

Dan half shrugged. "It's probably nothing, but whenever you say *grazie* in Italy, people always respond with *prego*. It's polite. And until now, I've never met an Italian who doesn't say it."

"Perhaps he's been told only to speak English," Alan said.

"Yes, that could be it."

They sipped their champagne, then Alan said, "We ought to go and mingle. I'd hate for people to think I'm hovering by the drinks."

"Sure."

They wandered through the crowd, smiling politely, though Dan didn't see anyone he recognised. After a while, they found a space near the glazed wall and stood, chatting. Dan asked Alan how his writing was going, and Alan, growing animated as the champagne did its work, rattled off the plot of his next adventure book.

Dan waggled his empty glass. "Fancy another?"

"Yes, but I could do with something to eat first."

Dan searched the crowd. "There's no sign of Daisy, but there's another young woman with a tray over there. It looks promising, but it'll take her ages to get over here. Let's go and see what she's got."

"It would be rude not to," Alan replied.

And then, like everyone else in the room, they froze.

The hollow boom that had silenced them faded away.

"Oh my God!" Dan said. "Was that a gun?"

Alan nodded. "Shotgun."

CHAPTER 16

A LONG WITH EVERYONE else in the conservatory, Dan stared out across the floodlit lawn. There was nothing to see, but still, no one moved. No one said a word.

And then they saw him.

A figure, clad in white, staggered into view, his head down, his hands clutched to his chest. He swayed, looked up, and then he fell, landing face down on the grass.

And Dan launched himself into action. Darting across the room, he found the exit and hurled himself against it, barging through. A split second later, he was kneeling beside the man's unmoving form. The man's face was turned to one side, and Dan's heart clenched. It was George, and his face was deathly pale.

"George," Dan called out. "Can you hear me?"

An unintelligible whisper escaped from George's lips, and Dan heard him take a ragged breath.

"He's alive! Ambulance! Call an ambulance!"

"I already have." Dan looked up to see Harry standing over him, a phone pressed against his ear. "Dan, what can you see? They're asking me to describe his injuries. Has he been shot?"

"We heard a gun, but I can't see anything while he's lying on his front. He was holding his chest. Ask them if we should roll him over."

Alan arrived and bent down to grab George's wrist. "He's got a strong pulse."

"Okay," Harry said. "They say we can turn him gently onto his side. Support his head and his neck."

Dan shifted his position. "I'll take his head. Alan, when I'm ready, roll him toward you."

"All right."

Dan cradled George's head. "You can move him but keep it slow."

Working together, they eased George onto his side. Dan expected George to cry out in agony, but he made no sound, and his silence seemed worse than any moan of pain.

And then Dan looked down at George's chest, and he gasped.

A red stain had spread across the white fabric, and protruding from his chest was the handle of a kitchen knife, its polished wood marked with a dark grain.

Without thinking, Dan's hand crept toward the knife, but a hand clamped around his forearm, holding him tight, and he looked up to see Harry glaring at him.

"Don't touch it," Harry said. "Wait." He spoke rapidly into his phone. Then, to Dan, he said, "Leave the knife where it is, or his lung will collapse, and he'll bleed out in seconds."

Dan pulled his hand free from Harry's grip. "There must be *something* we can do."

"Keep pressure around the wound," Harry replied. "Alan, go and find a blanket. Anything to keep him warm."

Alan stood, shrugging out of his jacket and passing it to Dan. "Use this until I get back."

"Sure." Dan draped the jacket over George's abdomen, then he reached for the wound, his fingers finding the hard edge of the blade through the tunic's thick material. He moved his fingers a little way from the wound and pressed down as hard as he dared. He glanced at George's face, but there was no reaction, no sign that he was suffering any pain as a result of Dan's efforts.

"Yes!" Harry exclaimed, staring into space, his phone still pressed to his ear. "That's right. There's a place they can land. I don't know how you'll find it in the dark, but maybe we can... I see. I didn't know that, but it's great. Thank you. Thank you very much."

He looked at Dan. "They're sending the air ambulance. They're on their way. I know Scott has had helicopters land here, but I didn't know the place was rigged for night-time landings. They said the crew can turn the lights on remotely when they get near."

"That's fantastic."

"Yeah." Harry let out a hoot of relief. "I just hope the downdraught doesn't blow the polytunnels away." He inclined his head and raised his hand in a show of submission. "Sorry, that was inappropriate. I don't know what I was thinking. It was the relief, you know? Help is on its way."

"It's understandable," Dan said. "How long until they get here?"

Harry returned to his phone, relaying Dan's question, then he listened, his expression growing solemn. "As far as I know," he began slowly, "no one else is hurt. I thought he'd been shot because I heard a gun, but it must have been something else." He caught Dan's eye. "You didn't see anyone else out here, did you?"

"No." Dan cast an anxious glance over his shoulder. The lawn was well lit by the outside lights positioned at strategic intervals around the house, but beyond their glare the garden lay cloaked in deep shadow. He could make out the darker shapes of a few scattered shrubs, but he'd never seen the garden in daylight, and he had no idea what was out there.

For all he knew, someone was watching him at that very moment. After all, George was hardly likely to have stabbed himself. And whatever Harry said, they had heard a gunshot, hadn't they?

"The helicopter will be here in ten to fifteen minutes," Harry said. "They want me to stay on the line." He glanced back toward the house. "Here comes Alan. Looks like he's found something to keep him warm."

"Good." Dan concentrated on George's wound, renewing the pressure. George's blood was wet and warm against his hand, and the bloodstain had grown, spreading inexorably through the white material. But at least he could hear George breathing, each breath crackling in his throat.

"Here we are." Alan appeared at Dan's side, bending to drape a soft blanket gently over George's body. "That should help." He laid his hand on Dan's shoulder. "Do you want me to take over?"

"No," Dan said. "I'm fine."

"Okay but tell me if you want to change places." Alan paused. "Scott is keeping everyone inside, trying to calm them all down. And I don't mind telling you, he's got a job on his hands."

"I can imagine."

"The older generation are keeping a stiff upper lip," Alan went on. "But some of the younger ones are very agitated. Scott's plying them with brandy."

"It'll take more than booze to sort this mess out," Harry said.

Yes, Dan thought. *Yes, it will.*

MONDAY

CHAPTER 17

DAISY WAS STILL in her bathrobe when someone rang the doorbell. She'd just come out of the shower, and her hair was still wet, but no one else was home, so she had to go down and answer the door.

Oh hell! It was *him.*

The man standing on the doorstep smiled. "Good morning, Daisy. We need to talk."

Daisy stood, fiddling with the belt of her bathrobe, pulling it tighter. The man's stare was unnerving: cold and hard. But Daisy gathered her courage. "What about? What do you want?"

The man shook his head. "Get dressed. I'll wait."

"No." Daisy stepped back, swinging the door shut, but the man was too fast. His hand was on the door, his fingers curled around the edge, and however hard she pressed, the door wouldn't budge.

"Don't be silly, Daisy." The man's voice was calm, as though they were having a nice chat. But his expression hardened, and he stepped forward, filling the door frame.

Daisy edged away. "Get out! I'll call my dad."

"No, you won't. I saw him leave. And the rest of your family. I saw them go." He half turned and pushed the front door closed. "It's just you and me, Daisy. Just you and me."

CHAPTER 18

A FTER A POOR night's sleep, Dan woke much later than usual, with a thick head and stiff muscles. Sitting up in bed, he checked his phone, opening a browser and scrolling through all the local news he could find. There were a few stories concerning George, but they all conformed to the same template, as if they'd been copied from an official statement.

Thanks to the Devon air ambulance, George had made it to the hospital in time, and after a life-saving operation, he'd been whisked to an intensive therapy unit pending further treatment. He was still in a critical condition and the incident was being treated as suspicious by the police.

Dan tossed his phone onto the bed and closed his eyes. Images from the night before flashed through his mind: the bloodstain slowly seeping through white fabric; the paramedics dashing across the lawn; the oxygen mask placed over George's nose and mouth; the needle slipped into his arm. And then, the swift choreography of purposeful movement that swept George up and whisked him away.

It had all happened so fast, and once the helicopter had clattered into the night sky, Dan and the others had stood and stared at each other in bewilderment.

Shortly afterwards, the police had arrived. Of course, there'd been questions, but Dan hadn't been able to tell them very much. Yes, he'd heard a sound that he'd believed was a gunshot. But no, he couldn't be sure. He hadn't seen a gun, nor was he aware of anyone, other than George, having been injured.

Dan could only relate what he'd seen and describe his part in it. The uniformed constable had noted everything down and then told him he could go, advising him to get some sleep.

If only, Dan thought. *I was awake half the night.*

He rolled his shoulders and then stretched out his arms, yawning. The vertebrae in his neck clicked and grated, and he knew there was only one thing that would revive him.

A few minutes later, he tied on his running shoes and headed out.

He'd worked out a moderately easy, circular route that he could run from his doorstep. It was only 7K, all of it on tarmacked roads, but it was ideal for days when he didn't feel like driving; days when he just needed to get out and run. The route took him through the village and then along a series of quiet lanes before bringing him back home.

He set off at a jog, but he hadn't gone far when a Volvo saloon pulled up at the side of the road, a familiar face peering out at him through the open window.

Dan jogged to a halt. "DS Spiller. I'd say it's nice to see you, but from the look on your face, I'd be wasting my time."

DS Spiller sent him a patronising smile. "Get in, Mr Corrigan. I'd like a chat."

"In your official capacity?"

"I'm a policeman, Mr Corrigan. Everything I do is official. But this needn't take long."

Dan locked eyes with Spiller, then reluctantly he nodded.

"Thank you," Spiller said. "Hop in. It isn't locked."

Dan climbed into the passenger seat and angled his body to face Spiller. Waiting.

But the policeman seemed intent on taking his time. Reaching into his jacket pocket, he produced a packet of mints and peeled back the paper wrapping with meticulous attention to detail. "Trebor extra strong. Something of a habit." He offered the packet to Dan. "Would you like one?"

"No, thank you. They're terrible for your teeth."

Spiller raised his eyebrows. "I've never had any trouble. But maybe that's because I brush and floss so thoroughly." He popped a mint into his mouth and sucked it thoughtfully. Eventually, he said, "I'm surprised."

"At what?"

"You didn't ask about George Hepworth. I'd have put good money on the first words out of your mouth being 'How's George?' But you haven't even mentioned him."

"I read the news online just before I came out, and if there'd been any developments either way, I'd have been able to tell from your expression."

"Then you're a better man than me," Spiller said. "You know, I've met plenty of coppers who reckon they've got an instinct for reading faces and such. They say they can spot a lie from a mile off. But you know what? It's all bullshit. People can be very clever when it comes to concealing what's going on in their minds. And not just bad people. Take doctors, for instance. They couldn't do their jobs unless they repressed their emotions. They learn to hide their feelings, their innermost thoughts. And after a while, it becomes a habit."

"Like your mints."

Spiller smiled. "Like my mints." He looked ahead, working his jaw as he sucked on his sweet.

"Does that mean you *do* have some news about George?" Dan asked.

"Not much. He needs another operation, but you can't

rush these things. For the moment, they're keeping him in the ITU. And like I said just now, you never know with doctors; they don't give much away. All I can say about George is, he's in the right place. He's got a fighting chance. But unfortunately for me, the poor lad is still heavily sedated."

"So, you haven't been able to speak to him yet."

"Regrettably, no." Spiller gave Dan an appraising look, as though deciding what to say next. "I don't know how you do it, Mr Corrigan, but you have an uncanny knack for being in the wrong place at the wrong time."

"Coincidence." Dan hesitated. "I'm guessing that you're about to warn me off, tell me not to get involved. But you needn't worry, Detective Sergeant, you can spare me the lecture about interfering in police enquiries. I have absolutely no intention of standing in your way, not even for a second."

"I'm glad to hear it. Surprised, but pleased, nevertheless."

"Right," Dan said. "Does that mean we're done? Can I go for my run now?"

Slowly, Spiller shook his head. "I'm afraid not. Because although I'm not going to lecture you, I do need to set you straight."

"About what?"

"About your involvement or otherwise," Spiller said. "You see, for all its strengths, the Devon and Cornwall Police is not a huge organisation. We talk. We attend meetings and conferences. And I bumped into a colleague recently, a detective constable from Newquay. She had a very interesting story to tell me."

"DC Kulkarni."

"Got it in one. A bright young woman with a very promising future if I'm any judge."

"She told you about the incident at the hotel."

Spiller inclined his head in acknowledgement. "She gave me a full account, and I must admit it was quite the tale. She had us all eating out the palm of her hand. So imagine my surprise when it turned out that the hero of the story was none other than a certain Daniel Corrigan."

Dan shifted uncomfortably in his seat. "What do you want me to say? It sounds as though you already know all about it. In which case, you'll know that I didn't do anything wrong."

"Indeed not. According to DC Kulkarni, if it hadn't been for you, the case might have come to a very different conclusion."

"That's probably true," Dan admitted. "But listen, whatever you're driving at, I wish you'd just get on and say it. I need to go for my run."

"It's like this, Mr Corrigan. I know that you're going to get involved in this case. I haven't the shadow of a doubt."

Dan opened his mouth to protest, but Spiller held up his hand to forestall him.

"So I've made a decision," Spiller went on. "As long as you do not interfere with or impede my investigation in any way whatsoever, I am prepared to turn a blind eye to your activities. With the important proviso that whatever you find, you come to me with it immediately. If you find even the merest trace of evidence, you do not touch it, but you get on the phone to me, so that I can have it properly received and processed. And if, in the unlikely event that you come across a credible suspect, you will not go haring across the countryside in pursuit of them. Instead, you'll do what?" He looked at Dan expectantly.

"Call you," Dan said. "But this is all academic."

"Then there's no harm in our having this little chat, is there? Call it a precautionary measure."

"Fine." Dan took hold of the door handle. "Is that everything?"

"It'll do. For now."

Dan opened the door and climbed out, closing it with a touch more force than was necessary. Immediately, the

Volvo's engine growled and Spiller drove away without a backward glance.

Pompous idiot, Dan thought. *He has no idea what he's talking about.* But as Dan jogged along Fore Street, the policeman's words niggled at the back of his mind. He didn't want to get involved in this case, but already it felt as though he would be drawn into it. He'd been there when it had happened. He'd kneeled beside George, willing him to survive, feeling the hesitant rise and fall of the young man's chest. And if Dan could do anything to help catch the person who'd done this terrible thing, then he'd have to try. There was no other way.

CHAPTER 19

A LAN SAT AT his kitchen table and switched on his laptop. *It's a normal Monday*, he told himself. *A workday.* Selecting the latest version of his work in progress, he opened the file and scrolled to the end, scanning the last few paragraphs. "Okay," he muttered. "Finish chapter three." He flexed his fingers, allowing them to hover over the keys. But a small voice piped up in the back of his mind: *You're only on chapter three? You should've finished the first draft by now.*

Alan took a breath. The deadline was months away. He had plenty of time. He just had to get on with it. Now, where was he?

He read the last paragraph again. Had he really written that? It seemed poor, wishy-washy, lacklustre. There was nothing for it; he'd have to rewrite it. But to do that, he'd have to go back further, making sure that any changes fitted in with what went before.

He scrolled back up the page, his frown deepening with each sentence he read. "This is awful."

Alan pushed the laptop away, sliding it across the table, then he sat back, staring into space. *Tea*, he thought. *I need tea.* He jumped to his feet and went to the kettle.

A couple of minutes later, watching the milk swirl through the tea as he stirred it, Alan forced himself to think about his book's plot. It should be simple. It was a light-hearted adventure for children, not *War and Peace*. But whenever he tried to picture Derek, the hapless explorer, or Jake, Derek's fresh-faced nephew, the characters slipped away from him, fleeing from the scene. Instead, he saw George lying on the grass, Dan kneeling beside him, Harry pacing back and forth.

Alan sipped his tea. *I need to work*, he thought. *I need to keep busy.* He moved back to the table, but before he could sit down, his phone rang. "Thank God for that." Alan snatched up the handset. He didn't recognise the number, but he answered the call; anything was better than the oppressive silence of the empty house. Even telesales.

"Good morning," Alan said.

But the voice on the line was anything but cheerful: "Hello? Is that Alan? Alan Hargreaves?"

"Speaking."

"It's Gemma. Gemma Nickleton. I'm sorry to bother you, but…"

"Gemma, what's wrong?"

There was a pause, and when Gemma spoke again, her voice cracked with emotion. "I know it's wrong of me to call you. After the way I treated you the other day, I've no right to expect you to listen to me. But I didn't know what else to do."

"It's fine. I'm glad you called. Forget about the other day. Just tell me what the problem is. If I can help, I will."

"Thank you. That's very kind. Thank you." He heard Gemma taking a deep breath, then: "After what you said about being questioned by the police, I thought you'd understand. You see, it's Billy, my brother, he's been arrested."

"What for?"

"It's awful. It's all a mistake. He can't have done it. It's just not possible."

"Wait," Alan said. "They don't think he had something to do with what happened to George, do they?"

"It's gone way past that. They've arrested him on suspicion of attempted murder. They've taken his clothes and his things. God knows, he didn't have much, but they've taken it all. And they've searched the house. It was the most humiliating experience of my life."

"I'm so sorry. I don't know what to say."

"He didn't do it," Gemma said. "He's stupid and lazy and frustrating, but he's never been violent. He's never hurt anyone. Even when he was a little boy, he never got into fights."

"What did the police say? They must have some reason for suspecting him."

"He's an easy target. He's just come out of prison, and he knew George. They were friends at school."

"I'm not an expert on these things," Alan said, "but that doesn't sound like enough to arrest him."

"Billy made it easy for them. You saw what he was like at the fair."

"Yes, but I don't see what that's got to do with it."

Gemma sighed. "He bumped into George and they argued. People saw them. And as if that wasn't bad enough, last night, he was stupid. Incredibly stupid."

"What did he do?"

"He broke his curfew. He's supposed to stay at the house at night, but he'd been out for a walk and he didn't get back in time. He has an ankle tag, and if he's not home when he's supposed to be, they know about it."

"What time was this?"

"He's meant to stay in after seven, but he was almost an hour late."

Alan's heart sank. "He was out while George was attacked."

"I know."

"What did Billy have to say for himself? Where had he been?"

"That's the problem. He won't say. He claims he was just walking on his own. He says he needed to get out of the house to clear his head."

"Do you believe him?" Alan asked.

Gemma whispered something so quietly that Alan had to ask her to repeat herself.

"No, I don't believe him," Gemma said. "I think he's lying, but I don't know why."

"Okay. I'm sorry to have to ask these uncomfortable questions, but it's best to get the facts straight from the outset. That way, we know where we're starting from and we can figure out a way forward."

"Does that mean you'll help me?"

"Of course I will. I'll try, anyway."

"Thank you," Gemma said. "That means a great deal."

Alan ran a hand across his brow while he tried to work out what to say next. *What on earth am I getting myself into?* he asked himself. *I must be mad.* But Gemma needed his help, and although he hardly knew her, he'd thought about her a great deal since the fair. Gemma was a very special woman; there was no way he was going to let her down. "I'd like to discuss this with Dan," he said. "Would that be all right?"

"Yes. Anything."

"We might want to come around and have a chat with you. Are you free sometime today?"

"Any time you like. I can't go to work. I'm far too stressed."

She gave Alan her address, and he scribbled it down on the notepad he kept in the kitchen.

"I'll give you a call later," Alan said. "Try not to worry. We'll get to the bottom of this."

"Thank you. And about the other day… I'm sorry. I really am."

"Think nothing of it."

Gemma said goodbye then she ended the call, and Alan stored her number in his phone. He was about to add her to his list of favourite contacts, but he changed his mind. *Don't get too excited*, he told himself. *She only called because she had nowhere else to turn.*

Alan took one last look at his phone, then he grabbed his jacket and made for the door. It was almost lunchtime, and with any luck, Dan would be busy in the kitchen. He just had to hope that his neighbour was in a good mood.

CHAPTER 20

DAN THREW THE kitchen knife into the sink. "Bloody hell!"

The damned thing had slipped while he was slicing a tomato, and he'd cut his finger. He wrapped a piece of kitchen towel around the cut, but he could see that it was nothing serious. The bleeding was stopping already. He had some plasters in the bathroom, but before he could go and look for them, Alan passed his kitchen window.

"It's open," Dan called out, and Alan's head appeared around the corner of the door.

"All right if I come in?"

"Yes. I'm making lunch, but you're welcome to join me. Come in."

"Are you sure? I heard a shout."

Dan held up his swaddled finger. "Just me being careless. It's one of those days. Give me a second." He dashed upstairs, dressed his cut with a sticking plaster, then hurried back down. But in the kitchen he paused, watching Alan carefully. "What's up? Has something happened?"

"Why do you say that?"

"Because normally, you'd have sat down by now and

made yourself at home. But you're standing there looking like a man who's lost a pound and found a penny."

Alan considered for a second. "It's not like you to come out with such well-worn phrases. Is that Sam's influence?"

"Don't try to beat me at my own game. Sit down and tell me what's happened."

Alan sighed and took a seat, but Dan rummaged in a drawer and produced a fresh knife, then he stood beside the table, examining the partially sliced tomato for traces of blood.

Alan waited then said, "Aren't you going to sit down?"

Dan shook his head. "I can work while I listen. It helps me to concentrate."

"Okay."

Dan sliced tomatoes and then peeled a portion of cucumber as Alan related his conversation with Gemma. When Alan stopped, Dan smiled and said, "Spiller was right. He said I'd get involved."

"When did you speak to him? Did he call?"

It was Dan's turn to report back, and when he'd finished, Alan nodded thoughtfully and said, "Well then. There we are. We have to help."

"We can try," Dan replied. "But it won't be easy."

"The best things in life never are. But we have to try. We have to do the right thing. That's what's important."

Dan sliced the cucumber as thinly as possible while he considered Alan's words. Alan liked to help others, but he was an idealist. He looked for, and often found, the best in people. Gemma had come to him for help, and of course he'd felt honour bound to step in. But there was something else going on here.

Whenever Alan had mentioned Gemma's name, he'd become more animated. He'd tried to hide it, but there'd been no mistaking the gleam in his eye: Alan had fallen for Gemma. It hadn't occurred to him that she might be using him; enlisting him as an ally in the defence of her brother. But was Billy worth defending? He was an ex-con with an attitude problem, a self-confessed troublemaker.

"You're being very quiet," Alan said. "What's the matter? You don't think Billy did it, do you?"

Dan looked up. "We have to admit that it's a possibility. He knew George, they'd argued, and whatever Gemma says, Billy isn't all sweetness and light. You saw him at the fair. He was spoiling for a fight."

"He was drunk. And I'll admit he was obnoxious, but that doesn't make him guilty. Everything you've said is true, but it's circumstantial."

Dan nodded. "Okay. But if we're going to do this, we'll need to keep an open mind. And if we find out that Billy is guilty, we'll have to tell Spiller."

"Agreed. So, where do we start?"

"I'd like to talk to Scott. It could be a coincidence that the attack happened at his house, but somehow I don't think so."

"You think he's involved?"

"I didn't say that," Dan replied. "I can't see Scott dealing in violence. It's not his style. And if he was tempted to strong-arm somebody, he's far too smart to do it on his own doorstep. But his house is the scene of the crime, so it's the logical place to start."

"Should we call and make an appointment?"

"No. Let's turn up on his doorstep and see what happens. If we take the car, we can be there in a few minutes."

"What about lunch?"

Dan regarded the small piles of sliced cucumber and tomato on his chopping board. Perhaps there was a spot of blood on the board, after all. "You know what? I've lost my appetite." Picking up the board and knife, he crossed to the counter and slid the sliced vegetables into his compost bowl. Drying his hands on a piece of kitchen towel, he turned back to Alan. "Do you want to drive, or shall I?"

"I'll take you up there. And you never know, if Scott's having lunch, we might be offered a bite."

"Do you ever stop thinking about your stomach?"

Alan grinned. "That's rich, coming from someone for whom the word *hangry* might have been invented."

"I don't..." Dan bit back his words, then he grabbed his keys. "Let's go."

The front door at Ironbrand Farm opened as soon as Dan and Alan stepped from the car, but it wasn't Scott who appeared in the doorway.

Carol Smethwick was dressed for a day in the office, her hair pulled back in a tight ponytail, and she greeted them with a faint smile.

"Good morning," Dan said as he strode toward her. "Did you hear us arrive? I think Alan's car needs a new exhaust pipe."

Carol inclined her head politely. "No, I saw you through the window, but I'm afraid I've come to head you off. Mr Benning isn't receiving any visitors today."

"Oh, that's a shame." Dan tried to peer past Carol. "Could you tell him we're here? He'll want to talk to us. It's about last night."

"That matter is being dealt with by the police," Carol said. "Mr Benning doesn't have any comment at this time."

"At this time," Dan repeated, keeping his tone light. "It's a strange phrase, isn't it?"

"Definitely," Alan said. "When you think about it, it's redundant. Everything happens *at this time*, but we don't feel the need to draw attention to the fact, do we?"

Carol's expression tightened. "This is all very entertaining, gentlemen, but I have to ask you to leave. If Mr Benning wants to talk to you, we'll be able to find your number."

"How about Mrs Benning?" Dan asked. "It would be great to have a chat with Jocelyn."

"No," Carol replied. "And before you start running

through every member of the household, please let me assure you that there is no one here who wishes to—"

"Who is it?" someone called out from within the house.

Carol turned, and a moment later, Harry appeared beside her, his features drawn and his face unshaved. Harry had the haunted look of a man with a terrible hangover. He stared at Dan, his eyebrows lowered, then he said, "Let them in."

Carol started to protest, but Harry sent her a disapproving glance, and she stepped to one side. "This way, gentlemen. I'll take you through to the library."

"No," Harry said. "We'll go to the conservatory. I want to have a chat with these two myself."

"Very well." Carol turned on her heel and set off, Dan and Alan trailing behind. Harry closed the door and then followed.

In the broad light of day, the conservatory looked very different. The white-clothed tables had been taken away, replaced with circular glass-topped tables surrounded by wicker chairs. In other circumstances, it would've made an ideal place to relax. But Dan couldn't keep his gaze from wandering to the lawn beyond the window, to the place where they'd seen George stagger and fall.

Perhaps sensing Dan's discomfort, Harry said, "I hope you don't mind coming in here. I know it's kind of weird, but I like the light. The rest of the house is gloomy, in more ways than one."

"It's fine. Helpful actually." Dan looked around the room, mentally rearranging the furniture to recreate the scene from the night before, committing it to memory. "It's good to see the place with fresh eyes."

Incomprehension flickered across Harry's expression, but he indicated a table where a laptop sat surrounded by scattered documents, and said, "Sit down." Then he took his own seat and shut the laptop's lid.

Dan and Alan sat opposite him, making themselves

comfortable, while Harry shuffled his papers into a single pile and stuffed them into a black bag on the floor beside his chair.

Carol loitered uncertainly. "Would you like me to stay, Mr Denton?"

"No, no. We're just having a friendly chat," Harry said. "Unless... Dan, Alan, would either of you like coffee?"

"That would be great," Dan replied. "Black for me, thanks."

"Same for me, please," Alan said. "Thank you."

"And you know how I take it, Carol. God knows I've had enough of the stuff this morning." Harry sat back, patting his stomach. "Come to think of it, I need something to soak up all that caffeine. I hadn't realised what time it was. Carol, could you throw us a few sandwiches together or something?" He looked to Dan and Alan. "Is that okay?"

"Yes, thank you," Dan replied. "But I'm a difficult customer, I'm afraid. I don't eat meat or dairy."

"That's no problem," Harry said. "There's a ton of stuff left over from last night. No sense in wasting it, right?"

"I suppose not," Dan admitted.

"I'll see what I can do," Carol said. "Everything's in a muddle. And since Marco hasn't—" She stopped herself short. "I'm sure I'll be able to find something." Carol hurried away.

"What's happened to Marco?" Dan asked.

"I've no idea. I'm guessing he hasn't turned up for work." Harry rolled his eyes. "It's no big surprise. I don't know where Scott finds these people. He's always hiring someone or other. I think he enjoys it."

"Like George, for instance," Dan said.

Harry met his gaze. "Yes. Like George."

"I've been thinking about that," Dan started. "I've been to a lot of corporate drinks parties, and when they're organising these things, the hosts are generally trying to impress. They tend to steer toward the usual luxuries. Caviar. Smoked salmon. Quails' eggs."

"Sure," Harry replied. "So what?"

Dan shrugged. "It's just that George was an unusual choice, wasn't he? He specialised in vegan food, and that might have been unfamiliar to a lot of the guests."

"That's exactly what Scott said. He'd already booked his regular caterers, but there was some problem or other, and we decided to cancel them at the last minute. I can't recall why. It was probably Jocelyn's idea. She's been on some kind of health kick recently. You know how it is. Last month it was fasting, next month she'll swear off alcohol." He paused. "Actually, she's done that one already this year. January was a hoot." Harry laughed, his guffaws growing louder and lasting longer than they should. But he seemed incapable of stopping.

"Are you all right?" Alan asked. "Do you want me to fetch you a glass of water?"

Harry held up his palms, his laughter rapidly subsiding. "Thanks, but no. I'm fine. Seriously. Fine." He wiped a tear from the corner of his eye. "It's been a hell of a night. A hell of a night. As you can imagine."

"It must have been difficult," Dan said.

"Yes, yes." Harry regained his composure, leaning forward. "But you didn't come here to make small talk. Am I right?"

Dan nodded. "Since we were involved in what happened last night, it's only natural we'd take an interest. We wondered if any new facts had come to light."

Harry shook his head firmly. "The police aren't giving us any information at all. It's a nightmare, and it means I can't help. There's nothing I can tell you. Sorry."

"Ah, like that, is it?" Dan hid his disappointment well.

"But you haven't had a wasted trip," Harry said. "I want

to discuss something with you. You see, Dan, I've been making some calls, asking around."

"About what?"

"About you, of course. And before you ask, there's nothing sinister about it. We thought you might be a useful guy to have on our side. Well spoken, articulate and passionate about the environment. It doesn't take much to see that you could be helpful when the time comes to win around local opinion for the solar farm."

"What about me?" Alan asked. "Did you poke your nose into my affairs as well?"

"Sure," Harry replied. "You're the other side of the coin, Alan. You're the man who's lived here for years but understands the need for change and progress. We wanted both of you."

Alan raised his eyebrows. "I see. And what did you find out?"

"About you? Not much. But on Dan, here, rather more than I expected. Quite the high-flyer in the corporate world, weren't you, Dan?"

"I've worked with some high-profile businesses in the past," Dan admitted. "But not anymore. I've moved on."

"But the skills are still there," Harry said. "And now we need you even more than before."

"I'd have thought all your plans would've been put on hold," Dan replied. "After last night, you can't expect to pick up where you left off."

"You must be kidding." Harry stared at each of them in turn. "The one thing we can't afford to do is stand still. We've been planning this project for a long time. We have a schedule. Components are being shipped from around the world. We have contractors standing by. If we hold things up, even for a few days, it will cost us a fortune. And that's money we can't afford to lose."

"The police might have other ideas," Alan said. "They

won't let you carry on regardless. Their investigation will take priority."

Harry grimaced. "The police have been and gone. The crime scene people stayed half the night, marching around in their masks and white suits. It was quite a circus — like something out of a TV show — but they've packed up and gone back to wherever they came from."

"Where were they looking?" Dan asked. "I still don't know exactly where George was stabbed."

Harry waved his question away. "At the back of the house. They sealed off the whole garden. No one was allowed anywhere near."

"So you don't know where the attack took place?"

"How could I?" Harry said. "I have no idea what was going on out there. Not a clue. But let's get back to the here and now. Are you interested in working for us or not? And by the way, the money will be good. Very good."

"I'm not sure," Dan replied. "What kind of work are we talking about?"

"I'd have thought it was obvious," Harry said. "I want your help in keeping a lid on this thing. I usually handle the press, but I'm up to my eyeballs in negotiations right now. These are high-level talks, and there's no way I can delegate. I have to deal with them myself, but that doesn't leave me any time for fielding enquiries from the media and so on."

"But you must have people to deal with your PR already," Dan said. "If not in-house, then you must have an agency that you use."

"In London, yes. But we need somebody on the ground. This is a fast-moving situation, and the vultures are circling already. There are plenty of other companies that would like to see Ironbrand fail. We need a full-scale damage limitation exercise. We've got to protect our reputation. But we can't waste our time trying to collaborate with people hundreds of miles away." Harry paused for breath, and when he spoke again, he chopped the air with his hand, emphasising each word. "We need somebody right here, right now."

Dan took a moment to think. The possibility of a job offer simply hadn't occurred to him, but it could be a useful way to get close to the residents and staff at Ironbrand Farm. Instead of being on the outside looking in, he'd be rubbing shoulders with the very people he wanted to talk to.

"If it's the fee that's worrying you, don't even think about it," Harry added. "We'd pay you handsomely. I've done my due diligence and I know you can handle this. My friends tell me you're good on strategy. They tell me you're a problem-solver and you can think on your feet. That sounds like an ideal skill set to me."

Alan cleared his throat. "Will you have time, Dan? There's that other matter we're dealing with at the moment."

"What's this?" Harry asked. "What other matter?"

"That needn't concern you," Dan replied. "But Alan is right, I do have other things on my plate."

Harry's expression darkened. "Are you turning me down? Because that would be an error of judgement."

"We'll see about that," Dan said.

"Yes, we will." Harry sat up straight, squaring his shoulders. "Why did you come here today, Dan? What do you want?"

Dan held out his hands, his fingers spread wide. "As I said, we're taking an interest. And we wanted to check in with everyone and make sure they're all right. When we left, Scott was clearly worried and Jocelyn seemed very upset."

"I don't buy that. You're up to something." Harry raised a finger. "When you first came in, you said it helped to see the place with fresh eyes. What did you mean? Help you with what?"

Dan offered an inscrutable smile. "I was refreshing my memory, that's all. Last night was a bit of a blur, and it's good to see the place under more normal circumstances."

"Don't bullshit me!" Harry snapped. "Did someone hire you to come up here and ask questions?"

"Certainly not," Dan said. "I can assure you that no one has hired me to do anything."

Harry pointed an accusing finger at Alan. "Then what the hell was he talking about just now? He said you had another matter to deal with. What did he mean?"

"There's no need to adopt that tone," Alan said. "We came here in good faith today. Scott and his wife are our neighbours, and believe it or not, we wanted to check they're okay."

Harry regarded Alan with a jaundiced eye. "More bullshit. Why did you try to stop Dan working for me? What's your angle? Have you been talking to journalists?"

"Now you're being ridiculous," Alan protested. "I don't want my name in the papers any more than you do. And I don't have to justify myself to you, but if you must know, Dan and I have agreed to help out a friend of mine. She's having some problems at home, and we promised to help her."

"Isn't that nice?" Harry sneered. "So you're a couple of do-gooders, is that it?"

Alan remained tight lipped, but he pushed back his chair, standing stiffly. "I think we'd better go, Dan. We're not achieving anything here."

"Agreed." Dan stood, just as Carol returned with a tray.

"Oh," she said. "Are you leaving?"

Dan nodded apologetically. "I'm sorry to have put you to so much trouble, but yes, we have to go."

"I see." Carol looked to Harry for an explanation, but he shook his head, scowling.

"You can leave the coffee but take that muck away," Harry snapped. "Fix me some real food. A ham sandwich or something."

Carol's cheeks flushed, but she said, "Certainly, Mr

Denton." Turning to Dan, she added, "I'll see you gentlemen out in a moment."

"That's all right," Dan replied. "We'll see ourselves out. We know the way."

Carol smiled gratefully and began transferring the coffee things onto the table.

Dan and Alan shared a look, then they made for the door, walking quickly. In the hallway, Alan said, "That went pear shaped very quickly, didn't it? What an awful man."

"Yes," Dan replied. "He reminds me of someone."

"Who?"

Dan smiled. "Me. I have a terrible feeling I used to be like that. Arrogant. Pig headed. No thought for other people's feelings."

"Who says you've changed?"

"I walked into that."

"Yes," Alan said as he opened the door and stepped outside. "Yes, you did."

CHAPTER 21

R EG STODDARD HUMMED a tune as he strolled along the lane, tapping his walking stick on the tarmac in time with his footsteps. The afternoon was warm with just the hint of a breeze, and it was a grand day to be heading out to the allotment.

Plenty to do, he thought. The risk of frost had passed, and he could start taking the plants from the greenhouse every morning to harden them off. He'd have to pop back each evening to return his treasured plants to the warmth, but after a few days they'd be ready for planting out. Soon, the gardening season would be in full swing, and he'd have his work cut out to keep up with it all.

Yes, it was going to be a busy few months, but he'd love every minute of it.

Arriving at the gate, Reg frowned. Someone had forgotten to close the catch, and the gate had swung open. That was careless. *Asking for trouble*, Reg thought, marching through and making sure the gate was properly fastened behind him. Leave an open gate, and the next thing you knew, there'd be all kinds of people wandering in. Dog walkers, ramblers, kids running all over the place. It didn't bear thinking about.

He cast an eye over the allotments, but there was no one else in sight. There were never many people around on a weekday afternoon; most people were at work. There'd be more amateur gardeners pottering about in their allotments over the weekend, but Reg tended to avoid the busier times. He liked it quiet. He could work the soil all day, needing no other company than the gentle sounds of nature drifting on the breeze.

Reg went straight to his plot, casting a critical eye over some of the other gardeners' efforts as he passed. It looked like Dave had a few French beans coming up. Madness. The nights were still too cold. But like every other living thing, the little plants had two chances: they'd live or they'd die, and that was that. Still, they might be lucky. The seasons weren't the same as when Reg was a lad. *Climate change* they called it. *The greenhouse effect*. It made sense. Nature needed to be left alone, not mucked about with. You couldn't keep churning out poisonous fumes and expect everything to be all right; it just didn't work like that.

People never learn, Reg told himself. *Not until it's too late.* Arriving at his allotment, he went straight to his shed, retrieving the padlock key from his pocket. But he stopped dead in his tracks.

Oh no! The door hung open; the wood splintered where the staple had been forced from the door frame. Reg marched up to the shed and yanked the door open. His rotary tiller was still there, and that was the only thing of value. His tools, too, were still arranged tidily along the wall. So why had someone gone to the trouble of breaking in?

Reg stepped into the shed, running his hands over the potting bench. He picked up the old biscuit tin that he used for storing seeds. It wasn't quite shut properly. Someone had opened it and then replaced the lid. Why?

His foot caught against something, and looking down, he saw a piece of cloth poking out from beneath the bench. He bent down to pull it out. It was an old hessian sack that had once held seed potatoes. But he didn't remember rolling it up like that, and anyway, he would never have left it on the floor, would he?

"Of course not," he muttered. He returned the sack to its proper place, hanging it from a nail on the wall, then he went back outside to inspect the damage.

The padlock was undamaged, and the staple and hasp could be reused. But he'd need to repair the door frame, and that meant going home to fetch some tools. He'd need a piece of scrap wood, some glue and some screws too. But maybe he'd be better off driving into town to buy something sturdier. A new staple and hasp wouldn't cost much, and you could get some high-security padlocks that would deter most intruders.

He glanced back inside the shed, then he shook his head and headed back along the path, one word repeating over and over in his mind: *Why?*

CHAPTER 22

I N THE AFTERNOON, Dan called on Monty Albright and found him in good form.

"Come in, old chap," Monty said. "I'll put the kettle on."

"Actually, I'm fine," Dan replied as he stepped inside. "I just wanted to check everything was okay."

"Fine. It's all sorted out. But come through to the front room. There's something I'd like to ask you about."

Dan followed Monty into the front room, and Monty took one of the armchairs, gesturing for Dan to take the other.

The old, winged armchair was surprisingly comfortable, and Dan sat back. Maybe he should get something similar. His sister had left behind a motley collection of careworn furniture, most of which he'd thrown out. Dan had transported his modern Scandinavian pieces from London, but they never looked quite at home in the old cottage.

"If you don't mind me asking," Dan said, "where did you get this armchair?"

"From my father. And he got it from his father before him. Where he obtained it, I couldn't tell you, but I suspect it's been in the family for generations. I've had it reupholstered, but the frame is solid oak. You can't beat it in the winter months. It keeps the draughts away." Monty smiled. "If you're looking for one like it, your best bet is an antiques dealer. It won't be cheap, but it'll last for a lifetime."

"I'll have a look online. There might be something on eBay."

"That's no way to choose furniture. A chair like that will become an old friend. You wouldn't pick your friends online, would you?"

"Well, that's pretty much the point of social media."

Monty wrinkled his nose. "Don't talk to me about that. People ought to stick to the proper forms of correspondence. Letters and postcards. Better all around. There's nothing quite so satisfying as completing a really good letter and popping it into the postbox. It sharpens the wits."

"It's a dying art," Dan said. "I don't know when I last received an actual letter."

"Bills and junk mail. That's all I get. Plus, the occasional unsolicited phone via courier, of course."

"Did you manage to get your money back?"

"Oh yes," Monty said. "They were very helpful. I spoke to a lady from India. She was very apologetic, and she dealt with the whole thing in two shakes of a lamb's tail."

"That's good. And you haven't had any more problems?"

"No. The old computer is behaving itself. But that's what I want to talk to you about. I've decided to scrap that one and invest in a new model. I thought you might be willing to help, for a fee, of course. Does that sound like something that would interest you?"

"Certainly," Dan said. "If you have a budget in mind, I can see what I can find. But…" He glanced across the room at the tower unit on Monty's desk. "I could upgrade your current machine. There's nothing much wrong with it, but a few upgrades would make all the difference. It would be cheaper, and from an environmental point of view, much better than scrapping a perfectly good machine."

"Perhaps, but I'd rather start afresh. I'm still worried that this one might be infected with a computer virus."

"I could replace the hard drive and install the operating system from scratch, preferably on a solid-state drive. That would be much faster, and I could add a brand-new hard disk for your documents and files. A couple of sticks of RAM and possibly a new graphics card, and it would be as good as new."

"Just like the old armchair, eh?" Monty said.

"I wouldn't bank on a computer becoming a family heirloom, but I can add a few more useful years to its life."

"I'm not sure. I've got some sensitive documents on that machine."

"You already have a good backup strategy," Dan said. "It's just a matter of restoring your backed-up documents to the new machine. But I can take your old hard drive and fit it into a caddie. That way, it becomes a portable hard drive, and the documents can be transferred directly."

"And that would be safe, would it?"

"Naturally, I'd check everything and run a couple of different scans to check for malware."

"And if I wanted the old documents destroyed?"

Dan raised his eyebrows. "I can wipe the old drive completely. I have a tool that runs a military-grade deletion process. Alternatively, I can physically break into the drive and damage the disk so it can never be used again. But both of those are irreversible."

"Good." Monty sat back, leaning his elbows on the chair's armrests and interlacing his fingers. "All right. It sounds like a good deal, so I'll take you up on it, on the condition that you complete the work here, including the destruction of the old disk. I don't want the machine to leave my sight. It's not that I don't trust you, but I have to be careful. Very careful."

"I understand. But that shouldn't be a problem. I'll need to order some parts, but they won't take long to arrive. I should be able to do the work in a few days. How about Thursday?"

"Perfect," Monty said. "All done and dusted before the bank holiday weekend, eh?"

"I'd almost forgotten about that."

"Tut, tut," Monty scolded. "You mustn't forget the VE Day celebrations. The seventy-fifth anniversary — it's going to be a big day."

"Yes, it's just that, with everything going on…"

"You mean that terrible business up at Ironbrand."

Dan nodded. "I was there."

"Good Lord! That must've been dreadful."

"It was."

Monty leaned forward and lowered his voice. "There are some strange goings-on up at that place. I heard the latest in the shop this morning. Do you know the gamekeeper, Sturridge?"

"Not personally. What's happened?"

"No one knows. He's disappeared. Vanished from the face of the earth. His poor wife has been going mad with worry, apparently."

"When was he last seen?" Dan asked. "Only, we heard a gunshot last night, at least we thought we did, just before we realised that George had been hurt."

"George? Is that the name of the fellow who was stabbed?"

"Yes. George Hepworth. Do you know him? He's from Embervale."

"I'm not sure," Monty said. "I knew a Jeremy Hepworth. Perhaps he was the boy's father."

"I wouldn't know."

Monty clicked his fingers. "Wait a minute. I remember Jeremy's boy from when he was a lad. He was always causing trouble. But that's how it often goes with teenagers around here. There's not much for them to do, so they misbehave, scrawling graffiti on the bus shelter, stuffing their rubbish in the hedgerows, leaving empty cans on the pavement."

"That doesn't sound like George. He's a hard-working young man."

"Perhaps he's grown up, but now that I think about it, the boy was called George. His father was at his wits' end. The trouble was, his lad was mixed up with some bad company. William Nickleton. A ne'er-do-well if ever there was one. He ended up in prison. Dealing in stolen goods."

"I've met Billy," Dan said. "He's out of prison. He turned up at the May Fair and made a nuisance of himself." Dan hesitated. "He's been arrested. The police think he might've stabbed George."

Monty gave Dan a knowing look. "I see. A tiff."

Tiff, Dan thought. *That's an odd word to use.* But then, Monty peppered his speech with phrases from a bygone age, so it probably wasn't significant. "I know they'd been friends in the past," Dan said carefully. "And they were seen arguing at the May Fair."

"That sounds ominous, but when it comes to the Nickleton boy, nothing would surprise me. He's a bad lot. When they were lads, they raised a few eyebrows, I can tell you. Back then, people weren't quite so forgiving about that sort of palaver."

There it was again: the hint of innuendo in Monty's tone. Was he suggesting that George and Billy were in a relationship? If so, why not come out and say it? Dan formed a direct question in his mind, but he held back from asking it. He didn't want to embarrass Monty, and anyway, he could find the answer by other means. The question was, need it concern anyone else? *It might matter to the police*, Dan thought. A quarrel between ex-lovers gave Billy a possible motive. But why hadn't Gemma mentioned any of this to Alan? Had she concealed it deliberately?

"Are you all right?" Monty asked. "You're looking a bit downcast."

"Sorry. I'm tired, that's all. After last night."

"The offer still stands if you'd like that cup of tea. I've got some Darjeeling. There's nothing like it for perking you up."

"Thanks, but I'm fine. And I have another appointment, so I really should be going."

"All right, if you're sure…"

Dan forced a smile. "Yes. I'll be in touch about your computer. I can remember the spec, and it's all fairly standard, so finding the new parts won't be a problem. It's not as if you'll be playing the latest games."

"Indeed not. I've never seen the appeal. I have my fun moving pennies from one place to another. It's addictive in its own way, I suppose. It certainly sets the heart racing from time to time, and when you win, it's quite a thrill."

"I'll take your word for it." Dan checked his watch. "I'd better dash."

"Okay. I'll see you to the door."

They parted company, and once Dan had left the peace of the secluded garden behind him, he set off along the street, pulling out his phone and checking his messages. He'd arranged to meet Alan at Gemma's house, and although Alan had reeled off a string of directions, Dan had told him to send the address via text message. "Google Maps will take you the long way around," Alan had protested.

Now, arriving at a junction of four roads, Dan wished he'd listened. He halted and checked the map on his phone. Alan had said something about cutting through a narrow lane, but one of the roads in front of him seemed to stretch the definition. Its surface was potholed, there was grass growing along its centre, and the hedgerows were creeping in from both sides as if to reclaim it. Dan had a hard time believing it was classified as a road at all. And yet, he had a feeling this was the shortcut Alan had told him about.

Dan looked for a signpost to give him a clue, but there was nothing in the narrow lane except for a notice forbidding wide vehicles. *No kidding*, Dan thought. He'd be safer sticking to the wider roads. But as Dan turned away, the sound of an approaching car drifted along the lane.

It's probably somebody local if they're braving that lane, Dan decided. *I could ask for directions.* He waited, and a minute later a small hatchback appeared, the driver taking it slow, hunched over the steering wheel and peering through the windscreen.

Ade, Dan thought. *What's he doing here?* Dan raised his hand in greeting, and Ade smiled, looking relieved. The car halted at the junction, and Ade wound down the window. "Hi," he called out. "Am I glad to see you!"

Rather than start a shouted conversation, Dan crossed the road. "Hello, Ade. Is everything all right? You look frazzled."

"I'm lost. I must've taken the wrong turning somewhere. I've been going around in circles. I think."

"Where are you trying to get to?"

"That wood where we camped, but my phone keeps sending me the wrong way."

Dan smiled. "You're not the only one to get caught out. It seems that satnav systems don't understand the complexities of Devon lanes. But are you sure you want to go back to Brandle Wood? After last time…"

"I know, but I lost something, and I really need to find it."

"What've you lost?"

"My ID badge. I've looked everywhere else, so it must be in the wood, and I need it tomorrow."

"I see. Is Maria not with you today? I hope she's not up there on her own, is she?"

"No. She's in Exeter. That's how come I'm lost. She's the one with the sense of direction."

"Okay," Dan said. "I can try and give you directions, but you ought to think twice about going up there on your own.

I'd offer to come with you, but I have an appointment and I'm running late already."

"Thanks, but I'll be okay. I'll be ten minutes at most and if I see that guy, I'll steer well clear."

"Actually, he's gone missing. No one's seen him for a while."

Ade raised an eyebrow. "I don't like the sound of that. I hope he's all right."

"I expect he'll turn up. From what I hear, he's a tough old character."

"Maybe. I hope so."

Dan saw the concern in Ade's eyes, and he thought back to DS Spiller's assertion that doctors repressed their emotions. Would Ade lose that spark of empathy when he qualified? *No*, Dan decided. *Spiller was wrong.*

Dan did his best to direct Ade to Brandle Wood, then he watched him drive away. Alone again, and still unsure of the way, Dan swallowed his pride and gave Alan a call. If a bright young man like Ade could admit when he was lost, then so could he. Alan was certain to tease him about it, but that was a small price to pay. And anything was better than going around in circles.

CHAPTER 23

Thanks to Alan's directions, Dan was only a few minutes late when he arrived at Gemma's house. Gemma lived in a semi-detached house on a tucked-away street, each well-appointed home boasting a neat front garden and modern double glazing. And apart from the handful of children riding their bikes up and down the road, the neighbourhood was quiet.

Gemma welcomed him at the door, and Dan couldn't help but notice the change in her. When he'd seen Gemma at the fair, she'd come across as proud, haughty even. But now, her cheeks pale and her eyes rimmed with red, she looked exhausted, as if the life had been wrung out of her.

"Please, come in," Gemma said, her voice wavering. She cast an anxious glance along the street, then she stood back, ushering him inside. As soon as Dan stepped over the threshold, she pushed the door shut, puffing out her cheeks as though the act had cost her some effort.

"Is everything all right?" Dan asked.

Gemma stared at him, surprised at so stupid a question.

"Let me guess," Dan said. "The neighbours have been twitching their net curtains."

"Nosy beggars!" Gemma blurted. "You'd think they have nothing better to do."

"I can sympathise. I know what it's like when you become the focus of attention in this village. If you can, it's best to rise above it."

"I know. I shouldn't let it get to me, but it's not easy." Gemma sighed. "Anyway, you'd better come through. We're in the kitchen." She led the way to the back of the house, and Dan found Alan seated at the kitchen table. "Make yourself at home," Gemma went on. "Would you like some tea? Or coffee?"

"I don't want to put you to any trouble." Dan sat facing Alan and saw that his neighbour had come prepared. Alan had a pen and pad in front of him, and he'd already scribbled a page of notes.

"It's no bother," Gemma said. "It's all I seem to be doing today, making tea and coffee. It gives me something to do; keeps me occupied for a couple of minutes. So, what would you like?"

Alan caught Dan's eye then inclined his head toward Gemma.

Dan took the hint. "Okay then. A cup of tea would be nice. Black, please."

"Right." Gemma filled the kettle and grabbed a mug. "Thank you for coming, Dan. I'm not sure what you can do, but I appreciate you making the effort. Both of you. I really do."

Hearing the desperation in her voice, Dan said, "That's kind of you to say, Gemma, but before we begin, I must stress that we can't make any promises. We're not professional investigators."

"But we'll certainly try," Alan put in quickly. "And we've had success in the past."

"That's true," Dan admitted. "But in each case, the circumstances were very different. There are no guarantees."

Gemma placed a mug of tea in front of Dan, positioning it carefully on a coaster made from glass etched with a floral design, then she sat next to Alan. "I understand that. But if there's even the slightest chance you can make a difference, it has to be worth trying. Billy is all the family I have left, and he didn't do this dreadful thing. He would never hurt anybody, especially not George."

"About that," Dan said slowly. "How would you characterise the relationship between George and Billy?"

Gemma stiffened. "Well, that didn't take long. Okay, so Billy's gay. So what? Does that mean he attacked George in some kind of jealous rage? Is that what you're getting at?"

"Not in the least," Dan replied. "But if they had a relationship, the police will probably regard it as being significant, and that means we have to take it into account as well."

"Why?" Gemma demanded. "Would you ask the same question if he was straight?"

Dan held her gaze. "Yes, I would. George wasn't caught up in a random act of violence. He wasn't mugged on the way home from a night out. He was on private property, attending an exclusive party in the middle of the countryside. I'm almost certain that he had some sort of connection with the person who attacked him."

Gemma started to protest, but Dan swept on, speaking quickly: "None of this implies that Billy is guilty, but it does mean we have to take steps to rule him out. I want to help you, Gemma, but we won't get anywhere unless you're frank with us from the outset. I hope that's understood."

Gemma regarded him levelly for a second, then she dropped her gaze and took a sip from her half-empty mug. She pulled a face and pushed the mug away. "It's gone cold. I'll make another." She stood slowly, and in a quiet voice said, "I'm sorry. You're right. I didn't mean to jump down your throat, but I'm tired." She glanced at Alan and offered a fleeting smile. "I see what you mean, Alan. But you'll have to excuse me for a minute. I won't be long."

Gemma walked from the room, and they heard her rapid steps on the stairs.

Alan turned on Dan. "For God's sake, watch what you say. The poor woman has been through enough. You need to be careful how you talk to her."

"It's best to be honest," Dan said. "But what have you been saying to her? Why did she say, *I see what you mean?*"

"I warned her what you're like, that's all. And after that display of tactlessness, I'm glad that I did."

Dan paused before replying. "You're quite taken with Gemma, aren't you?"

"No. But she's..." Alan shook his head. "Never mind. Let's concentrate on the case. I've been thinking. We can't question Billy directly, but we could get Gemma to ask him some questions over the phone, or in person if she gets to visit him."

"Possibly, but I'm not sure how useful that would be. I'd need to see his reactions. If Gemma asked the questions, we'd have to rely on her reporting back accurately, and I don't know if she's up to it."

"Up to what?" Gemma marched back into the room. She stood beside the table, folding her arms. "Go on. What am I not up to?" She fixed Dan with a reproving stare.

"I know it sounded as though I was being dismissive, but I didn't mean any offence," Dan said. "We were discussing the possibility of you questioning Billy on our behalf, but I don't think it will work. It's not that you're incapable, but you're close to Billy, so you can't be objective. And he needs you on his side. If he suspects you're interrogating him, he'll clam up."

Gemma pursed her lips.

"Dan was responding to my idea," Alan admitted. "And to be honest, he's probably right. You want to support your brother, and it was unfair of me to suggest anything that might get in the way."

Gemma turned away, then she crossed to the sink and leaned on the counter, both hands gripping the edge. She hung her head, took a breath, then whispered, "Bloody hell!"

Dan and Alan exchanged an anxious look, but Gemma roused herself, and she began filling the kettle at the sink. "Does anyone else want tea? No, of course you don't. Never mind."

She switched on the kettle then turned to face them. "After they arrested him, I was the first person Billy called. I tried asking him what he was doing last night, but you're right: the more I pestered him with questions, the more he got defensive. In the end, he refused to talk to me, and I had to give up. But I'll tell you what I know, and believe it or not, I can recount our conversation word for word. I have an excellent memory and I know my brother. I know when he's telling the truth and when he's being evasive. And that will have to be good enough."

"Thank you," Dan said. "Let's start at the beginning. On the night of the attack, did you see Billy when he arrived home?"

Gemma nodded. She started to say something, but she was distracted by the kettle boiling, and she fussed over her mug, spooning loose leaf tea into a small infuser and placing it carefully in the mug before pouring the boiled water. She took her time, swirling the diffuser around the mug until she was satisfied, then she carefully emptied the spent tea leaves into a compost caddy. When she was finally ready, she sipped her tea and said, "I was in the front room, watching the TV. I like the news on Channel Four, but when they started going on about cricket scores, I lost interest. And then Billy came in, so I switched it off."

"What time was this?" Dan asked.

"Just before eight. As I said, the news had almost finished, and the next programme started at eight."

"What were you going to watch next?" Dan said.

Gemma shrugged. "Nothing in particular. I sometimes channel hop until I find something."

"No Netflix?" Dan said. "iPlayer? Amazon Prime?"

"I can't be bothered with all that. By the time I've finished making lesson plans and marking books, I don't want to make any decisions. I sit back with a glass of wine for an hour or so, watching anything that catches my eye, then I go to bed and read." She frowned. "I don't know how we got on to talking about me."

"It's just background. The details help me to build a picture." Dan gave her an encouraging smile. "So, when Billy arrived home, you were relaxing with a glass of wine."

Gemma nodded. "Red. South African. Merlot, I think, but don't ask me any more than that. It was on special offer in the shop, and that's all I know."

"Shouldn't we be concentrating on Billy?" Alan said. "Gemma, tell Dan what you told me about when he came in; about the mud on his shoes."

"Oh yes. When he came in, Billy was in a foul mood. I called out, but he just grunted something without even sticking his head into the room to say hello. I heard him rummaging in the cupboard under the stairs, and the next thing I knew, the Hoover started up, so I went out to have a look."

Dan leaned forward. "What was he doing?"

"Vacuuming the hall. I asked him why, but he barely looked at me. He said something about treading in some mud, but he must've done a good job of cleaning it up, because I couldn't see anything on the carpet."

"When the police came to the house, did you tell them about the mud?" Dan asked.

"No. I didn't know what to say. I was worried I might make him sound guilty, like he had something to hide."

"I see," Dan said. "That might be a problem later. But going back to that night, I assume you asked Billy where he'd been."

"Obviously. He'd missed his curfew, and the phone had been ringing off the hook. His parole officer, or whatever they call themselves these days, had been ringing since just after seven, going on and on. Where was he? When had I last seen him? Did I have any reason to suspect he might've absconded?"

"Did you think Billy might've run away?"

"No. I checked his room. His clothes and things were all exactly where he'd left them."

"You must've been worried." Dan paused. "And yet earlier you said you'd been relaxing with a glass of wine. Merlot."

Gemma's eyes flashed. "Those were your words. I didn't correct you, but of course, I wasn't relaxed. Yes, I had a glass of wine. I needed it. If you must know, I was at the end of my tether, worrying myself ragged, wondering where he was. By the time he came home, I'd been watching the clock for almost an hour. All kinds of awful possibilities kept running through my mind. What if he really had run away? What if he'd hitch-hiked back to Plymouth? What if he'd been in an accident or worse? He'd been depressed, frustrated, angry. What if he'd... done something to himself?"

"Okay," Dan said gently. "But thankfully, Billy came home safe and sound. He must've known that he'd broken his curfew. What did he have to say for himself?"

"He refused to talk about it. All he'd say was that he'd been out for a walk and he'd lost track of time. He wouldn't say any more than that, and when I tried to reason with him, he just marched upstairs and shut himself in his room."

"Could we have a look at his room?" Dan asked.

"Why? The police took all his things."

"Even so, it could be useful," Dan said. "There might be some clue that'll help us to work out where Billy went last night. If he won't provide an alibi, we'll have to figure it out for ourselves."

Gemma looked doubtful, but she said, "All right. You can have a quick look, but that's all. I don't want you poking around. That wouldn't be right."

"Naturally," Alan said. "We won't touch a thing. Will we, Dan?"

Dan shrugged. "Whatever you say."

Gemma led them upstairs, and they followed, Dan looking around carefully as he went. The place had been redecorated recently, the walls painted in a subtle shade of palest purple, and the woodwork had been given a fresh coat of white gloss, but even so, this felt like the house of someone significantly older than Gemma. The prints on the wall, in their heavy frames of dark wood, were sombre landscapes in muted colours, and on the landing a set of narrow shelves held a crowd of small china dogs that had surely been collected by someone else.

Looking back from the top of the stairs, Gemma followed Dan's gaze and said, "Mother's menagerie. Souvenirs from holidays. Wherever we went, she'd hunt down the junk shops, and she wouldn't be content until she'd tracked down a china dog. I don't like them really, but I haven't the heart to get rid of them."

"That's understandable," Alan said. "I have a lot of keepsakes myself."

Dan didn't comment. How would a young man like Billy feel about coming back to his childhood home? He'd left prison behind, only to be entrapped by the four walls that had framed his younger self. At an age when he should've been striking out, he'd been reduced to living with his sister, surrounded by constant reminders of his former life.

"This was Billy's room." Gemma opened a door. "It still *is*. It's been used as a guest room for years, but it was Billy's when he was small, and it's his room again now, for as long as he wants to stay." She went inside and Alan followed. Dan took a last look around then he caught up with them.

Billy's room held a single bed, a wardrobe, a chest of drawers and a stack of plastic crates in the corner, but it was very much a spare room: devoid of personality. The surfaces were bare, and the shelves held only a row of dusty cardboard boxes, each one secured with brown tape and labelled in marker pen: *Billy*. Dan counted five small boxes bearing Billy's name: not many for a man of his age. Perhaps there were other boxes stored elsewhere, in the loft perhaps, or at another address, but somehow Dan doubted it. This room contained Billy's worldly goods, and judging by the way the boxes were still securely sealed, there was nothing here that the young man actually wanted.

Dan pointed to the shelf. "The police didn't take everything, then."

"No. I packed those up years ago. They're just old books and comics. Kid's stuff." Gemma crossed to the wardrobe and opened it, but there was nothing inside except for a few empty coat hangers. "You see? There's nothing left. There are a few things in the wash — the clothes he was wearing when he came home — but apart from that…"

"What about the drawers?" Dan asked.

"Empty." Gemma went to the chest of drawers and laid her hand on it. "Do you want me to prove it to you?"

"No," Dan said. "That won't be necessary."

Alan cleared his throat. "I think we've seen enough, don't you, Dan?"

"Yes. But I wonder why the police didn't take his dirty clothes as well."

"I suppose they didn't think about it," Gemma said. "When they arrived, the clothes were still in the machine.

Maybe I should've told them, but I was so distraught at the time. I've never had to go through anything like that before."

Dan paused for a second. Had Gemma intentionally withheld evidence from the police, or had she just been naïve? Watching her carefully, he said, "But Billy has been through this before, hasn't he? Tell me about that."

"There's not much to tell. He was living in Plymouth, and when he got into trouble, he kept it from me for as long as he could. I think he was trying to protect me. And Mum was alive back then. When she found out, she was mortified. I don't know if she ever got over it."

"That's very sad," Dan said. "But going back to the clothes, have you washed them already?"

"Yes, but don't tell me you want to look at his socks and boxers. What good will that do?"

"I was thinking about his jeans," Dan replied. "You said that he'd brought mud inside. Was it on his clothes?"

"Not really. His jeans looked fine to me, but he insisted on washing them anyway. His trainers too."

Dan raised his eyebrows. "Are his shoes still here?"

"Yes. He left them in the washing machine, but I've put them to dry on the windowsill."

"Show me," Dan said.

Gemma furrowed her brow. "All right. They're downstairs."

Back in the kitchen, Gemma took the pair of white trainers from a sheet of newspaper on the windowsill. "They're still damp. We get the morning sun on this side of the house, so they ought to be dry soon."

Dan held out his hands. "May I?"

"Sure." Gemma handed the shoes to him, and Dan turned them over to check the soles before peering inside. "Clean." He handed them back to Gemma.

"What did you expect? I told you, they've been in the

machine." Gemma replaced the shoes, lining them up on the windowsill.

"The question is, why did he take such great pains to wash them?" Dan asked.

"I don't know. He was always careful about his clothes. Fussy."

"There's more to it than that," Dan said.

Gemma sighed. "Look, this is all just speculation. It isn't getting us anywhere. Maybe I expected too much, but I don't—"

"Don't give up," Dan interrupted. "There's one more thing I need to check. Your Hoover. Have you emptied it since last night?"

"No. It wasn't full. It's one of those bagless ones."

"And it's under the stairs?"

"Yes, but…"

Before she could protest, Dan marched from the room, leaving Gemma and Alan to hurry after him. Dan found the cupboard under the stairs and flung the door open, retrieving the upright vacuum cleaner and lifting it to examine the dust container. It was half full of dust and fluff, but Dan needed a closer look. The canister could be detached by opening a catch, and Dan started to release it.

"Wait!" Gemma called out. "Let me get a bin bag or you'll make an awful mess."

Dan halted, his hand on the catch. "Okay."

Gemma disappeared into the kitchen, and Alan caught Dan's eye. "Take it easy," Alan said. "You're going over the top."

"No, I'm not. She wants results, and we need to move fast. Billy was obviously up to something, and it can't have been anything good. To tell you the truth, I'm worried about his state of mind. Fresh out of prison and he comes back to this place; it can't have been good for him."

"This house? What's wrong with it?"

"Nothing, so long as you like lace doilies and embroidered antimacassars."

"Now you're just being ridiculous," Alan grumbled. "It's a bit kitsch, but for all you know, Billy might appreciate being here. After all, Gemma took him in. Not everybody would do that."

"He's not the appreciative type, Alan. He's a malcontent. The first thing he did was make a nuisance of himself."

"I admit he can be difficult, but that doesn't make him guilty. We're here to help, remember?"

"That's why we need to act now. Billy might not have stabbed George, but he's been up to no good. One way or another, he's got himself into trouble. If you want to help him, we have to work out what he's done."

"You've got a point, I suppose," Alan admitted. "Even so, I don't want you upsetting Gemma. There's no need for it."

Dan held up his hands. "All right. Best behaviour."

"I should damned well think so. Here she comes."

Gemma bustled back into the hallway carrying a plastic bin liner, but she stopped short, examining Dan and Alan in turn. "What?"

"Nothing," Dan said quickly. "Shall I do the honours?"

"No. Let me." She took the Hoover from Dan, deftly removing the canister and positioning it inside the bin liner. "This thing is tricky but I know its foibles." She worked at the canister, muttering under her breath, then she withdrew it from the bag with a triumphant flourish. "Empty." She closed the top of the bag and held it out to Dan. "Take it outside, please. Don't open it in here."

"Hang on," Alan said. "If we do find something, it could be important evidence, but we'll have tampered with it. It won't stand up in court."

"It's too late to worry about that," Dan replied. "Anyway, I don't see the police rushing around here to try and get Billy off the hook, do you?"

"Maybe not, but—"

"We'll leave the shoes," Dan said. "We won't touch them."

"The shoes are clean," Alan argued.

"To the naked eye, perhaps, but there'll be traces. And in the meantime, we can get busy. Come on." Holding the plastic bag tight in his fist, he made for the front door, and the others followed him outside.

"You could've gone out the back," Gemma grumbled, but Dan took no notice.

While Gemma and Alan watched, Dan delved into the bag, sifting through the contents with his fingertips. At first, there was nothing but soft fibres and fine dust, but then he felt something harder, like an elongated splinter. He retrieved it, holding it up to the light. It seemed to be a dark sliver of wood, but it was partially decomposed, crumbling as he squeezed it.

"What is it?" Alan asked.

"I'm not sure." Dan returned to the collection of dust, and now he knew what he was looking for, he quickly found more of the woody fragments. He gathered a handful and showed them to Alan and Gemma. "There are lots of them. What do you think?"

"I've no idea," Gemma said. "It's nothing I've hoovered up; I'd have remembered."

Alan took a pinch of the crumbling wood and held it to his nose, sniffing. Then he smiled. "Pine needles. They're partially rotted, but that's definitely pine."

"Really?" Dan sniffed at the small pile of wood. "You're right. Gemma, do you have pine trees in your back garden?"

"No," Gemma scoffed. "I've got a lawn the size of a postage stamp and a couple of roses that have seen better days. That's all there's room for."

"So, where's the nearest pine forest?" Dan said.

"There's the plantation just outside the village," Alan replied. "That's the closest."

Dan nodded. "I've been there. It wasn't far away by Land Rover, but it would be quite a walk."

"Billy always liked walking," Gemma said. "He could go for miles. And it fits in with what he said at the time."

"Then why not admit where he'd been?" Dan asked. "Okay, so he might've been trespassing, but that's nothing to worry about. Unless there was another reason for him being there, and he doesn't want anybody to know about it."

"Ah, he could've been meeting someone," Alan said. "That would explain a lot."

"It's a possibility." Dan turned to Gemma. "Has Billy ever mentioned the plantation? Or has he talked about seeing anyone in particular?"

Gemma shook her head firmly.

"Were there any old acquaintances he might want to renew?"

"I doubt it," Gemma replied. "Billy didn't make friends easily. He was a loner. Apart from George, there were no childhood friends. He was bullied all through his teenage years. In the end, he hated it here. He couldn't wait to leave."

"He could've been meeting someone from outside the village," Dan said. "Did he have friends elsewhere?"

"There were a few people he hung around with in Plymouth, but I don't know their names, and from what Billy says, they were only pals until he got arrested, then you couldn't see them for dust."

"We could go up to the plantation and take a look around," Alan suggested. "But it's a huge area. I wouldn't hold out much hope of finding anything, not unless you have a trained bloodhound you've been keeping quiet about." Alan smiled wistfully. "I've been thinking about getting a dog for years."

"That doesn't help us now," Dan said. "We'll have to rely on our eyes."

"You want to go up there right away?" Alan asked.

Dan nodded. "It's our only lead." He gave Gemma a questioning look. "Unless you have anything else to tell us."

"No," Gemma said. "I'm sorry, but I can't think of anything."

"Okay. We'll get going, but you'd better take this." Dan made as if to hand the bin bag back to Gemma, but as she tried to take it, Dan held it tight. He looked her in the eye. "Don't throw it away."

"Of course not." Gemma held Dan's stare until he relinquished the bag. "I can be trusted," she added. "I'm not a complete idiot, you know."

"I know." Dan summoned a reassuring smile. "We'll try the plantation, and we'll let you know if we find anything. In the meantime, if there are any developments, please call us."

Gemma nodded. "I have Alan's number."

"You'd better have mine too." Dan gave her his number, then they parted, Gemma still clutching the plastic bin liner. Dan looked back as he headed for the road, but Gemma had already retreated behind her front door.

"Well?" Alan began. "What do you think?"

"I think we've got a lot of work ahead of us. But before we go tramping around the woods, we ought to equip ourselves with torches. From what I remember, it's shady beneath the trees."

"Agreed." Alan's gaze was fixed firmly on the ground as they made their way back through the village.

Eventually, Dan said, "Is something the matter?"

Alan looked up. "Something is bothering me about those pine needles. It must be a few miles up to the plantation, so why were so many of them still stuck to his shoes? Surely, most of the needles would've fallen off along the way."

"Maybe he stepped in a boggy patch or slipped into a ditch."

"That might explain it."

They walked on in silence for a moment, then Dan said, "Are you really thinking about getting a dog?"

"Yes."

"A lot of work."

"Good company, though. And it would make me get out for a walk every day." Alan smiled. "Plus, you can take them to the pub."

"Fair enough," Dan said. "And while we're on the subject, I think we should pop into the Boar later. I suspect we'll need a drink."

"You're on. And I'll get the first round. It's the least I can do."

"And that," Dan said, "is the best news I've had all day."

CHAPTER 24

"**D**AMN IT!" ADE thumped the nearest tree trunk with his fist. He was in the wrong place. He'd spent ages traipsing along half-forgotten paths in Brandle Wood, trying to retrace his steps, but it was much harder than he'd anticipated; one hollow in the woods looked much like another.

He was almost ready to give up. Why was he so hopeless when it came to directions? He could recall any number of diseases and conditions, along with their diagnostic tests and appropriate treatments, but give him a route through an unfamiliar environment and he could get lost in a heartbeat.

He was good with maps, but to use them properly you needed landmarks, fixed points of reference you could rely on. Here, there was nothing.

And then it came to him, the memory surfacing fresh and bright. "Idiot!" he muttered. "Why didn't you think of that before?"

He turned on the spot. He needed to find a certain thicket of shrubs that had grown alongside the path to their improvised campsite. The bushes were quite distinctive, heavy with white blossom, and he ought to have remembered them earlier.

It's where that bloke was poking around, Ade recalled. *I'd forgotten all about him.*

On their first morning in the wood, Ade had risen at dawn and slipped out of the tent to pee. Trying not to disturb Maria, he'd walked a little way from the tent. After a night sleeping on a thin foam mattress, he'd needed to stretch his limbs, and it had been good to fill his lungs with the chill morning air. And that was when he'd seen the man in the distance.

Ade had stood still, watching, but the man must've been oblivious to his presence, because he'd carried on, wandering slowly along the path, plucking blossoms from the shrubs as he passed.

Ade had almost laughed. In the early hours of the morning, it had seemed like a surreal scene, but he'd assumed that the guy had a good reason for his odd behaviour. Flowers and wildlife had never been Ade's thing. He'd learned to recognise a few edible plants during a survival training exercise with the OTC, but that was the limit of his interest.

The man had moved on, and Ade had backed away quietly before finding a place to pee undisturbed.

Today, Ade set off through the woods, searching with fresh eyes. A few minutes later, he almost whooped with delight. There they were, the clusters of white blossom dancing in the breeze.

Ade broke into a jog, finding the path and following it to the hollow. This was the place. He spotted the circle of stones that he'd used to stabilise the camping stove.

He began his search around the hollow's perimeter, moving slowly, his eyes on the ground while he kicked through the dead leaves. When he reached his starting point, he moved inward and resumed the hunt. Around him, the soft sounds of the wood scarcely penetrated his consciousness. He was dimly aware of the wind in the canopy overhead, the call of birds, and a faint rustling coming from somewhere in the undergrowth. But he didn't look up. If there was one thing Ade knew, it was how to focus.

"Are you looking for this, boy?"

Ade whirled around. "Jesus Christ! What the hell?" Ade's heart lurched in his chest. It was him. Sid Sturridge.

Sturridge cackled, his laughter soaked in scorn. From one hand, a set of plastic ID badges dangled from their lanyard. In the other, he held a shotgun, the stock pressed close against his chest, the barrel pointing at the ground. But it was the man's eyes that held Ade's attention.

Sturridge's expression was hewn from pure malice, his chapped lips pulled back to reveal his rat-like teeth. But his eyes, red rimmed and stretched unnaturally wide, glittered with a frenzied animosity.

"Give me my badge," Ade said. "That's all I came for. Hand it over now, and I'll go."

"Maybe you'd better come and take it from me, boy."

Ade swallowed his anger as best as he could. "Don't... don't call me that."

"Why not?"

"Because it's bloody offensive, that's why."

Sturridge snorted in contempt. "Offensive! What's offensive is you tramping around like you own the bloody place."

"Look, this is ridiculous. Just throw my badge over here and—"

"Ridiculous, am I?" Sturridge snapped. "Why don't you come over here and say that? See what you get."

"No, that's not going to happen." Ade shifted his stance, making it clear he was going nowhere. "Put my badge down and then step away."

"Don't give me orders."

"It's not an order, it's a statement of fact," Ade said. "You're going to put that badge down, then you're going to—"

"Shut up!" Sturridge shouted. "You want this, go and find it." Without taking his eyes from Ade, Sturridge swung the lanyard fast and let it go, sending it soaring into the air.

Ade watched it tumble into the undergrowth. "What did you do that for? I'll have to go and look for it, so I'll be here even longer. If you'd just handed it over, I'd be on my way home already."

"So what?"

Ade remained tight lipped.

"Go on then." Sturridge waved his arm. "Go and find your precious bit of plastic."

"When you've gone."

Sturridge cackled. "Oh no, sunshine. I'm staying right here. I'm going to enjoy this. I've been waiting for it. Waiting for a long time."

Ade looked Sturridge up and down. The man was swaying ever so slightly. His cheeks were sunken, his skin sallow, and taken with his strangely fixated facial expression, it could only mean one thing. "You're drunk. Dangerously so."

"Bollocks! I can hold my drink."

"That's what they all say. I've done my time in A & E, and every night someone came in who could hold their drink. Some of them were still alive in the morning, but some of them didn't make it."

Sturridge sneered. "Save your sob stories for someone who gives a shit."

"You need help."

With a growl, Sturridge swung the shotgun upward, pointing the barrel squarely at Ade's chest. "Go! Go and find your bloody badge! Go on. Grovel in the dirt."

Raising his hands to shoulder height, Ade took a step back. "All right. I'm going."

"Good. And be quick about it."

"Fine." Ade edged into the undergrowth, moving steadily away while keeping a watchful eye on Sturridge.

The man lowered his gun and reached into his coat pocket, pulling out a glass bottle. Unscrewing the cap with his thumb, he pressed the bottle to his lips and upended it, closing his eyes as he swallowed, gulping down the amber liquid as if his life depended on it.

Ade steeled himself. If he rushed Sturridge now, he could grab the gun, disarm him. The man's reflexes would be dulled by alcohol, but drunks could be unpredictable, and the man probably knew how to handle his weapon. *Do it anyway*, Ade told himself. *Overpower him now, before it's too late.*

But before Ade could make a move, Sturridge coughed, spluttering, flecks of spittle flying from his lips. He lowered the bottle but he kept hold of it, his eyes bulging as he choked, gasping for air. His pale face flushed crimson, tears rolling down his cheeks as a coughing fit wracked his body.

And now Ade knew what to do. Striding to the man's side, he wrenched the gun from his grip and laid it down carefully. "Mr Sturridge, I'm going to help you. Are you on any medication?"

Sturridge shook his head, clutching his chest, and the next moment his knees buckled.

Ade grabbed him, eased him to the ground, laying him on his side. A violent shudder ran through the man's body, and Sturridge closed his eyes, screwing them tight shut. Ade checked his airways and breathing, then he felt for his pulse and counted the beats. Sturridge's pulse was weak, but somehow he still clung to his bottle. Ade pried it from his fingers and tossed it aside, then he reached for his phone, dialling 999. Sturridge was suffering from a seizure, almost certainly brought on by alcohol poisoning. He'd be severely dehydrated and, judging by the sickly colour of his skin and his feeble heartbeat, he could be heading for multiple organ failure. But without the right equipment, there was little Ade could do on his own. The man needed urgent treatment, and as the call connected, Ade could only hope that help would arrive in time.

CHAPTER 25

I N THE PLANTATION, the gloomy shadows beneath the trees began to deepen, and Dan grumbled under his breath.

A few paces away, Alan turned in Dan's direction, his torch's beam flickering from one trunk to the next. "What's up?" Alan called out. "Have you found something?"

"No. Nothing at all."

"Me neither. What do you reckon? Should we call it a day?"

Dan didn't have to think too hard about his answer. "Yes. We're not achieving anything here. There's not so much as a footprint."

"No. The ground's too dry." Alan made his way over to join him. "I'm beginning to wonder if we were wrong about this place."

"I wouldn't rule it out just yet," Dan said. "If Billy wanted to meet someone in private, or if he just wanted to be on his own, this would be an ideal spot."

"I'm not so sure. There are plenty of quiet places all around the village, but on foot it would've taken him quite a while to get here."

"Maybe Billy wanted to put some distance between

himself and the village." Dan thought for a moment. "He might've been burying something. That would explain the pine needles on his shoes. The ground is dry on the surface, but if you dig down, I'll bet you find damp earth."

"Okay, but why here?"

"That's hard to say," Dan admitted. "Perhaps he's been here before and it has some special meaning for him."

"Hm." Alan looked around. "When I was a lad, we made dens in the woods. Hours of fun. But that was in a park. There were paths and picnic benches. This is a commercial forest, private property. I doubt whether the local kids ever come up here. They know the score. Come to that, we shouldn't be here ourselves."

"Billy's a loner. You've just described the kind of place he'd seek out."

"I don't think he'd come here by choice. He was a local lad once, but not anymore. This isn't his environment. You saw him at the fair. He's like a fish out of water. Some people take to village life, and some don't."

"True," Dan said. "And which camp do I fall into?"

"I'd say you've managed to fit in. Just about. It took you some time, but you're getting there."

"Thanks a bunch."

"You're welcome." Alan's grin faded, and he took a breath. "Actually, I've been meaning to say something, but I've never found the right moment. The thing is…" Alan left his words hanging in the air while he looked around as if seeking inspiration.

"What?"

"I can't help feeling that you haven't really found your niche."

"I didn't know I needed one."

"You know what I mean. Fixing computers."

"It pays the bills," Dan said. "Well, some of them at least."

"Yes, but it doesn't fire you with enthusiasm, does it?"

MICHAEL CAMPLING

"It has its moments," Dan replied. "But what are you really getting at? Because whatever it is, I wish you'd get on with it."

"Okay. You're keen on computers and you're good with them, but you never talk about your work. It's like you're going through the motions. But when I see you out here, searching for that one piece of evidence that'll make sense of the whole picture, it's as if you come alive."

"I'm here because you asked me for help, that's all."

"And I'm grateful for that," Alan said. "But the point is, I think you need a challenge. You thrive on it. When you're working on a case, I can see it in your eyes. Even when you were hunting through that plastic bag of dust, you were full of energy."

"I'm not sure what to say to that."

"Say you'll think about finding a new line of work. Something you can get your teeth into."

"All right. But I don't see myself as some kind of private investigator." Dan laughed, but when Alan didn't join in, he stopped abruptly. "Hang on. Is that what you're suggesting? Dan Corrigan, private eye?"

"Why not? Look at all the cases you've already solved. Look at what you're doing now. Is it so hard to imagine that you could solve a few more?"

"Yes, it is. I've no interest in becoming some kind of gumshoe. They spend most of their time taking photos of cheating spouses, don't they?"

"Probably. But you could set up in business in any way you wanted, and you'd name your own terms. You could help people, and I think you'd enjoy it."

Dan shook his head, unconvinced.

"Think about what DS Spiller said to you," Alan went on. "He guessed you'd get involved in the case, and he was prepared to let you run with it. He knew you'd get results. When it comes to this kind of thing, you're a natural."

"It's an interesting idea, Alan, but it sounds like a pipe dream to me."

"Don't dismiss it so quickly. I reckon you could make a go of it."

"In Embervale?"

"You'd have to cast your net a bit wider, but there are always people with problems. Most of us go through life blissfully unaware of the chaos behind closed doors, but you've opened my eyes to it."

Dan shook his head. "Then I've done you a bad turn. But you know what I think?"

"No."

"I think it's time for us to head back and get something to eat. You must be getting hypoglycaemic or something."

Alan laughed. "I am getting peckish. Why don't we eat in the pub? We were going to pop in later anyway, so why not go straight there? By the time we get there, the kitchen will be open."

"I'm not sure I'm ready for another veggie burger."

"They have other things. We can discuss the case while we eat. And it's my round, remember?"

Dan hesitated but not for long. "All right. Let's go."

Alan dropped his car off at home, then they walked to the pub, deep in conversation.

"Do you follow the cricket?" Dan asked.

"Not particularly."

"Me neither." Dan took out his phone, running a quick search. "Hm. That's odd."

"What is?"

"There weren't any major cricket matches yesterday."

"Okay. What about it?"

"Gemma told us that she was watching the news last night, but she lost interest when the cricket scores came on."

"I wouldn't read too much into it," Alan said. "It's just a turn of phrase, isn't it? She meant sports results in general."

"Maybe. But you saw how precise she is, how careful. In her small world, nothing is allowed to be out of place. I doubt she'd be so vague."

"She probably just forgot what she'd been watching. She had other things on her mind."

"But she claimed to have an excellent memory," Dan argued.

"What are you saying? Do you think she lied about watching the TV? Why would she do that?"

"Any number of reasons."

Alan paused before replying. "You don't like Gemma, do you?"

"It's not that. But we need to keep an open mind."

"We'd be better off focusing on Billy. He's the one we're interested in. We need to know where he went and why."

They reached the pub and Alan pulled open the door. "After you."

But before Dan could walk in, someone appeared in the doorway, and Dan stood back to let him pass. The man thanked Alan for holding the door, then he noticed Dan and stopped short. "Hello again."

"Hello, Ade," Dan replied. "I'm surprised to see you're still here. Did you find your badge?"

"Yes and no. I found it, but then it got lost again. Something came up."

"Oh? That sounds intriguing," Dan said.

"You don't want to know about it. But I needed a coffee afterwards, and while I was driving past, I spotted the pub, so I dropped in. And thankfully, they make a decent Americano, so it's all good."

"You've got Dan to thank for the coffee," Alan said. "He had a chat with the manager, and eventually she gave in."

"Nice one. I probably shouldn't have so much caffeine, but it's what keeps me going. And it's been one of those days." Ade offered a rueful grin as though the subject was closed.

"Something happened in Brandle Wood?" Dan asked.

Ade pursed his lips.

"I don't mean to pry," Dan went on. "But you look exhausted. Are you okay?"

"There was an incident, but I can't talk about it. Patient confidentiality."

"Oh dear," Alan said. "Was someone hurt?"

"Erm. Someone was taken ill. Fortunately, I found them, and the paramedics arrived in time, so everything was all right. I hung around for a while, trying to find my badge, but it was no use, so I gave up."

"Perhaps you'll find it another day," Alan suggested. "You could come back when there's more daylight."

"No," Ade said firmly. "I won't be back. I'll get another badge, and they'll cancel my old pass, so even if someone finds it, it won't do them any good."

Dan nodded. "Okay. Well, so long as you're all right."

"Yeah. It's been a funny few days. Ever since Thursday, things have been all over the place."

"Tell me about it," Alan said.

Dan frowned "Thursday? The May Fair was on Saturday."

"I know. But we arrived a couple of nights before. Neither of us had anything important to do on Friday, so we headed out of town for a break." Ade laughed. "Some break. No offence, but there are some odd people around here. We should've packed up and left as soon I saw that weird guy picking flowers from the hedge at the crack of dawn. I mean, who does that? Is there a bunch of druids around here or something?"

"Not as far as I know," Alan replied. "But I hope you haven't come away with a bad impression of Embervale. Some of us are quite normal."

"I'll take your word for it," Ade said. "Goodnight. I'm heading home."

But as Ade made to leave, Dan raised a hand to stop him.

"Could you just hold on a minute? If you don't mind, I'd like to ask you a couple of questions."

"About what?"

"This person who was picking flowers, did you get a good look at him?"

"Not really. He wasn't close. If it hadn't been so early, I probably wouldn't have spotted him, but it was quiet and you know how sound travels at that time in the morning."

"Young or old?" Dan asked.

Ade tilted his head to one side. "Hard to say. He wasn't as old as you guys."

"I beg your pardon," Alan put in. "We're not *old*."

"No, but if I had to guess, I'd say that this guy was nearer to my age than yours."

"Okay," Dan said. "What about his height?"

"Average. He wasn't as tall as me, and not as big either."

"And these flowers he was picking," Dan said, "were they by any chance white and growing on a bush?"

Ade's eyebrows shot up. "How did you know that? Friend of yours, is he?"

Dan looked at Alan. "It sounds like George. He goes out early to pick blackthorn blossoms for a recipe he uses. He told me at the fair."

"That makes sense, I suppose," Alan said. "Do you think it could be significant?"

"I'm not sure, but at this point, we'll have to consider every possibility."

"Okay," Ade said slowly, looking as if his suspicions about the locals had just been confirmed. "Nice to see you again, kind of, but I'm going back to Exeter. Bye." He breezed past them and headed along the street, already taking his keys from his pocket. The lights on a parked car flashed as Ade unlocked it with a remote, and then he was climbing inside and driving away.

"He was in a hurry," Alan said.

"I can't say I blame him," Dan replied. "But let's go and get that pint, and while we're at it, we'll see what we can find out about what happened in the wood."

"You think the rumours will be flying already?"

"Oh yes," Dan said. "And if I know Embervale, we're in exactly the right place to hear them."

And with that, Dan hurried inside.

CHAPTER 26

R EG STODDARD WAS ready. Sitting on a folding chair
behind the shed on his allotment, he stayed perfectly
still, out of sight. He was screened on one side by his shed,
and on another by a water butt, so he was tucked away where
no one would spot him. He'd stay for as long as it took to
make sure his shed was safe, content to watch and wait as the
sun dipped toward the horizon. The air grew cooler, but it
was a mild spring evening, and anyway, Reg never felt the
cold, even in the depths of winter. He glanced at the bag by
his side. He'd eaten his sandwiches, but the flask of tea was
still untouched, and it would warm him up later if he felt the
need. Beside the bag, his stout walking stick was within easy
reach. If anyone tried to break into his shed tonight, he'd see
them off and no mistake. *Let them try*, he thought. *Just let
them try.*

Reg smiled to himself. He'd done a good job of repairing
the shed door, and the new padlock was the best he'd been
able to find. It would deter all but the most persistent of
intruders. And as he'd fixed the new staple and hasp to his
shed, he'd thought long and hard about who might break into
his shed and why. Thieves had been the most likely

explanation, but nothing had been taken, so unless the intruder had been disturbed, they would surely have broken into several sheds, searching for anything of value. But Reg had taken a stroll around the other allotments, and as far as he could see, none of the other sheds had been damaged. *Mind you*, he thought, *with one or two of them it was hard to tell.* Not all the sheds were as sturdy as his; some were ramshackle affairs that would be hard pressed to stay upright come winter. And Reg knew exactly who owned these poor apologies for sheds: newcomers.

There'd been an influx of fresh faces on the allotments recently: people with young kids, or trendy types who hankered after organic fruit and veg. But while it was nice to see people having a go, some of them didn't have a clue. Weeds allowed to sprout all over the place, paths edged with upturned wine bottles, and perfectly good fruit bushes uprooted and thrown aside. These were just some of the strange sights that had met his disapproving eye as he'd made his rounds. But he'd had to admit that there'd been no sign of any forced locks or broken shed doors.

Eventually, Reg had been left with only one conclusion: someone had broken into his shed because it was a good sturdy one, and they were seeking a shelter for the night. That explained the rolled-up sack on the floor; someone had used it as a makeshift pillow. And they'd opened his old biscuit tin hoping to find food. Whoever it was, there was a good chance that they'd be back. All Reg had to do was wait.

Reg yawned. *You mustn't fall asleep*, he told himself. *That will be no good at all.* Maybe he would have that cup of tea, perk himself up.

He took the cup from the top of his flask and rested it on the ground, then he unscrewed the stopper, bending over to pour the tea. A thin cloud of steam rose from the cup, and the earthy scent of strong tea rose to his nostrils. He stoppered the flask carefully, setting it beside his chair, then he sat back to take a sip of tea. But he froze, his cup halfway to his lips. *Footsteps.* Someone was coming.

Reg sat still, listening. The sound was faint but there was no mistaking the rhythm of someone walking on the hard-packed earth of the path. Slowly, Reg lowered his cup to the ground and felt for his walking stick, wrapping his fingers tight around its handle. The footsteps faltered. Had Reg given himself away? He didn't think so. He hadn't made a sound, and there was no way he could've been seen. He'd chosen his position well.

The footsteps resumed, closer now, the intruder hurrying, anxious breaths seeming unnaturally loud, amplified by the still evening air. The hairs on the back of Reg's neck prickled. If this person was desperate, they might not be so easy to scare away. He'd heard all sorts of stories about drug addicts and the like. But then he heard the rattle of someone trying to open his shed door, and Reg's blood boiled. He rose swiftly to his feet, his stick ready in his hands, and he strode from his hiding place.

Whatever happened next, he'd deal with it.

"Right!" Reg growled, marching around to the front of his shed. "I've caught you!"

The slim figure in front of him let out a sharp cry and spun around, pressing back against the shed door.

Bloody teenagers, Reg thought. *They're all the same.* Clad in a shapeless baggy top, the dark hood pulled forward, the youth stood still, head hung low.

"What the hell do you think you're doing, breaking into my shed?" Reg demanded. "You have no right."

The teenager didn't reply, didn't move a muscle.

"Cat got your tongue, has it? I should bloody well think so too. You ought to be ashamed of yourself."

The teenager sniffed, mumbling something Reg couldn't quite hear.

"Speak up. Go on. What have you got to say for yourself?"

Another sniff. "Sorry."

Reg frowned. This wasn't what he'd expected. And there was something about the teenager's voice that didn't seem right. But even so, he'd have to deal with the ruffian, make them see sense. "It's all very well saying sorry," Reg said, "but you could at least look at me when you're talking to me."

The teenager looked up, the dark hood falling back slightly. And Reg's eyes went wide. "Daisy? Is that you?"

Daisy nodded. "I'm sorry, Uncle Reg. I really am. But I didn't know what else to do."

"Why aren't you at home? Has something happened?"

"I can't tell you."

Reg took a step closer and realised he was still hefting his stick. He lowered it, pressing it to the ground, using it to support his weight. "Are you all right? You're not hurt, are you?"

"No. But I'm in trouble. Terrible trouble. And I can't go home."

"Why not? Have you had a row with your mum?"

"No. Nothing like that."

Reg ran a hand across his brow. "Does your mum know where you are?"

Daisy shook her head. "I told her I'm staying at a friend's house. But you mustn't tell her where I am. She can't know I'm here. No one can."

"Daisy, you're not making any sense. Why can't you just go home?" Reg softened his tone. "Listen, I don't want to interfere, but this is no place for you to be hanging around at night. So unless you tell me what's going on, I'm going to take you home right now."

"No!" Daisy cried. "You can't make me. I need to stay out of the way."

"Why for pity's sake?"

"Because…" Daisy took a sharp breath as though she was stifling a sob. "Because he knows where I live."

A shiver ran down Reg's spine. "Who does?"

"I can't tell you. It's better if you don't know."

"I'll be the judge of that," Reg said. "But unless you tell me the truth, I shan't know what to think, shall I?"

"For God's sake!" Daisy hissed.

Reg fought the urge to grab Daisy by the shoulders and shake some sense into her. "This won't do, my girl. You tell me what's up, or I'll have to call your mum. That's all there is to it."

"Please don't—"

"I'll not hear one more word of argument." Reg pulled his phone from his pocket. "This might not be fancy, but I've got your mum on speed dial. Do you want me to call her?"

"No, of course, I don't," Daisy groaned. "But if I tell you, you mustn't be angry. I've done something stupid, I know I have. I wish I hadn't done it, but I've got myself in trouble and I can't undo it. So there's no point in giving me a lecture, all right?"

"Fair enough," Reg said. "Tell me all about it, and I'll listen. But that's the only promise I'll make, so don't ask for another, young lady. Don't even think about it."

CHAPTER 27

O N HEARING DAN'S request, Sam raised an eyebrow. "I don't know if we can fit you in. Have you booked a table?"

Dan made a show of looking around the room. The Wild Boar was almost empty. A middle-aged couple sat quietly in the corner, sipping their drinks, and local decorator and ex-police officer Jay Markham was on his usual stool at the far end of the bar.

"Do we need to book?" Dan asked. "It's not as if we had to fight our way to the bar."

"I like people to book," Sam said. "You could've called. It only takes a second. You have got the number, haven't you?"

Before Dan could reply, Alan intervened. "We just dropped in on the off-chance. I know it would've been better to book in advance, but we'd be grateful if you could fit us in."

Sam repaid Alan with a smile. "I'll see what I can do." She grabbed a tablet from behind the bar and tapped the screen.

"Do you have many bookings?" Dan asked.

"Quite a few as it happens. We've got a darts match on

later, and the book club are coming in too. They'll be wanting a couple of tables pushed together."

"I didn't know there was a book club," Dan said. "I thought that fad had died out."

Alan tutted. "There are thousands of active book clubs all over the country. Our local club is excellent. They asked me to come along as a guest speaker one week, and I had a great time. They were perfectly charming."

"I stand corrected." Dan drummed his fingers on the bar. "So, what do you say, Sam? Can we squeeze in before the literati arrive?"

Sam wrinkled her nose. "I'm really not sure. We're short staffed this evening."

From his end of the bar, Jay laughed. "Go on, Sam. Let the poor bugger off the hook. I can't bear to see him standing there for much longer with that little-boy-lost expression on his face."

"All right," Sam said. "We'll fit you in."

"Thank you. Could we have a look at a menu, do you think, or would that be too much trouble?"

Sam smiled sweetly. "Oh, you can have a menu, but there's no rush. The kitchen doesn't open for another ten minutes, and we don't take orders until it does. All right?"

Dan opened his mouth to argue, but Alan didn't give him the chance. "That's great. We'll have a drink while we wait. What're you having, Dan?"

"I don't know. Maybe I'll have a half of IPA."

"No, you won't," Alan said. "Sam, I see you've got a guest lager. That's a bit daring, isn't it?"

"You've got to ring the changes," Sam replied. "We can't always stick to the same old ales. Craft lager, that's what the younger customers want, and they don't mind paying a bit extra for the good stuff. This is a nice one. Tarka Pure. Brewed in Devon. Do you want to try a taste?" She sent Dan a sideways glance. "It's *vegan friendly*."

"Go on then," Alan said. "I don't need to taste it. I'm sure it'll be great. A pint for me." He turned to Dan. "Same for you?"

Dan shrugged. "Sure. Why not?"

"Two pints of Tarka Pure coming up." Sam grabbed a pair of glasses and began pouring. "So, what brings you two out so early on a Monday night?"

Dan and Alan exchanged a look. "Nothing much," Dan said. "We're looking into something."

"Very mysterious," Jay drawled. "I'll tell you what, you should've been here earlier. You missed all the excitement. It would've been right up your street."

"Excitement?" Dan asked.

"Aye. You know Sid Sturridge?"

Dan nodded. "I heard he was missing."

"Not anymore." Jay smirked. "Turned up in Brandle Wood. Needed an ambulance. That young man who just left, he found him. Saved his life."

"He told you that, did he?"

"Not exactly," Jay admitted. "But I saw an ambulance tearing through the village a while ago, and I overheard a couple of snippets and put two and two together. You know how it goes."

"Indeed, we do," Alan said. "But you ought to know better than to believe every bit of gossip that comes your way."

Jay grinned. "Get over yourself. You want to know the juicy details, same as everyone else. Anyway, it wasn't just me being nosy." He cast a sly glance at Sam and then lowered his voice to a stage whisper. "Sam used her charms on that young man, and before he knew what he was saying, she'd wheedled more or less the whole story out of him. Poor bloke didn't stand a chance."

"Very funny," Sam intoned. "I was just having a nice chat with a handsome young doctor. Nothing wrong with that."

"He's still a medical student," Dan said.

"Maybe," Sam replied, "but he's almost qualified. And he has such a nice way with him. You lot could take a leaf out of his book, that's for sure." She plonked two brimming pint glasses onto the bar. "There you go. Do you want to pay now or when you pay for your food?"

"We'll start a tab, please," Alan said. "I had to twist Dan's arm to come here, so I'm paying."

Jay made a show of clearing his throat, then he smiled at Alan. "I expect you'd like me to tell you what happened up in Brandle Wood, only my throat's very dry just now."

"Go on then, Sam," Alan said. "Give him a pint of whatever Australian fizzy beer he's drinking and put it on my tab."

"Ah, that's very decent of you, Alan. Same again, Sam, please." Jay slid from his stool and joined them, his watchful gaze on the pint Sam was already pouring.

"Well?" Dan said. "What can you tell us?"

Jay raised a hand. "Hold on, lad. All things come to those who wait." He received his pint from Sam, and after taking a long draught of lager, he smacked his lips. "That's better. Just what I needed. And it's cheaper than that fancy stuff you're drinking."

"Can we save the beer discussion for another night?" Dan asked. "You've got us on tenterhooks."

Jay laboriously wiped his mouth with the back of his hand. "All right. It's a simple enough story. I know Sid Sturridge of old, and he's always been a bit too fond of a drink."

"That's putting it mildly," Sam said. "He isn't allowed in here. He got barred ages ago."

"Did he cause trouble?" Alan asked. "I've heard he has a temper."

Sam shook her head. "That wasn't the problem. He'd just stand at the bar, necking down as much booze as he could afford, then he'd cadge drinks off the locals. But nobody liked him hanging around the place. It was depressing, watching him put it away like it was in short supply. No one wants to see that."

"But I've seen him around the village, and I never noticed anything amiss," Alan said. "I had no idea he was a heavy drinker."

Jay grunted. "He isn't. He's an alcoholic. It's like an occupation. It takes all his energy and willpower to keep pouring the stuff down his throat. He's an addict, and I know what that's like. You get crafty, keeping it hidden, making sure you don't get found out. Because once people know about it, you might have to stop, and that's the one possibility you can't face."

Jay looked down, and a heavy silence settled over the group until Jay placed his glass carefully on the bar and pushed it away. "I know what you're thinking, but before you say anything, that's my second pint and I might have one more before I go home. I can take it or leave it. Painkillers were my problem, nothing else, and I haven't had so much as an aspirin for months. I'm as fit as a flea. I had a day off the beer yesterday, and I didn't miss it one bit."

"That's good," Alan said. "It must've been hard for you. To come off the painkillers, I mean."

"Don't patronise me, Hargreaves."

"No, I meant it," Alan said. "You've turned things around, done well for yourself. I hear you're always busy. Business must be good."

Jay lifted his chin. "I'm not doing badly, but you don't want to hear about me. You want to know why Sid took himself up to Brandle Wood."

"Perhaps he'd hit rock bottom," Alan suggested.

Jay wrinkled his nose. "Yesterday, I was in the shop when his wife came in. Gary was behind the counter for once, and he made the mistake of asking after Sid. The next thing you know, she's having a good old moan. According to her, Sid had a real bee in his bonnet about Brandle Wood. He was always going up there, at all kinds of odd times."

"Ade and Maria," Dan said. "They were camping but they left on Saturday, after the fair."

"It wasn't them. This had been going on for weeks, according to his wife. It was driving her to distraction."

"Maybe he was after poachers," Sam suggested.

"Nothing much to poach up there," Jay said. "Scott runs a shoot, but it's on the other side of Ironbrand. You couldn't let those city types loose with shotguns in Brandle Wood: there's a bridle path right through the middle of it. Someone would get their head blown off."

Dan took a sip of his beer, thinking. Then finally, he said, "Does anyone know what Sid was so worried about?"

"Nope," Jay replied. "It's a mystery."

"Strange," Alan said thoughtfully. "It's not as if Sid owns the wood. If something was bothering the man, why didn't he go to his employer and let him sort it out?"

"I was wondering the same thing myself," Dan said. "It's quite suggestive, isn't it?"

Jay shrugged. "It suggests that Sid is off his trolley. Maybe he was seeing things, shooting at shadows."

Dan clicked his fingers. "The night George was stabbed, several of us heard a gunshot. At the time, we thought it had to be connected, but perhaps the two incidents were entirely separate."

"That would be quite a coincidence," Alan said.

"That's the thing about coincidences," Jay replied. "They happen all the time. But you mustn't put too much weight on things that probably happened by chance. That's one thing you learn when you're on the force. When you start seeing connections that aren't there, you're skating on thin ice."

"And how do you know the connections *aren't there* unless you test your ideas?" Dan asked. "You need to think scientifically; start with a hypothesis and then challenge it, pushing it to see if it holds up."

Jay shook his head slowly. "That's all very well for the geeks in white coats, but real life doesn't work like that. People do stupid things. Most of the villains I nicked were too lazy to think things through. They had no idea what they were doing. They were chancers. Mindless."

Dan was about to argue when the pub door opened, and they all turned to look at the new arrival.

Reg Stoddard stepped inside then he offered a nod. "Evening."

"All right, Reg," Jay said. "How's tricks?"

Reg made his way to the bar. "Not so bad."

"Pint of the usual?" Sam asked.

"Please," Reg said. "Are you doing food yet?"

Sam looked up from pulling Reg's pint and checked the clock. "Just about. I'll get you a menu in a minute."

"I see," Dan muttered. "Not everyone gets the third degree, then."

Reg glanced at Dan uncertainly.

"Ignore him," Sam said. "He's from London."

"Yes, I know," Reg replied. "We've met. But I don't need a menu, Sam. I just wanted something to take out. A pie or a pasty. Something like that."

"Okay." Sam grinned as she placed a pint in front of Reg. "What's going on? Is the wife not feeding you enough?"

Reg laughed nervously. "Nothing's going on. I just wanted something extra, that's all. I've been busy, and I worked up an appetite."

"Okay. Well, we've got Cornish pasties, or I can get you a cheese and onion slice."

"Cornish pasty," Reg said.

"Hot or cold?"

"Blimey." Reg ran a hand across his brow. "Cold. No, hot would be better. Thanks."

"Okay. Is that everything? I can get you a portion of chips on the side if you like."

"Good idea," Reg said. "And I'd better have a can of something. A soft drink. Lemonade."

"No problem. I'll get your food sorted." Sam bustled to the kitchen, and the four men at the bar sipped their drinks, studying each other with surreptitious glances.

"So, Reg, how's the woodwork?" Dan asked.

"You mean the shed?" Reg replied. "All fixed."

"I meant your woodturning," Dan said. "But was there a problem with your shed?"

Reg shook his head vigorously. "No, no. No problem. It needed a bit of maintenance. The door was sticking, so I had to put it right."

"I see." Dan watched Reg from the corner of his eye. When they'd talked at the May Fair, Reg had been chatty and relaxed, but now, the man could barely stand still. Reg was hiding something and he was not very good at it. But Dan thought of what Jay had said a few minutes earlier. It wasn't sensible to attach too much importance to every tiny event. Life was a messy business, and sometimes things happened for no reason at all. If Reg had a problem he didn't want to share, that was fine. Perhaps it was time to change the subject.

Dan placed his drink on the bar and said, "Reg, where would I find blackthorn around here?"

"All over. You find a bit dotted here and there in the hedgerows."

"Say, I wanted a lot of it, though," Dan went on. "For a recipe."

"For wine?" Reg asked.

"No, for a sorbet. But I'm guessing I'd need quite a bit."

Reg thought for a second. "Brandle Wood. That's the best place. There's any amount up there."

"Ah," Alan said. "So George could've been in the wood on Friday morning. It all fits."

"Young George Hepworth?"

"That's right," Dan replied.

Reg sighed. "Ah, it was terrible what happened to the poor lad. Terrible. He seemed like a nice young man."

"Do you know him?"

"Sort of. He took over his dad's old allotment." Reg smiled sadly. "Mind you, Jerry Hepworth would be turning in his grave if he saw what the lad was growing in his precious plot."

"Is George not much of a gardener?" Alan asked.

"Well, he tries, but he has some very funny ideas. I saw him planting seeds once, and he told me they were dandelions. I laughed. I said you want to pull them up, not plant the little blighters. But he said they were special ones for eating. Who ever heard of such a thing?"

"I have," Dan said. "They're a bit like endive. You put them in salads. It's quite fashionable. It used to be pea shoots, and before that, it was nasturtium leaves. People are always looking for something new."

Reg pulled a face. "Madness. Nasturtiums is one thing, but anyone who deliberately plants a weed wants their head examined. And then there's his fancy blueberries. They're not what I would've chosen, but they were going along right enough. And what does he do? He gets rid of the lot. I suppose he must've changed his mind. That's the problem with all this trendy nonsense, it's here today and gone tomorrow. I might be an old duffer, but I reckon the old ways are the best, especially when it comes to putting food on the table."

"Dead right," Jay said. "There's nothing wrong with meat and two veg."

Dan buttoned his lip. He was in no mood for an argument, and thankfully Sam returned with a couple of menus.

"There you go," she said. "Specials are on the board."

Turning to Reg, she added. "Your pasty and chips will be ready in a few minutes."

"Thank you." Reg raised his glass and took a long drink.

Studying the menu, Alan said, "I'm tempted to have a steak. It's from a local farm. That wouldn't bother you, would it?"

"No. Have what you like." Dan ran his eyes over the unpromising list. "I guess I'm stuck with the veggie chilli."

"Ah, you don't eat meat," Reg said. "You told me at the fair."

Dan looked up. "Yes. It seems like a long time ago, but it's only been a couple of days. So much has happened."

"And none of it good," Reg said bitterly. "None of it. The world's gone mad."

"You can say that again," Jay chipped in. "Have you heard about Sid Sturridge?"

Reg shook his head, and Jay related the details. Dan listened attentively, frowning when Jay peppered the tale with embellishments. Sid had been raving, firing his gun, chasing after the young medical student who subsequently saved him. Presumably, Jay was making these flights of fancy up as he went along. What would the story become by the end of the evening?

Dan caught Sam's eye, and she offered him a complicit grin. She was used to Jay's cock and bull stories, and they both knew it. Dan found himself returning her smile. Whatever he'd done to irk Sam, she seemed to have got over it.

A young man emerged from the kitchen and handed Reg a polystyrene takeaway container and a can of lemonade.

"Thank you." Reg produced a battered leather wallet from his pocket, then he paid his bill in cash before draining his glass. "That's me done. Time to head for home. Goodnight."

He headed for the door, and Dan watched him go.

"Reg is quite a character, isn't he?" Alan said. "A real countryman."

"Yes," Dan replied. "Yes, he is." But Dan was still processing what he'd just seen.

After he'd stepped outside, Reg had been clearly visible through the window, and the man had hesitated. He'd looked up and down the street as if he was frightened of being spotted, then he'd hurried away, his head down and his shoulders hunched.

Reg was definitely up to something, and though it was probably nothing important, Dan couldn't stop thinking about it. *Let it go*, he told himself. *There's probably a simple explanation*. Perhaps Reg was supposed to be on a strict diet, and he didn't want his wife to know about the pasty and chips. But that didn't account for the sudden change in Reg's behaviour. No. Something was going on, something that Reg didn't want anyone to know about, and sooner or later Dan might have to do some digging of his own.

TUESDAY

CHAPTER 28

SITTING UP IN his hospital bed, Sid Sturridge stared, unseeing, at the glossy magazine in front of him. Then he closed his eyes and let the tears roll down his cheeks. He couldn't remember the last time he'd cried, but now he couldn't stop. *You ought to be ashamed*, he scolded himself. *Man of your age, weeping like a child.* But there was nothing he could do about it. The fight had gone out of him. There was nothing left. Nothing but the loneliness and the recriminations and the awful silence.

They'd put him in a room by himself, and he'd been glad of it. But the solitude had given him too much time to think, and if there was one person he didn't want to be stuck with, it was himself.

I've been a bloody fool, he thought. *Stupid, pig-headed, ignorant bloody fool.*

Sid fumbled for a tissue from the box at his bedside, grabbing a handful and pressing them against his face, mopping his eyes. Lisa had brought the tissues from home, and they were the soft ones: the kind with aloe vera, the brand that she always bought. The faintly perfumed scent of the tissues brought him back to his senses, took him home for a moment. He should be there now, keeping Lisa company, sipping a mug of hot tea. Lisa made the best tea.

She'd been in to see him the night before, bringing him fresh pyjamas and a few essentials. It had been late, and she'd looked exhausted, the rosy glow gone from her cheeks. But she hadn't criticised him, hadn't complained. She'd just patted his hand and told him to get better.

She'd always been the strong one, the one to hold it all together. Now, it was up to him to get himself straight, to make things right, to make it up to her. And he made a decision. No more booze. Not one drop.

He'd told himself the same thing many times before, but never in a hospital bed, and this time, he knew it would stick.

A weight lifted from his shoulders, and he lay back against the crisp white pillows, the wad of damp tissues still clenched in his fist. He heard the door open and someone enter the room, but he didn't have the energy to open his eyes. It would only be one of the nurses. They'd been coming in regularly to check on him, but right now he needed a rest from all the poking and prodding, the intrusive questions. If he pretended to be asleep, they'd come back later.

But when someone spoke his name, it was not in the caring tones of a nurse or a doctor. The voice was cold, soulless. And he knew it immediately.

Sid's eyes shot open and his whole body tensed, a flush of perspiration prickling his brow. "What?" he croaked. "What do you want?"

Stalking toward Sid and staring down at him, Harry Denton smiled without any trace of warmth, baring his upper teeth. "That's no way to talk, Sid. I've come to see how you're doing. I wanted to make sure you're all right."

"I'm fine. Fine."

"Really? Because, from where I'm standing, you're not looking too good."

"I'm all right. I… stayed out too late, that's all. I had a funny turn."

"That's not what I heard," Harry said. "I heard a different story. So I hope you're not lying to me, Sid."

"No. It was a funny turn. I'll be all right." Sid stuffed the damp tissues under the bedclothes, making a show of straightening the sheets while he tried to pull himself together.

"We'll see." Harry cast a critical eye over the sparse furnishings. "This place isn't so bad. And you're lucky, having a room all to yourself."

"It's all right." Sid hesitated. "How did you know I was here?"

"Lisa. She was happy to tell me. More than happy."

Sid struggled to sit upright. "What do you mean? If you've upset her, I'll…" He mashed his lips together, struggling to find words strong enough.

"Relax, before you give yourself a heart attack. I paid a visit to your wife, and we had a nice little chat. Nothing for you to get worked up about. Up at the farm, we heard what happened and we had to check up on you, didn't we? Otherwise, what kind of employers would we be?"

Sid tried to swallow, but his throat was dry. He reached for the glass of water on his nightstand, and when he picked it up, he was shocked to see the way his hand trembled.

"Do you want some help?" Harry asked.

Sid shook his head, then he guided the glass to his dry lips and sucked gratefully, not caring that the water was lukewarm. "That's better." He slid the glass back onto the nightstand, and this time his hand was a little steadier.

"I expect you'd prefer something stronger," Harry said. "Silly me. I should've brought you a little something. Whisky, that's what you like, isn't it?"

"No. Can't stand the stuff."

"We'll see. Maybe I'll drop by later with a half-bottle of something decent."

"No, thank you. Like I said, I don't touch it. Not anymore." Sid eyed the call button beside his bed. If he pressed it, the nurses would come right away, but what would he say to them? How could he explain?

Harry followed his gaze and stepped closer, leaning over him. "You're a drunk, Sid. I can smell it on you, even now. It's coming out of your pores. What happened, did they have to pump your stomach? I'll bet that's no picnic."

"You can't…" Sid tried to protest, tried to look Harry in the eye, but he couldn't quite do it, so he stared across the room, his head low like a whipped dog.

"I can't what?" Harry whispered. "Tell me what I can't do, Sid. Go on. I'd love to know."

Sid licked his lips. "You shouldn't talk like that to me. I've been ill. I need to rest. The doctor said—"

"Ah, the doctor," Harry interrupted. "You must've had a long chat with the doctor. And a shrink, maybe?"

"No. Just a regular doctor."

"And what did you talk about with this regular doctor?"

"It's personal," Sid said.

Harry straightened his back. "Don't be obtuse, man. You know what I mean. I don't give a damn about your private life. But they must've asked you what you were doing in the woods, and I need to know what you said."

"Nothing."

"Nothing? Seriously?"

Sid met his stare for long enough to say, "That's right. Nothing. I said I was working, told them I'm a gamekeeper."

"And that's all?"

Sid nodded.

"And what about the guy that found you? What did he have to say for himself?"

Sid bridled. "Nothing. He's a good man. He saved my life. If it weren't for him, I'd be a goner."

"And the world would be a better place."

"Maybe."

Harry sighed. "God, you're a bundle of laughs, aren't you? I'm starting to wish I hadn't come."

"Then why did you?" Sid couldn't keep the note of insolence out of his voice, and it didn't go unnoticed. The next thing he knew, Harry's fingers were wrapped tight around his upper arms, pressing him back.

"Watch your mouth, Sturridge. Close it tight and keep it shut, do you hear me?"

"Get off!"

"I said, *do you hear me?*"

"Yes. I can bloody well hear you." Sid heard his voice wobble and hated himself for it. He was beaten, but he shouldn't show it, shouldn't give Harry the satisfaction of knowing he'd won.

"You had one job," Harry hissed. "One simple task to perform, but still, you managed to screw it up. What the hell were you thinking? Firing your gun, for God's sake. People heard you."

"I saw someone. I had to do something."

"Jesus Christ! I'm wasting my breath." Harry released him, grimacing and rubbing his hands together as though the contact had contaminated him. "God! What a bloody mess."

Sid rubbed at his arms, but he didn't even try to explain himself. There was nothing he could say to make this right.

"You've caused everyone a hell of a lot of problems," Harry said. "What are you going to do about it?"

"I suppose I'll have to leave the estate. As soon as I get out of here, I'll hand my notice in."

"Oh no, you won't. You'll stay with us, and you'll go back to work."

"But… I can't."

"You'll have to. Frankly, you don't have a choice. I need you where I can keep an eye on you. So you'll do what you're told."

"What about Mr Benning?" Sid asked. "Does he know? About the drinking?"

"I'll handle Scott. You needn't worry on that score."

Sid pressed the heels of his palms against his forehead. "I can't do this. I can't go on."

Harry's only reply was a dismissive grunt.

Sid looked up. "Let me hand my notice in. Please."

"No." Harry turned away, making it clear that the conversation was over. He focused his attention on the bag of clear fluid that hung from a stand at Sid's bedside, tracing the length of the plastic tubing with his fingertips. "What's this, saline? Or is it something more complicated than that?"

"I'm not sure. Fluids, they said. The doctor did explain it but…"

"Electrolytes probably. Very important." He looked Sid in the eye. "It would be awful, wouldn't it, if something were to happen to this little tube? If something were to go wrong with it when you were asleep, say. That would be terrible."

Sid's face fell, his cheeks sagging.

"The human body is a delicate thing," Harry went on. "Especially when you've been unwell. And thanks to the cheap whisky you've been pouring down your throat, your system has taken a beating. You're weak, Sid. Vulnerable. The tiniest thing could send you over the edge. A simple accident could squash you as easily as this." Harry took the plastic tube, squeezing it between finger and thumb, pressing it flat.

"No!" Sid tried to push himself up off the bed, but Harry placed his palm on the centre of Sid's chest and pushed hard, shoving him back.

"Stay there," Harry snarled. "Don't make me do something I regret." He let go of the tube, spreading his hands. "There's nothing for you to get so agitated about. I was making a point. Is it safe to assume that you understand the situation here?"

Breathing hard, Sid nodded once.

"Good. Then I'll get out of this dump. The smell is starting to get to me, and I'm not talking about the disinfectant." He made to leave. "Don't get up. I'll see myself out." Harry looked back as he opened the door. "And remember what I said, Sturridge. You need to keep quiet, or I'll have to come back here and deliver a reminder. And then I'll call in to see Lisa, and next time, I won't be so friendly. Do you understand?"

"Yes," Sid said. And as he watched the door swing shut, he leaned back and stared up at the ceiling. It had been a long time since Sid had been to church, and he couldn't remember the last time he'd said a prayer. But this was a good time to start. Because if there was a way out of this, he couldn't see it. And he needed something to keep him going; otherwise, he wasn't going to make it.

CHAPTER 29

D AN RUMMAGED THROUGH the contents of his kitchen cupboards, delving through the cans, cartons and packets, but it was no use. He was out of oat milk, and he'd set his heart on making a flat white for his morning coffee.

He could drink it black instead, but it wouldn't be the same, and it would only take him a few minutes to walk to the shop and back. He could pick up one or two other things while he was there, and besides, the fresh air and exercise would be good. He'd been cooped up all morning, hunched over a pad of paper, making notes and scribbling diagrams as he'd tried to piece together the events leading up to the attack on George. But he'd made scant progress. He needed that cup of coffee. And he wanted it to be just right.

He grabbed his reusable bag and left the house, setting off at a brisk pace, and a few minutes later he stepped into the cramped interior of Embervale's only shop.

Sitting behind the counter, a young woman looked up briefly but without any spark of interest.

"Morning," Dan called out. "It's another nice day. Getting warm already."

"Yeah," the young woman replied, then she returned her attention to the phone in her hand, her gaze dull.

She's not a patch on Sam, Dan decided. When Sam had worked in the shop, she'd had a kind word for every customer. Dan had enjoyed chatting with her and buying groceries had been a pleasure. But that hadn't lasted for long, and since Sam had taken over the pub, she'd seemed different, as far as her dealings with him were concerned, anyway. *She's friendly enough to everyone else*, Dan thought as he moved along the narrow aisle, scanning the eclectic mix of products on display. *Whatever it is that I've done to upset her, I wish she'd just come out and tell me.*

Dan plucked a can of chickpeas from the shelf, then he strolled to the end of the aisle, turning the corner to head for the chiller cabinet. But someone was blocking the way, a man standing still and staring at the brightly lit cabinet, his broad frame almost filling the aisle.

"Excuse me," Dan said politely.

"Sorry." The man half turned, looking over his shoulder at Dan, then he did a double take. "Oh, it's you again."

"Hello, Reg." Dan glanced at the cellophane packets in Reg's hand. "More pasties?"

"That's right."

"All that pastry," Dan said with a smile. "You'll have to keep an eye on your cholesterol."

"I wouldn't know about that."

"You're not on a diet then?"

"No. I get plenty of fresh air, and the allotment keeps me fit."

"That's all right then." Dan kept his tone light and friendly, but just like the night before, Reg was uneasy, his posture stiff and his expression wary. What on earth was making him so on edge?

"A pasty is handy, isn't it?" Reg said. "You can pop it in your pocket, save it for later. Keep yourself going."

"Well, that's why they were invented, wasn't it? For the tin miners. I'm told that, because the miners' hands were so dirty, they used to hold their pasties by the crust and then throw that part away."

"Best bit, the crust." Reg's smile was strained. "Right. I'll pay for these, then I'll be off." He picked up a wire basket from the floor and added the pasties to it.

Dan glanced at the meagre collection in Reg's basket: a toothbrush, toothpaste, a bar of soap and a bottle of mineral water. "Are you going away somewhere?"

"No. Why do you ask?"

"Your shopping. They're the kind of things you buy when you're going to be away from home."

Reg looked down at his basket. "Just stocking up. My wife likes to keep plenty of stuff in the cupboards. Living out here, you never know when you might run out of something. And if you can't get out to the shops, you're scuppered."

"I know all about that. When the roads were icy, I ran out of coffee. I learned my lesson, but I'm always having to pop out to buy something or other. I don't know how people manage if they haven't got a car. Do you drive?"

Reg nodded firmly. "I have a van. Ford. It's old but it keeps running, somehow. Just like me." He laughed but there wasn't much mirth in it, and Dan had the feeling Reg had trotted out the same line many times before. "Anyway," Reg went on, "it's useful for lugging lumps of wood around, and furniture when it's all put together."

"Ah yes, the woodturning. It must take a long time to finish a piece. Do you sell enough to make it worth your while?"

Reg shrugged. "Depends on the time of year. In the summer, I can shift a fair bit at craft fairs and such, but I can only make so much at a time. I've nowhere to store tables and chairs at home. It's only a cottage, not a bloody great farmhouse like some places I could mention."

A flash of anger glittered in Reg's eyes, and a stray thought made itself known in the back of Dan's mind. There was something that he ought to remember, some fact that he couldn't quite recall or a connection that he couldn't quite trace. But he couldn't put his finger on it, and before he had time to think, Reg changed the subject.

"I'm going out later, as it happens," Reg said. "Over to Exeter to visit Sid Sturridge, see how he's doing."

"Oh, are you a friend of his? You didn't mention it last night."

"Not a friend as such, but Sid's like me. He's been around the village all his life. Us locals have got to stick together."

"I hope he's getting better," Dan said. "We've never met, but it was awful to hear about what happened to him. Very sad."

"True enough. But there'll be plenty of folks around here who'll say he's brought it on himself. That's not exactly Christian, is it? Not right at all."

"Are you a churchgoer?"

"Every Sunday. The wife too. We never miss a service unless we can't help it." Reg paused. "I've never seen you there, but I'm sure you'd be welcome if you fancy coming along."

"It's not for me I'm afraid. I'm more of a humanist."

Reg tented his eyebrows. "Is that right? Well, I really must get going. I've a few things to do on the allotment before I head over to Exeter. Goodbye."

"Bye."

Reg strode toward the counter, and Dan turned back to the chiller cabinet. The shop had recently started stocking fresh oat milk, but its allotted space was bare, so Dan went in search of the long-life variety. He heard the bell ring as Reg left the shop, and Dan's mind went back to the odd mixture of items that comprised Reg's shopping. *Evian*, Dan thought. *I*

would never have pegged Reg as someone who'd buy mineral water.
He knew that the shop sold a couple of different brands, but
Reg had selected the more expensive of the two. It seemed
out of character. But then, he was having a difficult time
getting a handle on Reg. Perhaps that was because he and
Reg weren't just from different generations but from different
worlds. It sounded as though Reg had never lived anywhere
other than Embervale, and as someone who'd lived in several
parts of London, each one very different, Dan found Reg's
small world hard to imagine.

Dan discovered the long-life oat milk and took a couple of
cartons, heeding Reg's advice to stock up with more than he
needed. *I'm turning into a local*, he thought. *I'll be going around
in a tweed jacket next.*

Dan smiled to himself. Tweed might be going a bit far, but
perhaps a waxed cotton jacket would be just the thing for
rainy days. Besides, it would be worth it to see the look on
Alan's face.

Moving along the aisle and adding a couple of cans of
tomatoes and a can of kidney beans to his haul, Dan made his
way to the counter and handed over his basket. The young
woman huffed and put down her phone, then she removed
each item from the basket as slowly as possible, handling
each one with unconcealed disdain as she tapped its price
into the till.

Sensing that the young woman preferred not to engage in
conversation, Dan found his mind wandering back to Reg.
Why had the man been so shifty? Did he have something to
hide, apart from his Cornish pasty habit? Something was
bothering Reg, and Dan couldn't help but wonder what it
was. There was a loose thread here, and it was begging to be
pulled. *Strike while the iron's hot*, Dan told himself. *And this is
as good a place as any*. Smiling at the young woman, he said, "I
was wondering, are you from the village?"

MICHAEL CAMPLING

The young woman's eyes flicked toward him, and she regarded him with a sullen gaze. For a moment, Dan thought she wasn't going to answer, but she summoned the energy to nod before returning to her task.

"Excellent," Dan said. "So, the allotments, do you know where they are?"

"Yeah." The young woman frowned at the can of kidney beans, turning it around as though it held a secret. "Do you know how much these are?"

"No. Sorry."

Sighing, the woman pulled a dog-eared sheaf of papers from beneath the counter and began flipping through the pages.

"I can go and check if you like," Dan offered.

"No, I'll find it."

"Really, I don't mind."

"Ha!" The young woman jabbed her finger at a page. "Got it." She tapped at the till.

"You ought to have a barcode scanner."

"Mm. Is that everything?"

"Yes." Dan hesitated. She still hadn't given him directions to the allotments, but she was so reluctant to talk that it might be easier to find them on his own. *One last chance*, he thought. As he bagged his shopping, he plastered an inane grin across his features and said, "I'm Dan, by the way. Sorry, but I don't know your name."

The sullen look was back. "Elaine."

"Right. Nice to meet you, Elaine. Getting back to the allotments, could you tell me how to get there?"

"Go along Fore Street, and they're next to the orchard."

"The community orchard?"

"That's the only one as far as I know."

"Okay," Dan said. "So the allotments must be next to the field where they held the May Fair."

"No, the show field is on the far side of the orchard. The allotments are on this side, nearer the village."

"I see. Thanks, Elaine. You've been very helpful."

Elaine almost smiled. "If you want to get into the allotments, you have to go up the lane just before you get to it."

"I'm sorry? How can I use a lane before I get to it?"

"I mean, before you get to the allotments, obviously. There's a lane on your left. You have to walk up there for a bit, then you'll see the gate on your right."

"And this lane, does it have a name?"

"Don't think so." Elaine brightened. "Oh, you know the turning for Ironbrand Farm?"

Dan nodded.

"Well, it's the one before that. So at least you'll know if you've gone too far."

"Thanks." Dan paid for his shopping and left the shop, but when he met Fore Street, he headed away from the village centre, away from home. If he could catch Reg off guard while he was working on his allotment, he might be able to break through the older man's reticence. It had to be worth a try because Reg was up to something, and until Dan could find out what, he couldn't let it lie.

Dan marched along the road, and soon he came upon a promising lane. He recalled the route he'd taken up to Ironbrand Farm with Alan, and that turning was a little way further on. This had to be the right lane for the allotments, and Dan took it, striding along, swinging his bag of shopping at his side.

A tall hedge grew along the lane, and Dan tried to peer through it as he went along, but he could see very little. The hedge was dense, and it had been planted atop a typical Devon bank: a mound of rocks and earth almost as tall as Dan. After a few minutes, he saw a dark shape beyond the hedge and he moved closer, stretching up to peer through a gap in the branches. He could make out a wooden shed, and beside it, a tall figure, standing perfectly still.

Dan was about to call out a greeting, but something stopped him. *Scarecrow*, he thought. *It looks as though I've found the allotments.*

Dan followed the hedge until he came to a small wooden gate. The sign beside it warned that neither unaccompanied children nor dogs were welcome on the allotments, but Dan couldn't see anything prohibiting curious neighbours, so he lifted the metal catch and made his way inside.

Dan had seen plenty of inner-city allotments, usually through the windows of a train, and he thought he'd known what to expect. But these allotments were different. Rather than rows of neatly painted sheds and carefully tended plots, these allotments seemed to be altogether less formal. Some of the sheds were smart and sturdy, but many were ramshackle affairs, cobbled together from scraps of wood, old doors and discarded window frames. And the plots were anything but uniform. Many were pristine, with neat rows of plants untroubled by any sign of weeds or pests, but others were overgrown, and some had become completely covered by clumps of coarse grass and wild flowers.

A path ran along the edge of the allotments, and Dan made his way along it, studying the varied vegetable plots and guessing at the people who tended them: raised beds hinted at a tidy mind; a miniature spade must have been left behind by a small child; a row of compost bins suggested a keen recycler.

At first, it looked as though there was no one around, but then Dan spied a man hard at work, digging on a particularly neat plot. There was no mistaking the man's shock of white hair, and as Dan approached, Reg looked up and paused in his work, straightening his back.

Dan raised a hand in greeting, and after a moment's pause, Reg returned the gesture.

Offering a friendly smile, Dan strode over to meet him, but Reg stared at Dan from beneath lowered eyebrows, his mouth set in a straight line.

"Hello," Dan called out. "How's it going?"

"Right enough."

Dan made a show of admiring the plot. "This all looks very impressive. Lots of green shoots coming up. What are you growing?"

"Onions, potatoes, cabbages, carrots. Nothing fancy."

"I suppose it must take a lot of work to keep it looking so neat."

"Oh yes." Reg looked Dan in the eye. "Can I help you with something?"

"No. I just wanted to have a look around." An impressive wooden shed stood at one end of the plot, and Dan gestured toward it. "Is that your shed? The one with the door that needed fixing?"

"Yes."

"It's huge. What do you keep inside?"

"Tools. My rotavator. Wheelbarrow. Nothing interesting."

"I've been thinking about getting a shed for my back garden." Dan took a step closer to the shed. "Do you mind if I take a look inside?"

"Yes, I do mind, as it happens. That shed is my private property, and I don't like folk poking their noses around inside, thank you very much."

That touched a nerve, Dan decided. Spreading his hands, he said, "Okay. I understand. I didn't mean to cause any offence."

"That's as may be. But if it's all the same to you, I've got a lot of work to do, and I'd like to get on with it. You can walk around the allotments if you want, but I'd stay on the paths if

225

I were you. People don't like folks trampling about over their plots."

"That goes without saying."

"You'd think so, wouldn't you? But it isn't always so."

"I'll be careful," Dan said. "But before I go, would you mind pointing out George's plot to me?"

"Why?"

Dan was about to admit that he wasn't sure, but then it came to him: the fragment of memory he'd been trying to recall for some time. "It's something you said yesterday. You told me that George had got rid of some fruit bushes for no good reason, and you seemed to think it was a strange thing to do."

"It was a bit odd, I suppose."

"And when did he do it?" Dan asked.

Reg looked doubtful.

"From the state of your plot, I'm guessing that you're here almost every day," Dan added. "Is that right?"

"I'm here most days."

"And you have a keen eye for these things, so you would've noticed when it happened."

"All right. I reckon it was Sunday."

"The day George was stabbed."

Reg nodded.

"Could you show me his plot?"

"If you insist, it's over there, down at the end. Third one along." Reg pointed, and Dan counted off the plots.

"Thanks. I'll go and have a look."

"Suit yourself." Reg went back to his digging, pushing the spade's blade into the soft earth. "But watch your step. There's compost all over the path. He made a right mess."

"Okay, I'll be careful. Bye."

If Reg replied Dan didn't hear it; he was already marching along the path.

He reached George's plot in a matter of seconds, and he stood still, taking in the carnage.

At least a dozen bushes had been uprooted and flung across the plot, their branches broken, their roots laid bare. They hadn't even been placed in a pile but lay scattered as if thrown.

I knew it, Dan thought. *I bloody well knew it!* Because the neat, raised bed where the bushes had grown was not filled with ordinary soil, but with dark compost, and as Reg had warned, the stuff had been spread right across the plot and onto the adjoining paths. Squatting on his haunches, Dan plucked a chunk of compost from the ground, teasing it apart on his palm. "Pine needles," he murmured. And then he stood and headed back to the gate, already taking his phone from his pocket.

He'd stored the number in his contacts, and by the time he reached the road, his call had been answered.

"DS Spiller," Dan said, "I have some information for you."

"Go on," Spiller replied.

Dan hesitated. "Have you spoken to George yet?"

"No. And more than that, I will not say."

"Does that mean he's still sedated?"

"Mr Corrigan, you don't know how to take no for an answer, do you?"

"I'm just concerned for George," Dan said. "Surely, you can give me an idea of how he's doing."

"All right. He's stable, but they're keeping a close eye on him," Spiller said. "Now, what's this information you mentioned?"

"I know where Billy was on the night George was stabbed."

"So do I. Ironbrand Farm."

"No. He was somewhere else. And you'll be able to prove it. Listen for a second, and I'll tell you the whole story."

Perhaps Spiller caught the certainty in Dan's tone, and he didn't interrupt while Dan explained. Finally, he said, "I see."

"What do you think? Worth following up?"

"Yes," Spiller admitted. "Let's hope Billy's sister hasn't disposed of the shoes. Everything hangs on that."

"If she was going to throw them away, she would've done it before now. They're New Balance. Quite expensive. She was being careful to dry them out."

"Hm. Interesting."

"You sound suspicious," Dan said. "For what it's worth, I don't think Gemma was hiding the shoes deliberately. She had no idea of their significance."

"That's for me to determine."

"Okay, but you'll take the shoes in for testing, won't you?"

"Definitely. There's a chance they'll prove he was at Ironbrand Farm."

"I'd be very surprised about that," Dan said. "But just out of interest, will you be able to find soil traces even though the shoes have been washed?"

"Without doubt. Our experts can find the tiniest particles of soil, and then there's the pollen and even spores. People often try to wash clothes to get rid of evidence, but it doesn't work. They might look clean to the naked eye, but in my experience, the washing machine tends to work all the tiny particles into the fabric. They'll take the shoes apart, look inside the seams and so on. It takes a while, and it's also very expensive."

Dan heard the irritation in Spiller's voice and pictured him bridling. Tempting as it was to push him further, Dan held back; he needed to keep him sweet. "Since I've helped you out, how about a little information in return?"

"Such as what? You know I can't go into details. This is an ongoing investigation."

"I understand. But I'm assuming that you've finished with

the crime scene, so it can't hurt to tell me about it. Where was George attacked?"

There was a pause before Spiller replied. "We found evidence of bloodstains in the herb garden at the back of the house. It's a short distance from the kitchen door."

"He must've been gathering herbs. George likes to forage for natural ingredients."

"That's speculation, but it's not unreasonable."

"And he was stabbed with his own knife, so he probably took it outside himself."

"I can't confirm that."

"I can," Dan said. "The knives George uses are very distinctive. I saw one of them at the May Fair, and don't forget, I saw the one sticking out of his chest. I recognised it immediately as belonging to the same set. They're very expensive, and I doubt whether he'd have allowed anyone else to use them."

"More speculation. Anyone can pick up a knife."

"Were there any fingerprints on it?"

"The victim's, but that was about it," Spiller admitted. "More's the pity."

"Not even partial prints?"

"You've been watching too much CSI. But no, there was nothing we could use."

"Was there any sign of a struggle?"

"I know what you're thinking," Spiller said. "You're going to say that George got into a fight and his own knife was used against him."

"Well? Is that possible? Were there footprints? What kind of path is it?"

"Calm down, Mr Corrigan. The path is made from stone slabs, so we couldn't get much from it. No footprints, no sign of a struggle."

"But there was some blood."

"Yes, and I've already said more than I should have, so I'll say goodbye, Mr Corrigan. Thanks for letting me know about the shoes. I'll chase that up."

"Before you go, how's Billy holding up?"

Spiller grunted in disapproval. "You needn't worry about him. He knows the ropes, and he knows the custody clock is ticking. If we can't find enough evidence to charge him, we'll have to let him go. All we've had out of him so far is 'No comment.'"

"Perhaps that's because he's innocent."

"No comment," Spiller replied, then he ended the call.

CHAPTER 30

A LAN HAD TRIED to get some writing done. Really, he had. But the words wouldn't flow, and in the end, he'd taken a break for tea and toast. His snack finished, Alan picked up his newspaper and idly skimmed the pages, but he wasn't taking anything in. *Concentrate*, he told himself, but he couldn't summon enough enthusiasm to read about the problems of the world; there was too much happening on his doorstep.

Alan found the crossword. That ought to distract him for a while, but he stared at the obscure clues, uncomprehending. *What a load of nonsense*, he thought. *There must be something more useful I could be doing.* He tossed his paper aside. Maybe he should call on Dan, see if there'd been any developments. He stood, but before he could grab his jacket, someone knocked on his front door, and he hurried to see who'd come calling.

He found Gemma waiting outside. "Hello," Alan said. "This is a surprise."

But Gemma did not return his smile. Instead, she moved close, and when she spoke, her voice was heavy with suppressed emotion. "Can I come in? I need to talk to you."

"Of course." Alan stepped back and Gemma hurried past him.

The door to the kitchen stood open, and Gemma stood on the threshold. "In here?"

"Sure. Go ahead."

Gemma disappeared into the kitchen, and Alan took a moment to straighten his shirt. He ran his hand along his jawline, checking for stubble. Thankfully, he'd made himself reasonably presentable this morning, but his checked shirt and walking trousers were by no means smart. *You'll do*, he told himself, then he sauntered into the kitchen.

Gemma was standing by the table, distractedly looking around the room as though she wasn't sure how she'd come to be there.

"Have a seat," Alan said. "Can I get you anything? Coffee perhaps?"

"No. Thank you, but no." Gemma pulled out a chair and sat at the table, her posture upright, but her gaze fixed on the middle distance, like someone waiting for their turn in a dentist's surgery.

Alan's usual chair was directly opposite her, but it felt too formal to face her across the table, so he took the seat next to her, and leaning slightly forward, he said, "You seem upset."

Gemma nodded. "I'm sorry to come here like this. I don't mean to drop all my problems in your lap, but I had to talk to someone, and I didn't know where else to turn."

"That's all right. I'm glad you came."

Gemma's smile was fleeting but grateful. "I feel like I'm going mad. The police came to my house this morning. It was awful."

"Okay," Alan said gently. "Take a deep breath then tell me all about it."

"I was catching up with some work, trying to get back to some kind of normality, when they came to the door. There were four of them. They came in, and they went through the whole house. It made me feel... I don't know. It's as if my home isn't my own anymore. I've done nothing wrong, but that doesn't seem to matter. They can barge in whenever they feel like it and take whatever they want."

"Was it an official search? Did they have a warrant?"

"Yes, to both questions. They knew exactly what they were looking for. They started with Billy's shoes, then they went upstairs and went through every room."

"His shoes? The ones he'd washed?"

"Yes," Gemma said. "I explained what had happened, but they said it didn't matter. They're going to send them off to a lab somewhere. They gave me some paperwork, but I didn't even try to read it. It was like a bad dream."

Alan thought for a moment, choosing his words carefully, then he said, "Gemma, I hate to say this, but if they had a warrant, that probably means they're trying to get enough evidence to charge him with something. They must think they've got something to go on."

"Oh God," Gemma whispered. "That's what I was afraid of."

From the corner of his eye, Alan saw a shape pass his kitchen window, and a moment later, there was a knock at the back door.

Alan stood. "That'll be Dan."

"Oh. Should I leave?"

"No. Stay here for a while. Let's see what he makes of all this."

Alan opened the door and Dan bustled inside.

"I've got lots to tell you," Dan started, then he stopped short, blinking at Gemma. "Sorry, I didn't know you had company."

"Gemma's had a difficult morning," Alan said quickly. "The police have been to her house, and they had a search warrant."

"That was quick," Dan said. "I only called an hour ago."

Alan's expression froze. "Wait. Was this something to do with you?"

"Yes. I called Spiller and set things in motion."

"So you knew *an hour ago* that this was going to happen, but you've only just thought to tell me?"

"I didn't expect them to be so fast," Dan said. "And I had a few things I needed to check. I've been doing some research online, and you know how the time goes when you start trawling through the internet."

Alan lifted his chin. "If you'd come to me first, I could've helped with all that. That's what I usually do."

"I didn't even think about it."

"No. That's the problem."

"Look, I'm sorry if I've trodden on your toes," Dan said. "But let's concentrate on what's important." He turned to Gemma. "Did they take Billy's shoes?"

Gemma nodded.

"Excellent."

"I beg your pardon," Gemma said. "It was far from excellent. It was a horrible experience."

"But it's fine," Dan replied. "It's nothing to worry about."

Alan raised a finger. "Have a little consideration, Dan. Gemma has just been through a very traumatising experience. You'd better explain yourself, but I'm warning you, tread carefully."

"It's funny you should say that." Dan grinned, but his smile quickly withered beneath the force of Alan's glare. He held up his hands. "Is it okay if I sit down? I've got a few things to tell you. It's just as well that you're here, Gemma, because you need to hear what I've got to say. But there's no need for you to be worried. I think you'll be pleased. Trust me."

"All right," Alan said. "But only if Gemma agrees."

Gemma's gaze lingered on Alan, then she nodded. "I'll be fine. Thank you for being so kind, Alan, but I need to pull myself together. Whatever happens next, I'll need to face it. So go ahead, Dan. There's no need to spare my feelings. I want to know the truth."

"Okay." Dan sat down, then speaking quickly, he explained what had happened to George's allotment.

"You think that's where Billy was on the night of the party?" Alan asked. "Couldn't it just be a coincidence?"

"No, it couldn't," Dan said. "I've found a witness who says that the damage was done on Sunday night. The soil tests will do the rest. Blueberry bushes need certain conditions; I looked it up as soon as I got home. They like damp, acidic soil, and George knew that. He was a keen gardener, so he put pine needles around the plants, and he probably watered them a lot. That's why the soil was damp enough to stick to Billy's clothes and his shoes. Billy was angry at George, and he wanted to hit back at him, so he trashed his allotment."

"Oh no." Gemma hung her head, her fingertips pressing against her forehead. "The stupid boy."

"Hang on a minute," Alan said. "Billy had just come out of prison. How would he have known about George's allotment?"

Gemma looked up. "They used to play there when they were kids. The allotment belonged to George's dad, but George liked to help his father, and they would let Billy join in. George was always keen on growing things, even back then. He was a sweet boy. When he was a teenager, he used to come around to the house, and he'd bring me bowls of raspberries he'd picked himself."

"Does the allotment still belong to George's father?" Alan asked.

"George's dad passed away years ago," Gemma replied. "But George took it over. He loved it there. He said it gave him time to think."

Dan narrowed his eyes, and Alan knew why. When

Gemma had spoken about George, her voice had grown soft, and a smile had played across her lips. She was fond of George, but perhaps her feelings ran deeper. *Should I ask her?* Alan thought. *I'm not sure if I want to know the answer.*

Dan, though, had no such qualms, and he tackled the question head on: "Gemma, what's the nature of your relationship with George?"

Gemma drew a sharp breath, but she recovered quickly, shaking her head as though rousing herself. "What do you mean?"

"Precisely what I say," Dan replied. "But let me make it plainer. At any point, have you and George been involved in a romantic relationship?"

"George is gay," Gemma protested.

"Even so, the question stands," Dan insisted.

Gemma's hand had crept to her chest, and she looked down, fussing over the top button of her blouse. "You're being ridiculous."

"And you're being evasive," Dan said. "What's the answer, yes or no?"

"No." Gemma met Dan's gaze. "George was a friend of the family. He took Billy under his wing, and we were grateful to him for that. Of course, that was before we knew about… the rest of it."

"And after Billy came out?" Dan prompted.

"That wasn't easy. It was a different time. And we weren't the kind of family to talk about anything like that. I think Billy felt left out, as though he'd been rejected. I've often thought I let him down."

"You did no such thing," Alan said. "You've given him a roof over his head. He's lucky to have you."

"Thank you." Gemma started to reach out to Alan, but then, changing her mind, she sighed and laid her hand in her lap.

Poor thing, Alan thought, fighting the urge to move closer and put his arm around her shoulders. *She's beating herself up.* He opened his mouth to say a few words of comfort, but Dan put his spoke in first.

"There's one thing bothering me," Dan said. "How could Billy have known that George had taken over the allotment?"

"Oh." Gemma bit the corner of her lower lip. "That might've been my fault. I visited Billy a few times when he was in prison, and I think I told him about George. I'd bumped into him when he was coming back from the allotments, and we got talking."

"Where did you see him?" Dan asked. "Your house is nowhere near the allotments."

Gemma shrugged. "I don't remember, exactly. I must've been out for a walk one day."

"Does it matter where it was?" Alan said. "The point is, Billy knew the allotment was precious to George, so when they fell out, he went over there to vandalise it. What else do you need to know? Nothing."

"You've got a point," Dan admitted. "The main thing is that we've given Billy an alibi for Sunday night. Unfortunately, he might see it differently. If he confesses to causing all that damage, he could be sent back to prison."

"But that doesn't make sense," Gemma said. "If all he's done is a bit of vandalism, why doesn't he admit to it? Surely, anything's better than having an attempted murder hanging over his head."

"According to Spiller, Billy knows the system," Dan replied. "He knows he can only be held for a certain time, and then they'll be forced to release him. They call it the custody clock, apparently, and it's rapidly running out. Meanwhile, Billy's been refusing to answer their questions. He just keeps saying 'No comment' over and over. He's gambling that the case against him will collapse and they'll have to let him go."

"Madness," Gemma muttered. "He's risking everything."

"Perhaps," Dan said. "But looked at another way, he's

making a smart move. Think about it. If he didn't stab George, then how can there be any real evidence against him? There can't. And I'm almost certain that he never even went to Ironbrand Farm."

"Almost?" Alan said.

"Yes. I can't be one hundred percent certain, but the soil from his shoes will prove it."

"But he washed the shoes," Gemma protested. "You know that."

Dan smiled. "It doesn't matter. Spiller's confident about that. He says the lab can find tiny particles of soil trapped in the fabric. No washing machine on earth could remove every trace. They can even collect spores and match them up to precise locations."

"Then why didn't they do that in the first place?" Alan asked.

"Because forensic tests take time and they're expensive," Dan replied. "And anyway, they didn't have all the pieces of the puzzle. When we came to your house, you told us that Billy had left his trainers in the machine, so they were out of sight when he was arrested. And Billy hasn't been cooperating, so until I called, the police didn't know he had another pair of shoes."

"But what if you're wrong?" Gemma demanded. "What if it backfires and they prove he was near the farm?"

"They won't," Alan said. "I know Dan tends to charge into these things like a bull at a gate, but he's generally right. This will work out for the best, trust me."

Gemma's cheeks tightened. "I don't know. I just don't know. The allotments aren't all that far from Ironbrand Farm. They might say that if he was angry enough to tear up those plants, he could've gone to the farm afterwards."

"I don't think so," Dan said. "But the forensic tests will put him in the clear. They'll be able to prove that he hasn't been to the farm. If he'd told them about his shoes in the first place, he'd probably have been released by now."

Gemma didn't look convinced. "I hope you're right, Dan. I really do." She sent Alan a rueful smile. "Thank you for everything, Alan, but I think I'd better go. I've taken up enough of your time." She stood, but as Alan made to follow suit, she laid her hand on his shoulder. "It's all right, I'll see myself out. I've been enough of a nuisance already. More than enough."

Alan started to protest, but she bent down and planted a prim kiss on his cheek. "Bye for now," she murmured, then she headed for the back door, letting herself out without a backward glance.

Alan and Dan stared at each other in silence.

"Well." Alan's hand went to his cheek. "She kissed me. I didn't expect that."

"Didn't you?"

Alan shook his head.

"I did. I've seen it coming all along," Dan said. He sat back, folding his arms. "And the damned thing is, I did all the work, but I didn't get so much as a thank you."

"That's because you have no manners, Dan."

"Or maybe I'm just not her type."

"Hm." Alan stood and went to the counter. "Tea?"

"Tea," Dan replied. "And then we've got some thinking to do. Because if Billy didn't stab George, we'd better figure out who did."

CHAPTER 31

S ITTING AT THE table in Alan's kitchen, Dan and Alan discussed the case, batting ideas back and forward. But after a while, Dan slapped his palm on the table in frustration. "We're getting nowhere. If we could just talk to George…"

"Is there any news on that front?" Alan asked. "Did Spiller tell you anything?"

"Not much. George is stable. But reading between the lines, it sounds as though they're keeping him sedated. I guess it's going to take him a while to recover."

"Poor chap. At least he's young and fit."

"Meanwhile, whoever did this is still free. They could be wandering around the village, even now."

"You're assuming it's somebody local," Alan said. "Can we be sure of that?"

"No, but I still think there must be some connection between George and the person who attacked him. It makes sense to focus on the locals. Someone around here holds the key to solving this case. Somebody must have seen or heard something, and they might not have realised its significance, but it could help us to piece the whole thing together. The clues will be there; we just have to find them."

"Easier said than done." Alan sat back, his hand on his stomach. "Before we go any further, do you fancy a spot of lunch? I don't know about you, but I'm ready for it."

"Okay. What've you got?"

"I dare say we could knock up a sandwich or two. I've got plenty of salad and a loaf of bread. I've even got a lump of that vegan cheese. I didn't take to it, so it needs eating."

"That sounds ideal," Dan said. "Shall I give you a hand?"

"It's all right. I'll chuck everything on the table, and we can make our own sandwiches." Alan went over to the fridge and began sorting through it, selecting items one at a time and placing them in the centre of the table.

A few minutes later, as he assembled his sandwich, Dan said, "We should go up to Brandle Wood."

Alan had already taken a bite from his sandwich, but he chewed laboriously, then he said, "Why? What would we be looking for?"

"Well, we know that George was there to gather blossom, and it's close to Ironbrand Farm. There could be a connection."

"It couldn't hurt to retrace his steps, I suppose. But we've already been on one wild goose chase through a forest. I can't say I'm looking forward to another."

"Do you have a better idea?" Dan asked.

Alan took another bite from his sandwich, looking thoughtful as he chewed. "Hm."

"What?"

"I was just thinking that this sandwich is a bit dry. I need a drink to wash it down." Pushing back his chair, Alan went to the sink and filled a glass with water. "Do you want one?"

"Please."

Alan returned to the table, carrying two glasses of water, and as he retook his seat, he said, "You know, you could've been much more tactful in the way you broke the news to Gemma, but…"

"But what?"

"I have to admit that you did pretty well to figure out where Billy was on Sunday night. Blueberries and pine needles. I wouldn't have seen the connection."

"It was a fluke. If I hadn't bumped into Reg in the shop, I'd never have gone to the allotments."

"It was more than that," Alan stated earnestly. "You listened to your intuition, and it paid off. Once Billy is released, Gemma will appreciate everything you've done."

"Thanks. But I know that tone. You're going into teacher mode, and I'm about to get a lesson. So come on, Mr Hargreaves, let's hear it."

Alan smiled. "You may have found an important clue this morning, but it will only mean something when the forensic team get their hands on it. We don't have those resources. We could march around Brandle Wood all day and be none the wiser. Even if we find some fragment of evidence, we won't be able to prove where it came from, and we can't expect the police to analyse every scrap of rubbish we come across."

"I know that. But you think I'm getting carried away, don't you?"

"The thought had crossed my mind," Alan admitted. "It seems like you're on a roll, determined to chase down every lead. But I think we need to be more focused."

"So, where would you start?"

"I think we ought to go back to Ironbrand Farm," Alan said. "And this time, we should insist on speaking to Scott."

"We could combine the two. A quick walk through the wood to see if we can find where George was picking flowers, and then we could go on to the farm."

Alan sighed. "I can see it's no use trying to talk you out of it, so after lunch, we'll don our walking boots and head to the wood." He grinned. "And don't forget to bring your magnifying glass and deerstalker."

"Very funny."

They finished lunch quickly, then Dan popped home to change into his walking boots. He'd learned the hard way that on the subject of appropriate footwear at least, it was best to heed Alan's advice.

ENTERING THE COOL shade of Brandle Wood, Dan and Alan made their way through the gate.

"Same path as last time?" Alan asked.

"Sure. Why not?"

Alan set off at a good speed and Dan kept pace, sometimes following and sometimes, when the path was wide enough, at Alan's side. As they walked, Dan noticed a myriad of minor paths that branched out in all directions, but most of them looked as though they might peter out long before they led anywhere. Fortunately, Alan seemed to know where he was going, and Dan was content to let him lead.

After a few minutes of walking, Dan spotted a bush dotted with white blossom, and he pointed. "Is that it?"

Alan didn't even break his stride. "No, that's hawthorn. Similar, but no cigar."

"What's the difference?"

"The leaf shape, for one thing. Hawthorn has lobed leaves, but the blackthorn has a slightly serrated edge. And the blossom itself is different, too. On the hawthorn, the blossom is flatter, and the petals are more widely spaced. Do you want to go over and take a closer look anyway?"

"No. George would've known exactly what he was looking for. He wouldn't want to use the wrong plant."

"Agreed. Foragers tend to be very knowledgeable. You have to know your stuff, or you could easily poison yourself."

"Or somebody else. And that would've been disastrous for his business."

"He wouldn't have had much difficulty finding

blackthorn," Alan said. "It's very common. But that makes life difficult for us."

"Ade was near to his tent when he saw George. All we have to do is find their campsite, and we can work from there." He paused to look around. "The problem is, I'm not sure I can remember where it was."

"I can. No problem. We're heading in the right direction."

They walked on, Alan leading them away from the path and deeper into the wood. But it wasn't long before Alan halted, gesturing to a hollow in the ground. "Told you. That's where the tent was."

"Excellent." Dan turned on the spot, scanning the surrounding trees and shrubs, but Alan beat him to it.

"Got it." Alan pointed into the distance. "Over there. At least I think so. Let's go and check." Alan marched into the undergrowth, and Dan followed, peering ahead. He could make out several bushes bearing blossom, but they all looked pretty much the same to him.

Dan made heavy work of trudging through the treacherous tangle of bracken and brambles, but he pressed on.

"This way." Alan veered off to one side. "Look. There's a path. Perhaps George was following it."

"Let's see."

When they reached the path, Dan looked along the twin lines of bare earth that ran in parallel beside a dense hedge.

"It looks like we've reached the edge of Brandle Wood," Alan said. "Although, to be honest, I'm not sure what's on the other side of this hedge."

"Perhaps the track runs around the perimeter," Dan suggested. "It must be here for a purpose. There are definite tyre marks."

"Yes, but they're not big enough for a car. A quad bike? Quite a few farmers have them."

"Could be. I wonder if Sturridge has one."

"We could find out," Alan said. "At any rate, that's certainly a patch of blackthorn over there." He strode over to the hedge and plucked a leaf, holding it up to show Dan. "See?"

Dan nodded, then he turned to look back toward the hollow. "We don't know for certain where Ade was standing, but he saw George in the distance. I'd say we're in the right spot."

"Agreed. I wonder if George came into the wood this way. I presume it leads back to the lane, but I don't remember seeing a gate."

Dan smiled. "Then it must lead somewhere else. If we follow it back, we might find where George started."

"Hm. He could've picked up the path at any point, but it's worth a shot." Alan looked both ways along the path. "We don't know where he was coming from. It might be best if we split up, then we could cover both directions at once."

"We should stick together for now," Dan said. He was reluctant to admit it, but the tramp through the woods had thrown off his sense of direction. "Which way do you think George would've come?"

Alan pointed along the track. "That way takes us back toward the village. That's the best bet."

"All right. Let's try it." Dan brushed past Alan and set off along the track. He kept his gaze on the ground, but the bare earth was packed hard and there were no footprints, only the ridged tracks of rugged tyres. "Do you know much about quad bikes?" Dan called over his shoulder.

"Not a lot. Why?"

"These tyre tracks seem too narrow to me. I thought quad bikes had quite wide wheels."

"You're right," Alan replied. "These tracks are positively dinky."

"*Dinky?* That's a word you don't hear much anymore."

"All right, I'm old fashioned, but when you're a writer,

you never use two words when one would do. And for these tracks, *dinky* is perfect."

Dan was about to reply, but a distant shout made him stop and turn around. "Did you hear that?"

"It came from over there. On the left."

"Yes." Dan tilted his head to listen, but all he could hear was the low rumble of an engine, and the sound seemed to drift around him from several directions at once.

"That's probably a tractor," Alan said. "We must be getting close to the lane."

"Let's go on. We'll see what we can see."

They resumed their journey along the narrow track, moving more carefully now, their heads turning from side to side. The sound of voices grew louder.

"That doesn't sound like English to me," Alan said, keeping his voice low. "I could be wrong though. I can't quite make it out."

"No, you're right." Dan stopped walking. "We are allowed to be here, aren't we? I mean, people walk here all the time, don't they?"

"Well, strictly speaking, we should've stuck to the bridle path. This is private land, and it's enclosed. The right to roam only covers open countryside."

"We'd better be careful then. We might have to duck out of sight."

"Okay."

They crept forward, staying close to the hedge, and then Dan saw where the path led. The five-bar gate was closed and secured with a thick chain. Beyond it, Dan had expected to see a lane, but the track continued across an expanse of grass.

"Of course," Alan said. "I should've known. We've been heading toward Ironbrand Farm."

"Bingo," Dan muttered. "This is the connection we've been waiting for."

"Meaning what exactly?"

"Follow me, and we'll find out."

Dan edged toward the gate, Alan close behind.

"Blimey," Alan murmured. "I had no idea."

"They're enormous."

The field was huge, the ground flat, and stretching across it, row upon row of tall polythene-covered arches snaked into the distance.

"I've never seen such massive polytunnels," Alan said. "I had no idea they were here. You'd think you'd be able to see them from miles away."

"They've been carefully screened by the hedges; deliberately tucked out of sight."

"That's understandable. They'd be all right if they weren't so big. But these… They're a blot on the landscape."

"I wonder what they're for," Dan said. "It must be something worth growing. It must've cost a fortune to set them all up."

"We can ask Scott when we see him."

Dan clicked his fingers. "I've just remembered. Harry mentioned the polytunnels, right after George was stabbed. When we called the air ambulance, Harry said he hoped the helicopter wouldn't blow them away."

"Ah yes, so he did." Alan pointed along the hedge. "Look. I expect that's what made the tracks."

Dan spotted a curious little buggy sitting near the edge of the field. Alan was probably right; the buggy had small wheels, and it looked the right size to have made the tracks. But there was no one in the cab, and it had been left facing the hedge at an odd angle, as if it had been abandoned rather than parked.

"Sh!" Dan jumped back, pushing Alan out of the way.

"What's that in aid of?" Alan grumbled.

"Someone coming."

Keeping low, Dan leaned forward, pushing a branch aside so that he could peep through the hedge.

In the field, a group of four men emerged from one of the polytunnels and trudged across the field. More figures appeared from the other tunnels, forming a sizeable group of men and women, perhaps thirty or so, all walking in the same direction, and moving slowly, as though their limbs were heavy.

"It must be lunchtime for the workers," Dan said. Predicting their path, he spied a cluster of static caravans. He glanced back at Alan. "Come and see."

Alan crept to Dan's side. Meanwhile, the gaggle of workers dispersed, a few heading to each caravan. "I suppose that's where they live while they're working," Alan said. "I've heard about this. Lots of crops are picked by seasonal workers from abroad. But I didn't know it was happening on my doorstep."

"Doesn't that strike you as odd? You'd think we'd have seen them around the village."

"It does seem a little strange. But I suppose it's a sensitive issue. Especially with Brexit. People can be very small minded about migrant workers."

"Hm." Dan stepped back and Alan followed suit. They shared a look.

"Did George make the same discovery, do you think?" Dan asked.

"It's a distinct possibility. And that would give us a connection between him and Ironbrand."

"It gives us a thread, certainly. But where it leads, I'm not sure." Dan thought for a moment. "At the party, Jocelyn made some remark about Scott hiring too many workers. She mentioned immigration, but I put it down to snobbery. Maybe there was more to it than that."

"You think there's something fishy going on?"

"There could be. Do you remember the man who served us champagne? Marco."

"Of course," Alan said. "You thought he wasn't really

Italian. But why would he lie about it?" As soon as the question left Alan's lips, his face fell. "It's obvious, isn't it? They're here illegally."

"We don't know that," Dan said slowly. "But something isn't right. And if George discovered the truth, someone might've had good reason to silence him."

"So what do we do?"

"We can't just march up to the farm and start asking questions," Dan said. "We need a plan."

"Agreed. Let's head back home and figure something out."

"Good idea."

"Shall we reconvene at my house?"

"We'll go to mine," Dan replied. "I have better coffee. And frankly, I think we're going to need it."

CHAPTER 32

THE AROMA OF freshly brewed espresso filled Dan's kitchen.

Sitting at the table, Dan and Alan sipped from their tiny cups in reverential silence. Then they sighed.

"That's good," Dan said.

"Damned good." Alan set his cup down on the table. "When do my eyeballs start spinning?"

"Give it time."

"Maybe you should invite Scott over here and pump him full of caffeine. That ought to get him talking."

"He wouldn't come. But you might be on to something. We need to get him out of his castle; somewhere where he can't hide behind his minions. Neutral territory."

"We could invite him to the pub," Alan suggested. "That's about as neutral as it gets. And we know he likes a drink. He might relish the chance to slip out for a pint."

Dan shook his head. "Have you ever seen Scott in the local pub?"

"No. He probably thinks it's beneath him."

"Exactly. We need somewhere that appeals to his innate snobbery."

"There are plenty of places you could wine and dine him."

"I'd already thought of that," Dan said. "But I'm not sure I can afford to invite him to the kind of restaurant he'd like."

"I could—"

"No," Dan interrupted. "Anyway, fine dining isn't the answer. We need to find somewhere informal, put him at his ease. Ideally, we need to offer him something he can't resist. I wonder what his passions are."

"Hunting, shooting and fishing, I expect. Fox hunting is illegal, and pheasants are out of season. That leaves us with fishing."

"I wouldn't know where to start," Dan said.

"I do. I've been known to flick a dry fly at the water, and you could learn."

"I don't think that would work."

"Why not? Early May is an ideal time. They call it *duffers' fortnight* on the chalk streams. There are so many mayflies hatching, they reckon anyone can catch a trout or two."

"Me, fishing? I don't think so."

"But you eat fish, so you ought to know where it comes from. Surely, that's consistent."

Dan was stumped.

"I say we should give it a go," Alan went on. "I have all the gear we'd need, and if we invite Scott up to Kennick for a day's trout fishing, he'll be there like a shot."

"It's nice by the reservoirs," Dan mused. "I've been up there a few times for a run. But you must need a permit or something. Isn't it a bit expensive?"

"Not for a day ticket. You need a rod licence as well, but that doesn't cost much, and you can get one online."

"I don't know," Dan said. "I suppose it might work. A bit of male bonding, a friendly chat and Scott might let his guard down."

"Absolutely. Three blokes fishing together. What could be more natural?"

"Hm. I'm not sure Scott sees himself as a *bloke*. Come to that, neither do I."

"Come on, Dan. Lighten up. You know it's a good idea."

"He'll probably be an expert. He'll see right through us."

"That's easily dealt with," Alan argued. "We'll tell him that you're a beginner, and he'll relish the chance to show off his skill. Besides, trout fishing isn't usually a competitive sport."

"Isn't it? Don't you weigh the fish or something? See who can catch the biggest?"

"There are some official competitions, but most of us are amateurs, content to have a go."

Dan pictured the scene: the three of them chatting as they fished. He'd seen people fly fishing on TV plenty of times, and something about the idea appealed to him: the play of light on the water, the gentle rhythm of the rod, and the arc of the line floating through the air in perfect loops. And it could provide them with the ideal opportunity to wheedle information out of Scott.

"All right," Dan said. "It makes more sense if you call him. Explain that you're taking me out to show me the ropes, then invite him along. If he's interested, try and arrange it for tomorrow."

Alan took out his phone. "Give me his number, and I'll see what I can do."

Dan provided Scott's details, and Alan made the call. He looked at Dan and mouthed, "Voicemail," then he left a message and hung up. "Okay?"

"Perfect," Dan said. "You hit the right tone. All we can do now is wait."

Alan jumped to his feet. "I'll toddle off home. I can be getting on with some work. If Scott calls, I'll let you know."

"Perhaps we ought to be making some preparations."

"It won't take me long to get the gear ready, and it only takes two minutes to buy a licence. We can take care of all that later. I want to crack on with some writing." Alan grinned. "My fingers are itching for the keys. It must be that espresso."

"Don't get too hooked on it. You'll give yourself the jitters."

"Nonsense. I'll see you later. Bye." Alan headed for the door, and Dan was left sitting alone in the kitchen.

What am I getting myself into? he thought. And it wasn't the prospect of fly fishing that worried him. If Scott was deliberately employing illegal immigrants on his farm, then the stakes were high. Scott could face prison, and what would become of the workers? Would they be deported, or would they wind up in a detention centre? Dan had their fate in his hands. Should he call Spiller? Not yet. All he had were suspicions. He could be making a monumental leap in the dark. Yes, George had been stabbed, and there must have been some motive for that crime. But there was no evidence to connect the attack with anyone at Ironbrand. And for all he knew, the farmworkers were legitimately employed.

I can't stand by and do nothing, Dan decided. *I need to know what's going on.* And whatever he uncovered, he'd have to live with the consequences.

CHAPTER 33

PAUL SCARCELY SAW the houses and gardens flit past as he drove into Embervale, his old Ford Mondeo running smoothly for once. This place! God, he was sick of it. He'd been forced to stay late at work, watching the clock while he'd compiled last month's accounts for head office.

Along with the other reps, he sold satellite broadband, and the accounting system kept track of every transaction. A ten-year-old kid could've run the reports. It didn't matter if you had no idea what the figures meant. Did the morons at head office even read the damned reports? Probably not. The whole thing had been a waste of time.

There was only one good thing about working at DevonSat, and that was the customer database. He had full access to the names and addresses of everyone who wanted faster internet access and was prepared to pay for it. It was almost too good to be true.

But even so, he spent most of his working day making sales calls, sticking to the script, going out of his mind with boredom and frustration. And what did he have to come back to? A crappy little village where nothing ever happened.

Literally *nothing*. He was still living with his parents, for God's sake. He should've moved on by now, found himself a flat in a town somewhere, anywhere with a bit of life. He should be making money, meeting new people, having a laugh. He should be doing *something* with his life.

But here he was, stuck in a rut before he'd even got started, working in the same little office every day, and handing over most of his wages to his mum and dad for housekeeping. It was no wonder he'd taken to conning the local baby boomers out of a few quid. How else was he supposed to get enough money to get out of this place? And it wasn't like he was doing much harm. With their huge houses and their new cars, the old fools could afford to lose a bit of money without even breaking a sweat. A thousand pounds was nothing to them. A hundred pounds was loose change. But to him, every penny made a difference. Each pound he squirrelled away was another step on the road that led out of Embervale forever. Soon, he'd be ready.

But where the hell was Daisy? He had to find her. If she'd made a mistake, everything could fall apart.

"Stupid cow," he muttered. "Bloody useless."

Paul pressed the accelerator. It was early evening, and as usual, Fore Street was deadly quiet. No one about. Not a soul. Except for a single person: a lone figure shambling along the street.

Paul hit the brakes and turned the wheel, sending the Mondeo to a grinding halt at the side of the road. And then he was out of the seat and running, his shiny black shoes slapping against the pavement. "Hey!" he yelled. "Stop!"

Ahead, the figure stopped and turned.

Paul's footsteps faltered. He knew the man in front of him was Reg Stoddard, but he seemed different, a scowl transforming his features into a stony mask.

"What do you want?" Reg barked.

Paul jogged closer, squaring up to Reg. "Where is she?"

"Who?"

"You know who. Daisy. Where is she?"

Reg shook his head. "Who do you think you are, shouting at me in the street? You've got no business bothering me, so bugger off."

"Come off it, Reg—"

"Mr Stoddard, to you."

"Fine. Mr Stoddard. Whatever. You've got to tell me where Daisy is."

"How should I know?"

"Because…" Paul fought to find the right words. "Because you're family, and Daisy looks up to you. She's always talking about you."

Reg remained tight lipped.

"Please," Paul went on. "I'm worried about her. I don't know where she's gone, and it's doing my head in."

"You should've thought about that before you dragged her into your thieving."

Paul stared. "What?"

"You heard me," Reg growled. "I know what you've been doing. By rights, I ought to set the police on you. But unlike you, I don't want to see her in trouble."

"I don't know what you're talking about. I don't know what she's told you, but it's not true."

Reg moved close to Paul. "Don't waste your breath, lad. Daisy told me all about it. You ought to be ashamed of yourself, and not just on account of what you've stolen. You could've got Daisy hurt."

"No. She was never in danger."

"Of course she was, you bloody idiot! That man came to her house, and he threatened her, right there in her own home."

"Who? Who threatened her?"

"Denton," Reg snapped. "He found out what the pair of

you were trying to do at Ironbrand Farm, and he used it against her."

The blood drained from Paul's face. "Oh my God. What did he do to her?"

"Nothing. Not yet. Daisy had the good sense to get out of there. She's made herself scarce, and just in time. Who knows what he would've done to her? A man like that, he could do anything."

"Denton. I don't know him."

"And he doesn't know you, so you'd best keep it that way," Reg said.

"Daisy didn't give me up?"

Reg shook his head. "Denton reckoned she was put up to the job, paid by someone who wanted to spy on Benning and the rest of them. Daisy went along with it, spun him a tale."

"Bloody hell," Paul breathed. "What a mess."

"You've got that right. But it's no use standing around and complaining about it. You got her into this mess; how are you going to get her out of it?"

"I don't know. I'll think of something."

"You'd better. Because I've met Denton, and I know the type. He's like a dog with a bone. He won't let it drop just because Daisy's disappeared for a while. He'll go looking for her, and he won't give up until he finds her."

"I'll stop him," Paul blurted. "I won't let him hurt her. I'll smash his head in."

Reg snorted. "Don't be stupid. You're not in the playground now, sonny. You'll have to come up with something better than that. Denton isn't daft. Sooner or later, he'll put two and two together, then he'll come after you. He'll find you fast enough."

"It doesn't matter. He can go to the cops, but it'll be his word against mine. I was careful. They can try, but they won't get anything on me. I'm clean."

"Denton won't go to the police. If he was going to do that,

he'd have done it by now." Reg looked Paul in the eye. "Get this into your thick head: Denton is an evil bastard. I know what goes on at that farm, and believe me, you don't want to tangle with him."

"Huh! I've seen Benning and his posh mates. They don't scare me."

"Then you're even thicker than I thought."

"I've had enough of this," Paul snapped. "You don't get to stand there and call me stupid."

"Is that right?"

Paul didn't see Reg move, but suddenly the old man's hands were on him, grasping him tight by the arms.

"Listen to me," Reg snarled. "Those people have deep pockets, and they know how to get their own way. They'll come calling for you, and you'll regret the day you crossed them. Do you understand?"

"Bugger off."

"Do you understand?" Reg demanded.

"All right. I get it. Just get off me."

Reg glared at Paul for a second, then he released him and stepped back. "Keep out of my way, lad. And stay away from Daisy. Don't even try to find her, not unless you've fixed Denton first."

Paul glowered at him, biting back his words.

"I mean what I say," Reg went on. "Make this right, or you'll have me to answer to as well." He turned away and started walking, crossing the road and heading for the pub.

Paul watched him disappear into the Wild Boar, then he stalked back to his car, climbing inside and slamming the door. *Bastard!* Paul thought, then he started the engine and drove away, the Mondeo's worn tyres squealing on the tarmac.

This bloody place! Paul stared out through the windscreen, his jaws clenched tight enough to crack a tooth. Why did everything have to go wrong? Why did everything have to turn to shit?

"I'll pay them all back for this," he muttered. "Every one of them. They'll get what they deserve."

WEDNESDAY

CHAPTER 34

F OR THE SHORT journey up to Kennick reservoir, Alan
drove and Dan sat quietly, watching the scenery slide
past as Alan's VW Golf bowled along the hedge-lined lanes.
They'd arranged to meet Scott at the lake, and Dan wanted to
mentally prepare for the encounter. *He'll want to keep his cards
close to his chest,* Dan decided. *I'll have to tread carefully, let him
think he can relax.* Still, it shouldn't be too difficult to handle
Scott. Dan had dealt with more swaggering business types
than he cared to remember. But why had a sense of
foreboding settled on his shoulders? He glanced at Alan, who
was humming under his breath as he drove along. Alan was
in his element, looking forward to a few hours by the water.
But then, when they arrived at the lake, Alan would know
what he was doing.

I shouldn't have agreed to this, Dan thought. *I'm going to look
a fool.* But it was too late to back out now. Alan was turning
off the road, slowing the car as he took them onto a rough
rectangle of uneven gravel.

"We're here," Alan said. "Are you all set?"

"Sure," Dan replied. "I'm as ready as I'll ever be."

The only other vehicle in the car park was a mud-spattered black Range Rover, and as Alan parked beside it, its door opened and Scott climbed out and lifted his hand in greeting. Dan saw someone in the Range Rover's passenger seat, but they were facing away, perhaps retrieving something from the back seat, and he couldn't make out who it was.

"Who's that with him?" Dan asked Alan.

"I'm not sure. Let's go and find out."

They climbed out of the car and strolled across to meet Scott, then they exchanged a few brief words and even briefer handshakes. Already, Scott's smug superiority was on display, and as he cast a critical eye over Dan and Alan, he seemed to weigh them up and find them wanting. *So far, so predictable*, Dan thought. But when the Range Rover's passenger emerged, Dan tried to hide his surprise.

"Hello, Jocelyn," Alan said. "How nice to see you. Have you come along to watch?"

Jocelyn, looking relaxed and comfortable in her leisure gear, tented an eyebrow. "And miss the chance of a day's fishing? Certainly not." She eyed Dan's outfit. "Is that what you're wearing?"

"Yes." Dan looked down at his trousers and wellington boots. "I haven't got any waders, so I thought wellies would be all right."

"We'll be staying on the bank," Jocelyn said. "But we'll be on our feet all the time, and there's quite a lot of walking involved."

Dan smiled. "I'll be fine."

"I should've warned you," Alan said. "Sorry about that."

"Don't worry about it. As I said, I'll be fine."

"Okay." Alan hooked his thumb toward the car. "I'll go and get our gear." Alan bustled away, opening the Golf's boot and rummaging around inside.

Dan turned back to Jocelyn and found she was studying him with an amused glint in her eye. "What's so funny?" he said. "Should I have worn a special hat or something?"

Jocelyn shook her head, grinning. "It's you two. You're like an old married couple."

"Yes!" Scott guffawed. "That's it exactly, Joss. Nail on the head."

Dan humoured them with a fleeting grin. "Shall we get going? We don't want to keep the trout waiting."

"Oh, they can wait," Scott said. "They can wait all day and never show themselves, the slippery little sods."

Jocelyn pushed Scott playfully on the arm. "Don't put him off before he's begun, you bully."

Scott returned her smile, but his gaze flicked to the place where she'd pushed him, even though she'd barely made contact.

He didn't like that, Dan thought. *He sees himself as the alpha male, and he can't stand to be put down.* Dan stowed that insight away; it might well be useful later.

Breaking the turgid silence, Alan returned with a broad smile and his arms full of oddly shaped bags and plastic boxes. "Right. Let's get set up."

"We can do that when we find a good spot," Jocelyn said.

Alan's face fell. "I'd prefer to get ready before we go down to the water. I've got Dan's rod to set up as well as my own."

"Go ahead," Scott drawled. "I'm going to hop back in the car. I've got a couple of calls to make."

"Okay. This won't take me long," Alan said, but Scott was already climbing back into his Range Rover, slamming the door shut with a thump.

Alan looked to Jocelyn. "Have I offended him?"

"Who knows? But please, don't give it a second thought. He doesn't like to wait, that's all. My husband has many qualities but patience isn't one of them. Take whatever time you need, Alan. We'll be ready when you are."

"Right, Thanks." Alan smiled gratefully then held a long canvas bag out to Dan. "There's a rod in there. You'll need to slide the sections together. It's a ten-foot rod, but it's fairly forgiving so you should be able to handle it. It's my old one, but please be careful with it. Carbon fibre is flexible, but it can be damaged. I stood on a rod once — snapped it clean in two."

Dan took the bag and opened the top, untying the ribbon and unrolling the bag. Inside, the three lengths of rod nestled in their pockets, gleaming metal rings set along each one. And Dan had to admit that there was a certain elegance to the design. He took the thinnest piece out, and it weighed almost nothing. He waved his hand, and the rod whipped back and forth, almost as if it were alive. "Interesting," he said. "How do I fit them together?"

"You just line up the eyes — those are the metal rings — then you slide each section into the next."

"Isn't there a special catch or something?"

"Nope. They're made to fit perfectly. They won't come apart until you want them to."

"Okay." Dan assembled the rod, pleased with himself. This was all very easy. But he wasn't quite prepared for what followed. Alan took him through the procedure, and although attaching the reel was child's play, there was a lot of mucking around with lengths of line and elaborate knots. When Alan told him he had to spit on the knots before he pulled them tight, Dan almost laughed. But Alan wasn't pulling his leg, and it wasn't superstition; the saliva lubricated the nylon and helped the knots to form perfectly.

Finally, they were done, and they set off, Scott and Alan leading the way, Dan following, and Jocelyn bringing up the rear.

Dan plodded along the bank in his wellington boots, doing his best to keep up, and he could feel Jocelyn's eyes on him with every heavy step he took. It didn't help that his fishing rod was determined to slow him down. As Dan trudged over the uneven ground, the thin wand of carbon fibre wobbled alarmingly, its tip threatening to catch against the dense vegetation lining the path.

He shifted the rod from one hand to the other and somehow managed to snag a loop of his fishing line on a rhododendron bush. He yanked the rod, but the line had wrapped itself tight around something within the foliage, and it refused to come free. Holding the rod with one hand, he traced the line back into the bush with the other, muttering under his breath.

Jocelyn laughed, and Dan cast a disapproving glance over his shoulder.

"Sorry," Jocelyn said. "But I can't help thinking you're not cut out for this, Dan."

"It's a new experience, that's for sure." Dan found the leafy stem that was causing all the trouble. It was only thin, so he snapped it and removed it from the equation, allowing the line to slip free. "There. We'd better catch up with the others."

Jocelyn tilted her head to one side. "What's the rush?"

"No rush."

"Are you sure about that?" A smile curled the corner of Jocelyn's lips. "Are you sure you aren't a tiny bit worried about how it might seem? We've ducked out of sight behind a bush, you and me, and you're going to emerge looking rather flustered, aren't you?"

Dan felt the blood creeping up his neck. "No. I'm not flustered."

"How disappointing. I must be losing my charms."

"Not at all. You're a very attractive woman, but apart from the fact that you're married, you're completely out of my league."

Jocelyn laughed. "Good answer. I can see you're better at handling women than you are fly rods." She moved closer to him, taking hold of his fishing rod and angling it downward. "It's all in the grip. Be firm but gentle, and you'll be fine. Try to relax."

"I'll bear that in mind."

"Good." Jocelyn stepped back, breaking eye contact, then she peered along the path. "Now, where have those boys got to? We'd better find them before they hog all the best spots."

"Sure." Dan resumed his reluctant trudge along the path, and half turning, he said, "I would never have had you pegged as a fly fisher."

"Oh? Why's that? Did you have me pigeonholed as an empty-headed trophy wife?"

"No," Dan said, but Jocelyn wasn't listening.

"You know, that really is disappointing," she went on. "I thought you were a bit smarter than Scott's usual crowd, but perhaps I misjudged you. You're just like all the rest. You see a woman, and your first thought is to put her in her place."

"That's not true," Dan protested. "I didn't mean to offend you. It's just that I've never been fishing before, and my idea of the typical angler is a middle-aged man who wants an excuse to avoid DIY at the weekends."

"Well, you're wrong. Dead wrong."

They walked in silence for a while, then Jocelyn took a breath and said, "I'm sorry. I shouldn't have been so hard on you, but I get fed up with the way people see me as some kind of bimbo. They seem to think I'm a brainless woman who spends all her time shopping and preening herself. They might not say as much to my face, but I know what people are thinking. They all assume I married Scott for his money, but the truth is, it's the other way around. Scott came from a modest background, but my family have always been well off."

"Ah, does that explain your appreciation of vintage champagne?"

"You're doing it again," Jocelyn warned. "You're jumping to conclusions. Yes, I've had a privileged life, but it wasn't all fine wines and dinner parties and tiaras. I wasn't a spoiled brat. I was brought up to work hard, to better myself. I studied economics and management at Oxford, then I took an extra year to get my MBA. I've worked for some of the top companies in the world. Berlin, New York and London, of course."

"Impressive," Dan said. "I was based in London until I moved here. Perhaps we have some acquaintances in common."

"Possibly. But we won't talk shop. We've finally caught up with the others, and it looks like they've found a good place to start."

Jocelyn left the path, leading the way to an open stretch of grass beside the water, where Scott and Alan stood close together, deep in conversation as they stared out over the reservoir.

Alan turned around as Dan and Jocelyn approached. "There you are, Dan. What do you think of Kennick? Beautiful, isn't it?"

"It's impressive." Dan eyed the rippled surface. "It looks like the wind's getting up. It's quite exposed here. Maybe we should find somewhere a bit more sheltered."

Scott and Alan exchanged a pitying look.

"You'll need plenty of room to cast," Alan explained. "Believe me, when you're learning, the more space you have, the better."

"Definitely," Scott said. "This little breeze is nothing to worry about. It can be tough when there's a real gale blowing, but this is all right."

Jocelyn went to Scott's side, and he handed her a sleek leather cylinder without being asked. Jocelyn opened the case and began extracting slim sections of rod and fastening them together with practised ease. "I'll look after him. Why don't you two get started? We'll be fine here."

"Oh, I thought we'd stick together," Dan said.

Jocelyn arched an eyebrow. "You're not going to refuse my generous offer, are you?"

Dan glanced at Alan, but his friend offered only a sympathetic smile.

"My advice, Dan, is to stick with Joss," Scott said. "She's been doing this since she was a kid, and she's a first-rate teacher. She taught me everything I know, and I don't mind admitting it."

"Well, in that case, I'd be a fool to turn you down," Dan said to Jocelyn.

"Excellent. A wise decision." Scott pecked Jocelyn on the cheek, then he grinned at Alan. "Come on. Let's get cracking. The last one to bag a fish buys the drinks afterwards."

Alan nodded. "Count me in."

"I thought it wasn't competitive," Dan said. "I don't want to be a bad sport, but it's hardly fair."

Scott chortled. "This is just a bit of fun. And you never know, with my wife's excellent tuition, you might win."

"All right, I'll give it a go." Dan smiled, but he couldn't help noticing the mocking gleam in Scott's eye.

"May the best woman win," Jocelyn said. "Now, off you pop, you two. Dan and I have some serious work to do."

"I'll leave you in my wife's capable hands," Scott said to Dan. "But don't let her bully you too much, or she'll walk all over you."

Jocelyn flapped her hand at Scott, shooing him away. "Go. Poor Alan is champing at the bit."

"I'm in no hurry," Alan said. But his gaze slid sideways to the water, and he self-consciously adjusted his grip on his fishing rod. "Mind you, now that we're here…"

"Understood." Scott patted Alan on the arm, then they walked away, both men eying the water keenly.

Jocelyn laid her fishing rod carefully on the ground, then she stood, looking Dan up and down, her hands on her hips. "Right. Let's see you in action."

Dan smiled uncertainly. "Sorry?"

"There's no need to look so worried. I want to take you

through an overhead cast, then I'll see what I've got to work with." She nodded toward the reservoir. "Move down to the edge and we'll get started."

Dan did as he was told, following Jocelyn's instructions carefully as she explained how he should hold the rod, pointing it toward the water and flicking it gently to feed some line onto the surface. Then, under her watchful eye, he pulled some line from the reel and allowed it to lie on the ground at his feet.

"That's enough," Jocelyn said. "Now comes the hard part. I could let you try it on your own, but you'll only make a fool of yourself; everyone does the first time. It's much better if you let me help you, then you can feel what it's like when it's done properly."

"Okay."

Jocelyn stood close behind him, reaching around to hold his hands in hers. "With your left hand, you hold the line gently between finger and thumb like this. Just tight enough to stop it slipping through your fingers."

"What about all this line on the ground?"

"Patience. We'll come to that. Timing is everything." She tightened her grip on his right hand. "In a second, I'm going to bring your forearm up smartly, and then punch it forward. Imagine you're going to lift a hammer and then drive a nail into a wall in front of you."

"Got it. Ready when you are." Dan tried to keep his tone casual, but it wasn't easy when Jocelyn was standing so close. He could smell the heady musk of her perfume, and when she spoke, he wasn't sure whether it was the breeze or her breath that tickled the hairs on the back of his neck.

She shifted her grip on his right arm. "You're very stiff," she murmured.

"Am I? Sorry."

"If you're too tense, you'll never master it. You've got to relax, allow your muscles to move to the rhythm."

Dan tried for a careless chuckle, but his laughter sounded hesitant and nervous. "Are we fishing or dancing?"

"Oh, this is nothing like dancing, Dan. I'm a good dancer, but this is different. It's not an art, it's a primal urge to hunt, to survive. It's a craft. You have the tools in your hand, but you have to learn how to use them properly. You have to work at it. But first, you need to let me take control. Can you do that, Dan?"

"I'll try."

"Good. Whatever you do, don't cock your wrist. Treat the rod like it's an extension of your forearm. Do you understand?"

"I think so."

"Okay. Here we go." Jocelyn yanked his forearm upward and back, lifting the rod's tip and sending the line snaking through the air above their heads. Then she drove his arm forward, and as the line flew out across the water, she pinched his left hand. "Let it go."

Dan opened his fingers and the length of line coiled by his feet leaped upward and began sliding through the rod's eyes, tracing a straight line over the water.

"Gently lower the rod." Jocelyn guided his arm, and the length of line dipped toward the surface and touched down with a splash.

Dan smiled. "It worked."

"Not bad. Far too splashy. You'll frighten the fish if you keep doing that, but for a first effort, it was quite good." She let go of his arms and stood back. "Most people bend their wrists and end up hooking the trees behind them."

"I wouldn't have dared to make that mistake. Your instructions were *very* clear."

A sardonic tone had crept into Dan's voice, and Jocelyn didn't miss it. She sniffed, and when Dan looked back at her, she turned away, staring into the distance. "I'm not a complete monster, you know," she said. "I was trying to pay you a compliment."

"I'm sorry. I didn't mean to sound ungrateful. Honestly, I appreciate your help. You've been very kind."

She glanced at him. "Hm. You're forgiven. I don't think any woman could stay angry with you for long."

"You'd be surprised."

Jocelyn smiled. "And he has a sense of humour, too. How on earth are you still single?"

"Who says I am?"

"No one, but it's obvious just the same."

"So, what do we do now?" Dan asked. "About the fishing, I mean. Do we just wait?"

Jocelyn sighed. "You have to start retrieving the line. Here. Let me show you."

She stood at his side this time, pulling the line back through the eyes with a deft movement that formed the line into figures of eight in the palm of her hand. "And when you've retrieved enough line, you cast again."

"I see." Dan hesitated. "Jocelyn, do you mind if we just chat for a while?"

"It depends. About what?"

"The farm. The business."

Jocelyn shook her head. "I'm out of touch with all that."

"Really? I'd have thought that with all your expertise, you'd be helping to run the place."

"It doesn't interest me. It's small-time stuff."

"Even the plans for the solar farm?"

"That'll keep Scott out of my hair for a while, but in the scheme of things it's not a big deal." She gestured to the reservoir. "Are you going to try again?"

"In a minute. You mentioned that you worked in London. My area of expertise was start-ups, particularly in the high-tech sector. How about you?"

"Shipping. I was a consultant for a number of big companies. We shipped goods from all over the world, mainly in those huge container ships that get such a bad press nowadays." She smiled sadly. "People moan about the pollution, but with their next breath, they rattle on about their brand new gadget, boasting how they got it before anyone else. They just don't see the connection. What do they imagine — that their new TV floated all the way from China on its own?"

Dan dipped his chin to acknowledge her point. "And who are you working with at the moment?"

"No one. Not anymore. I'm taking a career break, assessing my options. I don't have to work, but I want to. I enjoy it." Jocelyn frowned. "But why do you want to know about the farm? Are you looking to invest?"

"No. I'm interested, that's all. I saw the polytunnels and wondered what they were used for."

"Fruit, I think. Strawberries. That type of thing."

"And the people who work there, are they local?"

"No, they're seasonal workers. Harry gets them from abroad. That's his job."

"What about Scott?"

"What about him?"

"Well, it's his farm, so he must be involved in hiring the staff."

"In the office, yes, but my husband doesn't like to get his hands dirty. He doesn't go tramping over the fields unless he's shooting pheasants." Jocelyn lowered her eyebrows. "Are you going to fish today?"

"Okay." Dan tried to repeat the movements she'd shown him, but he jerked the rod far too roughly, and the line whipped back and forth before landing on the water in an untidy tangle.

"Oh dear," Jocelyn intoned. "I don't know where to start with that one."

"It's harder than it looks. I can see the appeal, but as far as hobbies go, I think I'll stick with running."

"That might be for the best. Fishing is a passion for some, but I can see that your heart's not in it. I'm beginning to wonder if you contrived this whole outing just to pick Scott's brains."

"Guilty," Dan admitted. "At least on my part. Alan was genuinely keen, but I wanted to get to know Scott better."

"I don't believe you. You have an ulterior motive."

"What makes you say that?"

"I know your type," Jocelyn said. "You always have an objective. From the moment you climb out of bed, you start ticking off the items on your to-do list."

"I used to be like that, but not since I came to live here."

"Come off it, Dan. Tell me the truth. What's your interest in Ironbrand?"

Dan took a moment to compose himself, his mind working quickly. "Harry offered me a job, working for the estate, and I turned him down. But I'm reconsidering. I could use the money, but I'd want to know what I was getting myself into, and that means finding out about Ironbrand."

"What did Harry offer you?"

"I don't want to say too much. I'm keeping the idea under wraps until I've made my decision, so I'd rather you didn't mention it to anyone just yet."

"All right. But listen, I'd think twice before accepting any kind of offer from Harry. He's…"

"He's what?"

Jocelyn took a breath. "You know what they say: when you sup with the devil, be sure to use a long spoon."

"You needn't worry. I can handle Harry."

"No, Dan. You can't." Jocelyn laid her hand on his upper arm. "I'm serious. You don't know him, and you don't want to."

"Scott seems to trust him."

"My husband is easily taken in. You have to understand, Scott might be reasonably wealthy now, but he wasn't born that way. His parents worked their whole lives to buy their little bungalow in Walthamstow. That was all they wanted, but Scott had a vision, and he was prepared to work for it. He didn't go to university; he got a job in telesales and worked his way up."

"So, he's a self-made man," Dan said. "But he wouldn't have got so far without being a shrewd judge of character."

"You'd think so. But Scott's still a suburban boy at heart. Show him a big car, and he'll be impressed. Dangle the keys in front of his nose, and he'll follow you like a puppy."

"He's become greedy," Dan suggested.

"No, it's not that. It's more like he's fallen under Harry's spell, and I don't like it. I don't like what it's doing to him. I've tried to talk to him about it, to warn him, but he won't listen."

"And what is Harry doing that causes you so much concern?"

"I'm not sure, and that's part of the problem," Jocelyn began. "There's nothing I can point to and say it's not right."

"Are you sure about that? Sometimes, when there's a lot of money at stake, people cut corners, bend the law."

Jocelyn shook her head. "No. Scott wouldn't allow that, not knowingly."

"Then what? Maybe I can help, but you'll have to explain precisely what the problem is. Has Scott said something to you?"

"No." Jocelyn looked away. "It's a hundred little things. I hear Harry's name more and more, but whenever I ask what they're up to, Scott fobs me off. He used to share his work with me, but not anymore. I know he's excited about his solar farm project, but he won't tell me the details. And all those people at that awful party — I didn't know any of them. And neither did Scott."

"Really? I got the impression they were his business contacts, his investors."

"They might be putting money into the solar business, but I've never laid eyes on any of them before, and when I asked Scott to introduce me, he made all kinds of excuses and changed the subject. But I know when he's bluffing. And that night, he was out of his depth, floundering while Harry marched around as though he owned the place. It made me see red, I can tell you."

"That explains a lot."

Jocelyn sent him a sharp look. "Was I beastly to you? I wouldn't be surprised. It was such an awful night. And then that poor boy was hurt. It was—" She broke off abruptly, her voice catching and her eyes growing moist. "I don't know if I'll ever get over it."

"Maybe George won't get over it either."

Jocelyn's face fell. "I'm sorry, that didn't come out the way I meant it to. Of course, I can only pray that George recovers. He's so young and so gifted. It breaks my heart to think about him." She dabbed at her eyes with her fingertips. "Is there any news, do you know? I tried ringing the hospital, but they wouldn't tell me anything."

"The last I heard, he was in intensive care, recovering from an operation. He's not out of danger yet."

"Oh dear. I keep wondering if it wouldn't have happened if only we hadn't hired him."

Something in Jocelyn's tone made Dan pause. She'd spoken casually, a throwaway remark. As far as he knew, Jocelyn had hired George, but she certainly hadn't sounded contrite or as if she was taking any part of the blame herself. And she'd said *we* not *I*. Choosing his words carefully, Dan said, "George was your choice for the catering, wasn't he?"

Jocelyn looked at him blankly. "Of course not. Scott had our usual firm lined up, but Harry changed the arrangements at the last minute. I was fuming at the time, but I climbed down off the ceiling when George arrived and I saw what he could do."

"*Harry* hired him? But he said..." Dan didn't finish his sentence. He was too busy wondering why Harry had lied.

"Are you all right?" Jocelyn asked.

Dan nodded.

"You look upset, but we must try to keep things in perspective. George is young and strong, and he's got so much to live for. I expect his girlfriend will be waiting at his bedside, and she'll help him to pull through. These things make a difference."

"I'm afraid that's unlikely," Dan said without thinking.

"What do you mean?" Jocelyn's hand went to her mouth. "What are you saying? Is he worse than you're letting on?"

"No, I've told you everything I know about his recovery. It's just that I'm pretty certain George doesn't have a girlfriend."

"But I've seen them together," Jocelyn insisted. "They looked so sweet. He had his arms around her."

"Where was this?" Dan asked.

"In the village. I was driving through and I saw them. This was before I knew George, but I recognised him immediately when he turned up at the farm. He's a good-looking boy."

"Who was the girl? Do you know her name?"

"No. I guessed she was a local, but to be honest, I didn't see her face. She had her head on his shoulder."

"And what makes you think she was from the village?"

Jocelyn shrugged. "Her clothes maybe? I'm not sure. I thought she might've been that girl who used to work in the shop."

"Sam?"

"I don't think I ever knew her name. I haven't been to the shop for ages, but there used to be this girl who worked there, and I always thought she'd be quite pretty if she made a bit of an effort, do you know what I mean?"

Dan declined to answer.

"Anyway, I think George was with that young woman," Jocelyn went on. "And he wasn't just giving her a friendly hug, they were holding on to each other as only young lovers can. That's all I can tell you."

"I see," Dan said. "Well, you've given me a lot to think about."

"I don't know about that, but what about this fishing? Are you going to have another go?"

"No." Dan turned the reel to wind the line back in. It only took a few seconds, and as soon as he was done, he laid the rod on the ground. "Could you keep an eye on that for me?"

"Yes, but where are you going?"

"I'm going for a walk around the reservoir. I need to stretch my legs."

"What shall I tell Scott and Alan?"

"Tell them to give me a call when they've finished, and I'll meet them at the car park. There's no rush."

"Shall I come with you?"

"No. You stay and enjoy yourself. I don't want to spoil everyone's fun, but you were right earlier. This isn't for me."

"But what about the bet?" Jocelyn asked. "You don't want to look like a bad loser, do you?"

"No, but if I'm buying, I get to choose the venue, and I nominate the Wild Boar."

Jocelyn looked put out. "Scott won't go there. He can't stand the place."

"Then I guess it'll be a cheap round. You'll be welcome to join us, although I can't promise champagne."

Jocelyn didn't reply.

"I'll see you later," Dan said, then he turned his back on

Jocelyn and the lake, and he started walking, picking a path and following it without knowing where it led.

Alan would be disappointed in him for giving up so easily, but that couldn't be helped. Dan had a lot to think about, and fishing was the last thing on his mind.

CHAPTER 35

I T WAS GETTING dark when Paul parked in a lay-by in a little-used lane. He sat in the car for a minute, waiting and watching, but there was no one around. It was time.

He set off on foot, walking quickly without looking back, and he didn't pause until he was halfway along the narrow lane that led to Ironbrand Farm.

Paul cocked his ear. Was that a car approaching or just a breeze in the treetops? He waited. The sound grew louder, became the drone of an engine. Someone was coming.

Paul made out the glow of headlights filtering through the hedgerow. Although the vehicle was growing closer, it wasn't on the same lane as him, but on a wider road that ran at right angles to it. It sounded like a truck or perhaps a Land Rover. Something big. It would probably stay on the wider road, passing the turning toward Ironbrand Farm. If Paul waited for a few seconds, it would be gone.

But the vehicle slowed. Paul heard the crunch of gears, and a moment later, a van trundled into the lane. Paul jumped back, pressing himself against the hedge and turning his face to one side. Thorns scratched his cheek, but he stood still. He'd chosen dark clothes, and his baseball cap shaded his face. Unless the driver looked straight at him, everything would be all right.

The van was close now, but the driver was taking his time, as though he wasn't sure where he was going. *Bloody couriers*, Paul thought. *Always getting lost.* Paul lowered his head, shielding his face with the peak of his cap, and he held his breath. If the driver stopped to ask for directions, Paul would have to run. He'd have no choice.

But the van passed by, and Paul let out a long breath. He watched the van's tail lights dwindle in the distance until they disappeared. The driver must be heading for the farm; the lane led nowhere else. A courier, if that's who it was, would make a quick delivery then head back the same way. And next time, the driver might be more observant.

Paul stepped back into the lane and hurried toward the farm. He didn't have much time. He thought about running, but that might make too much noise, and you never knew who might be about. Instead, he strode along the lane as quickly as he could, listening for the sound of the van. But he heard nothing, and soon he saw the farm's entrance. The wrought-iron gates stood wide open, and beyond them, the wide yard was lit by powerful floodlights.

The van was parked in front of the house, but there was no sign of the driver. That was good news, but even so, Paul's courage faltered. He hadn't bargained on anyone else turning up. The van was an unknown, a variable he hadn't accounted for; the kind of thing he hated.

Paul took a step forward, keeping to the shadows beside the hedge. *I don't like those floodlights*, he thought. *Maybe I won't get a chance today.* But he didn't turn tail. He patted his jacket pocket, feeling the hard outline of his butterfly knife. He'd be needing that. But first, he had to wait, watch, choose his moment. *I'll be all right*, he told himself. *I can do this.*

Paul crept closer to the gate. There was no going back. He pushed his doubts aside, and he breathed easier, felt his heart rate slow. It was getting darker all the time, and lights shone at most of the farmhouse's windows. From inside the brightly lit rooms, the lane beyond would be swathed in darkness. Even if someone looked in the right direction, there was no way they'd see him. He was safe.

Beside the iron gates, a low brick wall stretched out on both sides. He could climb over it in a second, but the yard beyond offered no hiding places. He'd be better off making his way to the back of the house.

Staying low, he followed the wall until it turned a corner. There were fewer windows on this side of the farmhouse, and Paul straightened his back. Here, the grass underfoot was soft, and he broke into a run, hardly making a sound. At the back of the house, the wall gave way to a wooden fence. Made of smooth vertical boards, the fence was taller than him and offered no footholds. It might be tricky to climb, but despite that, it still felt like the best way in. He jumped, gripping the top of the fence with both hands, then he hauled himself up until he could peek over the edge.

Paul smiled. The garden was dark and there were clumps of shrubs that he could hide behind. Between him and the house, there were several brick outbuildings: large sheds or garages. They would be worth a look. If there were tools in there, he might find something he could use; something that would cause some real damage.

Paul didn't hesitate. In one movement, he pulled his body up and over the fence, dropping silently onto the soft ground below.

He was in.

THURSDAY

CHAPTER 36

DAN OPENED THE door, coffee cup in hand, and stared blankly at the man waiting outside.

"Mr Corrigan?" the man asked.

"Yes."

The man smiled. "Thank goodness for that. I've been driving around these lanes for the last hour. The blooming satnav sent me the wrong way."

"That happens a lot. But what can I do for you?"

"Parcel for you, Mr Corrigan. I'll fetch it from the van. I wanted to make sure I'd finally found the right place. Yours is the third door I've knocked on this morning."

The man retreated to his van, returning a moment later with a large cardboard carton. "Here you go, Mr Corrigan. Sorry that it's late."

"Late? It's only just seven, isn't it?"

"Yes, but this was meant to arrive yesterday. Sorry about that. The driver couldn't find the place, so he took it back to the depot."

Dan took the carton, studying the label, and realisation dawned: the components for Monty's computer had finally arrived. "I'd almost forgotten I ordered this." Dan tucked the box under his arm, thanked the driver, then closed the door and headed through to the kitchen, a spring in his step.

It was always good to open a freshly delivered parcel, and Dan grinned as he ripped off the tape and unfolded the flaps. He retrieved the delivery note and checked off each item in turn. All the components he'd ordered had arrived intact. He had everything he needed, and that was very satisfying. *Back to normal life*, he thought. *Back to doing the things I'm good at.*

You knew where you stood with computers. Select the right parts and assemble them in the correct way, and you had a machine that worked: a computer that did its job. An operating system might not always behave in the way you expected, and sometimes errors could appear to come out of the blue. But whatever the problems, you could always get to the bottom of them if you were persistent enough. It was just a question of following a logical routine.

If only people could be so straightforward, Dan thought. His mind wandered back to his disastrous fishing trip the day before. Alan had learned nothing useful from Scott, and it was beginning to look as if Jocelyn was a fantasist. George with his arms around Sam? It was possible, but did it make sense? He could've asked Sam about it, but when they'd left the reservoir, Scott and Jocelyn had gone straight home, and Alan hadn't wanted to go to the pub. All in all, it had been a washout.

Forget about it, Dan told himself. *I've helped Gemma, and that's all I was asked to do.* The attack on George had been terrible, but it wasn't Dan's responsibility to solve the crime. And anyway, he'd run into a brick wall. There was something shady about Ironbrand Farm, but either Scott and Jocelyn were very good at concealing the truth, or they didn't know what was going on. The finger of suspicion pointed at Harry, but what could Dan do about it? He couldn't march up to the farm and search for evidence, and he had no right to interrogate anyone. It was time to let the police handle things.

"I'm just a computer repair man," Dan muttered, and he took out his phone and dialled Monty's number. As he waited for the call to connect, Dan eyed the cardboard box. He could carry it over to Monty's house, but it would be better to take the car. *I'll drive*, he decided. And at that moment, he heard Monty's unmistakably cultured tones on the line.

MONTY WELCOMED DAN into the house. "Good to see you, Dan. Come in. Coffee?"

"Yes please." Dan squeezed into the hallway, the cardboard box under one arm, and a plastic toolbox in his other hand. "I have all the parts ready, so this won't take long. All right if I go through?"

"Be my guest. You know where it is. I've made some room."

Dan went through to the front room. The place had been neat and orderly on his last visit, but now it was immaculate. He sat down at the desk and began unpacking the new components.

Monty appeared with a mug of coffee and set it down on a coaster on the desk. "Do you have enough light?"

"Fine, thanks," Dan said. "It's all very tidy in here. You put me to shame."

Monty tutted. "I usually have a cleaner once a week, but she let me down. I've had to do all this myself."

"Well, you've certainly done a good job."

Dan checked that Monty's computer was switched off, then he pulled it closer, sliding it carefully across the desk. "Before I begin, have you backed up everything?"

"Yes. All up to date."

"Excellent." Dan felt around the back of the computer and began unplugging the peripherals. "This part of the process isn't very interesting," he began. But then his fingers found an unfamiliar shape nestling among the cables. "What's this?"

"Something wrong?"

"I'm not sure." Dan pulled out the power cable, and then he turned the tower unit around. A small device the size and shape of a memory stick, its case made from smooth black plastic, protruded from the back of the computer, a USB cable trailing from it.

"I don't remember that," Monty said. "It looks like an adapter of some kind."

Dan reached for the device, but he stopped short. "You're sure? You've never seen it before?"

"Never."

"Your keyboard is plugged into it. Did you connect it, or did someone do it for you?"

"I'm telling you, I've never seen the damned thing before," Monty said. "I set the computer up myself. I'm not some old duffer who doesn't know one end of a cable from the other."

"I know. But I'm worried about this, Monty."

"Pull it out then."

"No. Wait." Dan took out his phone and ran a search. He soon found what he was looking for, then he turned his phone around, showing Monty the screen. "It's similar, yes?"

Monty craned his neck to peer at the screen. "Not quite the same, but near enough. What is it?"

"Monty, that's a keylogger. It records every keystroke you make and stores them. The data can be collected later."

Monty paled. "Is that how…?"

"Yes. Someone has been trying to steal your identity, to access your accounts. Devices like this can't be detected by your security software. They don't break into your system. They simply sit there, collecting keystrokes."

"Passwords?"

Dan nodded. "Account numbers, PINs, the answers to security questions. Everything."

"Oh my God. What about documents? Could they have downloaded my files onto that thing?"

"I don't think so, but the passwords could give someone remote access to your files."

"My documents are encrypted. Will they be safe?"

Dan nodded. "Hopefully. I have to say, I'm impressed. You're much more security minded than most people."

"I've always been careful. Even so, this is a disaster."

"At least we've stopped it. And we can find the culprit. We need to make a list of everyone who's been in this room."

"But no one comes in here without me," Monty said. "Except for…" His hand went to his mouth. "The girl who does the cleaning. Daisy."

"Then it must be her. We need to call the police."

"Yes. Yes, of course." Monty stared into space, his cheeks sagging. "When we thought I'd been targeted by some damned hacker in Russia or China or somewhere, it was bad enough. But to have my privacy invaded like this, in my own home, that's so much worse. And she seemed like such a nice young woman. I trusted her."

"Could it be anyone else?"

"No. It has to be her." Monty moved away, heading for the door. "I'll call the police from the other room."

Dan stood. "Do you want me to talk to them?"

"No, it's all right." Monty roused himself. "Thanks, Dan, but I'll deal with this. You may as well head home. We can't do anything until the police arrive."

"Okay. I'll pack up my tools, but we mustn't touch the computer. I expect they'll want to take it."

Monty stopped in his tracks. "I can't allow that." He faced Dan. "Perhaps we should take some other course of action."

"I don't think—"

"Hold on," Monty interrupted. "Let's just hold our horses

for a minute. What she tried to do is awful, but she didn't get away with it. I sent that phone back, and I've been through all my accounts with a fine-toothed comb. As far as I can tell, I haven't lost a penny."

"That's not the point."

"Isn't it? From where I'm standing, it's very important indeed."

"She's broken the law," Dan argued. "And for all we know, she's targeting others."

"Granted, we have to stop her. But that doesn't mean we have to go straight to the police."

"I disagree. I'm sorry, Monty, but if you won't call them, I'll have to."

"That's not on, old boy." Monty moved closer to Dan. "Listen to me. We can work something out. After all, I was the intended victim, not you. And when we stop to think about it, what damage has been done?"

Dan furrowed his brow, lost for words.

"Why don't we talk it over?" Monty went on. "Stay and finish your coffee. Let's see if we can't put our heads together and come up with a solution that suits everybody."

For a second, Dan didn't respond, then slowly he nodded.

Monty clapped him on the shoulder. "That's the spirit. Now, make yourself at home for a minute. I'll just go and fetch my coffee from the kitchen. I may need to add a drop of something stronger to it, eh? What do you say?"

"Not for me, thanks. I drove over here."

"Suit yourself."

Monty ambled out of the room, and Dan sat alone, staring into thin air. At first meeting, Monty had been the model of a stiff-upper-lipped gentleman: courteous and unflappable. He'd shown a flash of anger over the mobile phone ordered in his name, but that was understandable. If anything, his outrage showed that the man was a stickler for law and order. *He was a magistrate*, Dan thought. *What's got into him?*

A crime had been committed. Was Monty seriously suggesting they should try to conceal it?

Dan turned his attention to Monty's computer. *That's the key*, he decided. *Monty changed his tune as soon as I said the police would want to take it away*. And Monty had been very cagey about the upgrades, insisting that he must be in the room when Dan did the work.

"Here we are." Monty strolled back into the room, a mug in one hand and a bottle of whisky in the other. He waggled the bottle in the air. "Are you sure I can't tempt you, Dan? You look like you need something to revive your spirits."

Dan shook his head firmly. "Monty, what's on your computer? What is it that you don't want anyone to see?"

Monty's expression froze. "I told you before. Financial details. I trade in stocks and shares."

"Then unless you're doing something illegal—"

"Certainly not!" Monty snapped. "All my business affairs are above board, and my accounts are in order. I declare all my earnings and I pay my taxes in full. I've never cheated anyone out of a single penny, and that includes Her Majesty's Revenue and Customs."

Dan held up his hands. "Okay, but there's something you want to keep hidden, and it's on that computer. Unless you tell me what it is, I shall have to call the police and tell them about the keylogger."

The two men locked eyes, but Monty blinked first. "All right," he began, "but what I'm about to tell you must not leave this room. Do I have your word on that?"

"Within reason, yes. But if you tell me about something illegal, I'll have to take action."

"There's nothing that's against the law; nothing that concerns anyone but me." Monty drew breath. "I was married for over forty years. My Mary passed away some time ago, and I miss her every day. We never had children. Mary fell pregnant twice, but after the second miscarriage, the doctor told her never to try again. It was a source of disappointment for both of us, but we stuck together through thick and thin, right until the end."

"I'm sorry for your loss," Dan said.

"Thank you. But our marriage was not entirely happy. There's a bitter irony, you see. Mary's first pregnancy was the reason we married. We were young and careless, and back then, if you got a girl into trouble, you married her. It was the only thing to do. But my heart belonged to someone else. It still does."

"Are you telling me that you had an affair?"

"No. I was never unfaithful except, perhaps, in my heart. I carried a torch for my first love for a very long time, but I couldn't make contact with her. I knew she'd married; it was in the papers. Her husband was a wealthy man, a well-known figure in society, and I couldn't risk calling her or writing her a letter. So I tried to convince myself that I'd put her out of my mind. And for many years, that was that."

"But something changed," Dan suggested. "You tracked her down online, didn't you?"

Monty nodded. "The internet made it easy. I reached out to her, and we began a correspondence. It was foolish of me, I know, but I couldn't help it. I had to let her know how I felt."

"Was this while your wife was still alive?"

"Regrettably, yes. Mary never went near my computer, so my secret was safe."

"I'm sorry, but I don't see why you're being so secretive about this now. You're no longer married."

"Yes, but my correspondent *is*. And her husband parlayed his wealth into political influence. He's a powerful man, a household name."

"Who is it?" Dan asked.

"I'm not going to tell you. Suffice to say that if my correspondence with his wife came to light, it would be on the front page of every tabloid in the land. Our lives wouldn't be worth living."

Dan thought for a moment, then said, "I think I should go."

"All right, but first, tell me what you're going to do.

"I haven't decided."

"Then stay for a minute and finish your coffee. Ask me any questions you like. I'll answer if I can, but I won't give you any names."

"No. I'm going to head home. I need to think about this."

"Listen, why don't we just forget about the whole thing?" Monty said. "I'll talk to Daisy, and once she knows the game's up, she'll see sense. She won't try anything like this again."

"No," Dan said quickly. "That's not a good idea. I'll go and see Daisy myself."

Monty started to protest, but Dan cut him off. "It's either that, or I'll call the police right now. What's it to be?"

"I see. That's the lie of the land, is it?" Monty regarded Dan from beneath lowered eyebrows, then he said, "All right. We'll play it your way. For now."

"Okay. Do you have Daisy's address?"

"I'll scribble it down for you." Monty went to the desk and opened a drawer, taking out a pad and pen. He wrote down the address, then he tore off the top sheet and handed it to Dan. "It's not far."

Dan went to take the paper, but at the last second, Monty pulled it away. "What are you going to say to her?"

"I'm going to make the position plain, and then I'll ask her some questions," Dan said. "I need to know if she's targeted anyone else, so I'll have to get a list of places where she's worked. They'll all have to be checked. And I need to find out whether she's working alone."

"Then what?"

"I'm not sure. It depends on how she reacts. I may have to go to the police after all."

"If you do that, will you give me some warning? I shall need to destroy some files."

Reluctantly, Dan nodded.

"Thank you." Monty handed over the address.

Dan glanced at the sheet of paper before tucking it into his pocket, then his gaze fell on the cardboard box of components. "I suppose I'd better take those with me."

"You can leave them here. I hope you'll still want to upgrade my machine."

"I don't know. In the circumstances…"

Monty waved his concerns aside. "I'll pay you for the parts and for your time as well. Send me the bill and add on a little service fee while you're at it. Say, an extra couple of hundred. To cover the inconvenience."

"No. I haven't done the work, so you can pay for the components if you want to keep them, but that's all."

"Fair enough. You play a straight bat. I'm happy to accept your terms." Placing his mug on the desk, Monty extended his hand for a shake.

Without a word, Dan shook his hand.

"Good man," Monty said. "I'll see you out."

Monty ushered him through the hallway, but they didn't speak until Dan stood on the threshold.

"You know, I'm relying on your professional discretion," Monty said. "I trust you'll do the right thing."

"So do I," Dan replied. "So do I."

CHAPTER 37

I T DIDN'T TAKE Dan long to find Daisy's house; it was part of a cluster of relatively modern homes that stood on the edge of the village. He parked on the quiet street and looked around. *There's no character to the place,* he thought. *I could be anywhere.* The homes had been designed to emulate the style of typical Devon cottages, but there was no disguising the new slate roofs and the plastic bargeboards. Besides, the houses were far too alike, each one a carbon copy of its neighbour.

But Dan hadn't come to study the architecture; he had a job to do.

Checking the house number, he marched up to the front door and rang the bell. A moment later, the door swung open and a stern-faced woman regarded him with undisguised hostility. "What do you want?"

"Hello. I was given this address by Mr Albright. I'm looking for Daisy Pugh. Have I found the right place?"

"Maybe. What's it about?"

Dan offered a reassuring smile. "I'd like to talk to her in person. Is she in?"

"About a cleaning job, is it?"

"Yes."

"Well, she ain't here," the woman said. "I haven't seen her for days. With her boyfriend, I expect."

"Does she have a phone?" Dan asked.

"I'm not giving you her number. You could be anybody. Besides, she doesn't answer the damned thing most of the time."

Dan gathered his reserves of patience. "I presume that you're Mrs Pugh, Daisy's mother."

"That's right."

"Then please listen carefully, Mrs Pugh. Daisy is in trouble, and unless I talk to her soon, the next person to call at your house will be a police officer."

"Hang on a minute. Who are you anyway?"

"My name is Dan Corrigan. I live in Embervale, and I'm helping Mr Albright. Daisy has done something very foolish, and she's broken the law, but if I can talk to her, perhaps we can put things right without involving the police. Do you understand?"

Mrs Pugh eyed Dan warily. "What's she done this time?"

"I'd rather not go into that. At least, not here on the doorstep. I need to talk to Daisy in private."

"Well, you can't. She ain't here. And I'll tell you the same as I told that other bloke: I'm only her mother, not her personal assistant. Goodbye."

She made to slam the door, but Dan called out, "Wait!"

Mrs Pugh stopped to stare at Dan, her eyes cold. "What now?"

"What other man?" Dan asked. "Who else has been looking for Daisy?"

"I don't know. Some smarmy sod or other. I didn't like him, and I don't like you, so you'd better go before I fetch my husband."

"I'll go in a second," Dan said. "But please, try and remember the man's name. Was he with the police?"

"No. He just said to call him when Daisy got back. I don't know who he thought he was, throwing his weight about, giving me the evil eye. I told him to bugger off. He insisted on giving me his card, but I threw it in the bin."

Dan groaned inwardly. "What did he look like? Was he my age?"

"How should I know?"

"What about height? Hair colour?"

Mrs Pugh shook her head. "I'm not going to stand here playing guessing games. I've got things to do."

"I understand, but this is important."

"Oh yeah?" Mrs Pugh folded her arms. "Owe somebody money, does she? Well, I'm not paying, so don't ask. She's old enough to stand on her own feet."

"It's not about money," Dan insisted. "Daisy could be in danger."

Mrs Pugh's expression didn't alter. "Is that so?"

"Yes. I don't want any harm to come to your daughter, but I'm not so sure about the man who came here. It's best if I find Daisy before he does, so if you can remember anything about him, it could help to keep Daisy safe."

"I don't know. Sounds like a cock and bull story to me. But…" Mrs Pugh let out an exasperated sigh. "The bloke's name was Denby, something like that."

"Denton? Harry Denton?"

Mrs Pugh nodded. "Know him, do you?"

"Yes. He works at Ironbrand Farm."

"That's all right then. Daisy's been working up there, doing a bit of cleaning, so it was probably just to do with that." Mrs Pugh rolled her eyes. "And here's you, coming up with daft ideas and giving me palpitations over nothing."

Dan didn't reply. Harry Denton wasn't the kind of man to make friendly visits to the cleaning staff. If he'd been looking for Daisy, it was almost certainly because she'd been up to no good at Ironbrand Farm. And she'd been found out.

"Are you done asking stupid questions?" Mrs Pugh demanded. But before Dan could answer, she added, "I reckon so." Then she closed the door.

Dan headed back to his car, deep in thought. Harry Denton's name had cropped up once again, and it didn't feel like a coincidence. It seemed more as though Harry was at the centre of a web, pulling on the invisible threads, manipulating all those who were caught in his sticky trap.

From what Jocelyn had said, Harry was the one in charge at Ironbrand Farm. *He tried to hire me*, Dan thought. *He didn't want to protect the business, he wanted the attack on George covered up.* Dan recalled the night of the attack. Dan had reached George first, but Harry had been the second one to arrive. Was that because he was already outside? Dan couldn't quite believe he hadn't thought of that before. It was so obvious.

Dan reached his car and climbed inside. He started the engine, but he sat still, gripping the steering wheel, staring straight ahead. He wasn't sure what to do next, but one thing was for certain: he had to find Daisy before it was too late.

CHAPTER 38

URING HIS LUNCH break, Paul slunk out of the office. He headed for Exeter city centre, his head down and his hands in his pockets. Only when he'd left the office far enough behind did he stop and look around. A few people were walking nearby, mostly office workers by the look of them, in search of sandwiches and coffee. Fortunately, there was no one he recognised.

He took a final glance back toward the office, then he strode away, ducking into a narrow side street. He changed direction a couple of times, trying hard not to look too conspicuous, then he headed toward the River Exe. When he came to a flight of stone steps that led down to the riverbank, Paul hurried downward, taking the uneven steps as fast as he dared.

Soon, he was strolling along the broad pavement beside the river. He took his hand from his pocket, his butterfly knife held tight, pressing the slim handle against his body so that no one would see it. Then he stepped to the water's edge and kneeled down as if fastening his shoelace. A final check that no one was watching, then he tossed the knife out across the rippling water. It flew over the surface for a few metres, then it met the river with barely a splash and disappeared.

Paul stood, brushing his hands together. It was done. He marched back along the pavement, grinning to himself. And when he climbed the old stone steps, he took them two at a time.

CHAPTER 39

"I'VE HAD ENOUGH," Dan said. Sitting in the kitchen at home, he'd been toying with a vegan sausage roll, but he pushed the plate away and sat back.

Facing him across the table, Alan said, "You've barely touched that."

"I'm not hungry."

"You really ought to eat something." Alan took a bite of his sausage roll and chewed earnestly. He seemed to be having difficulty swallowing, but when he finally succeeded, he offered an encouraging smile. "It's not that bad. Quite tasty in its own way."

"I know, but I can eat later. I can't sit around all day. I need to get moving. I need to *do* something."

"But where do we start? If Daisy doesn't want to be found, we haven't much chance of finding her."

"So we try a different tack," Dan said. "We concentrate on Harry."

"On what grounds? From what you've told me, there's no evidence that Harry has done anything wrong. I don't like the man, but that doesn't mean a thing."

"What about the night of the party? When I got to George,

Harry appeared very quickly. Are you sure you didn't see where he came from?"

"I've told you already, he came out of nowhere. All I know is that he didn't pass me on the way."

"Then how did he get to George before you? You were standing next to me, right up until the moment I went outside."

"You took off like a hare," Alan protested. "It took me longer to react, and in the meantime, Harry could've noticed the commotion and dashed after you. In a house that size, there'll be more than one exit. He probably used another door."

Dan thumped the table in frustration. "If Harry is innocent, then why is he looking for Daisy?"

Before Alan could reply, Dan swept on. "Think about it. Just before George was stabbed, we were looking for some food, but Daisy was nowhere in sight. It's reasonable to assume she'd gone to fetch some more canapés, and if she was in the kitchen, she might easily have seen something. That's why she's gone into hiding. Harry has worked out that she's a witness, and now he's after her."

"That's sheer speculation."

"Yes, but it fits the facts, doesn't it?" Dan pushed his chair back from the table, then he stood, looking around with a sense of purpose.

"Where are we going?" Alan asked. "Ironbrand Farm?"

"No. You were right when you said we have no grounds for tackling Harry. Not yet, anyway. So we need to find out what he's up to. We need to figure out what's going on at Ironbrand, and we can start by poking around, gathering some background information."

"Okay. What do you suggest?"

"We're going to the one place in this village where we might find out something useful."

Alan raised his eyebrows hopefully. "The pub?"

Dan nodded, and Alan jumped to his feet. "I'm ready when you are."

"What about your lunch?" Dan said. "Do you want to take it with you?"

"I'll grab something in the Boar."

"Okay. Let's go."

Outside, Dan and Alan marched toward the Wild Boar, but they slowed their pace when they saw the pair of police patrol cars parked on Fore Street.

"I don't like the look of this," Alan said. "I wonder what's going on."

"We might find out in a minute. Sam might well have seen them arrive."

"Two cars. That must mean something. I hope it's not more bad news."

"Let's wait and see," Dan said. "It's not necessarily connected to our case. Don't jump to conclusions."

Alan sent Dan a sideways look.

"All right," Dan added. "Pot, kettle. Point taken. Even so, there's no point getting excited until we know more."

"On that, we can agree." Alan led the way into the Wild Boar, and Dan followed. Sam was behind the bar, chatting to a customer. But as Dan and Alan approached, the customer turned around and regarded them with a wry smile.

"Well, well," DS Spiller said. "If it isn't my two favourite amateur sleuths."

"Afternoon," Dan replied. "I see you've come with reinforcements today. Has something happened, or did you just pop in for a pie and a pint?"

Spiller maintained his smile, but it looked as though it cost him some effort. "I'm here on official business, Mr Corrigan. It's a serious matter and not to be treated lightly."

"Sorry," Dan said. "I didn't mean to be flippant. Is everyone okay?" He turned to Sam. "Are you all right? I mean, you look fine. Better than fine, actually. But I would hate to think…" He left his sentence unfinished, Sam's smile derailing his train of thought.

"You needn't worry on my account," Sam said. "I'm all right."

"Good. Excellent." Dan regained his composure. "So, what's happened?"

"I'm here to ask a few questions, that's all," Spiller replied. "And Ms Ashford has been very helpful."

"I haven't been able to tell you much," Sam said. "Mr Denton never comes in here. I met him at the May Fair, but after that, I don't think I've ever seen him in the village."

"It helps us to form a picture," Spiller replied. "How about you two? Have you seen Mr Denton recently?"

"We saw him at Ironbrand Farm," Dan said. "But that was on Monday, and I haven't seen him since."

"The same goes for me," Alan chipped in. "Monday."

"And what were you doing at Ironbrand Farm?" Spiller asked.

"We went up to see Scott," Alan replied. "But we never got a chance. Harry collared us the minute we arrived."

"*Collared?*" Spiller said. "A strange turn of phrase, Mr Hargreaves. What are you implying?"

Alan looked nonplussed. "Nothing really. We were hoping to offer Scott some support. We're his neighbours, after all. But Harry had his own agenda."

"That's right," Dan said. "Harry was worried about the farm's reputation. He'd found out about my business experience, and he asked if we'd help him handle the PR."

"Did you agree?"

Dan shook his head. "We turned him down, and he was none too pleased about it."

"Do you mean he was disappointed?" Spiller asked. "Or was there more to it than that?"

"He was angry," Alan replied. "But then he was tired and overwrought."

Spiller seemed to consider this. "Did either of you say anything that might have made him angry? Were you, by any chance, asking questions about the assault on George Hepworth?"

"It came up in the conversation," Dan said. "But why are you so interested in Harry? Has something happened to him?"

"That remains to be seen," Spiller replied. "Officially, Mr Denton is missing, but unfortunately we have reason to suspect foul play."

"What kind of reason?" Dan asked. "Had someone been making threats against him?"

"We're not releasing that information yet," Spiller said. "But we have cause for concern, so we're carrying out enquiries."

Dan and Alan exchanged a look, and then Alan shook his head. He clearly thought Dan should keep his theories about Harry to himself.

Spiller missed nothing. He moved closer to Dan. "You know something about this, don't you? What is it?"

"Nothing, at least, not for sure," Dan said.

"Tell me anyway," Spiller replied. "Mr Denton might come to harm at any moment, so if you have any information that might help us find him, you need to tell me *now*."

Dan looked down for a moment, thinking. This situation required careful handling. There were too many moving parts to this case. Some of them would have to be eliminated, and in that regard, Spiller could be useful. Dan looked up and said, "I was doing some work for a client—"

"What kind of work?" Spiller interrupted.

"Upgrading his computer. But I discovered his machine had been tampered with, and I suspected the young woman who does his cleaning. Her name is Daisy."

"And who is this client?" Spiller asked.

"It's not important," Dan said quickly. "He didn't want to

take action against Daisy, so I agreed to have a chat with her on his behalf."

Spiller furrowed his brow. "And what does this have to do with Mr Denton?"

"Daisy was at Ironbrand Farm on the night George was stabbed. She'd been hired to serve food and drinks."

"And her full name is?"

"Daisy Pugh."

"Go on but get to the point. I haven't got all day."

"When I got to her house, I was told that Harry Denton had been looking for her. And it occurred to me that she may have been a witness to the attack. She might've seen who stabbed George, or perhaps she saw something significant."

"All the staff were interviewed at the time," Spiller said. "Why wouldn't she have come forward when she had the chance?"

"Possibly because she'd been up to no good," Dan replied. "I know she tampered with one computer, so she may have done something similar at Ironbrand."

"Is that all you've got?" Spiller asked.

"That, and the fact that Harry appeared on the scene very quickly after George was stabbed," Dan said. "I think he might've been outside already."

Spiller looked down his nose at Dan. "Thin. So thin I can practically see right through it."

"Then why was Harry looking for Daisy?" Dan asked. "Why would he go to the effort of calling at her house?"

"Any number of reasons," Spiller replied. "It doesn't give me much to work with, that's for sure. I'll follow it up, but it feels like a dead end to me."

"Okay, but you won't find Daisy at home," Dan said. "According to her mother, she's spent the last few days with her boyfriend." Dan paused. "His name is Paul. I met him at the May Fair."

"Hang on!" Sam blurted, and they all turned to look at

her. "Paul. Is that the guy who came into the beer tent to ask about his bag? The one who said he'd lost his wallet?"

"That's right," Dan said. "I saw him with Daisy at the fair, and afterwards in Brandle Wood."

"Oh my God." Sam's hand went to her mouth. "What if…?"

Spiller sent her a sharp look. "Is something wrong?"

"I don't know," Sam replied. "But I saw Paul the other day, through the window. I knew I'd seen him before, but I couldn't place him. I suppose that was because he was in smart clothes like he'd come straight from work. Then I remembered about the fair. But the next thing I knew, he started kicking off in the street, having a right old barney."

"Who was he arguing with?" Spiller asked.

"Reg Stoddard. He's one of my regulars. He came in afterwards for a drink. He didn't say anything, but I could tell he was shaken up. I felt sorry for him."

Spiller glanced over at the window. "You have a good view of the street. Could you see what caused the argument?"

"I could see all right. Reg was walking along, minding his own business, and Paul drove up, jumped out his car and started having a go at the poor bloke. I couldn't hear what they said, but I could see the look on Paul's face. He was spitting blood. And after what you said just now, it made me wonder." Sam blushed. "I know it might not mean anything, but it shows he's got a temper, doesn't it?"

"A lot of people have bad tempers, especially when they're behind the wheel," Spiller said. "They could've been arguing over a parking space for all we know."

"But Paul was in a rage," Sam argued. "He was losing it. Don't you see what I'm getting at?"

"I do," Dan said. "You think that if Harry Denton was hassling Daisy, Paul might've done something about it."

"It's a possibility, I suppose," Spiller admitted, "but it doesn't follow."

"Worth checking though," Dan said. "Harry can be an abrasive character, and Daisy's mum took an instant dislike to him. She said that Harry had been throwing his weight about, and she obviously resented it."

Spiller nodded thoughtfully. "What's Paul's full name?"

Dan and Alan looked at each other blankly, but Sam brightened. "I've got a card somewhere." She disappeared beneath the bar, then she bobbed back up, a handbag in her hands. She began rifling through it. "I usually throw cards away, but it was something to do with getting faster broadband, and I thought it might come in handy for the pub. For the Wi-Fi." She smiled and produced a business card. "Here you go. Paul Sanderson. DevonSat."

Spiller strode over to the bar, and when Sam offered the card to him, he snatched it up. "Thank you very much, Ms Ashford. We'll have a chat with Daisy Pugh, and with her boyfriend too." He looked at Dan and Alan. "Is there anything else you can tell me?"

"Nothing relevant," Dan said.

"Are you sure? No mysterious footprints or bits of twig? Nothing like that?"

Dan shook his head.

"You do disappoint me."

"When we find something, we'll call," Dan said. "Meanwhile, I presume you've released Billy Nickleton."

Spiller smiled but there was no humour in it. "You presume wrong. But I won't go into details."

"What about the forensic tests?" Dan asked. "Haven't you had the results back yet?"

"Don't push your luck, Mr Corrigan." Spiller cast a searching glance around the room, then he nodded to Sam. "Thanks for your help, Ms Ashford. Nice place you've got here."

"Thanks," Sam said. "Pop back at any time. We do food. You could bring Mrs Spiller."

"What makes you think I'm married?"

Sam arched her eyebrows. "Seriously? Do you want me to answer that?"

"No, it might be better if you didn't." Spiller gave her a sanguine smile, then he headed for the door. A moment later, he passed the window, his phone pressed to his ear.

"Job done," Dan said. "We don't have to go looking for Daisy anymore. We can let Spiller take it from here."

"Are you sure?" Alan asked.

"Yes. The police will find her faster than we could. Let's have something to eat, and we'll talk things over. I don't like the way Harry has suddenly disappeared. We'll put our heads together and see what we can come up with. I'm buying."

"Okay. You can get the drinks, but I'll pay for my own lunch."

"Fine."

They leaned on the bar. "I fancy a bottled beer for a change," Alan said. "Something different."

"We've got some Avocet in." Sam took a bottle from the chiller and placed it on the bar. "It's a nice ale from Exeter Brewery. It's organic *and* vegan friendly."

"That sounds perfect," Dan said. "I'll have one of those. Same for you, Alan?"

Alan nodded firmly. "Just what the doctor ordered."

They took seats at the bar while Sam poured their drinks.

"Sam, when you've got a minute, could we have a couple of lunch menus?" Alan asked.

"Sure. And there are some new things you might like, Dan. Vegetable samosas and onion bhajis. They're both vegan."

"You're too good to me," Dan said.

"You can say that again." Sam slid two full pint glasses across the bar. "But don't tell the other customers. They just think they're getting fancy Indian food. If you tell them it's vegan, they'll moan about it and say we're going trendy."

"No one could accuse the Wild Boar of that," Dan replied, quickly adding, "but we like it just the way it is. You've done wonders with the place. We wouldn't change a thing, would we, Alan?"

"Certainly not," Alan said. "You've given the old place a certain charm."

"All right, that's enough smooth talk for one day. Here you go." Sam handed Dan and Alan a menu each, and though she tried to look stern, Dan noticed the hint of a smile hovering on her lips.

"Thanks," Dan said. "I don't suppose DS Spiller let slip any details about the case, did he?"

Sam shrugged. "Not really."

"Did he say why they're so worried about Harry?"

"Oh, it was his car. Somebody slashed the tyres, apparently."

"Where did this happen?" Alan asked. "Somewhere in the village?"

"No. It was up at Ironbrand. Somebody broke into the back yard and did a proper job on the car. One of those four wheel drive jobs. BMW."

Dan sat up. "Didn't the alarm go off?"

"I don't know. He didn't say."

"Ironbrand has floodlights all over the place, and a valuable car like that ought to have been parked somewhere secure," Dan said. "Scott might be a bit pompous, but he isn't careless."

Sam shuddered. "Don't talk to me about that man. He goes after anything in a skirt. He even had a go at me, at the May Fair."

Dan bridled. "He did what?"

"You know, he had a go at me."

"You mean he flirted with you?"

"No. I'm used to that in this job. It's like water off a duck's back."

"Well, that's not okay," Dan said slowly. "It's not right at all. But what did Scott do to you?"

Sam folded her arms. "Calm down, Dan. I don't need you to fight my battles. If you must know, he put his hand on my arse while I was collecting the empties. But I set him straight, all right? I told him where to get off, and he got the message. End of story."

Dan and Sam stared at each other in silence.

Then, from somewhere in the back of the pub, a metallic crash rang out.

Sam sighed. "That'll be Jordan. He's just started in the kitchen, and he's still finding his feet. I'd better go and see how he's getting on. I'll be back in a minute to take your orders."

She bustled through the door that led to the kitchen, leaving Dan and Alan sitting awkwardly. Alan sipped his drink then studied his menu as if committing it to memory.

Unsure what to say, Dan picked up his menu and let his gaze wander over it, though he hardly took any of it in.

After a few long seconds, Alan said, "Well, what do you think?"

"I'll probably go for a couple of samosas with an onion bhaji on the side."

"No, about what Sam just told us."

"I think… I think she's right. She doesn't need me to stand up for her." Dan took a gulp of his beer. "I'd still like to get my hands on Scott and teach him a couple of things about harassment, but Sam wouldn't thank me for it, so what can I do?"

Alan opened his mouth to speak, but Dan carried on. "I mean, I've got no grounds to be jealous. It's not as if Sam and I are together."

"Right. And if you were together?"

"Well, we're not, are we? But even so, I feel like going up to Ironbrand and punching Scott in the face."

"Good. There's hope for you yet. But to be honest, I don't think he's worth it. You heard what Sam said. She's dealt with him already."

Dan stared straight ahead, scowling at nothing in particular.

"It's none of my business," Alan began, "but if you want to show Sam how you feel, there are better ways than thumping the nearest idiot."

Dan looked at Alan. "But that's just it. When it comes to Sam, I don't know what to think. She's great in so many ways, but we're completely different. We have absolutely nothing in common. And recently, whenever I talk to her, I seem to say the wrong thing."

"You say the wrong thing to everyone, Dan. But with Sam, you notice."

"Is that supposed to make me feel better?"

"Not really," Alan said. "But it's true, and I work with what I have."

"Right."

They drank in silence for a minute.

"Maybe, when this case is over, things will be different," Dan said. "Right now, everything is in a mess."

"Yes. First George and now Harry. I wonder what's happened to him."

"I don't know. Harry's the kind of man who enjoys making enemies. I'm starting to think we should stand back and let the police handle the whole thing."

"Yes." Alan took a gulp of his beer. "Paul might have a temper, but somehow, I don't think he could've hurt Harry. Do you remember when we met Paul in the wood? He was like a frightened rabbit, running away rather than facing Sid Sturridge."

"I agree. I don't know what's happened to Harry, but I don't seriously think Paul has anything to do with it."

Alan furrowed his brow. "But you let Spiller think Paul was in the frame. You *encouraged* the idea."

"Spiller needed a lead, and I gave him one. I wound him up and sent him on his way."

"Why?"

"Because we need Daisy to be found, and as you pointed out earlier, we don't stand much chance of finding her on our own. But the police have resources. They'll find her in no time."

Sam emerged from the kitchen, wiping her hands on a towel. "What was that?"

"We were talking about Daisy Pugh," Dan replied. "We were going to look for her, but the police will find her soon enough."

Sam frowned. "You reckon she's done something to somebody's computer, is that right?"

"It looks that way." Dan took a sip of his drink. "This beer is very good. There's a hint of citrus, isn't there?"

"It's the hops." Sam looked into the middle distance, her gaze growing soft. "It's funny, you talking about Mrs Pugh earlier. I remember her from when I was little. She used to help out at the school, teaching us to dance around the maypole. She was a right laugh. She had us in stitches."

"That must have been a very long time ago," Dan said.

Sam glared at him. "I'm not that old, you know."

"No, I didn't mean…" Dan held up his hands, his fingers spread wide. "I just meant that she's changed. When I talked to her, I got the impression she hasn't laughed for quite a while."

"Well, I suppose it was quite a long time ago," Sam admitted. "It was definitely before she got married. She was plain old Miss Stoddard in those days."

Dan froze with his glass halfway to his lips. "As in Reg Stoddard?"

"She's his sister."

Dan looked at Alan. "I think I know where Daisy is."

"What makes you say that?"

"Cornish pasties. They're the ideal food to take to someone who's on the run. And the other day, I saw Reg buying a toothbrush, and when I asked him about it, he was very evasive."

"I'm not surprised. Most people wouldn't like to be quizzed about their shopping."

"But don't you see? She must be staying with him. Harry intimidated her, so she went into hiding with her uncle."

"That makes sense." Alan set his glass down on the bar. "We could go and ask him, but I'm not sure where he lives."

"I know," Sam said. "He has a little cottage. I could tell you where it is."

Dan took out his phone. "It's all right. I have his number." Dan made the call, and it was answered quickly.

The woman's voice on the line was hesitant: "Hello?"

"Hello, I'm Dan Corrigan. I met Reg at the May Fair. Is he in?"

"No."

"Ah. Do you happen to know where he is? I'd like to talk to him about some carpentry I need doing."

"Well, he's not in his workshop, so I expect he's where he always is. On his allotment."

"Right," Dan said. "Do you happen to know his mobile number?"

"No, but it wouldn't do you much good if I did. He never takes the blooming thing with him."

"Okay, thanks anyway. Bye."

Dan ended the call, then he slid from his seat. "I know exactly where Daisy is. Let's go, Alan. I'll explain on the way."

CHAPTER 40

DAN AND ALAN hurried along Fore Street, striding past the school and on toward the edge of the village.

"Hang on a second," Alan said. "If you're so sure about this, shouldn't we call the police?"

"Good idea." Without slowing, Dan took out his phone, and Spiller answered his call straight away. Dan launched into his message, speaking quickly, explaining where they were heading and why.

"I see," Spiller intoned. "As it happens, I've just talked to Mrs Pugh, and you were right, Mr Denton seems to have made himself unpopular. I'd better have a chat with young Daisy. I'll be there in five minutes."

"I'll meet you, show you where she is."

"No, you need to keep out of the way," Spiller said, but Dan ended the call. Pocketing his phone, he grinned at Alan. "He said we should go ahead."

"It didn't sound like that to me."

"The signal was poor. Anyway, they'll be here soon, but we can beat them if we run." Dan broke into a brisk jog.

Doing his best to keep up, Alan said, "This is rash, even for you. I thought we were letting the police find Daisy."

"That was when we were stumped. It's different now. We've got a head start. You don't want to give that up, do you?"

Alan didn't reply.

Soon, they reached the allotments, and Dan opened the gate and carried on, jogging along the path.

"I've been thinking," Alan began, but Dan cut him off.

"Come on. We're almost there." Dan raced ahead. They were almost at Reg's allotment, and though there was no one to be seen, Daisy would be hiding in Reg's shed. She had to be.

Dan ran to the shed and took hold of the door handle, but the sight of the sturdy padlock stopped him short. The shed was firmly locked.

Alan caught up, took one look at the locked door and grunted under his breath. "That's what I was trying to tell you. Reg wouldn't have left Daisy in a shed. She's his niece, for crying out loud."

"But I was so sure." Dan went to the shed's grimy window and peered inside, pressing his hands against the glass to cut out the reflections. But apart from the neat row of tools hanging from the opposite wall, Dan could see nothing.

"There's no one in there, is there?" Alan said.

"No." Dan stepped back. "But you weren't with me when I came here before. Reg was so secretive about his shed. He was hiding something, I know it. It all adds up."

Alan regarded him balefully, and in the silence, a shout echoed across the allotments: "What the hell do you think you're doing?"

DS Spiller stormed down the path toward them, his colleague, DC Collins, in tow.

"Oh dear," Alan muttered. "This is going to be painful."

Dan waited, his hands in his pockets. Alan was right. *I've done it this time*, Dan thought. *I've made a complete fool of myself.*

But there was no escaping this embarrassment. There was nothing for it but to own up and face the consequences.

"I told you to keep out of the way," Spiller fumed. "Which part of that didn't you understand?"

"I'm sorry. But anyway, our being here didn't make any difference." Dan drew a breath. "I've made a mistake. She's not here. There's no one here."

Collins smirked, but Spiller looked like a man chewing a wasp. "Are you telling me that you've completely wasted our time?"

Dan nodded.

Spiller growled under his breath, then he strode to the shed and eyed the lock. "Have you touched anything?"

"Just the door handle," Dan admitted. "And the window pane. I had to look inside."

"You've been very foolish," Spiller said. "You've jumped to a conclusion based on no real evidence, and you've taken us away from our enquiries. I've got a good mind to charge you with wasting police time."

"It was a genuine mistake," Dan replied. "I really thought—"

"Well, you thought wrong," Spiller interrupted.

"Yes, but in my defence, I was on the right track. Reg is Daisy's uncle, and he's hiding her somewhere. She's probably at his house. Please check. His surname is Stoddard. He has a cottage in the village. Sam knows where it is."

"Enough!" Spiller snapped. "Goodbye, Mr Corrigan. Some of us have work to do."

Dan moved closer to Spiller. "What are you going to do? Are you going to check Reg's house?"

"That is none of your business."

"What about Paul?" Dan asked. "Did you find him?"

"Of course we did," Spiller replied. "We do know what we're doing, you know. He was at work, and my colleagues in Exeter are bringing him in."

"That's good," Alan said. "I expect he'll be interviewed under caution."

Reluctantly, Spiller nodded. "We'll have a word with him, and we'll find out what he knows. After that, we expect to find the girl very quickly. So you see, we're not asleep at the wheel, Mr Corrigan. We get things done."

"Me too," Dan said. "And I haven't finished yet."

Spiller bristled. "I'd have thought you'd learned your lesson but let me spell it out for you. I told you before that you're on thin ice, but you didn't listen. Now, that ice is melting fast. I can't stop you from trying to work out what's been going on around here, but one false step and it won't be just your feet that get wet."

"That's a very colourful turn of phrase," Dan said. "What do you think, Alan?"

"Not bad. I might use it in a story."

"Be my guest." Spiller nodded to Collins. "Come on. We have work to do." Spiller marched away, and pausing just long enough to leer at Dan, Collins followed.

"Maybe Spiller's right," Alan said. "We should step back from this. We tried, but we've outstretched our reach. I've been feeling out of my depth for a while. I should've said something."

Dan shook his head. "This is all on me. I cocked it up. I should've known better."

"All the more reason to let it go."

Dan didn't reply. Instead, he stared out across Reg's allotment. Some earth had been freshly turned, and a wigwam of thin poles had been erected and fastened with string, but otherwise the place was unchanged. It was a quiet spot, and perhaps that was why he'd thought it would be a perfect hideaway for Daisy. But it was also the meeting place for a small community of gardeners. Any new arrivals would be noticed and talked about. He should've realised that immediately.

Maybe Alan's right, Dan thought. *I've made a mess of this from start to finish.* But George's life hung by a thread, and the person responsible was still at large. If it was Harry, then he ought to face charges and be answerable to the law for what he'd done; he shouldn't be spirited away by persons unknown, nor should he be allowed to disappear. And that thought gave Dan pause.

"Is it likely that someone in Embervale would grab Harry?" Dan said.

"Not likely, no, but possible. What's the alternative?"

"What if Harry staged the whole thing?" Alan looked doubtful, but Dan swept on. "Think about it. He knows that George could recover soon, and once he's awake, George can point the finger. And Harry knows Daisy has seen something, so he risks breaking cover and goes to her house. When he can't find her, Harry feels the net closing in. He's desperate, so he trashes his car and makes a getaway."

Alan winced. "Dan, you're doing it again. This isn't like you. You're all about logic and reason, not flights of fancy. Where's the evidence?"

"There isn't any, but that's because we haven't found it yet. We've been looking in the wrong places."

"Where are the right places?" Alan asked. "You can't want to go back to—"

"Ironbrand Farm," Dan interrupted. "That's where we should've been concentrating our efforts all along."

"We've scarcely managed to get past the front door. They've kept us at arm's length, and our fishing trip yielded nothing except a couple of rainbow trout."

"We should've been more persistent."

Alan sighed. "You could be right. We could've had access if you'd accepted Harry's job offer, but you turned him down."

"It wouldn't have helped much. Harry wanted to keep an eye on me, to make sure I didn't get too close."

"That sounds dangerously like paranoia."

Dan grinned. "You know what they say: if you're not paranoid, you don't know what's really going on."

Alan rolled his eyes, but Dan was not to be discouraged. "Come on, Alan. Let's go up to Ironbrand right now."

"You heard what Spiller said."

"Yes. He said he can't stop me, so what are we waiting for?"

"But the place will be crawling with police. It'll be a crime scene. You won't be able to get near Harry's car."

"I know that. We won't go anywhere we're not supposed to, but we need to talk to Scott and Jocelyn. They must know something about all this, and we'll get it out of them."

"The police will have interviewed them already."

Dan nodded. "But they'll relax when they talk to us. We're friends."

Alan looked down, intent on prodding at a dandelion with the toe of his shoe. But when he looked up, there was the suggestion of a smile on his lips. "All right. I don't know why I'm going along with this, but all things considered, it's worth trying."

"Good man. We could walk from here."

"No, I think we should nip back home first, then go by car. I'll drive."

"Okay, but we'll just grab the car and go. I don't want to be cooling my heels while you go rooting about in your kitchen for something to eat."

"I need to keep body and soul together."

"Later," Dan insisted. "Right now, we haven't got time."

"You're impossible," Alan grumbled. But Dan was already marching along the path.

CHAPTER 41

ALAN STEERED HIS VW Golf through the open gates at Ironbrand Farm. Dan half expected to see police cars parked across the yard, but the place was quiet with not a police uniform to be seen.

"It looks like things have calmed down," Dan said. "With any luck, we'll be able to have a proper talk with Scott."

"We'll see," Alan replied. "Don't get your hopes up." Alan parked the car and Dan climbed out, making straight for the front door and pressing the doorbell. As Alan caught up with him, the door was opened and Jocelyn stood on the threshold. "Oh," she said. "It's you."

Dan presented her with a smile. "Yes. Is it okay if we come in for a minute? We thought we might be able to help."

"Help? How?" Jocelyn peered at them scornfully. "I really don't think—"

"Please," Dan interrupted. "We need to talk."

"Oh, for God's sake. Haven't I had enough to deal with this morning?"

"We understand how you feel," Alan said. "You've been through a very trying time, but believe me, we're not here to cause you any inconvenience. And sometimes it helps to have someone to talk to."

Jocelyn's looked as though she was on the point of sending them away, but then her expression softened. "You may as well come in. It'll make a change from talking to the likes of Detective Sergeant Spiller."

She stood back to allow them in, and once they were inside, she closed the door. "We'll sit in the front lounge. It's lovely at this time of day. It gets the sun." She led the way into a spacious living room, and Dan and Alan followed.

"Have a seat." Jocelyn indicated the trio of sofas that occupied the centre of the room. "Can I get anyone a drink? Tea? Something stronger?

"Tea would be nice." Alan made himself comfortable on a sofa then added, "We haven't had lunch."

"Neither have I," Jocelyn said. "I'll get Marco to put something together. He's very good at that kind of thing, and we have some excellent olives. He'll fix up a feast in a trice." She focused on Dan. "You're a vegan, aren't you? I'll see what we can do."

"Thank you. That's very kind."

"I'll eat anything," Alan put in. "Anything at all."

"Then you'll be easy to please," Jocelyn said. "I'll be back in a tick."

She bustled from the room, and Alan breathed a sigh of relief. "Result. Food. I thought she'd never ask."

"Mm. But we didn't come here for lunch." Dan crossed the room to a chest of drawers, leaning forward to study the tastefully arranged photos displayed on its surface. Several showed Scott with his arm around an attractive woman, and it wasn't Jocelyn. "I wonder if Scott was married before," Dan said. "And if so, what happened to her?"

"What happened to who?" Jocelyn's voice made Dan turn around with a guilty start. She had reappeared silently, sweeping into the room, and she stood facing Dan, her hands on her hips.

"I was admiring your photographs," Dan said. "There's a woman in several of them, and I wondered who she was."

"That's Evelyn. Scott's first wife." Jocelyn cast a disdainful glance at the photographs. "But there she still is, staring out at me every damned day."

"I'm sorry," Dan said. "That's obviously a sore point, and I didn't mean to pry."

"Yes, you did," Jocelyn replied. "But I'll forgive you, just this once. She was a beautiful woman. But then, those who leave us when they're young never age in our imagination, do they? We cling to an idea of the person as they were at the time. She's probably run to seed by now, but to Scott, she'll always be as you see her there: a classic English beauty. That's the power of the old flame."

Dan stood slowly, and he thought of Monty, still nurturing his feelings for a love that he'd lost so long ago.

"Oh dear, have I embarrassed you?" Jocelyn went on. "I'm sorry. I didn't mean to sound so bitter. I'm not jealous of the poor woman. After all, I've got Scott, and she hasn't. But let's talk about something else. I can't take any more doom and gloom." Jocelyn sighed. "You must've heard about poor Harry."

"We know he's missing," Dan replied. "And we know his car was damaged, but that's all."

"Then you know as much as I do," Jocelyn said. "We've no idea what can have happened. It's enough to drive you to drink, it really is."

"When did you realise he was missing?" Dan asked.

"This morning. I went out after breakfast and saw the state of his car, but when I came inside to tell him, his room was empty, and his bed hadn't been slept in."

"That's one of those things people always say in books," Alan put in. "But I always wonder about it. I generally straighten my bed when I get up, and when I'm done, no one would know whether I've slept in it or not."

"That's because you're not a slob," Jocelyn replied. "Harry only has to walk through a room, and you can tell where he's been from all the mess he's left behind. The man is a walking disaster area."

Dan frowned. "Do you have a housekeeper? Someone who makes the beds up?"

"Not at the moment. There was someone, but she left. And I don't know what's going on with her replacement. She doesn't seem to have started."

"Then Alan's point stands. How can you be sure his bed hadn't been slept in?"

"Oh, I don't know. It was just the impression I got." Jocelyn wandered over to the window, staring outside. "It's a shame there's no view from this room. All you can see is the yard and those awful stone troughs full of, what are they, geraniums?"

"Pelargoniums," Alan said. "They give a splash of colour, don't they? I rather like them."

"Do you? To my mind, they're cheap and gaudy. Like something you'd find outside a village pub."

Dan stood and joined Jocelyn by the window. "Going back to last night, did Harry join you for dinner?"

"Yes. He was hitting the red wine rather heavily and so was Scott. They were getting a bit unbearable, so I left them to it. I had a bath and an early night."

"You didn't hear anything in the night?" Dan asked.

Jocelyn shook her head. "Like what?"

"Well, for one thing, I'd have thought Harry's car alarm would've gone off."

"I didn't hear it. But then, I was out for the count. I didn't want Scott to wake me when he'd finished carousing, so I'd taken a sleeping pill."

"Surely Harry and Scott would've reacted to a car alarm," Alan said. "It's quiet out here. They would've heard it."

Jocelyn shrugged. "No one tried to break into the car. The tyres were slashed but that was all, so perhaps the alarm didn't go off."

"That's a good point," Dan admitted. "If someone was careful and made sure the tyres deflated slowly, it might not have triggered the alarm. But it seems odd."

"How so?" Alan asked. "The perpetrator would be afraid of being caught in the act, wouldn't they?"

"Possibly, but on the other hand, they might've damaged the car in an attempt to lure Harry outside. If not, then why slash the tyres at all?"

"Maybe they wanted to make sure Harry couldn't get away," Alan said.

"There are plenty of other cars here," Jocelyn replied. "And none of those were touched. Just Harry's."

"That's very suggestive but we need to know more," Dan said. "Could we ask Scott if he saw or heard anything?"

"After lunch, perhaps." Jocelyn clasped her hands together. "I'll go and see how Marco's getting along."

Alan shuffled forward on his seat. "Would you like us to come through?"

Jocelyn waved him back. "No, you stay where you are. I'll have him bring it through here." She smiled, then she waltzed from the room.

Dan paced back and forth until Alan said, "Why don't you sit down? You'll make everyone uncomfortable, prowling around the room like that."

"Fine." Dan sat down heavily next to Alan, but far from relaxing, he leaned forward, his elbows resting on his knees.

"What do you reckon?" Alan asked. "Do you still think Harry could've staged his own disappearance?"

"It's a possibility. Harry's not the kind of man to give in without a fight, and yet no one saw or heard anything, so I find it hard to believe he was abducted. And the slashing of the tyres doesn't fit. If you've come to grab someone, you'd want to do it fast. You wouldn't hang around just to vandalise a car. Someone might see you and call the police."

"It could've been done to intimidate him. They drag him outside and say, 'We've slashed your tyres, and if you don't play ball, you'll be next.'"

"We?"

Alan nodded. "Two or three people, working together, might have been able to subdue Harry very quickly. That would explain a lot."

"That sounds like something from a film. You think a bunch of heavily built thugs bundled Harry into the back of a black car?"

"It's as likely as anything you've come up with," Alan said. "And you saw all those fat cats at the drinks party. I'll bet most of them have dealings with private security firms. A quick phone call is all it would take. And you've said it yourself; Harry had a knack for making enemies."

"It's an intriguing idea. Professionals would make quick work of snatching someone. But where's the motive?"

"When there's money at stake, there's greed. Harry was swimming with sharks. Maybe one of them turned on him, ready to bite."

Before Dan could comment, Jocelyn returned with Marco in tow. Marco was carrying a large tray, and Jocelyn waggled her fingers at the coffee table. "Set it down there, Marco. Thank you."

"Of course, Mrs Benning." Marco placed the tray carefully and began arranging the contents neatly around the table.

Jocelyn watched him like a hawk, then she pointed an accusing finger. "What's that?"

Marco flinched. "Sorry, Mrs Benning. Have I done something incorrectly?"

"That bowl," Jocelyn said. "Where has it come from?"

Marco looked unhappily at the table. There were several small bowls containing dips, olives, fruit, salad leaves and cherry tomatoes, and Marco ran his eyes over them all, seeking the source of Jocelyn's irritation.

"The one with the grapes in," Jocelyn snapped. "The wooden one."

"Ah, it was in the kitchen," Marco said. "Would you like me to replace it with a different one?" He plucked the bowl from the table. "I have to go back anyway, to get the tea."

"It doesn't matter. You can leave it there, Marco. It's just that I haven't seen it before. Scott must've bought it from somewhere. He's always coming home with bits of tat, and I have to throw them away when he's not looking."

"So, it's okay?" Marco asked.

"Yes. You can fetch the tea, Marco. And don't forget the oat milk. Put it in a jug. A small one."

Marco nodded and put the bowl back on the table, then he hurried from the room.

Jocelyn fussed over the plates, moving each of them a few millimetres further apart. "He's very good really, but you do have to spell things out for him." She offered them a smile. "Please, help yourselves. The flatbreads are fresh. Marco makes them himself. And the dips too. He adds just the right amount of seasoning. They're so much better than the shop-bought stuff."

"It all looks wonderful." Alan leaned forward, helped himself to a plate and began loading it.

"That's what I like to see," Jocelyn said, "a man with an appetite. Go on, Dan. Dig in."

Dan complied, taking a plate and adding a flatbread, a spoonful of houmous and some salad to his plate. His hand hovered over the bowl of grapes, then on an impulse, he picked it up to admire it. The bowl had been polished to a deep sheen, the wood's dark grain curling along its sides in an intricate pattern. "I wouldn't describe it as tat," Dan mused. "It's rather fine."

"But it doesn't match the others," Jocelyn said. "I wonder where he bought it. If you've finished with it, pass it here."

"Certainly." Dan handed her the bowl, and he watched as she turned it around in her hands.

"Hm. It's not my style at all. It'll be from John Lewis, I expect. If it's still got the sticker on, I might take it back the next time I'm in Exeter." Jocelyn held up the bowl to examine its underside. "Oh."

"What is it?" Dan asked.

Jocelyn dismissed his question with a shake of her head. She set the bowl down on the table. "Do have some more to eat. There's plenty. And Marco will be here with the tea in a minute."

"It's all delicious." Alan took another flatbread. "Better than anything we'd have had in the pub, eh Dan?"

"Yes. Much better." But Dan didn't take any more food. Instead, he picked up the bowl of grapes and lifted it to eye level. The base of the bowl was just as smooth and polished as its sides, but there was a small symbol carved into the wood: a triangular shape with a curl at each corner and a circle in the centre.

"Dan, what are you doing?" Alan asked.

"Just showing an interest," Dan said. "Here. See for yourself." He handed the bowl to Alan.

Jocelyn watched with raised eyebrows, but she remained tight lipped.

Reluctantly, Alan peeped beneath the bowl. "Ah yes, it's a kind of triskelion. An ancient symbol. Some people ascribe them to the Celts, but they don't usually have that circle in the middle. I'd say this is a maker's mark: a kind of signature, put there by the person who carved it."

Dan turned his attention to Jocelyn. "Are you sure you've never seen this bowl before?"

"Positive."

"But when you looked underneath, you saw the maker's mark, and you recognised it."

Jocelyn nodded. "It's probably just a coincidence, but it looks familiar. It's very like the mark we have on the table in the conservatory. Scott made a point of showing it to me. It's underneath, on the frame."

"And the two marks, do they look similar or are they identical?"

"I can't remember." Jocelyn smiled. "You can have a look if you really want to."

"Thanks. I will." Dan set his plate on the table, then he jumped to his feet and headed for the door.

"I wasn't being serious," Jocelyn protested, but Dan pretended not to hear.

"I'll find my own way there." Dan marched from the room, finding the conservatory easily and making straight for the large oak table. He crouched to look beneath it and heard footsteps hurrying over the terracotta tiles.

Alan kneeled beside him. "Can you see anything?"

"Not yet. Where's Jocelyn?"

"She went to get the tea, but from the look on her face, I'd say she disapproves of your behaviour."

"Doesn't everyone?"

"That's the consensus. But now you're here, you may as well find the mark." Alan took a small flashlight from his pocket and handed it to Dan. "Here."

"A tactical light. It's just like mine."

"Yes. Yours has come in handy a few times, so I found one online." Alan gestured to the table. "Go on then. Use it."

Dan turned on the light and played its beam along the table's underside.

"He'll have put the mark out of sight," Alan said. "He wouldn't want to spoil the look of the thing."

"Right." Dan shuffled further under the table, craning his

neck and training the flashlight's beam into the dark nooks and crannies. "There." Dan stared at the mark carved into the wooden frame. "Got it."

"Is it the same?" Alan asked. "Does it have the circle in the centre?"

"Yes. It's identical." Dan backed out from beneath the table and climbed to his feet. Alan followed suit, brushing himself down, but before they could speak, Jocelyn appeared in the doorway.

"Have you quite finished?" she asked.

"Yes, thanks," Dan replied. "At the party, you told me that a local craftsman made the legs and frame for this table. Was his name Reg Stoddard?"

"Yes," Jocelyn said. "What is this? Are you in the market for a couple of chairs?"

"No. I'm on the trail of a dangerous criminal."

Jocelyn blinked. "What on earth are you talking about?"

"I need to have a word with Marco." Dan pointed to the door. "It's this way to the kitchen, isn't it?"

Jocelyn nodded. "First door on your left, but—"

"I'll explain later, but you can come with me if you like. You too, Alan." Without waiting for a reply, Dan made for the door, vaguely aware of Alan and Jocelyn trailing behind him.

The door to the kitchen stood ajar, and Dan let himself in.

Standing at a granite-topped island unit, Marco looked up, a flash of alarm in his eyes. "Sir? Can I help you with something?"

"Yes," Dan said. "That wooden bowl, the one that Mrs Benning mentioned, where did you find it?"

Alan and Jocelyn arrived in the kitchen, and Marco's gaze went to his employer.

"It's all right, Marco," Jocelyn said. "There's nothing to worry about. You can answer the question, ridiculous as it may seem."

"Er, I'm not sure. Maybe it was on the counter this morning."

Dan noticed the twitch at the corner of Marco's mouth and the way the man's eyes roamed around the room in search of inspiration. He was lying. "Come on, Marco," Dan said. "You can tell us the truth. You won't be in any trouble." When Marco still didn't answer, Dan added, "Did you find the bowl somewhere strange? On the floor, perhaps?"

"Why would it be on the floor?" Jocelyn asked. "You're not making sense, and you're confusing poor Marco."

Dan turned to face her. "I think Reg Stoddard, or someone associated with him, was here. I think he turned up at the house, saying he'd come to deliver the bowl. He's been here before, and so his visit would've seemed reasonable. Someone let him in, and there was a scuffle. Harry was dragged outside, and the bowl was left where it fell."

"Look, why don't you forget about the damned bowl? I probably made a mistake. Maybe we've had it for months, and I'd just forgotten all about it."

Dan shook his head. "You have a keen eye for this kind of thing. You wouldn't make a mistake like that. The bowl is new. That's right, isn't it, Marco?"

Reluctantly, Marco nodded. "Yes. But I didn't find it on the floor. Miss Smethwick brought it into the kitchen this morning. That's all I know."

"That's Carol, Scott's PA," Jocelyn explained.

"We've met," Dan said. "I need to talk to Carol. Where can I find her?"

Jocelyn's expression gave nothing away. "She'll be in the office. I can take you, but what about your lunch?"

"Sorry, it'll have to wait."

"All right. It's this way." Jocelyn swept from the room. Dan gave Marco an apologetic smile, then he followed Jocelyn, Alan at his side.

"Are you sure about this?" Alan asked under his breath.

"Not entirely," Dan replied, "but it's worth following up."

"Maybe. But go carefully. Remember what Spiller said."

"You needn't worry, I won't make the same mistake again. We'll check the facts before I call Spiller. If it doesn't amount to anything, we'll forget all about it."

"Fair enough." Alan smiled. "It's good to be back on the trail though, isn't it?"

"Yes. Yes, it is."

CHAPTER 42

I N A SERVICE station off the A38, DS Spiller was sitting in
his car, sipping coffee from a paper cup. His phone
vibrated in his pocket, the harsh ringtone blurting into life,
unnaturally loud in the confines of the Volvo saloon. It
jangled Spiller's nerves, and he ground his teeth together. It
was probably someone back at HQ, wondering where he'd
got to. He'd been called back to base to interview Paul
Sanderson. The lad was playing silly buggers, and Detective
Inspector Riley reckoned Spiller could talk some sense into
the daft sod.

Can't I have five minutes peace to grab a coffee? Spiller asked
himself. He'd a good mind to let the call go to voicemail, but
that would never do. He'd answer the phone; he always did.

Sitting next to him, DC Collins extended his hand and
Spiller passed him the cup. "Thanks."

"No problem, Sarge. But next time, get a car with a cup
holder, yeah?"

"Fat chance. This car will last longer than I will." Spiller
retrieved his phone and inspected the screen. The call was
from a young DC at Exeter HQ, Barry Clarke, and Spiller
swiped the screen to accept it. "Spiller, here. All right, Barry?"

"Yes, but there's something I thought you'd like to know."

"Go on."

"You're on both of the Embervale cases, aren't you – the GBH and the MisPer?"

"For my sins," Spiller intoned. "And I don't like the look of the Denton case. It's something more than just a missing person. So I hope you're calling to cheer me up. What've you got for me?"

"Well, it might turn out to be nothing, but we've had a bloke calling in. He says he's from Embervale and he wants to confess."

At one time, those words might've caused Spiller's heart to flutter, but not anymore. "Crank caller?"

"Maybe, but we don't think so. He mentioned a couple of places in Embervale, and they checked out. He sounded like a local."

"All right, I'll bite. What's he confessing to?"

"He wouldn't give the details on the phone. He says he wants to meet in person, and he'll only talk to the person in charge. He claims to have committed a serious crime and says he has important information."

"Don't they all? And do we have a name for our civic-minded caller, or did he keep that a secret in case the little green men were listening?"

"That's a good one, Sarge, but he gave his name. It's a Mr Sturridge. Sid Sturridge."

CHAPTER 43

A T IRONBRAND FARM, Dan and Alan followed Jocelyn outside, crossing the yard to a large stone building that had been subtly modernised, its double-glazed windows set into frames of wood rather than uPVC.

"It was originally a barn," Jocelyn said. "It's where Scott does all his office work. I won't have a computer in the house. I can't stand cables trailing all over the place."

"Will Scott be in?" Alan asked.

"Let's see, shall we?" Jocelyn pulled open the door and waited for them to enter.

The sound of Scott's voice could be heard, and Dan's spine stiffened, his fists clenching involuntarily as he remembered what Sam had told him about the way Scott had treated her. But as if sensing his tension, Alan sent him a warning look, and Dan pushed his anger aside. He affected a grim smile, and Alan seemed to understand. It would be all right. They had more pressing matters in hand, and Dan marched inside with Alan hard on his heels and Jocelyn following.

The open-plan office was larger than Dan had anticipated, and at its far end, Carol was seated at a large desk with Scott standing next to her. Scott was leaning on the desk, concentrating on the pair of screens, but he straightened as Jocelyn, Dan and Alan approached.

· "Hello." Scott looked only at Jocelyn. "Is something the matter?"

"No. Dan and Alan wanted to ask Carol about something, that's all."

Scott frowned. "Darling, you know I'm working. I don't like to be disturbed."

"Blame me," Dan said. "I insisted, I'm afraid."

"And what's so important that it couldn't wait?" Scott asked.

"We're trying to work out what happened to Harry," Dan replied. "And it looks like we're onto something."

Scott let out a dismissive grunt. "The police are already looking into it."

"With respect, all the police have is a missing person and some malicious damage to a car. How much time and energy do you think they'll devote to that?"

"All right," Scott said. "What do you want to know?"

Dan turned his smile on Carol. "Hello again. This morning, did you give a small wooden bowl to Marco?"

"What a strange question," Carol replied. "But yes, I did."

"Where did you find it?"

"It was on the hall table, by the front door."

"Empty?" Dan asked.

Carol nodded. "Yes, but I knew it shouldn't be there. Mr Benning doesn't like clutter, so I took it through to the kitchen."

"And what time was this?"

"First thing," Carol replied. "I arrived just before eight, and Mr Benning was already in the office. He asked me to pop into the house and make a cup of coffee."

Dan glanced around the office and spied a small kitchen area. "Don't you have coffee-making facilities in here?"

"Yes. We have one of those pod machines, and it's fine for me, but Mr Benning likes his coffee freshly ground."

"Very wise," Dan said. "It's so much better."

"This is ridiculous," Scott snapped. "Did you really disrupt my work to ask how I take my coffee? And what's all this about bowls? I don't know what you're getting at, but it sounds like nonsense."

Dan paused before replying, and when he spoke, he kept his tone level. "Carol's right; there's never any clutter in your house, Scott. So that bowl would've been noticed if it had been left there during the day. That means it was almost certainly put there last night, the night on which Harry vanished. It's possible that someone gained entry to your house by pretending to deliver the bowl. And that someone was probably connected to Reg Stoddard."

"All I'm hearing is 'possible' and 'probably'," Scott said. "I remember Reg. A nice old chap. He made our table. But what the hell has he got to do with Harry?"

"Reg has a niece, and she's been working here."

"Really?" Carol asked. "Who?"

"Daisy Pugh. She was at the party when George was stabbed."

"Oh." Carol wrinkled her nose in distaste, and a sudden realisation hit Dan between the eyes. Daisy had been an employee, so she'd almost certainly been in this very room. Had she tried to steal data from here?

Dan looked at the computers ranged around the office and counted four, plus a couple of laptops.

Dan focused his attention on Carol. "Daisy has been in here, hasn't she?"

"Just once," Carol said. "She came in after her interview with Mr Benning. I needed her details for our payroll system and so on."

"Was she ever in here alone?"

"Oh no." Carol hesitated, her cheeks colouring. "That is,

not for long. I left her briefly while I went to fetch some paper for the printer, but I was only a couple of minutes."

"Where was she sitting?" Dan asked.

Carol indicated a chair facing her desk. "She was right there."

Dan went to Carol's side. Her desktop PC was mounted on a shelf below the desk, and Dan gestured toward it. "Excuse me, but do you mind if I take a look at your computer?"

Carol looked to Scott, apprehension in her eyes, and her employer squared up to Dan, his shoulders back. "You're damned right I mind," Scott said. "I mind a great deal. There's no way you're going to interfere with our computers. I don't know what your game is, Dan, but you've wasted enough of my time. You'd better leave."

"I can't do that," Dan said. "I need to check every computer in this room. Daisy also worked for a client of mine, and she planted a device on his computer. She used it to steal confidential data, and she might have done the same thing here."

"She did *what?*" Scott's jaw slackened. "No. She's just a kid, a girl we hired to do some cleaning."

"And she used that as a cover for her real intentions. Now, you could call in a cybersecurity expert, but that will take time. Or I can give you an answer right now. I know exactly what I'm looking for, so if she's planted anything on your machines, I'll see it. One look is all I need." Dan inclined his head. "It's up to you, Scott. What's it to be?"

Scott cursed under his breath. "Carol, shut the computer down, then go around the whole office and make sure every computer is switched off."

Carol grabbed hold of the computer's mouse, clicking it rapidly, then she stood. "Done. What about the laptops?"

"We can leave those for now," Dan said. "First, I'll check

the desktop machines. I could look at your laptops later — if you want me to, that is."

Scott stared at Dan as though making up his mind, then he turned to Carol. "You heard the man. Dan needs to see all our computers, so I want you to gather them all together and put them where he can see them. But make sure they're all shut down."

"Right away, Mr Benning." Carol hesitated, twisting her fingers together. "I should never have left that girl alone. I had no idea what she was capable of. She seemed so ordinary."

"You weren't to know," Scott said. "I was the one who hired her. But let's not get too carried away. She might not have done anything." Scott patted Carol on the back, and she stiffened.

"I'll get started with the computers." Carol hurried over to the nearest desk, and Dan saw the way Scott's eyes lingered on her as she bent over to shut down the computer.

"Scott, darling," Jocelyn said, her voice a little too high, a little too bright. "I'm going back to the house. I'll leave you boys to sort all this out, but whatever you do, don't give Carol a hard time. You can't run this place without her."

"Absolutely." Scott gave his wife a saccharine smile. "I'll see you later, darling. I'll let you know how we get on."

"If you must." Jocelyn turned on her heel and strode for the door, and though Scott watched her leave, his smile had gone.

To Dan, Scott said, "You'd better get started. But whatever you find, it has to be kept between us, all right? I don't want anyone to get even the slightest whiff of this."

Dan didn't reply. There was no way he could agree to Scott's terms, so he made his expression blank and kneeled in front of Carol's computer. He slid the machine forward on its shelf, then he felt around the back, tracing the keyboard's cable. And there it was: the same, smooth plastic shape he'd detected at Monty's house. Leaving it in place, he disconnected the other cables and pulled the computer out completely, setting it on the floor. Then he stood to deliver the bad news. "There it is, Scott. Can you see it?"

Scott bent down to look. "That little thing? What is it?"

"It's a keylogger," Dan said. He explained how the device worked, and Scott listened in silence, his gaze growing colder by the second.

When Dan finished, Scott sat down heavily. "It's a bloody disaster. An absolute bloody disaster. This explains everything."

"What do you mean?" Dan asked. "Has something happened? Something that made you suspicious?"

"*Suspicious?* If only it were that simple." Scott stared into space as though he'd forgotten the others were there. He mumbled something, but Dan couldn't quite catch it.

Carol rejoined them. "All the computers are off, so you can go ahead." Her gaze went to the machine on the floor and to the small device dangling from a USB port. "It's a tiny thing, isn't it? I'd never have known it was there. Mr Denton certainly didn't spot it."

"That's hardly surprising," Alan said. "I wouldn't have known what it was unless—"

"Hang on," Dan interrupted. "Carol, why did you mention Harry? The keylogger was completely out of sight, so how *could* he have seen it?"

"Well, he works in here sometimes. And the other day, when I came in, he was looking under the desk. He said the network cable had come loose, although…" Her gaze swept the room as if retracing an imaginary path. "I don't know. It must've been a coincidence."

Scott snapped out of his trance and sat up straight. "I don't believe in coincidences. Go on, Carol. Tell us the rest. What was he doing? What did he say?"

"As I said, he was under the desk and he claimed he was

fixing the cable. But now that I think about it, it seemed odd at the time. I mean, the cables are concealed and the plugs click into place, don't they? I remember wondering how it could've come loose, because I'd been using the computer the day before, and it had been working perfectly."

"When was this?" Scott demanded.

"Monday. Monday morning."

"The day after the party," Alan said. "Could the two things be connected?"

"Not necessarily." Dan let his gaze rest on Scott. "But there's one thing I'm fairly sure about: Harry knew what Daisy had been doing. That's why he went to Daisy's house. And that's why she went into hiding. Harry knew her secret, and he tried to use that knowledge to control her."

"But how did Harry find the device in the first place?" Alan asked. "It was hidden, and this isn't his desk, is it?"

Carol shook her head. "It's my desk, and no one else uses it. There's no need. We have plenty of space."

"Hm." Dan looked out of the window, running through different scenarios in his mind. Surely he could come up with a version of events that matched the known facts. But his flow of thought was interrupted by Alan saying, "And here's another thing. If Harry knew what Daisy was up to, why didn't he tell anyone?"

"That's easy," Scott replied. "Dan must be right; Harry was using her. He's been gathering ammunition to use against me, and that damned girl must've helped him. It looks as though Harry has been trying to oust me as chairman of Ironbrand. He's staging a takeover."

"Is that a possibility or a certainty?" Dan asked. "Do you have any evidence?"

"Not exactly. He's been too careful. I've had my suspicions for a while, but I didn't want to believe them. I thought we were friends. But now that he's disappeared, it's pretty obvious what he was up to. Suddenly all my backers are running for the hills. Investors I thought were rock solid have pulled out, and no one is returning my calls. I was beginning to think Ironbrand had become a toxic investment overnight, but the business is the same. The only thing that's changed is that Harry isn't here."

Silence filled the room. Scott leaned his elbows on the desk and covered his face with his hands. His shoulders shook, but not a sound came from him.

Dan watched him for a second. Was Scott play-acting? He didn't think so. Scott had just revealed a reason why he might want to harm Harry, but it was either a spectacular bluff or the genuine shock of a man who was in danger of losing everything he valued. And Dan knew what that looked like; he knew what that *felt* like.

Dan nudged Alan with his elbow. "We should go."

"But what about the other computers?" Carol asked.

"The situation has changed," Dan replied. "It looks as though Harry has been involved in a serious financial crime. You shouldn't touch the computers. Call the police and explain what's happened. They'll deal with it."

Scott looked up; his eyes rimmed with red. "No! Not the police."

"You have no choice," Dan said. "The police are already searching for Daisy and they're looking into Harry's disappearance. Whatever he's done, it will all come out soon. The only smart move is to get ahead of it, make sure your version of events goes on the record."

Scott didn't respond. He sat very still, his cheeks pale and his gaze darting around the room, like a man looking for an escape and finding every way barred.

His chickens have come home to roost, Dan decided. *He's trodden on the backs of others, and now that he's fallen down, no one will rush to help him.* But Dan kept the thought to himself. Scott could be arrogant and obnoxious, but he'd been taken in by someone far worse. Harry was the real villain here, and

Dan couldn't bring himself to kick Scott while he was down. Instead, he headed for the door, and Alan followed him outside.

"So, Daisy has graduated from cybercrime to corporate espionage," Alan said. "Who'd have thought? She seemed like a nice girl."

"You think everyone's decent," Dan replied. "You bring out the best in people."

"Well, in most people, perhaps." He looked expectantly at Dan as though expecting him to share the joke, but Dan didn't feel like smiling.

Dan turned to face the house. "The other day, when we were talking about the attack on George, I thought Daisy must've been in the kitchen when George was stabbed, but what if she was somewhere else?"

"Like where?"

"She could've been right here. The thing with keyloggers is that you have to collect the data from them. Sometimes you can access them remotely via Wi-Fi, but even so, Daisy would've wanted to retrieve the device sooner rather than later. The longer she left it in place, the greater the chance it would be noticed."

"Ah! I see what you're getting at. Usually, her work as a cleaner allowed her to come and go, planting the keylogger and retrieving it whenever she wanted. If she wasn't due to clean, she could easily come up with a pretext. She was trusted, and that made it easy for her to cover her tracks."

"Exactly. I found the one at Monty's house by chance. If Daisy hadn't gone into hiding, she probably would've removed it, and I'd have been none the wiser."

Alan looked thoughtful. "But during the party, the office would've been locked, wouldn't it?"

"Possibly. But they're not exactly security conscious here, are they? There's no CCTV and no burglar alarm that I can see. Nothing but a few floodlights. Daisy might've fancied her chances, so while the party was in full swing, she ran over here to try her luck." Dan turned on the spot, picturing Daisy's dash across the darkened yard. She was young and fit. It would've taken her only a few seconds.

"Did you notice how nervous she was that night?" Dan went on. "She was clumsy, almost stumbling into people. I thought it was because she was a fish out of water, but now we know the real reason; she was gearing herself up for a bit of breaking and entering."

"I think we might be getting somewhere," Alan said. "What's next?"

"That's a good question. Let's run with the idea that Reg has managed to grab Harry."

"All right, but we can't be certain Reg was here. Someone else could've brought that bowl."

"Unlikely. Reg knew it would gain him admittance because he'd been here before when he made the table. Who else would've thought of bringing the bowl?"

"Daisy? She was Reg's niece, so she must've visited him at home. She could've seen the bowl and taken it on an impulse."

"No," Dan said. "Daisy was an employee at the farm. She didn't need an excuse to show up here, so she didn't need the bowl. And anyway, can you imagine her overpowering Harry?"

"She could've lured him outside."

"You're grasping at straws, Alan. Reg is our man. He may be older than Harry, but he's big enough and strong enough to have grabbed Harry and forced him into his van."

"Does Reg have a van?"

"Yes," Dan said. "He told me about it when I met him in the shop. A Ford."

"Then they could be miles away by now."

"I think not. Reg would want to stay on familiar territory. They won't be far away."

"You already have an idea, don't you? Are you going to tell me, or do I have to guess?"

"Do you remember that wigwam of wooden poles we saw on Reg's allotment?"

Alan shrugged. "Vaguely. They're for growing runner beans."

"I guessed that much. But they weren't canes, were they? They weren't bamboo. They were much more substantial."

"I dare say they were hazel switches. It's common in the hedgerows."

"But these weren't ordinary bits of stick," Dan argued. "They were very uniform, very straight. And a man like Reg, a craftsman who works with wood, might be picky about the kind of poles he uses to grow his beans."

"Maybe, but it's not much to go on."

"It's not conclusive, but it set me thinking. And then I remembered the hand-carved walking sticks. Reg was displaying them at the fair. He makes them himself."

Alan rubbed his temple as though he sensed an incipient headache. "Will you get to the point?"

"Think about it. There's somewhere nearby where he might have got his supplies. It's a short drive, a parked van wouldn't attract attention, and it happens to be an ideal place if you wanted to disappear for a while."

"Brandle Wood!"

Dan grinned. "Let's go."

CHAPTER 44

D S SPILLER RAN his eye over the cottage's exterior. The house was small but well cared for. The white-painted walls were clean and bright, and the windowpanes were free from dust and grime. Beside the paved path, the square of lawn had been mown, its edges trimmed, and by the garden fence, the borders were planted with small shrubs that had been clipped to a uniform height.

No flowers, Spiller thought. It was as if the garden had been constructed according to a strict plan, and no room had been allowed for the wanton untidiness of colourful blooms.

Behind Spiller, DC Collins shuffled his feet. "Are you going to ring the bell, Sarge, or shall I?"

"Have patience, Collins. It's always best to look around before you do anything." Spiller took a last glance around the garden, then he stepped up to the door and rang the bell. He didn't have to wait long for it to be answered, and he smiled as the cottage door swung open.

A woman appeared in the doorway, eyeing him doubtfully. She wore a woollen cardigan over her floral print blouse, and her jeans were dark blue and spotless, as though they'd been freshly laundered. But although the woman's clothes looked brand new, her expression was altogether more careworn.

"Mrs Sturridge?" Spiller asked.

The woman nodded.

"I'm Detective Sergeant Spiller and this is DC Collins. We're from Devon and Cornwall Police. Your husband's expecting us."

Lisa Sturridge allowed herself a tiny sigh. "You'd best come in. He's in the lounge." She remained in the doorway, her lips tightening as though there was something she wanted to say.

"Is everything all right?" Spiller asked.

"Sid's just come home from the hospital. He's not well. I don't want you upsetting him."

"We'll do our best. This is an informal chat, Mrs Sturridge, nothing more."

"All right." Lisa stood back. "He's in the front room. It's this way. Shut the door behind you." She set off along the cottage's narrow hallway, and Spiller stepped inside, closely followed by Collins.

"Nice place," Spiller said. "Shut the door, Collins."

"I heard her, Sarge."

Spiller smiled. "I know. So why did I just repeat it?"

"Because, as usual, you want to remind me that you're the boss."

"That's right. Well done, Collins. We'll make a detective of you yet." Spiller fixed his colleague with a look. "It sounds like the man is in a fragile state, so we'll need to handle this carefully. We'll sit back and let him do the talking. Understand?"

"Yes, Sarge."

"Good. Now, watch and learn, Collins. Watch and learn." Spiller strolled into the cottage's front room and paused to look around while Collins followed him into the room and stood quietly by the wall.

Sid Sturridge sat in an upholstered armchair, a thick blanket draped over his knees, and his hands clutched together in his lap. His wife stood beside him, upright but anxious, as if waiting for bad news.

"Nice place you have here," Spiller said. "Very cosy."

"It does for us," Lisa replied.

Spiller indicated the sofa. "Mind if we sit down?"

"Of course not," Lisa said. "Do you want a cup of tea or…?" Her gaze went to her husband. "I don't mind making a pot of tea, m'dear, but would you rather I stayed here with you?"

Sid shook his head.

"A cup of tea would go down a treat." Spiller sat down on the sofa, making room as Collins joined him. "And I'm sure my colleague would agree."

"Actually, I'd prefer coff—" Collins began, but Spiller didn't let him finish.

"DC Collins takes his tea white with two sugars, but I'll just have milk, please. I'm supposed to be watching the calories. My wife tried to get me onto those sweeteners, but I'd rather do without."

Lisa scrutinised Spiller as though struggling with the idea that he might have a wife, let alone one who cared enough to watch his calorific intake, then she made for the door.

Spiller let a couple of seconds pass, fixing an enigmatic smile on his face as he watched Sturridge shift uncomfortably in his seat. The man still hadn't spoken, but for now, Spiller was prepared to wait.

The clock on the mantelpiece ticked.

Sid drew a long breath, then he said, "I shot at him."

"You shot someone?" Collins blurted. "Who?"

Spiller turned a stern glare on Collins. "I expect Mr Sturridge is coming to that."

"No. That's not…" Sid's fingers worried at the stubble on

his chin as he fought to find the right words. "What I said was, I shot *at* him. I didn't hit him, thank God."

"I see," Spiller said. "This is a very serious matter, Mr Sturridge, whether you hit someone or not. But you'll need to tell us more. At whom did you shoot? And when?"

"I don't know who the bloke was, I wasn't near enough to tell, but it was on Sunday night. I was in the wood and it was dark. I saw someone running, and..." Sid broke off, looking down. "I shouldn't have done it. Never. But there was no way I hit him. He was too far away, and I didn't aim at him. I fired too high on purpose. But I didn't mean to fire at all. It was more of a... what do you call it when you do it without thinking?"

"A reflex," Spiller said.

Sid nodded. "That's it. It was like I couldn't help it. I was afraid of what might happen."

"Are you claiming it was self-defence?" Spiller asked.

"Not exactly."

"What do you mean by that?"

"It's hard to explain. I'll get to that in a minute. But first, I need you to understand that I never hurt anyone. The bloke was trespassing on Mr Benning's land, heading for Brandle Wood, but he was a long way away."

"And you're absolutely sure no one was hurt?"

Sid nodded firmly.

"Sarge, we've had no reports of anyone injured by gunshots," Collins said. "Not recently."

"I'm aware of that, thank you," Spiller replied. "But on Sunday evening, several guests at Ironbrand Farm reported hearing a gun being fired nearby." He turned his piercing gaze on Sid. "So that was probably you, yes? A shotgun, was it?"

Sid nodded unhappily. "It was only loaded with four-ten cartridges. It's what I use for rats."

"Nevertheless, we can't have people taking potshots at passers-by," Spiller said.

"I know, sir. I suppose I'll lose my licence now, and that means I'll be out of a job, but it can't be helped. I had to get it off my chest. I'm making a clean start."

Spiller considered the matter. The man had fired a warning shot at a trespasser. He wasn't the first overzealous gamekeeper to do it, and he wouldn't be the last. And God knows, the man regretted what he'd done. Even so, he'd have to be cautioned. He'd let Collins handle that; it would give him something useful to do.

"Here we are." Lisa Sturridge breezed in carrying a tray, then she stood uncertainly, searching for somewhere to put it down. "Sid, pull Reg's table over here, would you?"

Leaning sideways from his chair, Sid took a magazine and a pair of reading glasses from a small table beside his chair, then he pushed it toward the centre of the room. "There you go."

"Thanks." Lisa placed the tray on the table, then she passed a mug to Sid. Turning to Spiller, she added, "The Chiefs mug is the one without the sugar."

"Thank you." Spiller picked up the mug emblazoned with the yellow and red logo of the Exeter Chiefs. "I haven't been over to watch the rugby for years. Do you follow the team, Mr Sturridge?"

Sid raised his eyebrows. "Of course. I used to play when I was a lad. You can't beat it."

"I prefer football," Collins said, earning frowns of disapproval from Sid and Spiller alike.

"I'm just saying." Collins took his mug. "Thanks for the tea, Mrs Sturridge. Very kind of you."

"You're welcome."

Spiller sipped his tea appreciatively, then he said, "That's a nice little table. Just now, you called it *Reg's table*. You wouldn't happen to mean Reg Stoddard, would you?"

"Oh yes," Lisa replied. "Reg made it."

"Fancy that."

Sid perked up. "He's a craftsman, is Reg. He gave us that table when we got married."

"Friend of yours, is he?"

"Not as such," Sid said. "Why?"

"We want to ask him a couple of questions. Do you happen to know where he might be?"

"If he's not on his allotment, he's usually at home." Sid slurped his tea. "What do you want him for?"

"It's a routine enquiry," Spiller said. "But we've tried his house and his allotment. No luck."

"Did you look in his workshop?" Sid asked. "It's down at the bottom of his garden."

"It was checked."

Sid shrugged. "I don't know then. We don't speak much these days."

"You haven't seen him recently, then?"

Sid pushed out his bottom lip, thinking. "Not for a long while."

"They used to be thick as thieves, those two," Lisa put in. "Isn't that right, Sid?"

Sid summoned a sad smile. "When I was a nipper, Reg sort of took me under his wing. I used to get into scrapes, you see. I had three brothers, and once my old dad passed away, Mother didn't know what to do with us."

"Four boys," Spiller said. "That must've been a handful."

"We were that, all right. There was always someone fighting over one thing or another. First, it was rugby, then it was girls. And later on, it was the beer that caused all the trouble. I can see that now."

"So, Reg was like a father to you."

"In a way. He showed me some of the old crafts, took me with him when he went to fix a barn or put up a fence. It was him that first took me to Ironbrand, and I met Mr Knowles — he was the estate manager in those days — and I reckon Reg put in a good word for me. The next thing I knew, Mr Knowles was knocking on the door, asking if I fancied helping the gamekeeper with the birds. He only offered me a few pounds a week, but it was my first proper job. I thought all my Christmases had come at once."

Spiller smiled. He'd got the man talking. Now, they were just a couple of blokes having a chat, and the rest would be easy. "What kind of man is Reg, would you say?"

"He's a hard-working man. Steady." Sid's eyes clouded as if at an unhappy memory, and Spiller didn't miss it.

Leaning forward, Spiller said, "What is it?"

"Nothing really." Sid let out a rueful sigh. "Times have changed, haven't they? People don't approve of it now, but back then, if a youngster misbehaved, he got a clip round the ear. And Reg was like a lot of blokes. He'd tell you once, he'd tell you twice, and if that didn't do the trick, he'd fetch you a thump that'd make your head spin."

Spiller set his mug back on the tray, the tea forgotten. "Did he hit you often?"

"Only when I deserved it. But it was a different matter if anyone mucked around with his Rosemary. She was a handsome maid, and there was many a local lad who went home with a shiner if Reg thought they'd tried anything on with her."

"Was Rosemary a girlfriend?" Spiller asked. "I've spoken to his wife, and her name is Patricia, isn't it?"

"Everybody calls her Trish," Lisa replied. "But you're barking up the wrong tree. Rosemary is his sister."

"This would be Mrs Pugh," Spiller said.

Lisa was suddenly wary. "That's right. How did you know that?"

"I've had a chat with Mrs Pugh. Would you say that Reg was still very protective of his sister?"

Sid looked doubtful, but before he could reply, Spiller added, "And what about his niece, Daisy?"

"What do you want to know about her for?" Lisa asked. "She's all right, isn't she?"

"We're having trouble finding Daisy," Spiller said carefully. "No one seems to know where she is."

Sid grunted. "That's young folk for you. Flighty." He went on for a while, grumbling under his breath, his Devonian accent growing thicker. Spiller could make out maybe one word in three, but he got the gist: young people were feckless, work-shy and too soft for their own good.

"You're getting tired, Sid," Lisa said. "Do you want to go and have a lie down?"

Sid sighed. "Don't make a fuss. I'm all right. As it happens, I've just had an idea where Reg might be."

"That would be very helpful," Spiller said.

"The only thing is, it's the wrong time of year."

Spiller's encouraging smile faded. "I don't follow."

"Well, I was going to say he might be in Brandle Wood," Sid replied. "Reg sometimes goes up there. He makes walking sticks and sells them at fairs and such. But he wouldn't be doing that now. You only cut wood for sticks in winter."

"I see. Brandle Wood is local, is it? Could you spell that for me?"

Sid obliged with the correct spelling, and turning to Collins, Spiller said, "Pop that in your phone. You'll need to give me directions."

"Are you going up there?" Sid asked.

"Yes. It's worth a look." Spiller grabbed his mug and took a quick slurp of tea, then he placed the mug back on the tray and smiled gratefully. "Thanks for your time and for the tea. You've been very helpful, but we must get moving." He nudged Collins in the ribs. "Come on. We've got some ground to cover."

Spiller and Collins stood together, and Sid made to get up, thrusting his blanket aside.

"No need to see us out," Spiller said. "We can find our own way."

But Sid rose to his feet. "If you're off to Brandle Wood, I'll have to come with you."

"That's not necessary," Spiller replied. "We'll find it."

"But you won't find Reg. You won't know where to start, but if he's there, I'll find him. Nobody knows those woods like I do."

Spiller opened his mouth to protest, but he didn't get the chance. Pulling himself up to his full height, Sid said, "Those woods are private property. I don't know the ins and outs of your business, but I reckon your life would be a damned sight simpler if you had permission before you went stomping all over the place. And I'm still the gamekeeper. So do you want me to take you there right now, or would you rather waste your time with a load of paperwork and red tape?"

"Actually, Sarge, he's got a point," Collins put in. "We don't have a good reason for going into this wood; nothing that'll stand up if the landowner makes a complaint."

"He can't complain if I'm with you," Sid stated. "And I can finish what I was telling you before, about when I fired my shotgun. There's more to it."

"I'm going to regret this," Spiller said. "But if you're sure you're feeling up to it, you can accompany us to the wood, Mr Sturridge. Just to point us in the right direction."

"That's settled then." Sid lifted his chin. "What are we waiting for?"

"Sid," Lisa began in a warning tone, but then she changed her mind. "I'll get your coat. And you'll need your boots." She bustled from the room, then they heard her call out, "Come and get yourself sorted out then. I'm not your servant."

"I'll be back in a tick." Sid left Spiller and Collins alone.

"I don't know about this," Collins said. "It feels like another wild goose chase to me."

"Collins, you know what I always say about sticking to procedure and following the rules. Well, that's good advice. But only for about eighty percent of the time. For the other twenty, you need to go out on a limb, seize the initiative. So yes, we are going to take a trip into the great outdoors. But remember this: don't ever question my authority in front of a member of the public. You can say what you like in the station. My shoulders are broad enough, and I can take a bit of banter. I've heard it all before. But out here, in the real world, it's important for us to look like we know what we're doing. So if your sentence begins with 'Actually, Sarge,' you'd do well to keep it to yourself. Do you understand?"

"Yes, Sarge. Sorry. It won't happen again."

Spiller nodded. "Good. And while we're setting the record straight, we do have a legitimate reason to go onto that land. According to Mr Sturridge, Reg has visited the wood on several occasions. That makes it a known haunt of a suspect: a man we're actively looking for in connection with a suspicious disappearance. If Reg has found out that Harry Denton was bothering his niece, he might well have taken matters into his own hands. And from what we've just heard, Reg can cut up rough. Harry Denton is in danger. If we don't follow every lead, we'll be failing in our duty. But unless you want to stay here for the next few hours while we organise a search party, we need Mr Sturridge's help."

"Got it, Sarge."

"Good lad. Now, get ready for some action, Collins. As soon as Mr Sturridge is ready, we'll be on our way. And we won't be hanging about."

CHAPTER 45

"LOOK!" FROM THE passenger seat of Dan's Toyota RAV4, Alan pointed through the windscreen. "That has to be Reg's van."

Dan nodded. The white Ford Transit van sat alone in the lay-by beside Brandle Wood. There was just enough room for Dan to park behind the van, and he tucked his car in as best as he could.

Without needing to discuss it, Dan and Alan climbed from the car and circled the van, peering in at the windows.

"No sign of anything suspicious," Alan said. "Shall we try the doors?"

"Yes."

Alan tried the front doors while Dan yanked at the handle on the rear, but they were all locked.

"Reg must be in the wood somewhere," Alan said. "It's too big for us to cover on our own. Maybe we should call the police."

"After last time?" Dan shook his head. "Anyway, I'm almost certain Reg will have stuck to the main path, at least to start with. He was probably forcing Harry to walk, and that would've been difficult if they were trying to push their way through the undergrowth."

"I'm not so sure about that. I only know of one main route through the wood, but Reg will be much more familiar with the place. He could've headed off in any direction."

"Even so, we could start on the main path and take it from there," Dan said. "We might see or hear something, pick up their trail."

"I'm game."

They made their way through the gate and set off along the path, moving as quietly as they could. Dan strained his ears, but all he heard was the drone of insects and the chirrup of birdsong that seemed to come from all around him.

"I've been thinking," Dan whispered. "Reg would've wanted to find a hiding place fairly quickly. The longer he stayed on the path, the greater the chance of someone else coming along."

"You sound as though you have somewhere in mind."

Dan nodded. "That hollow where Ade and Maria were camping. It was tucked out of sight, but it wasn't a long way from the path."

"That feels too obvious."

"How so? Reg doesn't know we've been there."

"Good point," Alan said. "And the students would've been following the same thought process. They wanted somewhere out of sight, and they wouldn't have wanted to lug their camping equipment too far."

"Exactly. And I think I can remember the way."

"You don't sound too sure. But don't worry, I can take you straight there. I found it last time, and I can find it again."

They trudged onward for a little longer, and then Alan struck away from the path, marching resolutely through the undergrowth. Dan followed close behind. There was nothing to confirm they were going in the right direction, and Dan looked in vain for any sign of trampled plants that might show where two men had passed. But soon he spied the ridge that marked the edge of the hollow.

Dan tapped Alan on the arm and said, "We need to take this slowly. We have no idea what we'll find. Be prepared for anything."

Alan nodded, his expression grim, then together they crested the ridge.

Below them, the hollow was empty.

"Dammit!" Dan muttered. "We'll have to—"

"Listen." Alan raised a finger. "Do you hear that?"

Dan tilted his head on one side. At first, there was nothing except the background sounds of the forest. But then he realised that the only birdsong was very faint. No birds sang in this part of the wood. Perhaps something had frightened them away. Was that what Alan had meant?

But Alan's expression was growing darker by the second. What had he heard?

Dan tried again, closing his eyes. And this time, he detected the unmistakable sound of a man in pain: a low moan carried on the breeze.

"This way!" Alan started running, skirting the hollow and crashing into a patch of bracken. Dan followed, keeping pace easily. He could run at this speed for hours and barely break a sweat, but today an unnamed fear coursed through his veins and his heart thudded heavily in his chest.

They headed deeper into the forest. The moaning was louder now, and despite the noise they were making as they trampled through the bracken, Dan could pinpoint where the pitiful groans were coming from. He picked up the pace, and from the corner of his eye, he saw Alan matching him stride for stride.

Ahead, a stand of spindly trees grew close together, their thin trunks forming a natural screen. Without hesitation, Dan and Alan barged through, pushing the leafy branches aside. And then Dan halted, his eyes wide.

A short distance away, in a clearing, a man sat slumped against a gnarled tree trunk, his head covered by a hessian sack, and his head hung low so that his chin must have been resting on his chest. The man's legs stretched out on the ground in front of him, his hands clasped in his lap, and around his chest, thick coils of rope held him fast against the tree.

"Come on!" Dan charged across the clearing, Alan hard on his heels.

The man's head snapped up, turning toward them, and he let out a frightened yelp, his feet scrabbling against the ground as they fought for purchase on the soft earth.

"It's all right," Dan called out. "We're here to help you."

Dan and Alan reached the man together, and they kneeled at his side.

"This sack is tied around his neck," Dan said. "Have you got a knife?"

"Ahead of you." Alan held up his Swiss Army knife. "Hold still," he said to the man, then pulling the thin rope tight, Alan slid the blade underneath and cut it away from the man's neck.

Alan took hold of the sack, but Dan laid his hand on Alan's shoulder to stop him.

"Close your eyes," Dan said to the man. "We're going to take the sack off, and the light might hurt your eyes."

The man let out a resigned grunt, and Dan nodded to Alan.

Working carefully, Alan lifted the sack. And there, his eyes screwed tight shut and a gag wrapped around his mouth, was Harry Denton. His features were haggard, and a gash showed where he'd been struck on the nose, but apart from that, he appeared unharmed.

"It's all right, Harry," Dan said. "You're safe now. I'll get this gag off you. Alan, can you deal with the rope around his hands?"

"Of course." Alan took Harry's hands in his and inspected the rope while Dan untied the strip of fabric that had been forced into Harry's mouth.

Harry opened his eyes a slit, and when Dan pulled the gag away, Harry took a shaky breath. He coughed, his chest heaving, then he laid his head back against the tree, blinking at Dan and Alan in turn.

"All night long," Harry mumbled. "I've been out here all night."

"Don't worry," Dan said. "We'll get you out of here. We'll make sure you're safe."

"Safe!" Harry spat the word. "What good is safe?"

Dan hesitated. Harry's eyes were wild. He was traumatised. He probably didn't know what he was saying.

"I'm having trouble with his hands," Alan said. "The rope has cut into his skin. We might have to get a doctor to take a look at it."

"I'll call an ambulance." Dan stood, taking out his phone.

"Wait!" Harry said. "I don't need a doctor. Just get me out of here before that man comes back. He wandered off — he didn't say why — but he warned me not to move. He said he'd only be a few minutes. He could turn up at any second."

Dan froze. Had he just heard someone approaching? There it was again: the snapping of a twig beneath a boot. Dan saw the look on Alan's face and knew he'd heard it too.

Dan bent down, running his hands over the rope holding Harry to the tree. It was thick nylon rope and it had been tied tight, the knots bunched together in an ugly lump, impossible to unpick.

Dan turned to Alan. "Leave his hands for now. We need to get him on his feet. Try your knife on this rope."

Alan moved to the tree trunk and set to work, gamely sawing at the tough rope. "This is going to take too long. Someone's knotted each loop separately then tied them all together."

Harry moaned. "Please, you have to try. The man is unhinged. I don't know what he's going to do."

"The man who did this, was his name Reg?" Dan said. "Reg Stoddard?"

"I think so." Harry nodded uncertainly. "Yes. Reg. That's what he said."

"Was he armed?" Dan asked. "Did he have a weapon?"

"I didn't see. He hit me, put a bag on my head, and I felt something hard against my throat. He said he'd cut me. He must have a knife and he's crazy enough to use it. The man's a maniac. Don't you see? He was the one. He stabbed George."

The words left Dan's lips before he could stop himself: "That's a wild guess. You couldn't have seen anything. You were by the office at the time."

Harry stared at Dan, "How did you know?"

"You found Daisy trying to break in, and you found out about her keylogger. But you decided to leave it in place because you're working against Scott."

"Are you kidding?" Harry said. "You're doing this *now*?"

"It's as good a time as any. We'll help you, Harry, but remember, you made this mess worse when you tried to coerce Daisy."

"*Coerce?* You think…" Harry let out a hysterical guffaw, his mouth stretched wide. "I never forced her to do anything. I offered to pay her, and she agreed. How was I to know she'd panic and run away?"

"You went to her house," Dan insisted. "You intimidated her."

"I had to make sure she'd take it seriously, but I wasn't going to hurt her. I was going to pay her more money than she'd ever see in her lifetime. But she couldn't hack it, so you have to make me the villain. You're as bad as bloody Reg. You're out of your minds, both of you!"

"Shush!" Alan hissed. "Someone's coming."

But Harry raised his voice even louder. "Let them. What do I care? It's over. Whatever happens, I'm finished."

"Tell me one more thing," Dan said quickly. "You hired George to cater for that party, but only because you wanted to keep him onside. He saw the farmworkers, didn't he? He figured out they were illegal immigrants."

"Wrong again. They're all here legally. They've all got passports. But George stuck his nose in. He wanted to stir things up, cause trouble. I had to sweeten him somehow, so I gave him a job. These so-called social justice warriors are all the same. Show them the money and they change their tune."

Dan's mind worked quickly. Harry's bluster was a charade, an act he was putting on because, despite everything, he was still hiding the real story. He would never have hired George unless there was something at stake. But Harry had seemed genuine when he'd said the workers weren't illegal immigrants. So what was he hiding? Something worse?

And then Dan realised the truth, and a shudder of revulsion ran through him. Fighting to keep his voice level, Dan said, "It's funny. Just now, when I mentioned the workers, you immediately started talking about their passports. Devious people often take a grain of truth and work it into their lies. You visualised the workers' passports because you have their papers under lock and key, don't you? You're keeping those people on the farm against their will. Modern slavery, that's what you're involved in, isn't it?"

Harry glared at Dan. "Don't be ridiculous. What are you basing that on? Where's the evidence?"

"I'll find it," Dan replied. "Perhaps I'll start with Marco. He may have spent time in Italy, but he's not Italian. Where is he really from? Judging by the food he makes, I'd say Turkey. George was selling flatbreads at the May Fair, and he told me they were made locally and to a Turkish recipe. He must've met Marco before the party. Interesting. It sounds as though

Marco had a little sideline. No doubt he was desperate for money. Am I right?"

Harry's only reply was a scowl.

"We can sort all this out later," Alan said. "The important thing is to get to safety before things get out of hand."

"Agreed," Dan replied. "You keep working at the rope, and I'll try to buy us some time."

"All right. But what are you going to do?"

"Whoever's coming this way, I'm going to meet them head on. If I find Reg, maybe I can hold him up while you get Harry free."

"It sounds like a plan," Alan said. "But be careful. He could be dangerous."

"Of course he's dangerous," Harry spluttered. "You can't go anywhere near him. He's deranged. There's nothing you can do."

"Don't bet on it." Dan strode for the clearing's edge, his fists clenched. Reg was a big man, but he'd be slow. Dan was younger and fitter. If it came to it, he could stop Reg. He'd have to.

CHAPTER 46

DS SPILLER SENT his Volvo along the narrow lane as fast as he dared. It had been a long time since he'd taken the advanced driving course at work, and the lane was bordered by a tall bank that looked distinctly solid. If he met an oncoming vehicle, there'd be no room for him to swerve, and he wasn't convinced he'd be able to avoid a collision.

In the back seat, Sid Sturridge hooted. "Bloody marvellous, this."

"Take the next right," Collins said. "It's a hard turn."

Spiller nodded; his jaw clenched tight.

"There's the turn!" Collins cried. "Brake."

Spiller braked, changed gear and threw the Volvo into the turn. Tyres rasped over loose gravel as the Volvo's rear end slid sideways, and then they were off, roaring along the lane.

"Bloody hell, Sarge," Collins murmured, and hearing the grudging respect in the younger man's tone, Spiller smiled.

"It's just up there," Sid called out. "That's Reg's van."

A blue Toyota was parked tight behind the van, so Spiller drove his Volvo diagonally in front of the van and stopped. If they missed Reg in the woods and he made it back here, he wouldn't be able to drive away.

Spiller and Collins jumped out of the car, and Collins went to help Sid clamber from the back seat. The colour had returned to Sid's cheeks and his eyes were alight with new-found energy.

"It's this way." Sid marched straight for the gate, Spiller and Collins following close behind.

They trooped along the path, Collins regarding his surroundings in disapproval.

"What's up?" Spiller asked. "Not afraid to go into the woods, are you?"

"Don't be daft, Sarge. It doesn't bother me. But where do we start? He could be anywhere."

"No," Sid replied without slowing. "Most people don't want to get lost, so they stick to the same old familiar spots. Reg is no different. And I've been thinking about it. I know exactly where he'll be."

"Enlighten me," Spiller said.

Sid pointed to the right of the path. "There's an old hazel coppice. Nobody looks after it anymore, but it's a good place to cut sticks, and I've seen the signs. Someone has been taking branches every winter, and it has to be Reg."

"How can you be sure?" Spiller asked.

"Well, a few years back, Reg asked me if it would be all right to take a few sticks, and I said it would be fine. This must have been five or six years ago, but the branches still get cut every year, nice and neat, and he always takes them when they're the right size. I've never seen him at it, but every time I pass that coppice, I think of old Reg, and I have a look to see if he's been."

"Makes sense," Collins said. "Has he been here recently?"

Spiller tutted. "Weren't you listening? The time to cut sticks is in the winter. Isn't that right, Mr Sturridge?"

"Right enough." Sid stopped walking, and he indicated a trail of flattened undergrowth. "See? That's where he's gone."

"How far is it from here?" Spiller asked.

"Not far. It'll only take a few minutes to get there."

Spiller patted Sid on the arm. "You've done a good job, but you'd better let me lead the way."

"All right, but you still need me to come with you, otherwise you might miss it."

"Okay, but you'll have to stay behind me. Stick with DC Collins, Mr Sturridge. He'll look after you."

Reluctantly, Sid stepped to one side, allowing Spiller to march into the undergrowth.

This is it, Spiller thought. *Finally, this case is about to crack open.* But it wasn't over yet, and he had a very bad feeling about what they might find. He just had to hope he'd be in time.

CHAPTER 47

D AN STOPPED TO listen. Someone was stomping clumsily through the forest, and they were getting closer.

Turning on the spot, Dan scanned his surroundings, searching for some position that might give him an advantage. But the ground was flat here, without so much as a mound of earth for him to stand on.

He spotted a dead branch on the forest floor and he grabbed it, testing its weight in his hands. The branch felt too light, as though it was half rotten and ready to snap. It wouldn't be much use as a weapon, but perhaps it would serve as a deterrent in case Reg was tempted to rush him.

It'll have to do, Dan decided. *There's no time to look for anything better*. Just a few strides from where he stood, something stirred behind a clump of bushes. Dan froze, watching. A shadowy figure flitted across a gap between the shrubs, then the branches parted, and Reg marched into view.

Dan drew a sharp breath. The shambling old man was gone, replaced by a vengeful demon in human form. Reg's hair was awry, his lips were pulled tight in an angry line, and his eyes burned with a simmering rage.

But Dan's gaze slid to the long, sturdy blade dangling from Reg's hand. Some kind of saw, its edge was deeply serrated, the vicious teeth glinting, and Reg gripped it tight, hoisting it to waist height as he glared at Dan.

"You," Reg growled. "What the bloody hell are you doing here?"

Dan held the man's furious gaze. "Hello again, Reg. I might ask you the same question. What are *you* doing here?"

"Never you mind. I have every right to be here."

"Is that so?" Dan glanced at the saw in Reg's hand. "What's that for? Are you planning to cut down a few trees?"

"Don't talk daft. It's a pruning saw. I was going to cut some sticks if you must know."

"Really? Does Scott Benning know that you come in here to hack lumps off his trees?"

Reg grimaced. "I don't rightly know, and I can't say as I care. But I know Sid Sturridge, and he said it's all right, so that's that." He took a slow step closer to Dan. "For townies like you, it's a different matter. You have no business being here, so why don't you bugger off?"

"I can't do that, Reg. You see, I'm not here alone. And we've found Harry. My friend is with him now, and we know what you did."

Reg froze, his face a stony mask. "What did you just say?"

"It's over, Reg. It's time to put down your weapon and give up."

"This isn't a weapon." Reg waggled the saw in the air. "I told you, it's for cutting sticks."

"And no doubt it put the fear of God into Harry. But you don't need it anymore. Whatever Harry's done, he's paid the price, don't you think? The poor man is frightened out of his wits."

"Poor man! Poor bloody man!" Reg stormed toward him, and Dan raised the dead branch, holding it across his body.

The half-rotten wood was too weak to stop a direct blow from the saw, but perhaps it was strong enough to deflect a swipe or two.

"Have you any idea what he did?" Reg demanded. "Do you even know what that bastard is capable of?"

"I have my suspicions, and I'll make sure to tell the police what's been going on around here."

Reg came to a sudden standstill, staring at Dan in disbelief. "He went to my sister's home, barged his way in and threatened my niece. She was petrified. He had no right to do that, no right at all."

"I agree," Dan said. "I presume Daisy hid in your shed for a while, but then you spirited her away. You told me you were going to Exeter to visit Sid, but I don't believe that. You said you weren't even friends, so where were you really going? There's a station in Exeter, so you could've sent Daisy anywhere from there, but you mentioned a brother in Sheffield. Is that where she is?"

Reg didn't reply, but a flicker of astonishment raced across his features.

"Family is very important to you, isn't it?" Dan went on. "You talked a lot about your relatives when we first met at the May Fair. I remember what you said about your uncle and his sheepdog. A young child shouldn't be exposed to that kind of brutality. It makes me wonder how you were brought up. Was your dad a bit free with his fists, Reg? Is that why you're carrying around all this anger? I bet it is. And you know what? I feel sorry for you, Reg. I really do."

Reg mashed his lips together, then he said, "You're trying to tie me up with words. But you didn't shout for help. That's because you're on your own, aren't you? There's nobody else here. You're lying."

"You're wrong about that. I haven't lied to you, Reg. I wouldn't do that. Believe it or not, I don't want you to get into any more trouble. And it's not too late. You can still walk away from this. You haven't hurt anyone, and I don't think you intend to, otherwise you'd have done it already. You could've hurt Harry when you arrived at the farm, but you didn't. The only thing you've damaged is his car, and that—"

"What car?" Reg interrupted. "I never touched any car."

"Someone vandalised Harry's car. The tyres were slashed."

"Not me. I don't even know what his car looks like."

Dan examined Reg's expression and felt certain he was telling the truth. But that could be checked later. In the meantime, he had to work out a way to get through to the man before his temper flared.

"I believe you, Reg, and I'm glad to hear it wasn't you. Someone else must've damaged the car, and you can explain that when we talk to the police."

"Police be damned." Reg spat on the ground. "I've had enough of this. You reckon you're a smooth talker, but I've never heard so much rubbish in all my life." Reg nodded as though coming to a decision. "But you're right about one thing. It's not too late. I've still got time to finish the job. I'll take care of Harry Denton, and God help anyone who stands in my way."

Dan raised his hand. "Reg, no."

But Reg wasn't listening. He brandished the saw, raising it to shoulder height, then he charged at Dan, letting out a bellowing roar that vibrated in Dan's chest.

For a fraction of a second, Dan considered standing his ground. Reg's attack was all sound and fury, intended to frighten Dan away. There was no way he'd swing saw as a weapon, was there? But Dan's instincts took over, and he darted to one side, bracing himself against a sturdy tree trunk. The tree would shield him on one side and give him something to duck behind if needed. But still, he felt exposed, with nothing but a stick to defend himself.

Get ready, he told himself, holding his dead branch with both hands. *You'll only get one shot at this. Make it count.*

Dan held his nerve as Reg thundered toward him. The man was two strides away. One. Reg swung the saw back over his shoulder, his teeth bared in a cruel snarl, his bloodshot stare fixed on Dan. And then he lashed out, bringing the saw down in an arc toward Dan's head. The blade flashed in the sunlight, and Dan ducked, dropping into a squat. He heard the saw sink its teeth into the tree trunk above him, and Dan struck out with the dead branch, driving it with all his might into Reg's right kneecap.

Reg grunted in pain and staggered back, but he stayed upright, and the saw was still in his hands. "You bastard!" Reg growled. "Why did you have to poke your bloody nose in? Why don't you mind your own bloody business for once, eh? You shouldn't even be here. You don't belong."

Dan locked eyes with his assailant, then very slowly he stood. He tossed the branch aside. There was only one course of action open to him now. He would have to make a dash for it, and the branch would've slowed him down. He could outrun Reg easily, leading him away from Alan and Harry, taking him toward the road. There was very little chance of finding a passer-by to help, but the chase would tire the older man, and that would even the odds in Dan's favour.

Dan tensed his legs, ready to dart forward. Mentally, he picked out a path through the trees, then he drew a slow breath, taking the air deep into his lungs.

Reg advanced on him once more, silent this time, placing his feet carefully, focusing on his task. There was no sign of mercy in his gaze, only a savage sense of purpose.

Dan steadied himself against the tree, ready to push away from it.

And in the distance, a man's yell split the air: "Police! Drop your weapon!"

Reg flinched, looking to his left, and Dan saw DC Collins haring through the forest, his long legs making easy work of the uneven terrain. Behind him, Spiller followed, his arms pumping wildly as he ploughed through the clumps of undergrowth that Collins had leaped over.

"Give yourself up, Reg," Dan said. "Don't do anything stupid."

"Bugger that." Reg dropped his saw, then he turned and fled, hobbling as he lumbered off into the forest, quickly disappearing from view.

"After him, Collins," Spiller shouted. "I'll be right behind you."

Dan could only stand and watch as Collins sprinted through the trees in pursuit.

Spiller jogged to a halt in front of Dan, gasping for breath but grinning. "All right, Mr Corrigan? Still in one piece?"

"Just about. But I must admit, I've never been so glad to see a policeman."

"All part of the service." Spiller's hand went to his side, and he exhaled noisily.

"Stitch?" Dan asked.

Spiller wrinkled his nose. "Not really."

"I'll take your word for it. Aren't you going to go and help DC Collins?"

"No. He can handle an old man. Besides, it's good for his arrest rate. Let the lad have his moment of glory. He'll call me if he needs help."

"We've found Harry Denton," Dan said. "He's okay, but he's a bit shaken up. Alan's with him now."

"Was he near a hazel coppice by any chance? Lots of thin branches?"

"Yes. How did you work that out?"

Spiller glanced over his shoulder. "Mr Sturridge brought us here. I don't know where he's got to."

"I expect he'll turn up," Dan said. "I'll take you to Harry. He has a lot to tell you."

"Lead on, Mr Corrigan. Lead on."

Sid Sturridge wandered back to the path. He'd seen Reg squaring up to that man, seen the set of his shoulders, and it had brought back memories, memories that made his gut squirm. He'd done his best to wipe the bad old days from his mind, and for most of the time, he'd succeeded. But one glance at Reg had brought it all back. *I was only a child*, he thought. *He'd no call to treat me like that.*

Reaching the path, Sid paused, leaning against a tree to steady himself. Whatever happened next, he'd let the policemen deal with it. He was suddenly worn out, his leg muscles aching. Since he'd come off the drink, he seemed to tire so easily.

I need to get fit again, he decided. *Start afresh.* It wouldn't be easy, but Lisa would stand by him. She hadn't said as much, not directly, but he knew. He'd seen it in her eyes. He'd won the lottery when he'd married Lisa and no mistake. She was worth ten of any other woman. No, that wasn't enough. She was beyond any measure he could dream of. And to think, he'd almost thrown it all away.

Sid sniffed, wiped the corner of his eye on the back of his hand. *You'll be all right*, he told himself. *It'll all work out in the end.*

A noise made him look up, and he turned to see a man creeping out onto the path. *Reg!*

Staring at Sid, Reg froze, a flash of fear in his eyes. Reg looked like a deer caught in the headlights, and something snapped in Sid's mind, a spark of outrage firing in his belly. Reg had tormented him for long enough. The man wasn't to be feared. He was a bully, a coward. And he was trespassing on Sid's turf.

Pushing himself away from the tree, Sid pulled himself up

to his full height. "Reg Stoddard! You'd better stay right there."

"Shut up, you bloody idiot." Reg marched toward him. "Get out of my way. This doesn't concern you."

"It does." Sid puffed out his chest. "I'm the gamekeeper in this wood, and you'll answer to me. What the hell have you got yourself into? The police are after you, and I've been helping them. What do you say to that?"

"I say, why don't you mind your own business, you bloody drunk? You've never been any good. You were a pathetic little brat and you're no better now. You're weak, always have been. Now, get out of my way." Reg barged past Sid, storming along the path, making a desperate bid for freedom.

But that wasn't going to happen. Taking a run-up, Sid threw himself at Reg, launching himself at the man's legs. It might've been a good number of years since Sid had played rugby, but his muscles still knew how to execute a perfect tackle. His arms locked around Reg's legs, and the big man went down hard, landing heavily on his front with a dull thud. Reg cried out, struggling to get free, but Sid held on tight, pressing Reg's legs tight against the ground. He wasn't going anywhere; not today.

"Bloody hell," someone said, and then DC Collins was kneeling beside him. "Are you all right, sir?"

It took Sid a moment to realise the policeman was talking to him. "Yes. Yes, I'm fine."

"Good man. You can get up now. I'll take it from here."

Sid disentangled himself and stood shakily, light headed. He had an urge to laugh, but that wouldn't be right.

Collins manhandled Reg to his feet. "Mr Stoddard, you can come with me and assist us in our enquiries, or I can arrest you right now. What's it to be?"

Reg tensed, but Collins had a tight grip on the man's arm and he simply repeated his question.

"All right," Reg snapped. "Don't keep going on. I'll come with you." Reg shook his head, but his shoulders slumped. The fight had gone out of him.

"Good. That'll be easier all around." Collins winked at Sid. "By the way, sir, that was one hell of a tackle. Well done."

"I told you," Sid replied. "Rugby. It's a great game. You can't beat it."

CHAPTER 48

A LAN CUT THROUGH the last thread of rope, and with the aid of DS Spiller, Dan helped Harry to his feet.

"Are you all right, Harry?" Dan asked. "Can you stand?"

But Harry raised a shaking hand to point. "Keep him away from me."

Dan turned to see Collins leading Reg by the arm, with Sid Sturridge at his side.

"You've nothing to worry about, Mr Denton," Spiller said. "We'll get you fixed up, then you can both come down to the station and we'll sort it all out."

"Reg isn't the only one with a case to answer," Dan said. "You'll need to ask Harry about the conditions at Ironbrand Farm, and you'll need to interview all the workers."

Before Spiller could reply, Sid hurried over to join them. "That's right. That's what I was trying to tell you about."

"Shut up, Sturridge," Harry snapped. "Keep out of things you don't understand."

Sid bridled. "I understand all right. I know what's been going on, and I'll tell anybody who'll listen." He wagged an accusing finger at Harry. "It was all *him*. He wanted to scare the poor devils he's got cooped up over there, so he told me to march around with my gun and my dogs. I didn't know what he was up to, not at first, but he got all the workers together, and he told them I'd shoot them if they tried to get away. Then he made me drive around the farm at all hours of the day and night, just to make sure they were all too scared to run away."

Spiller stared at Sid. "So, when you said you shot at someone…"

"It was one of the workers making a run for it. I drove over the field, but the buggy got stuck in a ditch, so I had to jump out. I tried running after him, but it was no use. And Mr Denton had got me into such a state, I did exactly what he'd told me to do. I fired my gun."

Harry sneered. "He crashed our utility vehicle and he fired his gun because he was drunk, as usual."

"No. I got drunk because I couldn't live with myself. I couldn't live with what you made me do."

"For God's sake," Harry muttered. "Why are we wasting time with this nonsense? Let's go. I want to press charges against that old man for a start. Then I'm going to sue Corrigan for defamation. My lawyers are going to have a field day."

"We'll see about that," Spiller said. "All in good time."

"And don't forget the criminal damage to his car," Collins chipped in. "That'll have to be cleared up too."

"That wasn't Reg," Dan said. "Someone else slashed the tyres; someone who wanted to take revenge for the way Harry tried to intimidate Daisy." Dan clicked his fingers. "It was almost certainly her boyfriend, Paul. He was seen arguing with Reg in the street. Paul was angry, and now we know why. He found out that Harry had paid a visit to Daisy's house, and he wanted to hit back."

"We'll look into it." Spiller took Harry by the arm. "Let's get going. There's a lot to unpick."

"I'll come with you to the police station," Sid said. "I want to make a statement."

"Later perhaps." Spiller looked to Dan. "Was that your Toyota I saw in the lay-by?"

"Yes."

"Excellent. Could you run Mr Sturridge home? He's played his part, but he's been unwell recently. It's time he had a rest."

"Of course," Dan replied. "I'm happy to help, but you'll need Alan and me to come to the station, won't you?"

Spiller smiled. "It depends on how cooperative these gentlemen are. But we'll contact you if we need you. And that goes for you too, Mr Sturridge."

"Oh." Sid looked a little deflated. "What about me firing my gun? Will I have to go to court?"

Spiller and Collins exchanged a look.

"Just now, he stopped the suspect from getting away," Collins said. "I don't know how the old man gave me the slip, but if it hadn't been for Mr Sturridge, things might've worked out differently."

"There you go then." Spiller winked at Sid. "I don't think you've got anything to worry about, sir. But if I were you, I'd stay off the sauce. It seems like you fare better without it."

Sid nodded firmly. "I'll never touch another drop, don't you worry."

Reg had remained silent, staring at the ground, but now he lifted his head to stare balefully at Sid. "Sorry, lad, for what I said. I shouldn't… I should never have…"

Sid looked away.

"Right," Spiller said. "Let's get down to the station. I don't know about you lot, but I could do with a cup of tea." He grinned. "But not for you, DC Collins. You can have coffee."

The policemen and their suspects made a strange group as they walked away through the forest. Dan, Alan and Sid stood and watched them go, then they eyed each other warily.

"Are you ready, Mr Sturridge?" Alan asked.

"Yes, thanks. I'm ready for home." He licked his lips. "But listen, gents, do me a favour. Call me Sid."

Alan smiled. "No problem. Are you all right to walk, Sid?"

"Fine."

"Maybe you could show us the best way," Dan said. "I expect you know all the little paths."

"Every one of them," Sid replied. "Like the back of my hand."

FRIDAY

CHAPTER 49

D AN WAS STILL asleep when his phone rang, but he
grabbed it almost instantly, snatching the handset from
his bedside table before his eyes were fully open. "Hello?"

"Good morning, Mr Corrigan. It's DS Spiller here. I hope I
haven't called too early."

"No. It's fine. Is everything all right?"

"Yes. I just wanted to let you know that William Nickleton
has been released. The soil tests proved he'd been on the
allotments, and faced with the evidence, Billy changed his
tune and owned up to damaging the plants. We found no
evidence that he'd been at Ironbrand Farm, so we're inclined
to believe his story."

"Right. That's good news. Thanks." Dan wasn't sure what
else to say. Spiller hadn't thanked him for finding the crucial
evidence, but his tone was much more companionable than
usual.

"There's something else you might like to know," Spiller
said. "Reg Stoddard has been cooperating, and he's admitted
to abducting Harry, so that makes life easier."

"Have you found Daisy? Did you get my message? I sent
it yesterday."

"I received your text, and your guess was correct. Reg put her on a train to Sheffield and arranged for her to stay with his brother. She's been interviewed under caution by the South Yorkshire Police, and she had a lot to say. According to her, at the time of the knife attack at Ironbrand Farm, she was with Harry Denton. He'd just caught her trying to break into the office, and she's confident of the exact time. She'd slipped away from her duties, so she was watching the clock to make sure she wasn't too long. Of course, that means she's inadvertently given Mr Denton an alibi, so he's in the clear when it comes to the knife attack. You'd think he'd be grateful, but he's not. Unfortunately, he's being less than helpful."

"Have you talked to the workers at Ironbrand?"

"Oh yes," Spiller replied. "We took a team up there yesterday, and I won't go into the details, but let's just say that we've started a full-scale investigation."

"That's good to know," Dan said. "Is it modern slavery?"

"That remains to be seen, but I've had a pat on the back from the top brass, and even better, a few drinks were sent my way in the pub last night. It didn't hurt that I was the one who got Paul Sanderson talking. He's been singing like the proverbial canary. Once he knew we had his girlfriend, there was no stopping the lad."

"I take it that he was the one who slashed Harry's tyres."

"Correct. But that was just the start of it."

"You sound very pleased with yourself," Dan said. "Does that mean he owned up to the computer crime as well?"

"Got it in one. That keylogger you found at Ironbrand Farm was a big help. But what you don't know is the extent of Sanderson's little enterprise. He's asked for thirteen other cases of identity fraud to be taken into account. So with one stroke, I've cleared up a whole batch of cases."

Dan thought of Monty. "Will you have to investigate each one?"

"It depends on the individual circumstances. To start with, we'll warn the victims, offer them advice and support, that sort of thing."

"I see. And what about Paul and Daisy? Will they go to prison, do you think?"

"Oh yes, and quite right too," Spiller said. "All in all, things are going well. The only fly in the ointment is that we still haven't tied up what happened to George Hepworth, so if you get any more bright ideas, give me a call, eh?"

"I will. How is George? Any news?"

There was a pause before Spiller replied. "Sadly, he needs another operation. It's going to be carried out today. Fingers crossed for the lad, but..." Spiller sighed. "Put it this way — in my experience, surgeons don't usually operate on a bank holiday. Not unless they really have to."

"That sounds serious," Dan said. "I hope he pulls through."

"You and me, both. But looking on the bright side, it means they've found a problem and they're fixing it. They'll take care of him."

"Yes. Well, thanks for letting me know."

"No problem, Dan. Keep in touch. Bye."

The call ended and Dan flopped back in his bed. Had DS Spiller just called him Dan? *Yes*, Dan decided. And throughout the call, there'd been no snide remarks, no thinly veiled exasperation. What had got into the man?

He's not so bad, Dan thought. Yes, Spiller had dragged Alan over the coals in the past, but the man had only been doing his job. And the Detective Sergeant might be a bit flat footed when it came to solving problems, but whatever his faults, he'd turned up in the nick of time and saved Dan's bacon. More than once.

∾

LATER THAT DAY, Dan stood by the window in his front room and looked out. Red, white and blue bunting had been strung back and forth across Fore Street, and though it was early afternoon, trestle tables had already appeared on the pavement in readiness for the VE Day street party.

Dan's contribution, a batch of vegan scones, was cooling on a wire tray in the kitchen. They'd risen a treat, and he was looking forward to handing them out and then revealing that they contained neither butter nor milk. How would the locals react? Would they be pleasantly surprised, or would they roll their eyes at just another example of the strangeness of townies?

Am I still a townie? Dan wondered. He thought of the VE Day events that would be taking place in London. They'd be on a grander scale, with crowds gathering to catch a glimpse of the Royal Family, and there'd be marching bands, troops on horseback and a fly-past by the Red Arrows. But it all felt very distant; like something happening in another country.

Reg's bitter words in Brandle Wood came back to him: *You shouldn't even be here. You don't belong.* But the old man had been wrong. This was exactly where Dan should be, and this *was* where he belonged. This was home.

Dan watched a pair of women, both in long cotton dresses for the occasion, struggling to fasten down a tablecloth that was flapping in the spring breeze, and he smiled. But there was one thing that prevented him from feeling completely at ease: George's attacker was still at large.

Dan stayed by the window for a few minutes, thinking about the case, still trying to piece together a sequence of events that made sense. He stared out at Fore Street, lost in thought, and a new arrival attracted his attention. A young woman had stopped to help with the errant tablecloth, and working together, the women wrestled it into submission. The young woman had her back to Dan, and she cut a distinctive figure in her colourful 1940s outfit, the long dress pinched tight at the waist and accentuating the curve of her hips. Her fair hair had been arranged into the kind of elaborate swept-back style that Dan had only ever seen in wartime dramas on TV, but even so, there was something familiar about her.

"It's Sam," Dan whispered. "Wow!"

But then the young woman lifted a basket from the ground, and as she turned, Dan realised his mistake.

Gemma transferred her basket to the crook of her arm, then she crossed the road as if heading for Alan's house, a skip in her step.

"Well, well," Dan said. "Alan will be pleased."

He moved away from the window and went through to the kitchen, intending to make a cup of coffee. But something stopped him.

It was strange how he'd mistaken Gemma for Sam. It must've been the unfamiliar clothes and the unusual context. But now that he thought about it, Sam and Gemma had a similar build, and their hair was roughly the same colour. Seen from behind, anyone might make the same mistake.

Like Jocelyn, for instance. She thought she'd seen George hugging Sam in the street, but what if it had been Gemma? In the past, George had been a frequent visitor to Gemma's house, and she'd said something about him bringing raspberries to her because they were her favourite.

So George and Gemma might still be close. Old friends. But what did that mean? *It's a link to the victim*, Dan decided. *Something to think about*.

Gemma had been very certain that her brother was innocent, but she'd never explained why she was so sure. Could she have been the one to wield the knife?

On the night of the attack, Gemma had said she'd been watching TV on her own, but she'd made a remark about the cricket scores that hadn't checked out. Dan had assumed she'd made a simple mistake, but there could be more to it.

Dan paced the room. As far as he knew, Gemma had

absolutely no reason to attack George. But then, that was the problem with this case. No one seemed to have a motive. Harry might've wanted to threaten George, but he had an alibi. Who else would want to harm the poor guy? Dan could think of no one, but he was certain of one thing: the attack had not been motiveless.

Dan went to the kitchen table and sat down, pulling his laptop toward him. Research: that was where the answer lay. He thought of Monty Albright, and of the secrets tucked away in his past. Almost everyone had some past deeds that they preferred to keep hidden, and that was precisely the kind of thing Dan needed to unearth.

He began with Gemma, searching for several combinations of her forename, surname and initials, checking all the social media channels he could think of. He learned very little, but that wasn't surprising; as a primary school teacher, she'd have taken care to ensure her online reputation was squeaky clean.

Who next? Jocelyn was referred to in several news articles, all of which centred on her wedding to Scott. Dan found her maiden name, but it yielded nothing much except for an announcement from Oxford University, confirming that Jocelyn had graduated with first-class honours in economics and management, and was planning to stay on to complete an MBA.

Dan paused. Jocelyn had told him how she felt excluded from Ironbrand's business. Perhaps that was down to Harry. He could've been working behind the scenes to make sure she was sidelined. It was one thing for Harry to pull the wool over Scott's eyes, but with Jocelyn's skills and experience, she might have realised that something was very wrong at Ironbrand Farm. Harry would've wanted to make sure she couldn't challenge him, so in his mind it would've been logical to freeze her out.

Harry thwarted her at every opportunity, Dan thought. *He even overturned her catering arrangements for the party.* It was hardly surprising that Jocelyn had been in a bad mood that night. She'd been forced into the background, feeling like an outsider in her own home, surrounded by strangers. And she'd been keen to get her hands on the champagne. Was Jocelyn a drinker? It was hard to tell. She certainly seemed highly strung. She'd mentioned that she took pills to help her sleep. And some medication reacted badly with alcohol.

Had Jocelyn been out of control that night? George was a good-looking young man, and Jocelyn hadn't known that he was gay. Had she made a pass at him and then been angry when she'd been rebuffed? It was a possibility. Dan recalled the fishing trip and the way she'd teased him, standing too close and murmuring in his ear.

A harmless flirtation, Dan told himself. *She knew the boundaries, and she took care not to go too far.* Dan frowned. Jocelyn was a highly intelligent woman, but was there another side to her personality? He thought of their conversation in the lounge at Ironbrand Farm, remembering her carefully controlled expression when she'd talked about Scott's first wife. She'd tried to cover it up, to explain it away, but there'd been something there: an edge of bitterness in her tone, a shadow of a long-held grudge, even a hint of repressed anger. Why?

Dan ran one more search on his laptop, his fingers darting over the keys. He selected the most promising result, and his eyebrows rose steadily up his forehead as he read. Returning to the search results, he picked another link to follow, read the article quickly, then repeated the process.

"My God," Dan muttered, then he jumped to his feet and headed for the door. He had to talk this through with someone, and only Alan would understand.

A few seconds later, Alan ushered him inside with a bright and cheery smile. "Dan! You're just in time. Gemma's here. Go through to the lounge. I'll just be a tick."

"Thanks." Dan made his way into the front room, a sense of dread settling on his shoulders. Alan was in high spirits, but Dan had a feeling he was about to spoil the mood.

Gemma was sitting on the sofa, her back straight and her hands in her lap. She smiled as Dan walked in, but when she saw the look in his eyes, her smile dimmed. "Hello, Dan. Nice to see you again."

Dan nodded. "You too. I heard that Billy's been released."

"Yes, that's right. It's wonderful, isn't it?" Gemma perked up. "That's why I'm here. I came to say thank you."

Alan joined them, three wine glasses in his hand. He set the glasses on the coffee table and straightened up. "Has Gemma told you the good news?"

"Yes," Dan said. "But I'd already heard from DS Spiller. He called this morning."

"To thank you?" Gemma asked.

"He didn't quite go that far, but I don't mind. Billy's home and that's for the best. After all, we both know that he didn't attack George, don't we?"

Gemma nodded. "I suppose it seems crass to be pleased with the way things have turned out. After all, Billy's still going to be in trouble. What he did was wrong and very stupid, but he would never hurt anyone."

"What will happen to him?" Alan asked.

"We're waiting to hear from his probation officer. There's a chance he'll have to go back to prison, but he might be lucky and get away with a warning."

"Let's hope for the best," Alan said. "And guess what, Dan. DS Spiller might not have shown much gratitude, but Gemma's brought a bottle of wine to say thank you. Since you're here, I thought we'd share it."

"Yes." Gemma bent down to retrieve a tall gift bag from her basket, and she handed it to Alan with a shy smile. "I didn't know what kind of wine you'd like. I hope it's okay."

Alan beamed as he opened the bag and started to

withdraw the bottle. "I'm sure it will be—" He broke off suddenly, his lips tightening.

Gemma leaned forward. "Is it all right? I don't normally drink white wine, so I know nothing about it. I prefer red. I'd never get through a bottle of champagne on my own, but the label looked good, so I thought you'd like it."

"It's too much," Alan said. "This must've cost a fortune."

"Not at all. To be honest, it was a gift from a friend. But as I said, I don't usually drink it, so I hope you don't mind. Regifting; that's what they call it, don't they?"

"I believe so." Alan took the bottle fully from the bag and turned it around to show Dan the label.

"Krug vintage champagne," Dan read. "1988. Well, well. That's the final piece of the puzzle."

"Is it?" Looking to Alan, Gemma said, "I don't know what he's going on about, but shall we open the bottle? We don't want it to get warm."

"We can't drink it, I'm afraid," Dan replied. "We wouldn't want to be accused of destroying important evidence."

Gemma paled. "Evidence of what?"

"I think you know, Gemma." Dan took his time, watching her carefully. "You see, Alan and I had the same champagne recently. It was very good, so I looked it up afterwards. You might be interested to learn that it sells for over six hundred pounds a bottle."

"Goodness! I had no idea." Gemma laughed nervously. "I should've sold it on eBay."

Alan offered her the bottle. "If you'd like to take it back, we'd be just as happy with a pint of ale in the Boar."

"No. I wouldn't hear of it. It's a gift. But you needn't open it now. You could keep it for a special occasion."

"Is that why it was given to you?" Dan asked. "For a special occasion?"

"Yes. That's right."

Dan smiled. "What occasion was that?"

"Erm, my birthday. Last year."

"That was nice. You must have a wealthy friend. What's his name?"

Gemma's hand fluttered to her chest.

"Or was it a woman?" Dan went on. "A relative perhaps. It would seem strange if it was a friend. A friend would know that you don't normally drink white wine."

"Yes, well it was a relative. I have an aunt who's quite wealthy. She's always sending inappropriate gifts. It's embarrassing."

"I wish I had an aunt like that," Dan replied. "All I ever get is a pair of socks at Christmas. But if the champagne was from your aunt, why did you say it was from a friend?"

"I wasn't thinking. I made a mistake."

"We all make mistakes," Dan said. "For instance, on the night of the party, you said there were cricket scores on the news. That was another mistake, wasn't it?"

"I beg your pardon."

"What's your aunt's name?" Dan asked.

"What is this?" Gemma turned to Alan. "You warned me about your friend, but I won't be talked to like this." She gathered her basket and stood. "I'm sorry, Alan. I came to say thank you and to give you a gift in good faith, but I have to go."

"I'm sorry too," Alan said, his voice heavy. "I really am."

"You've got nothing to apologise for," Gemma replied. "But I still have to leave."

She made to move toward the door, but Alan raised a hand and said, "Wait. You see, Gemma, the reason I'm sorry is that you're not going to like what I have to say. But you ought to answer at least one question. Where did you get this champagne? And please, tell us the truth."

"I've already told you the truth. It *was* a gift."

"Was it from Marco?" Dan asked. "Is he your friend?"

Gemma lifted her chin in tight-lipped defiance.

"Come on, Gemma," Dan said gently. "This champagne is from Ironbrand Farm. Their cellar is full of expensive wine, and I know they keep it locked. I also know that Marco was allowed to use the key."

"That doesn't prove anything," Gemma replied. "Who says the wine came from Ironbrand?"

Dan held her gaze. "It certainly didn't come from the village shop. And don't tell me Scott gave it to you, because I won't believe you."

"I don't care what you believe," Gemma said. She was putting on a brave front, but Dan had seen her flinch at the mention of Scott's name, and there'd been a hint of disgust in the curl of her lip. This was the moment he'd been waiting for.

"Let me ask you something," Dan said. "Does the name Walker-Brown mean anything to you?"

Gemma shook her head. "No. Should it?"

"Not necessarily. The family are wealthy and one of them made a splash on the news sites a while back. Her name was Evelyn, and Walker-Brown happens to be the maiden name of Scott's first wife." Dan paused, and there it was again, that twitch of disgust in Gemma's expression.

"What's this got to do with anything?" Alan asked. "I don't see what you're getting at."

"You will, Alan. You see, Evelyn Walker-Brown was born into a life of wealth and luxury, and after a whirlwind romance, she married Scott when she was just eighteen. She was due to inherit a fortune on her twenty-first birthday, but she was only twenty years old when she divorced Scott — on the grounds of adultery."

Alan's eyebrows lowered. "So he must have cheated on her within the first few years of their marriage."

"It appears so," Dan said. "The divorce happened very quickly, and everywhere I checked, there were claims that Scott had been granted a substantial settlement. It was rumoured that Evelyn's father had paid him off to avoid a long legal battle. Ms Walker-Brown refused to comment, but she did say that it had been worth every penny to be free from her former husband. Her friends were less discreet. According to them, Scott had made Evelyn's life a misery."

Alan wrinkled his nose. "That man. It makes your blood boil."

"Yes," Dan said. "And it made me wonder what kind of man behaves like that. We know that Scott harassed Sam. He thought she was fair game, just because she happened to be working behind a bar. And I'd bet he's the kind of man to go further. He's the kind of man who'd lay his hands on a woman without giving it a second thought."

A tiny sound escaped from Gemma's throat. She tried to hide it, covering her mouth and clearing her throat, but Dan heard it all too clearly.

Alan must've heard it too because, keeping his voice soft, he said, "Gemma, did Scott do something to you?"

Gemma blinked. And then she nodded.

"It happened on the night of the party," Dan said. "It happened at Ironbrand Farm. That's right, isn't it?"

Gemma stared at him without replying, her cheeks tight.

It was time for Dan to go out on a limb. "You went to the farm to see Marco, didn't you, Gemma?"

"What?" Alan sent Dan a sharp look. "Where did you get that idea?"

"When we went to Ironbrand the day after the party, no one knew where Marco was," Dan explained. "I should've put it together sooner, but I think Marco was the man Sid saw running away."

"You think Marco attacked George?" Alan asked.

Dan shook his head. "Marco ran because he'd seen the attack on George, but he went back to the farm because he had no choice. I suspect that Harry was holding his passport."

"You've lost me," Alan said. "Do you know who stabbed George or not?"

"Yes. The problem with this case has always been the lack of a credible motive. But when I saw Gemma today, I began to put the pieces together. I had the beginnings of an idea, but for it to make sense, there had to be another person at the party, someone who wasn't supposed to be there. And Gemma fitted perfectly. She *knew* her brother wasn't guilty, because she was there." Dan paused, turning to Gemma. "Until just now, I thought you'd gone to see George. But the champagne changed everything. I'm sure you were at the farm that night, but you were there to see Marco, weren't you?"

"I…" Gemma gazed at Dan for a second, then: "I hate the way they call him that. It's not his name. It's as if he's just some foreigner and they can call him anything they want. They think they can take his name from him, his religion, his identity. But they can't do that. They can't. His name is Halil."

"Go on."

"We met in the village shop. I think he was treated better than the rest. At any rate, they let him go out on errands. I was buying a sliced loaf and a piece of cheese, and he made a joke of it; said that English bread was awful. I told him I'd always wanted to bake my own but didn't have time, and he said he'd show me. I don't know what made me agree, but I knew I was safe with him. He's such a gentle man, and maybe I could see he needed help. I took him back to my house, and we had coffee and a chat, nothing more. But it was enough. We knew something had started, and we arranged to meet again. After that, he'd come to see me whenever he could slip away, and we became close. Very close. And eventually, he told me how he'd come to be here. It's a harrowing story. You wouldn't want to be in his shoes, believe me."

"Oh, I believe you," Dan said. "But let's go back to the party at Ironbrand. Why were you there?"

"I went because Halil called me," Gemma replied. "He was at his wits' end. He couldn't take the way they treated him. He was going to run away, but he was terrified of what might happen. You were right; they'd taken his passport, his papers. They'd told him he'd be deported. He didn't trust the authorities, so I had to go to him. I wanted to help him, to make sure he got away safely."

"So, you went to the house, and you waited for Halil in the back garden," Dan said. "But then it all went wrong. Scott saw you, didn't he?"

Gemma looked down, grimacing. "He grabbed me. I tried to push him away, but he slobbered all over me. It was disgusting."

"Didn't Halil help you?" Alan asked.

"He saw what was going on, but he was too scared. He panicked, ran away."

"How could he?" Alan said. "That's unforgivable."

Gemma shook her head. "You don't know what he's been through. In Turkey, he was beaten by the police. He's never really recovered. He's still so fragile."

"So you were alone with Scott," Dan said. "Is that when George came back from the herb garden?"

"I don't know where he came from. He appeared out of nowhere, and when he saw me struggling, he went mad. He grabbed Scott and pulled him off me." Gemma sniffed, pressed her fingertips against her eyes. "They were fighting. It was horrible. It happened so fast."

"Did you see what happened with the knife?" Dan asked.

"Not really. It was dark, and I was terrified. But George let out this awful cry like he was in terrible pain, so that must've been when it happened. That must've been when Scott stabbed him. But then I heard the gunshot. I was sure someone was shooting at Halil, so I had to go and find him. He could've been hurt. He could've been killed."

"I presume you found Halil," Dan said.

"Yes. He turned back when he heard the gunshot. He practically ran into me. It was pure luck that I found him so quickly."

"Where did you go?" Alan asked. "You said you were at home when Billy came back from the allotments, and that can't have been much later."

"We cut across the fields. I grew up here, remember? I know my way around. I'd left my car in a lane, not far from the farm, and we drove back to my house."

"Did Billy see you with Halil?" Dan said. "Is that why he wouldn't answer any questions when they took him in? Was he covering for you?"

Gemma shook her head. "No. I was prepared for a row with Billy when I got home, and I was shocked when he wasn't there. But I didn't have time to think about it. I hid Halil upstairs, and then I just had time to smarten myself up before Billy came in. But I needn't have worried. He was in such a foul mood, he hardly noticed me. He stomped about, hoovering up the mud he'd brought in, then he went to his room and slammed the door. I didn't see him again until late the next morning, and by that time, I'd managed to persuade Halil to go for a walk. I thought it would settle his nerves, and I had to get him out of the house. I needed time to think."

"So, Halil..." Alan seemed to change his mind mid-sentence. He looked uncomfortable, then said, "He was all right. He was unharmed."

Gemma nodded.

"So why didn't you go to the police?" Alan went on. "They would've been able to help him."

"I couldn't do that to Halil. He begged me not to say a word."

"Nevertheless," Alan began, but Dan raised a palm to stop him.

"We understand, Gemma," Dan said. "You'd just been through a terrible experience."

"I didn't really think about myself. I was more concerned for Halil. He was in a terrible state. Physically shaking. He was so worried about what might happen to him. He said we mustn't say anything until he'd had a chance to get his passport back."

"Is that why he went back to Ironbrand?" Dan asked.

"I tried to reason with him, but he wouldn't listen. His passport is everything to him. Without it, he lives in fear, always looking over his shoulder."

"You must've been scared yourself," Alan said. "Did Scott try to find you?"

"Not as far as I know. I'm almost certain he didn't know who I was."

"Didn't he recognise you?" Alan asked.

"No. When I'd had a chance to calm down, I realised that he'd assumed I was there to wait on tables. I had my hair tied back, and I was wearing a light-coloured blouse. But he didn't care, one way or the other. I was just an object to him. Even when he grabbed me, he didn't really look at my face, so I was sure he didn't know my name or where I lived. For the time being, I was safe."

"And then Billy was arrested," Dan said. "You knew he wasn't at Ironbrand, but you withheld the evidence of his clothes and shoes because you suspected he'd been up to no good."

"I... I thought he must've done something wrong, but I couldn't be the one who sent him back to prison. I wanted to say something to the police, but I couldn't bring myself to do it. I've never felt so torn. I had no idea what to do."

"So you came to us," Dan prompted.

"Yes. I hope you'll forgive me, but Alan threw me a

lifeline and I grabbed it. I thought, between you, you'd get Billy out of trouble, and maybe you'd figure out that Scott was to blame for what happened to George. That way, I could keep Halil out of it. I didn't even tell him what you were trying to do. He'd sworn me to secrecy."

Dan hesitated. "And you wanted to keep your name out of it too."

"I suppose that was part of it," Gemma admitted. "When you teach in the village school in a little place like this, it's like living in a goldfish bowl. Everyone knows your business, and most of the time, that's okay. It's the life I chose. But if people knew what had happened, I couldn't carry on. I couldn't face the knowing looks and the gossip. I'd have to leave."

"But you were a victim in all this," Alan protested. "Surely that counts for something."

"To you, maybe. You're a good man, Alan. Perhaps you don't have double standards, but everyone else does." She smiled sadly at Alan. "I owe you an apology. You've been a good friend to me, and I took advantage of that. I'm sorry."

"You should've told me the truth," Alan said. "I'd have helped, regardless."

"I know you would've done your best, but you would've gone to the police." Gemma sighed. "I can't justify what I've done. I was wrong. And now it'll all come out anyway." She turned to Dan. "Unless there's some way you could keep Halil out of it. After all, he did nothing wrong."

"It's too late for that," Dan replied. "The police have already been to the farm, but they'll look after all the workers, including Halil. They'll make sure they're all safe."

The colour drained from Gemma's face. "Oh. That just leaves me then. Stuck in the middle."

"You should go to the police before they come to you," Dan said.

"I don't know if I can do that."

"Look at this way," Dan replied. "You've always been close to George, haven't you?"

"Yes. For a long time, when we were teenagers, he was my only real friend."

Dan softened his voice. "Then you'll want to make sure he gets justice. You'll want to make sure that the man who put George in hospital pays for what he's done. Do it for George. Do it for your friend."

Gemma nodded, tears trailing down her cheeks. "You're right. Of course you are. I'll call them today."

"Do you have your phone with you?" Dan asked.

"Yes."

"Then call them now. We'll give you some privacy." Dan headed for the door. He went straight through to the kitchen and filled the kettle. No doubt Alan had things he wanted to say to Gemma, and that was between them. But afterwards, Alan might need a cup of tea. Or possibly something stronger.

CHAPTER 50

AFTER GEMMA HAD left, Dan and Alan put in an appearance at the VE Day street party. Neither of them were much in the mood, but they took their places at the trestle table and drank tea and ate cake. They smiled and nodded to their neighbours and talked about the good weather. And had they heard about the goings-on at Ironbrand Farm? Yes, they had, and it was, indeed, shocking.

Alan checked his watch.

"Yes, I'm ready to go home too," Dan said. "I'll give it five minutes more, then I'm off."

"It wasn't that," Alan replied. "I was thinking that Gemma will be at the police station by now. I hope they're not being too rough on her."

"She'll be okay. She's tougher than you might think."

Alan looked unconvinced.

"I'm sorry things didn't work out," Dan said. "I know you liked her."

Alan waved his words away. "Some things just aren't meant to be." He hesitated. "How did you know about her and Marco, I mean, Halil?"

"I didn't know for sure until I saw that bottle of

champagne, but there were lots of little things that added up to form the bigger picture. It's a shame it took me so long to piece it together. If I'd known sooner, I'd have told you. If there'd been any other way…"

"I know. It's not your fault."

Dan picked at the crumbs of scone on his paper plate. "I've just remembered. I was supposed to give Reg a quote for a laptop, but I never got around to it."

"Probably just as well."

"Yes. To be honest, I'm thinking about giving up the computer repairs."

"Oh?"

"I thought about what you said when we were up at the plantation, and you were right. I like working with computers, but it isn't me. It isn't enough."

"What will you do instead?" Alan asked.

"I've licked my wounds for long enough. I'm ready to go back to some kind of consultancy work, but I won't find it in Embervale."

There was a pause before Alan said, "Does that mean you're going to leave the village? Will you move back to London?"

"It probably won't come to that. There must be plenty of companies in Devon who might employ me. I could try freelance, play the field."

Alan nodded fervently. "There are lots of businesses in Exeter, and there's Plymouth. It's a bit further, but it's only a forty-five-minute drive. That's nothing for a commute."

"Very true. That's settled then. I'll stay in Embervale. See how it goes."

"And if another case comes up?" Alan asked.

"Well, we might find the time to look into it," Dan said. "It would be rude not to, wouldn't it?"

"I'll drink to that." Alan raised his teacup and sipped, then he pulled a face. "It's gone cold."

"Mine too. I'm sure there's more tea in the urn, but if you'd prefer something different, I've got a couple of beers in the fridge at home."

"Lager?"

"Certainly not. IPA."

"Rapidly becoming my three favourite letters." Alan stood. "Come on then. What are we waiting for?"

"Nothing at all." But as Dan stood, someone clapped a hand on his shoulder, and he turned to see Monty beaming at him.

"Going somewhere, chaps?" Monty asked.

"Just nipping home for a bit," Dan said.

Monty shook his head then checked his watch. "Not yet. Give it a few more minutes." He cocked his ear. "Ah, here it comes."

Monty pointed to the clouds, but Dan could see nothing. And then a sudden roar hammered down from the sky, a crackling energy filling the street and rattling through Dan's body until he felt it in his fingertips.

The plane appeared like an avenging angel, soaring over the rooftops, majestic and yet strangely terrifying.

"A Spitfire!" Alan cried, and when everyone cheered, Dan joined in as loudly as anyone.

When the plane had disappeared into the distance, Monty laughed at Dan and Alan's incredulous expressions. "Before you say anything, I was too young for that particular war, but I did my bit afterwards. I've still got a few chums in the RAF, and they put me in touch with the right people. I thought it would give everyone a treat. A bit of excitement."

"I didn't know you were in the RAF," Dan said.

"Then you don't know everything, old boy. You don't know everything." He tipped them a wink, then he marched away, swinging his arms as he went.

Dan turned to Alan. "This place continually amazes me."

"Me too," Alan said. "IPA?"

"IPA."

They replaced their chairs at the table, and Dan noticed that all his vegan scones had been eaten. He took the empty plate, and as he headed for home with Alan at his side, he thought, *There's hope for Embervale yet.*

EPILOGUE

WHO'D BE A *medical student?* Ade thought. *Everyone else is on holiday, but where am I?* He sat down heavily at the nurses' station and logged on to the system. On most days, life on the ward was hectic, but things were quiet because most surgical procedures had been scheduled for after the public holiday. There was only one new admission today and Ade read through the notes. The patient was called George Hepworth, and he'd been transferred from the Intensive Therapy Unit after a successful operation to repair a previously undetected intra-abdominal injury. A diagnostic laparoscopy had revealed a small perforation of the anterior surface of the stomach. The perforation had been closed and no other injuries had been found.

Reading through the rest of the notes, Ade reckoned the prognosis looked good. The young man would need careful monitoring, but the surgical team were happy for him to leave the ITU, and that was a very good sign.

He glanced at the patient's address. Embervale. *What are the chances? Ah well, it's a small world.*

Ade stretched his back. There was nothing that needed his urgent attention, and the afternoon sunshine still shone tantalisingly through the windows. He could take a break and grab a few minutes of fresh air. It would do him the world of good.

Outside, Ade headed across the car park. There was a grassy area with a bench where he sometimes spent his breaks when the weather was fine. But before he reached it, he saw a man hurrying toward him. Ade stopped. It was the man from the wood, wasn't it? Mr Sturridge. Sid.

"Hold up," Sid called out. "Please."

Ade knew Sid had been discharged, but it had happened on someone else's shift, and Ade hadn't minded that at all. He was in no hurry to see this particular patient again, but something in the man's expression made him wait.

Sid came to a breathless halt in front of him. "I brought you something." He held out a carrier bag, its sides stretched into an unusual shape.

Ade eyed it uncertainly. "I see."

"It's a brace of pheasants. For you and your young lady. I thought you might like them."

"Oh."

"Don't worry, I've drawn them and hung them for a bit, and Lisa, that's my wife, she's plucked them and all that. They're ready for the oven." Sid frowned. "You do eat meat, don't you?"

"Yes. We both do. But I've never had pheasant before."

"There you go then. Ideal. My way of saying thank you."

Sid handed the bag over and Ade took it. "Thank you, but there's no need."

"Yes, there is. And, truth be told, it's not just to say thank you. It's by way of being an apology. There's things I said and did, and they shame me. They really do. I know a couple of birds can't make up for it, but I don't know what else I can do, except to say that I'm sorry."

Ade nodded slowly. Working in the hospital, he'd witnessed the worst and the best in people, and he knew that this man was in earnest. But he'd seen a lot of sincerity in the newly sober, and too often, he'd seen the same faces a short while later, back on the ward and in a worse state.

Maybe this time would be different. "Mr Sturridge, if you want to thank me, there's one thing you can do. You can stay sober. It's hard to do on your own, but there are plenty of people who can help you. We've got some information sheets inside, and if you like, I can help you go through them, then you can decide what to do."

"Thanks, but they gave me a handful of leaflets before I went home." Sid smiled. "I'm not a great one for reading, but Lisa said she'd sort through them and tell me where to go. She says I ought to start next week, after the holiday. And what she says goes."

"That's all right then. It sounds as though you're in good hands."

"You can say that again. Well, thank you, doctor. Thank you for everything."

"I'm not a doctor yet. I'm still a student."

"Well, I reckon you'll make a good one. Goodbye." Sid turned and headed back across the car park.

"Hang on a sec," Ade called after him. "How did you know where I'd be?"

Sid looked back with a grin and tapped the side of his nose, then he walked away.

Ade peeked inside the bag, and there, nestling on top of the plastic-wrapped pheasants, was his lanyard and ID badge. He took the lanyard out and looked through the collection of cards and badges. They were all there, and every one of them was spotless, as if they'd been cleaned. He'd been issued with a new set, but even so, it was good to have the old ones back. They'd been with him for a while, and for the last few years they'd been part of his identity.

He stuffed the old lanyard in his pocket then he headed back inside. He still had his shift to finish. It would be another five hours before he could go home, so until then, where on earth was he going to keep a couple of raw pheasants?

Thank you for reading Mystery in May
I hope that you enjoyed it.
Here's the next in the series:
Accomplice to Murder

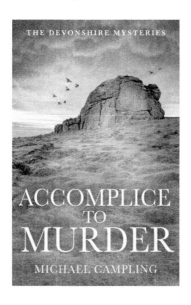

Find it on your favourite store
Accomplice to Murder
Visit: books2read.com/atmurder

AUTHOR NOTES

Is Embervale a real place?

Embervale is a fictional village, but its imagined location is within the real Teign Valley in Devon. The area is named after the River Teign, which is pronounced 'Teen'.

Where real places are referred to, they are used in a fictionalised way. Shops, pubs and businesses are fictional, but are often inspired by real places, e.g. The Wild Boar is an amalgam of a range of country pubs that I've visited. What I try to capture is the atmosphere of the Devon countryside, and the feeling of life in a small village.

Brandle Wood is inspired by a woodland called Bearacleave Wood. Ironbrand Farm is entirely imaginary, and I know of no large-scale fruit farms or solar energy installations in the Teign Valley area; if they exist, it's purely a coincidence.

Kennick Reservoir is real, and you can buy a permit to fly fish for trout. It's a beautiful lake with rhododendrons growing wild along the banks, but it's a tough place for a beginner to fish, so it's no wonder that Dan became so frustrated.

Are you inspired by real events?

The May Fair is distilled from the village fairs in the area. At one fair, I had a go at woodturning on a pole lathe (bodging), and I made use of that experience at the start of the book. At the time, I made a note in my notebook because I'd spotted a large home-made mallet on display: "Murder weapons — big mallet... then burned." It occurred to me that the mallet was made entirely of wood, so could easily be burned, destroying the weapon completely. This detail didn't make the cut, but the woodturning did.

A real event that inspired a chunk of dialogue was when Sam asked Dan if he'd booked a table in the pub. This happened to Mrs C and me in Yorkshire. The pub was practically deserted, but the surly landlord wanted to know if we'd booked a table. Eventually, he told the much friendlier young woman behind the bar that we could be given a couple of menus, then he cast us a sour look and wandered off. I used this in the scene where Sam is venting a little of her frustration with Dan. There is an element of tension between those two. Will they ever get together? We'll have to wait and see.

I recorded another note in my notebook after listening to some older residents in a small village discussing the past. It says, "Long-ago events seeming recent because people haven't moved, so childhood friends still near." They were talking about events from decades ago, but their shared memories made it sound as though these things were very recent. There is something of that feeling in this book. Sid is haunted by events in his youth. He's never been allowed to escape from his past, because he's remained in the same small village all his life. Perhaps Reg sees himself as protecting that small world, but his perspective is terribly skewed, and he's blind to his own faults. Paul and Daisy don't want their lives to play out on such a small stage. They feel trapped in the village, but to escape, they choose a somewhat desperate plan.

On a more sombre note, I must make it plain that the depiction of modern slavery is completely fictional and not inspired by or based on any real case or situation. This is a heinous crime and more common than most of us imagine.

Racism rears its ugly head in this book. Coming from London, Dan would notice that Devon doesn't offer much in the way of cultural and ethnic diversity. It's a fact that most people in rural communities in Devon are white, but in no way do I mean to imply that bigotry and ignorance are more prevalent here than anywhere else. All I know is that racism is a scourge and everyone must do what they can to combat it.

Can you camp on Dartmoor?

Yes, but it's important that this beautiful landscape isn't spoiled. There are certain areas where camping is allowed, but only if you follow the rules. Alan knows what he's talking about.

Do you have a recipe for blackthorn sorbet?

I'm afraid not. You can use blackthorn blossom to make a cordial, and I know that you can make elderflower sorbet, so I put the two ideas together. There are links to recipes in my online notebook (see sources below), but you must be careful when foraging. I'd hate for anyone to be poisoned!

I am looking into the possibility of creating a slim volume of Embervale recipes, and the best place to find out about that is on my website at michaelcampling.com

What's going on with the allotments?

In the UK, allotments are areas of land that are divided into plots and rented out to individuals, usually for growing food. They have a long history, stretching back over a thousand years to when the Saxons cleared land for common use. Now, they are typically owned by local government bodies, such as town or parish councils. Rents are usually very low, and in some places, the interest in organic and home-grown food has meant that there are long waiting lists of budding gardeners. Often, the allotment holders will form an association to establish rules governing the use of the plots, e.g. setting down the maximum size for sheds and greenhouses. I've had allotments for many years, and it occurred to me that the sheds would make good hiding places. A neighbour, whenever he was putting out new plants, would always say, "They've got two chances. They'll live or they'll die." That snippet stuck with me, and it became one of Reg's thoughts.

While I'm on the subject, you really do need acidic soil to grow blueberries successfully, so in the UK, some people use compost made from pine needles.

Can you tell me more about the VE Day bank holiday?

2020 marked the seventy-fifth anniversary of VE Day. This was a real public holiday, and I wanted to incorporate it into the story. Unfortunately, the real-life holiday was affected by the Covid-19 restrictions, and I'd already decided not to include the pandemic in the Devonshire Mysteries. In reality, the planned street parties became individual garden parties, with people sitting in front of their houses to drink tea, eat cake, and say hello to their neighbours from a safe distance. Dan and Alan experience the day as it might have been.

In the summer of 2020, there were spitfire flypasts to honour the NHS, and there were some flypasts on the VE Day holiday. I wanted to bring the spitfire to Embervale because I had a personal experience that I could use. Many years ago, I lived in Moreton-in-Marsh in Gloucestershire, and one Remembrance Sunday, I was walking into town when a spitfire roared over the rooftops. It was awe-inspiring, and I've never forgotten it.

Is the Devon Air Ambulance real?

It certainly is. Run by a charity, these fine people manage to keep their helicopters flying all year round. Devon's narrow lanes and rural landscape are lovely in many ways, but it can take far too long for help to arrive by road. The air ambulance teams save many lives each year, bringing medical aid to those who urgently need it. They have several sites rigged for night landings with lights that can be switched on remotely. These sites are vital, because trees, power lines and other obstructions can spell disaster for helicopters. I often see one of the distinctive red air ambulances flying past my house, and it's good to know they're out there, doing such great work. I support them in my own small way, and if you have something similar in your area, you might consider donating. There's a link to the Devon Air Ambulance Trust on the sources page (see below).

Is a keylogger a real device?

Yes. There can be legitimate reasons for using them, but they can also be used to steal sensitive information. The software mentioned is also real, but I didn't want to get the reader too bogged down with technical information. Dan isn't a cybercrime expert, but he knows enough to get by, and the story follows his train of thought.

The mobile phone scam mentioned is based on reports of real-life events.

They're drinking beer again?

Yes, Dan and Alan aren't going to become teetotallers any time soon. The brands of beer I mention are all authentic. No one from any brewery has ever rewarded me for mentioning them. You'd think they'd try, but no.

Can we see some of the sources you used for research?

Certainly. Here's a link to my website, and from there, you can view a list of links in the online notebook that I used:

michaelcampling.com/mystery-in-may-sources

Will you talk to my book group?

Yes, if we can arrange a date and time, I'm happy to chat with your group via an online call. Please get in touch at:

michaelcampling.com / contact

Anything else?

That's all I have for you at the moment. I hope these notes add a little extra background to your reading experience.

Thank you very much for joining Dan and Alan on their adventures. I'm planning new stories for the pair, and the best way to find out about upcoming books is via my VIP Readers Club where you can also claim exclusive free books and content. Here's the place to learn more:

michaelcampling.com / freebooks

Happy reading and take care,
    Mikey Campling
    February 2021
    Teign Valley,
    Devon

BECOME A VIP READER

MEMBERS GET FREE BOOKS,
EXCLUSIVE CONTENT AND MORE

Visit: michaelcampling.com/freebooks

ABOUT THE AUTHOR

Michael (Mikey to friends) is a full-time writer living and working on the edge of Dartmoor in Devon. He writes stories with characters you can believe in and plots you can sink your teeth into. His style is vivid but never flowery; every word packs a punch. His stories are complex, thought-provoking, atmospheric and grounded in real life.

You can start reading his work for free with a complimentary starter library when you join Michael's VIP Readers' Club. You'll receive free books and stories plus a newsletter that's actually worth reading. Learn more and start reading today at: michaelcampling.com/freebooks facebook.com/authormichaelcampling

x.com/mikeycampling

instagram.com/mikeycampling

amazon.com/Michael-Campling/e/B00EUVA0GE

bookbub.com/authors/michael-campling

ALSO BY MICHAEL CAMPLING

One Link to Rule Them All:

michaelcampling.com / find-my-books

The Devonshire Mysteries

A Study in Stone

Valley of Lies

Mystery at the Hall

Murder Between the Tides

Mystery in May

Death at Blackingstone Rock

Accomplice to Murder

A Must-Have Murder

The Darkeningstone Series:

Breaking Ground - A Darkeningstone Prequel

Trespass: The Darkeningstone Book I

Outcast — The Darkeningstone Book II

Scaderstone — The Darkeningstone Book III

Darkeningstone Trilogy Box Set

ACKNOWLEDGMENTS

THANK YOU TO Sue Campling for a million and one things.

Special thanks to supporters Diana Johnson, Chriss Jones and Cynthia Wenslow.

Thanks also to these eagle-eyed beta readers:

Loretta Blimline, Deanne Charlton, Bridgit Davis, Judith Dickinson, Doreen Fernandes, Rosemary Kenny, Pat Kidd, Patty Mele, Essie Munro, Robin Panza, Bev Priest, Jean Soderquist, Linda Taylor, Helen Valenzuela, Kathleen Veglio, Julie Warwick, Gary Webber, Saundra Wright.

The cover was designed by Patrick Knowles. The book was edited by Andrew Chapman.

Printed in Great Britain
by Amazon